He pirouetted rapidly and unsteadily to see if he could spot where his own clothes had been cast down. No part of his body thanked him for this manoeuvre; worse, not only didn't it reveal what he was searching for, it also caused him to topple sideways across the room. Trying to regain his balance, he performed that peculiar arms swinging, legs crossing dance that music hall entertainers liked to use to work their way off the stage; he'd have needed only a cane, a straw boater and a peppy rendition of 'Knocked 'em in the Old Kent Road' from the orchestra to have secured a week of matinees at the Alhambra on the strength of it. Except, rather than ending in appreciative applause, it ended with his crashing into the bedroom door with the top of his skull. The noise this made inside his head could not be measured using human science; it was something like the level of sound you'd hear if you chewed on a hydrogen bomb. Unfortunately, even outside his head, it generated what was, objectively speaking, an awful bloody racket. He bounced back from the woodwork and pluckily wrestled with man's ancient enemy, gravity, in a bid to steady himself.

A few feet away, Strange Woman stirred from her sleep and asked, 'Mmmmeeerrrum-m-m-m?'

Chris would swear on anything you cared to name that, at this point, he actually felt his testicles freeze, constrict and then flee upwards into his abdomen.

Mil Millington is the creator of the cult website www.thingsmygirlfriendandIhavearguedabout.com and co-founder of www.theweekly.co.uk. He writes for various newspapers and magazines and lives in the West Midlands with his girlfriend and their two children.

By Mil Millington

Things My Girlfriend and I Have Argued About
A Certain Chemistry
Love and Other Near-Death Experiences
Instructions for Living Someone Else's Life

INSTRUCTIONS FOR LIVING SOMEONE ELSE'S LIFE

MIL MILLINGTON

PHOENIX

A PHOENIX PAPERBACK

First published in Great Britain in 2008
by Weidenfeld & Nicolson,
This paperback edition published in 2009
by Phoenix,
an imprint of Orion Books Ltd,
Orion House, 5 Upper St Martin's Lane,
London WC2H 9EA

An Hachette UK company

1 3 5 7 9 10 8 6 4 2

Copyright © Mil Millington 2008

The right of Mil Millington to be identified as the author
of this work has been asserted by him in accordance with
the Copyright, Designs and Patents Act 1988.

A CIP catalogue record for this book
is available from the British Library.

ISBN 978-0-7538-2627-0

Typeset by Input Data Services Ltd,
Bridgwater, Somerset

Printed and bound in Great Britain
by Clays Ltd, St Ives plc

The Orion Publishing Group's policy is to use papers
that are natural, renewable and recyclable products and
made from wood grown in sustainable forests. The logging
and manufacturing processes are expected to conform to
the environmental regulations of the country of origin.

www.orionbooks.co.uk

For my mother and father

ACKNOWLEDGEMENTS

I can no longer remember how long I've been on this island. Sometimes I think I've been here always; that what I believe was my earlier life is nothing more than a dream that's been forged to the hardness of memory by heat and isolation. But then I remind myself that I'm wearing clothes I constructed from empty, plastic, microwave rice packets. I must have lived in a world beyond this place at some time, I *must* have – it says 'Savoury Chicken Flavour' all over my trousers.

Now my days are filled with nothing more than eating seafood and near-relentless masturbation, but it was once so different; once there were days, sometimes weeks, when I ate hardly any seafood at all. Back then I had an editor, Helen Garnons-Williams, whose professional wisdom matched her thorough personal loveliness and, twice, her shoes. Often, remembering, I become teary just thinking about her. Until, after indiscriminately tearing things for a while, I slowly regain the understanding of homographs that solitude has eroded and recall a second editor. When our work was done, Helen took her sweet face and her collection of erotic exclamations to a lucky new publisher, and I moved onto the lap of Jon Wood. The very idea of male editors is, of course, an affront to God and nature; thus, it speaks prettily of Mr Wood that, in his cupping palms, there was satisfaction (and – I blush – on occasion almost pleasure) in a relationship so intrinsically collied and bestial. Yes, he persistently uses the telephone instead of email (and we all know what *that* says about a person), but his hard work and his good humour and his repeated declaration that his entire reputation should rest solely on how well *Instructions for Living Someone Else's Life* fares in the nation's bookstores is tremendously winning.

Purposelessness is the carrier of despair, so, to keep myself busy and maintain structure during the endless, empty hours, I have devised a strict routine. On Tuesdays, for example, I pick at my feet. Sometimes, while doing this, I imagine myself once more back in the world beyond these confining shores, and I picture Ali Gunn. Who is fearful. Like a literary agent from the id. It's a great comfort to know that she's chosen to stand by my side, though I wouldn't want to be around if anyone ever decides to dig up her patio.

Finally, sustaining me through the long, lonely nights here with consoling memories of love, support, companionship and shouting is the precious image of Margret. If I could have only one thing from my lost life with me on this island, it would be pizza. But, if I could have two, then the other one would be Margret. Being able to put things down for one damn second without their being tidied away to some ridiculous place where I'll never find them again, I now realise, is small compensation for the simple yet perfect pleasure of being able to feel the touch of her hand in mine and hear the unremitting movement of her mouth. My heart will always be with her, even if my body, and any kind of right of attorney over my financial affairs whatsoever, remains forever in this cursed place.

And so I cast this message into the sea. If you've found it, then that's enough. That you know I was once a man like you, unless you're a woman, in which case you'll have to pretend you're a man for little while, but not in any sexual role-play way – that's weird, actually, that you'd think of that; let's hope that no one sitting by you right now is somehow aware you're having those kind of thoughts, eh? Anyway, as I was saying, I hope nothing more than that you see this note, understand, perhaps run your fingers gently over the words, then realise what I had to use to write them, and go and wash your hands.

0

Something's about to happen to Chris.

Actually, it's not quite that simple. From *Chris's* point of view (and, coincidentally, from ours) it's about to happen. From the point of view of the people around him, it doesn't happen until much later. And, when it does, it's an entirely different thing that happens anyway. Really, in one sense, you might say that nothing at all happens to Chris, but – at the moment that it doesn't – long, slow things happen to everyone else.

Right: I'm glad we've cleared that up.

Anyway, the important things to consider are ... No, enough. You can pick them up as we go along. Let's get on with the story now – Chris is waiting.

Or was waiting. As you'll discover, time really isn't on anyone's side here.

1

Simon Mayo had leapt, mid-sentence, into Chris's ear.

It had been a bit of a jolt at the time, but Chris was over it now. Now, he was happily eating a slice of toast while he looked through the window at the busy street beyond. There wasn't much distance between the front of his undesirable ground-floor flat and the pavement that marked the beginning of the not-sought-after neighbourhood as a whole. With the curtains pulled back, he could easily connect visually with any passer-by and, as he nibbled his burnt Mother's Pride, he occasionally waved at one and made an expression of surprised, *fancy-seeing-you-walking-here!* recognition. He didn't actually recognise any of them; he simply liked to watch as they, instantly and instinctively, returned his cheery gesture; outwardly unfazed but, if you knew to look, with a frantic, 'Christ! Where the hell do I know him from?!' just *howling* behind their eyes.

He was in a jolly mood this morning. Normally, he would never do anything so puerile as standing at his window greeting random strangers simply to see if they'd greet him back out of panic. No, this wasn't Chris's normal behaviour. Normally, he'd do it on the Tube; he'd wait until he heard the beeping alert begin then (apparently having just spotted them) brightly call out, 'Hi! Great to see you again!' to the person directly beyond the shutting-in-three-seconds train doors.

This was the ideal place for the game. Those who didn't respond (mostly because they were simply stunned inert by confusion) would then find themselves peered at oddly by the fellow passengers with whom they were trapped. *Why had this person completely ignored their friend? What terrible secret or psychological defect might explain that?* Usually, the opposite happened – and this was even better. The person *would* respond, then be whisked away almost immediately to spend who knew how long racking their brains trying to recall where they might possibly have met Chris before; but, better still, because they'd been tricked by their own reflexes into mirroring Chris's wide and merry gesture before they could think about it, they'd been outed. The dead-faced, insulating shell that everyone in a commuter train wears would have been shattered, and there they now were: on the Tube, exposed as human.

But, best of all, was Chris's fantasy. It wasn't a consuming fantasy, far less the intention of the whole exercise – not *remotely* – but it was one he enjoyed having from time to time. In this dream he would unleash his bright, booby-trap salutation to some woman, and she, lightning fast, would slip out before the doors closed and acknowledge him twice as warmly. 'My God! It's so wonderful to see you again!' This she would do in the full knowledge that she didn't know who the hell he was, and that he knew she didn't: it would be done to call his bluff. (Right, smart-arse, what are you going to do *now*, eh?) If a woman ever did that, Chris thought, he would, there and then, ask her to marry him.

In his fantasy, she always replied to his proposal with, 'No, you twat.' Which rather annoyed him; not because she'd say it (of course she'd say it), but because it was *his* fantasy, after all. In the real world he already had a very attractive girlfriend and he wasn't looking for another one (that's to say, a 'different one' rather than 'another one'; women can be picky about such semantic distinctions), but that wasn't the issue. The issue was that it's a bit unfair when even your own fantasy ends with your being called a twat. Still, it was merely an idle dream purely for entertainment purposes so he was easily able to shrug off its going a bit pear-shaped at the end.

He was resilient. He was, let's not forget, someone capable of coping with Simon Mayo leaping, mid-sentence, into his ear.

Simon Mayo did this almost every weekday, because of Chris's six-minute-sized declaration that he was not a number, but a free man. It would have been easy (too easy, that was the point) to set the radio alarm by his bed to activate at an o'clock or a half hour, to start with the beginning of a news report or the pips. But Chris had deliberately programmed it to go off six minutes past the unthinkingly obvious.

'Get up,' he had said to his muscles in response to the abrupt arrival of today's *Breakfast Show*. He wasn't a morning person. He never had been. His birth, his father had often told him, had taken hours longer than expected. Twenty-five years ago optimistic midwives had predicted he'd emerge at four or five a.m., but his mother had been in labour until ten. This was almost certainly because unborn-Chris's final in-womb act after the contraction alarm went off was to repeatedly hit a snooze button on the cervix and go back to sleep. He understood that, for some people, waking up was a brisk change of location – one moment *there*, the next *here*. For him, however, it was slow, precarious, and not especially pleasant: no swift hop out of slumber, but rather more like being sucked back into consciousness through a thin straw.

Even this morning, the morning of a day he'd been planning for months (a day he was looking forward to: a Day of Action), had slumped on top of him out of the mouth of Simon Mayo and had to be manhandled off his eyelids like a fat corpse before he could claw his way into himself proper.

'Get up,' Chris had told his muscles again as he'd reluctantly opened his eyes to look towards the digits on the clock-radio. At first, his vision had been still too blurry with sleep to read them, but seeing their snot-green glow at all had informed him that Katrina wasn't there.

How *Who-takes-which-side-of-the-bed?* comes about is one of the bigger mysteries of relationships. Rarely, if ever, is it discussed – it simply happens, as though preordained. Nonetheless, it's fixed very early on, and thereafter changes only if you get a new partner, or a new house. When Katrina stayed, she always slept on the right, between him and the radio – her shoulder blocking the view from where he lay. No snot-green glow: Katrina. No Katrina: snot-green glow. Chris had reached into his still-sleepy memory and managed to pull out that she hadn't come back with him the previous night because she'd been all fired up about the new painting she was working on and wanted to keep in the flow. He'd decided to leave her to it and get a good night's sleep at his own place. He had a Monday to prepare for: and a big Monday at that.

By the time Chris had successfully remembered all this Mayo had begun playing Nick Kamen's 'Tell Me', for who knew what possible reason.

But that had all been twenty-five minutes ago – a lifetime away. Generally, once he'd managed to break through the sticky, surface tension of the waking barrier he was fine – and, this morning at least, he'd raise that assessment to fine *and* dandy. The unaccountably huge and wondrously addictive weight of the duvet was no longer pinning him down; now he stood eating buttery toast at his front window, casually disconcerting random strangers with his waves, and full of eagerness to begin putting his plan into effect. He chewed, and smiled, and savoured the keen anticipation.

This was going to be a very good day.

2

Someone (inexplicably, not Wilde) observed that 'Friends are God's apology for relatives.' No one, however, has yet given us an explanation for colleagues.

Now, workmates *can* be the people with whom you go out drinking and dancing as well. But almost as common is for them, instead, to be stupid, pestiferous, freeloading gits you can't wait to see the back of every day, and who – if you think about them outside work at all – cause your hands to spontaneously warp into rigid claws.

OK, it might be that a particular workplace brings like-minded people together. If you get a job in a tanning salon, it's no surprise to find yourself in the company of someone who also feels that lipliner is central to her life; if you set to work as a builder, then no disinterested person is going to think it unreasonable of you to expect to find yourself with other liars and thieves. That's perfectly understandable. But it's equally likely that the people across the office or with whom you share staff toilets are more or less a random collection of humans; it's simply a lottery. A good proportion of you will spend more time in the company of your work colleagues than with anyone else in your lives. Yet, unlike friends, you don't choose them, and, unlike relatives, you're not bound as confederates by your DNA's timeless struggle to keep itself in the gene pool either.

Chris worked for Short Stick Media and everyone he worked with hated him.

Much as it often felt like it, hating Chris was not actually company policy. There wasn't even an unofficial 'Us and Them' (or, rather, 'Us and Chris') attitude dividing the staff into, on the one hand, a coherent, unified group of people who didn't like Chris and, on the other hand, Chris. His colleagues' enmity wasn't organised, or even openly declared; it was a deeply personal thing that they kept to themselves and, though they were always on the lookout for ways to make his life less pleasant, they were also always careful that their doing so wouldn't reveal that they regarded this as an end in itself. Publicly, between each other, they expressed a professional admiration for Chris. Each of his colleagues believed that he or she was the only one who didn't like him. This made their dislike all the more intense – due to the aggravation of believing that, while they hated him, everyone else seemed to think that the sun shone out of his backside.

The reason for all this ill will landing on him was a combination of his ability and his attitude. After leaving university, Chris had spent a few years learning his craft in a series of fairly short-term positions at a number of different firms. He absorbed many important facts, had an epiphany or two, and, when he chose to start at the Short Stick Media advertising agency, he'd pretty much made up his mind that he essentially knew it all. He wasn't brash or arrogant about this. It was simply that he'd realised, correctly, that he had a natural talent few could match: he just seemed to have an innate aptitude for producing cheap and nasty campaigns. Operatic scores, elegant photography and vast spectacles with purple silk were not his forte. But, while there were only a small number of accounts of the Guinness or British Airways variety, there were many, many thousands of clients who needed shrill adverts for local commercial radio stations, say, or something exactly crude and jarring enough to sit well across a full page in some monstrously uninteresting trade journal. And when it came to producing copy that was taut, punchy and crass enough to sell (for example) anodised copper fasteners to their target audience – irrespective of the fact that if anyone else accidentally read it they would become angry and upset – then Chris was a rock-solid maven.

Short Stick Media itself was surging from strength to strength. In fact, the company was so successful that, although a relative newcomer, it had already acquired two other, smaller businesses in the field of advertising and promotion, and its creator, David Short, was – it was widely agreed – going places (some even suggested that, in a few years, he might dominate the downmarket). It was a company with a drive to win and a clear

7

sense of direction: a one-stop shop where, rapidly and at highly competitive rates, a campaign could be taken all the way from an inchoate, appalling notion to a Christ-awful reality. Though Chris didn't have a senior position at Short Stick, everyone knew that he was by far the most gifted member of staff there. Not only did he produce exactly what was required – create what was, within its own terms, perfection – but doing it was, for him, almost effortless. Chris Mortimer was the Mozart of tat.

Being extremely good at your job is, of course, a sure way to piss off all your colleagues. But you're really in unpopularity's fast lane if, on top of this, you turn out everything you do with what amounts to a relaxed yawn while they have to work as hard as they can to squeeze out something that, it's instantly obvious to all concerned, is far, far worse.

Is it possible to improve upon this neat combination, if you especially fancy being the target of a full forty hours of varyingly concealed, low-level hostility each week?

Well, yes it is.

Almost always in life you really enjoy and value the things you do well. Brilliant mathematicians love maths. Splendid bassoon players are filled with joy and fulfilment from playing bassoons. Even people with a talent for football not only get pleasure *from*, but also feel there's meaningful value *to*, the ability to run around and intermittently kick something quite accurately. You'll have noted that this phenomenon is specifically as stated: you enjoy and value the things you do well. It's not simply the result of effort – borne of consideration and desire. You are *not* necessarily good at the things you enjoy and value. Any number of people would dearly love to play the piano well, or draw wonderfully, dance in a way that made them even remotely attractive to the opposite sex – but they can't, and they know they can't. This fact makes the point unarguable: the point is, it's as if we're programmed – as if there's a routine running secretly in our subconscious – so that, when we happen across something we have an aptitude for, we like that thing. Perhaps it helps to focus our energies where they will be most effective. Perhaps it's just Nature taking pity on us: when it turns out that the only thing you're any good at is not getting completely lost, well, then the Pity Protocol kicks in and ensures that you develop a real passion for orienteering, at least.

It's psychology making a virtue out of necessity, basically.

Chris, however, was an aberration – the exception that proves the rule. He didn't like what he did very much, and he *certainly* didn't regard it as having any worth. The bleak, unsightly stupidity of what he produced was something he wearily commented on almost daily. Chris regarded this as his own personal misery. But, as misery is, let us say, solipsistic, all his colleagues saw was someone declaring that what *they* did (they were doing the same thing as Chris, after all) was utterly without merit.

Put these factors together and you can understand the (unspoken, quietly festering) attitude of Chris's workmates. They didn't actually wish him dead – he was too obviously an asset to the company and thus, by extension, to each of them as individuals. But they did hope he would fall badly on the stairs, ideally chipping the bone in his shin on the edge of a step.

However, none of them gave any thought to the possibility that Chris might be thinking, 'Bugger this for a game of soldiers.' His burden of aptitude made him prominent professionally, but, by nature, he was too unassuming for them (dynamic and thrusting and dynamically thrusting as they all were) to think he'd do anything ... well, that he'd do *anything*. Oh, he complained all right; he didn't conceal his cynicism and discontent, that was plain enough. But it was *so* near-constant that the impression it created was that he enjoyed moaning as an activity – he'd never actually act on the moans, because the moaning itself was sufficient. It was also well known that he was prone to Pointless Acts of Trivial Rebellion. Someone, for example, now always checked the initial letters of the sentences if his idea used a number of lines descending the page or poster, as Chris found it hard to resist the temptation of a childish acrostic. Or take the fact that, recently, and to everyone's puzzlement, he'd been very insistent about the precise piece of dialogue that needed to be delivered by one of the two child actors due to record a radio ad for some biscuits. What had baffled his colleagues was that the 'dialogue' wasn't even words – it was nothing but 'enthusiastic speech made completely unintelligible because the child's mouth is full'. 'What do you think?' Child Actor One was to ask, and Child Actor Two's reply would be mere (but obviously happy) mouth sounds, as he couldn't bring himself to stop chomping away. Why, then, was Chris so determined that the garbled words *absolutely must* make the noise 'Jouma ... sewapskiet ... pap'? That nothing else quite conveyed the innocent, totally consuming, biscuit-eating ecstasy. The answer accidentally emerged when, by pure coincidence, it turned out that the technician at the recording studio happened to come from South Africa; and he couldn't help mentioning how bizarre it was that the random 'I'm a child with an unstoppable love of this biscuit' line sounded *exactly* like '*Jou ma se wap skiet pap*' – a common Afrikaans curse meaning 'Your mother's twat shoots porridge.'

This kind of puerile behaviour was Chris's league. If he had any strategy at all, it was probably something like, 'Come the revolution, I'm going to knock on your door and run off.' His colleagues assumed that they could depend on his getting on their nerves daily, forever, at a more or less stable, low-level intensity. That was Chris, they all knew: he was a target, not an arrow.

'I'll be there,' Andrew insisted, holding the telephone receiver between his shoulder and his ear – giving a sort of 'hanged man' flop to his neck. He was glancing through a stack of invoices; placing them into piles on the table one by one, like dealing cards.

Chris snorted. 'You always say you'll be there, then you cry off at the last minute.'

'That's not true.'

'Yes it is. You say you'll be at the pub, and you say you'll be at the pub, and you say you'll be at the pub, and then you stay at home watching *Dynasty* or something, like a big girl.'

'No I don't. I—'

'Oh, crap – I have to go.' Chris had spotted his boss approaching. 'Somewhere there is a crime happening.'

'What?'

'*RoboCop*.'

'What?'

'*RoboCop*. "Excuse me, I have to go. Some—"'

Chris put the phone down before Andrew could continue. Andrew, he knew only too well, couldn't stop himself pouring out everything that happens in a movie you haven't seen. You had the feeling that he *tried* to, but the thing was simply bigger than his will to resist it: 'I'll ... I'll ... I'll just tell you *this* bit ... ' Once the fragile membrane holding it back had been pierced by your accidentally enticing him with an opportunity, it all came gushing out unstoppably. And Chris had missed *RoboCop* when it was on at the cinema a few months ago, having made the tactical error of going to see it with Katrina. She'd wrinkled her nose, and pushed a strand of her hair back behind her ear in an especially cultivated fashion, and – to maintain his position as sophisticated and thoughtful – he'd had to sit through *Babette's Feast* instead (a film during which – despite its being many, un-BBFC-cut minutes longer than *RoboCop* – nothing whatsoever blows up).

'Personal call?' asked Chris's boss with a broad, I'm-one-of-the-lads-just-like-you grin that left no room for any doubt that he was genuinely narked about it.

'No,' Chris replied.

David Short decided to respond to this by remaining silent.

Chris decided to let him.

To get a psychological submission by forcing a nervous and hurried scramble for an obviously invented explanation, the head and founder of Short Stick Media carefully applied the extended, awkward pause like a martial artist digging a thumb into a pressure point. Like some other kind of martial artist, Chris reached into his drawer and took out a bag of crisps.

The person next to Short shifted uneasily from foot to foot. His name was Euan and this was his first day. He'd been introduced only briefly to the others in the office, and was anxious about who it would be expedient to befriend and who he should make a point of disliking – the latter aspect reinforced the former (your friendship is valued more if you appear to be choosey about your friends, and hating the same person is a useful bonding technique too). Was Chris the alpha male in this place, or was he the office wanker? It's always tricky to make that particular call.

Short gave a big, loose laugh and turned away to nod towards Euan. 'This is our new gofer,' he said.

Witnessing this surrender – a shaming acceptance of defeat in the face of his plucky counter-attack of silence – Chris tingled inside, deep down where he suspected his soul used to be. Usually, he wouldn't have had the slightest interest in any kind of silly ego wrestling, but today was different. Today he was going to allow himself a bit of satisfaction – and, obviously, while you get some satisfaction from doing something that gives you pleasure, you get even more from doing something that annoys someone you don't like. In that sense, this was a perfect start to the morning: if you wanted to hit Short where he lived, then what you needed to do was deny him a petty victory.

'Hi there,' said Chris, offering Euan a crisp.

'Euan,' said Euan.

'Cheese and onion,' said Chris.

Short put his hands deep into the expensive pockets of his foreign trousers to signify that nothing concerned him less than whether or not he got offered a crisp too. 'Chris will teach you all the basics, Eu, yeah? Show you a rope or two.' He placed three beats here and, on the third, the cheery brightness of his face gave way to an abrupt intrusion of fearful anxiety. 'That *is* OK, Chris, right?'

Having him train a newcomer, while still doing all his other work, and the whole carefully seasoned with the insinuation – for Euan's benefit, of course – that he might not be up to it. Top notch.

'Yep, that's fine, David,' Chris replied with a smile. It really was remarkable, he thought to himself, how sanguine you can be about everything when you know that, a fortnight from tomorrow, you won't be there.

That was at the centre of Chris's plan. Well, at what would have been the centre, had there been any actual plan to go around it. But we'll come to that detail later.

'Well, if there's anything you need ...' Short said; after a careful moment he completed the sentence with a substantial slap across Chris's back that could equally well have meant either 'I'll be in my office' or 'you can sod off'. With that, his Gucci'd feet turned snappily, he spun on his designer balls, and Chris watched him saunter away across the office.

'So, what's the story, Euan?' Chris asked. 'Straight out of uni?' He popped another crisp into his mouth.

Euan nodded. 'Yes.' He supposed that being introduced as 'the new gofer' didn't exactly create the impression that he'd been headhunted after single-handedly conceiving and running the whole Levi's campaign, but he was a little irritated that Chris had made the assumption all the same. After all, there was surely only two or three years difference in their ages. 'Business Studies,' Euan added. 'Got a first, in fact.'

'Really? Excellent.'

There's not much that's worse than doing a Business Studies degree, thought Chris, except, that is, for doing it well.

Chris's attitude to education was rather hedonistic. Which is to say that he felt its chief good lay in studying something because you enjoyed (or were at least interested in) the subject; not because it was a means to an end. Nobody, of course – other than some kind of inhuman freak – was going to be interested in Business Studies, and the idea that there was a mind on the loose somewhere out there that might actually *enjoy* it made the hairs on the back of his neck stand up. It was the type of course that attracted people who would be happy enough to go to the lectures sufficiently often, or to copy out someone else's essays, or to just sit in a tin bath full of baked beans for three years, if it resulted in a bit of paper that would statistically raise their projected post-graduation salary into a higher percentile. Even to consider the question, 'What will this degree be worth in practical terms?' before choosing a course spoke, Chris felt, of a dismal excess of clinical focus for an eighteen-year-old.

Andrew was an accountant now, and that was fine (for him). He'd taken the qualification post-grad, after realising that otherwise, within two years, he'd probably be back living with his mother or end up working in a library. *That* was how you ought to make practical decisions about your financial future: in a panic, when things are looking desperate. It didn't reflect badly on Andrew that he was an accountant – Chris didn't think any less of him. He, like Chris himself – like Neil too, amazingly – had taken a Humanities degree. So, the fact that they were all doing reasonably well career-wise was certainly not the result of bleakly sensible choices made while they were still studying for their A levels. Who'd want to have their life plotted out at that stage? You shouldn't have a plan that maps your whole journey from clearing to pension. You should have nothing but a hasty list left in your pocket during the wash, a list reading, 'Complete assignment; buy even sillier trousers; continue attempts to lose virginity.' The roads ahead might lead in wonderful, unexpected directions. Finish your A levels, then do a Humanities degree, and you'll arrive at twenty-one still not heading anywhere at all. That's how it should be.

Chris, casting a black crisp into the waste-paper basket, mused that Euan had appeared before him not much more than a minute ago, and had said under ten words, but already he'd made many sweeping – and less than positive – decisions about the newcomer's character, motivations and moral worth. He scolded himself inwardly and, for the eighty-thousandth or so time in his life, resolved to stop doing that.

'Well, I suppose—' Chris began, but he was interrupted by a hand coming down on his shoulder from behind. He turned to look at it, and then traced his eyes upwards along the attached arm and neck until he reached the face of Abigail. It wasn't worth the journey.

'What's the ETA on the completed Thurston proposal?' she asked. She was holding a pencil lightly in the fingers that weren't pawing Chris, and, as she finished speaking, she brought it up to her mouth and laid it vertically across her lips – carefully constructing the image of a young, fiercely intelligent businesswoman. Chris thought she looked like the first frame from a 'Stripping Secretary' photo series in *Fiesta*.

He got as far as almost considering the question then, a sudden joy leaking through his insides (as though the shell of the sweet his spirit had been sucking had just split, exposing a chocolate centre), he replied, 'Three weeks.'

'You're sure you'll have it done in three weeks?'

'My assessment is absolutely, definitely, that it'll take three weeks to make everything perfect.'

'OK. Great.' She pointed her pencil at him. 'I'll be holding you to that.' As she started to walk away, she realised that she hadn't smiled – so 'I'll be holding you to that' had probably come across not as a friendly threat made with good-spirited humour (which is what she intended), but rather as 'Don't you dare be a second late, you little shit' (which is what she felt). She pulled up, glanced round at Chris, smiled, then turned again and continued striding over to her desk.

Chris twisted his attention back to Euan. 'Right – where were we?'

'I think you were going to start telling me everything I need to know,' Euan said. He still wasn't entirely sure, but he was leaning more and more towards the assessment that Chris was someone of little political importance, so his reply – which could easily have been strategically fawning – gravitated in the direction of sarcastic.

Euan quickly rebuked himself for jumping the gun with his nuances like that. He prided himself on his ability to be cool when not under fire. In fact, this was one of the brilliant personal insights that he knew would lead him to success. He'd realised that people like to think of themselves as the sort of person who would – if the circumstances ever arose – be solid when the chips were down. When pushes were coming to shoves and when shit was hitting fans, they would impress with their cool heads and brave hearts. They further assume that others can just, kind of, 'sense' this about them. But, in reality, others don't sense it; it's nowhere in their heads at all – because they're fully occupied with thinking about themselves. And what's far, far more important is that, for the vast majority of the time, there isn't a crisis exploding all around – our world is vastly more the dull slog than the big push. And even when things *do* become hectic, it's often too much of a disorientating blur for anything much to sink in or be remembered properly. Euan had instinctively seen, therefore, that a person will do best not by focusing on pulling off the big coup. That might be how it works in films, but films are about drama not about reality. Instead, he should attend to making the right impressions and alliances during what most regard as the trivial, day-to-day times. It's better (and, frankly, easier) for a soldier to get ahead by being popular and clever with how he presents himself during the long dreary months in the barracks than by concentrating on doing something impressive during a sudden firefight: target the long periods of boredom, not the brief flashes of violence.

Euan was, then, annoyed at his own carelessly premature snideness. But, as it turned out, his lapse accidentally paid dividends. He saw that Chris hadn't noticed his little dig anyway. Well, that confirmed it. If he wasn't sensitive to when people were taking the piss out of him, then Chris was *definitely* a no-hoper. That was one person in the company labelled and pinned to a board nicely; a good start so early in his first day.

'Hmmm, OK.' Chris peered into his crisp packet. 'Where to start ...'

'I suppose it's quite a complex operation.'

'I suppose so.'

'That's fine. I'm a quick learner. Complexity is no problem. I can cope with that. High pressure too – I'm sure it's a pressurised career.'

'Pressurised? No, I wouldn't use the word *pressurised*, exactly.'

'What then?'

'Erm, "wearing". Yes. It's a very *wearing* career.'

(Was this banter? Euan wondered. He tried to fake a laugh. But he didn't try very hard.)

'Ha.'

(Still, he'd better keep it upbeat; someone else in the office might overhear – it was open-plan and people were all around. One or more of these others might matter.)

'I bet it's satisfying to create something and see it realised, though,' he continued, quite loudly.

'You'd think so, wouldn't you?'

Chris had decided on his next crisp now but, as he reached into the packet to take it out, the phone on his desk rang. He scowled at it. Then looked at his selected crisp again. Then reluctantly sucked the salt off his fingers and reached for the receiver.

'Chris Mortimer ... Yeah ... Yeah ... Uh-huh ... Three weeks.'

3

The yellow bounced off three cushions, clipped the black, ran into the cue ball (which had been ricocheting around the table completely unrelatedly since their first meeting a short time ago) and, with a provocative wriggle between the jaws on the way, slipped into the left-hand corner pocket.

'You utter bastard.'

Neil picked up the chalk and applied it carefully while considering the position of the balls.

'Played for it,' he said.

Chris looked over at Andrew and appealed to him for support. 'Andrew, tell him he's an utter bastard. He'll listen to you. You have that idiot savant quality that intrigues him.'

Andrew took a sip from his beer and shook his head solemnly. 'I believe him. Pool is as much about honour as it is about skill. There's a sort of samurai code. He *must* have played for it – I don't think a person would lie about something like that.'

Neil lifted his glowing cigarette up from the ashtray and drew on it like a cool, hard-bitten detective considering a situation of immense intricacy and peril.

'The thing you miss, my poor, doomed Christopher, is that pool is just an extension of life. And what do we know about life?'

'That it's not fair. Terrible diseases strike down people who are honest and deserving. Poverty and injustice oppress whole communities. And, meanwhile, utter bastards completely fluke yellows.'

'That's my point exactly.'

'No it isn't. It's *my* point. You don't have a point. You point thief.'

'Tch. I didn't mean your laughably banal interpretation. I meant

17

that the crucial thing about life, if you look at it scientifically, is that you are rubbish, and I am splendid.'

'Just put your fag down and take your shot, will you?'

Katrina, grinning, raised a hand and flapped it lightly in a 'slow down' motion. 'Hold on, Chris. I want to see where this is going.'

'Up his own arse, that's where,' Michelle said with a sigh at one end and a smile at the other. 'That's where everything he says is ultimately heading.'

Though turning his eyes to Chris, Neil reached across and patted her shoulder. 'My girlfriend is being self-deprecating on my behalf,' he said. 'It's understandable. You look at me, Christopher, then look at yourself ... and despair is sure to follow. She'd like to spare you that. *I* would too, of course, but *I* must serve the higher calling of speaking the Truth.' He raised a hand to sweep the foppish flop of his almost-unarguably-too-long fringe from his eyes, and adopted the pose of a poet gazing into some imaginary, shining distance.

'Jesus. Play the bloody shot.'

'In a moment – after I've finished being brilliant.'

Chris shook his head. 'You know, I always thought that people who were successful in sales did it by talking persuasively. But I bet people will buy whatever the hell you're offering them, just so long as it makes you shut up.'

Neil raised a finger in the air, and then slowly brought it down to point at Chris. 'The key is to *play for the flukes*.'

'You can't play for a fluke. If you've played for it, it's not a fluke. Get a dictionary.'

'Fff – I write my own dictionary.'

'That's just plain ridiculous. You can't write your own dictionary.'

'Dr Johnson did.'

'*Play the bloody shot!*' Chris looked across at Michelle. 'God – you actually sleep with this man? How on earth do you have sex with someone that annoying?'

She shrugged. 'It's no picnic, but at least it's quick.'

Chris turned back to Neil. 'You – even you, lying bastard that you are – cannot tell me that you intended that yellow to go in.'

'I intended *a* yellow to go in.'

Katrina, holding a lager and black, paused with the glass

halfway to her mouth. 'Wow. That's incredibly Zen,' she breathed, impressed.

Chris glanced at her, and wondered if she perhaps had a bit of a thing for Neil.

Neil didn't give her a reply, and seemed hardly to have noticed she'd spoken at all. He just absently rolled the cue over in his hands and moved slightly closer to Michelle.

'It's odd,' he continued, 'that you – of all people, Christopher – are so hung up on the balls that are being hit, instead of the person who's hitting them. I'm what's important. The human element. The ineffable, fabulous magic that is me. I strike the white with flair and confidence' – he mimed striking with flair and confidence – 'and just *know* that one of my balls will more than likely go into a pocket. It might not be the most obvious ball going into the pocket I was aiming for, but that's hardly the issue, is it?'

'Yes, it is.'

'It's not. Like I said: as with pool, so with life. You're forever hearing someone or other mumble that so-and-so "always seems to land on his feet", or that, "Them what has, gets." It's because people affect the world far more than the world affects people. If you're wonderful, and know that you're wonderful, then wonderfulness runs into your open arms as inevitably as the key points of a woman's personality and mental state are revealed by her shoes. If you're a bit crap, and spend your time reflecting on your a-bit-crapness, you attract crap to yourself out of the ether. As we've agreed, I'm very marvellous indeed ... so the yellow's going to go in. That's all there is to it.'

'That's fascism,' Chris responded, pointing at the pocket into which Neil's ball had disappeared.

'No it isn't.'

'It is. It's all Nietzsche, and Leni Riefenstahl filming people holding torches, and it being your destiny to bomb Warsaw.'

'I bet Hitler was terrible at pool,' Andrew said. Everyone turned their eyes in his direction. 'No – I bet he was, though. You can just tell by looking at him.'

Everyone turned away again.

'Nature–Nurture,' Chris went on. 'We're a product of our society, culture and environment – *Nurture*. If you think we're

Nature, you're a fascist. I did an essay on it in year two's The Rise of Nationalism module, remember? I got an A3.'

'Cuh. I'm not saying that anyone who can't beat me at pool should toil underground to provide my tank factories with coal. And I'm not saying my natural ace-ness is the expression of divine law either. I was merely lucky enough to be born magnificent, that's all. If I can help those less fortunate than myself, then I will. I'm no more worthy than they are: I'm simply more super ... I may even deliberately miscue on an important shot later, Christopher, just to give you a chance. You watch and see if I don't.'

'It's the odd humility in his nauseating arrogance, isn't it?' Michelle said to everyone and no one. 'You're not sure whether to slap him, or kiss him, and then slap him.'

'I think Chris is heavily on the kissing side,' Andrew muttered, hunching forward and burying a grin in his lager.

Chris flinched away from this comment, as though the surprise of it was similar to unexpectedly leaning against a hot stove. 'You *what*?'

'You guru him. Admit it.'

'I do *not* guru him!' he replied, his face practically concertinaing down to half its size with the expression of astonishment he'd thrown onto it.

'OK.'

Chris swung to look at Michelle. 'I do *not*.'

'Andrew's winding you up – it's just a joke,' she soothed, rolling her eyes. Though, privately, she marvelled at the interweaving currents that flowed through man dynamics. Did Chris guru Neil? Well, she thought, he certainly spent a very large proportion of any time they were together publicly making derogatory remarks about him – albeit in a non-malicious, jokey fashion. That was a clear sign, in man language, that he had a good degree of respect and affection for Neil. (Equally, she could tell by the fact that Neil aimed many more digs at Chris that he felt closer to him than he did to Andrew.) Whether Chris guru'd Neil wasn't what she found intriguing here. What puzzled her was why Andrew had made the remark, when *he* so obviously guru'd Chris. Smokescreen, maybe? And, that aside, she was totally baffled by why Andrew should guru Chris anyway. That wasn't to say anything against Chris, whom she liked a lot. It was purely that, if Neil was the alpha male of the three (the idea of her boyfriend – who had gone to Alton Towers and been sick, on the monorail – being an 'alpha male' struck her as very funny indeed, but that was another matter), then why didn't Andrew guru *him*? Was it yet one more impenetrable rule of male interaction that you guru'd not the person at the top of whichever mini-hierarchy you happened to be in at the time, but only the person one or two rungs above you?

Michelle was completely captivated by men: they could look very agreeable in boxer shorts, and yet you could also study them like ants.

Neil tapped Chris's shoulder to get his attention. 'Your shot.' He gestured towards the pool table. 'Come along – we haven't got all night.'

'What? You've . . . Ah, missed, then? Ha.'

'I've developed the balls. And given you a Tao. I consider that's enough for one visit.'

Andrew opened his mouth to say something funny in a Neil/Steve Davis-crossover manner, but pulled himself up. However clever the joke, he bet that what would happen was that everyone would picture him at home alone watching live coverage from the Crucible into the early hours, like a saddo. No one would take in his amusing comment because they'd all be too busy imagining him sitting there glued to the Embassy finals; in their minds, he'd probably be wearing cords and a tank top, and eating small cheese sandwiches off a plate balanced on his clamped-together knees too. So he kept his mouth shut and merely adjusted the position of his beer glass instead.

'Anyway,' Neil continued as Chris stood considering whether or not to go for a risky double, 'I don't want to be too fascinating. It's your night, isn't it? And at some point, you're surely going to tell us *why* it's your night. Why you insisted we all came out to the pub this evening, but why you wouldn't reveal what the special occasion was beforehand.'

Chris turned his attention from the balls and leaned back against the edge of the pool table. He took the opportunity to smile in a way that – he was fairly confident – everyone would find inscrutable, try as they might to scrute it.

'Well . . .' he began, but then unexpectedly found himself stepping into a small falter. Actually, he realised, he didn't really want to say, now it came to it. It had reached that point where keeping back a secret or a surprise has overtaken whatever the secret or surprise is. The means has almost become the end, and you suspect that once you let it out you'll feel sort of 'emptied'; tangibly void of looking forward – like that hollowness you find in your stomach when you first step back into your house after returning from a holiday.

'Well . . .' he repeated, and took a self-urging breath. 'I'm leaving Short Stick.'

No one said anything in response to this for long enough for their continuously not saying it to become quite awkward.

Michelle sighed inside. She saw that Katrina was twisting her lips as she peered with no little intensity at her own lap – indicating that she'd clearly known nothing about Chris's news before now. Her boyfriend had made a big Life Decision without mentioning it to her at all, and then announced it publicly. Though Katrina was entirely blameless, Michelle knew that this situation would be widely considered to diminish her status as a girlfriend and as a woman. (If Neil ever did something like this to her, she thought, her vengeance would surely be protracted and barbaric.) So she empathised with Katrina's obvious humiliation, and knew that the poor woman wouldn't want to draw attention to herself still further by saying anything just yet. Neil and Andrew's motionless silence was doubtless due to their both trying to think of something sarcastic to say in reply. This was a significant emotional and psychological moment for their friend, and thus – unless they could come up with an appropriate gag – they'd have to address it like mature human beings and, as a result, be consumed by fire. Michelle realised it was up to her.

She was sure she'd got a 'fairly good' to 'absolutely airtight' hypothesis already (these things simply came to her, luckily). Chris's mother had died when he was still young – nine or ten, if she remembered correctly. So you have one aspect, right there: a need to fill the hole that was left – searching, restlessness, always longing for an ineffable something. Then – she knew for a fact, because she'd been seeing Neil already by this point – his father had passed away while Chris was in his final year at university. And he was only in his mid-fifties when he'd died too. OK, that was a few years ago now, but the shock of these things can take a long time to finally hit home. Put this all together, and it was clear to Michelle that Chris was wounded in his core by the absence of his mother, in addition to being nervous about his own mortality as highlighted by the early death of his father. *That's* why he was dramatically changing his job. She was itching to explain this to them all, but thought she'd better allow the others time to settle first, so that they could fully appreciate and enjoy her analysis. Something that moved things on, but also left them open, was what was needed right now, she concluded.

'Wow,' she said absolutely without inflection, so that everyone listening could colour it with whichever one they preferred.

'Yes,' replied Chris, thankful for, at last, a sign of astonishment and admiration. 'I'm giving them my two weeks' notice first thing tomorrow morning.'

'*Tomorrow* morning?' Michelle squinted. 'You're giving notice on a *Tuesday* morning? Why didn't you give it to—'

Andrew cut in before she could finish. 'Because he's Chris, of course. He's deliberately avoided doing the obvious thing. Everyone gives notice at the start of the week, or at the end of it. So he couldn't possibly do that.'

It's a demonstration of his individuality,' added Neil, nodding. 'He's a puckish free spirit, our Christopher. Unconcerned with the accepted mores and the only master of himself.' He tapped ash off his cigarette. 'Also, he's inadvertently revealing – yet again – that, for all his Marxist Soc ranting and his A3 essay, he knows I'm completely right about our not being a powerless product of what happens around us.'

'Or,' Chris said, 'it might simply be that I want to bugger Short Stick about as much as I can, and resigning on a Tuesday seems like a good way to do that.'

Andrew raked his fingers through his hair. 'You're actually destroying capitalism from within.'

'How can he be destroying it from within if he's leaving?' said Neil.

Michelle sucked on her teeth. 'Well, he'll still be destroying it from within. Just a different bit of it. So – where *are* you moving to, Chris?'

'I'm glad you asked me that, Michelle. I am moving . . .' He held his arms wide, like someone in musical theatre at the very end of

23

a song about making it big in musical theatre. 'To nowhere.'

'What do you mean?'

'I mean that I'm not leaving to go to another job. I'm just *leaving.*'

Katrina finally spoke. 'I don't understand ... What are you going to do?'

'I haven't decided, Kat. It could be anything, or nothing.'

'How can it be *nothing*? What about money?'

Chris laughed. 'You're always saying how money isn't important – that the only important thing is being true to yourself.'

'For *me*, yes. I didn't mean ... Well, for a start, what are we supposed to do if you can't afford to run a car any more?'

'I'll walk wherever I need to go.'

'What? With half a dozen bloody great canvases?'

'I don't have any ca—'

'No, but I do! You don't seem to be thinking about anyone but yourself.'

Abruptly, the situation had developed from being unsure where it wanted to go to standing on a precarious edge demanding one good reason for not stepping off it.

No one wants to have a row with their partner while in company. But, even more, no one wants to let a row with their partner while in company end without it being plain to the company that they are in the right. It's easy to lose it totally in these circumstances, because you're so enraged by the pounding injustice of it all: there's little that's more infuriating than your partner prolonging an embarrassing scene purely because they're too irrational with anger to do the sensible thing of admitting you're correct and just letting the damn thing lie.

Katrina, twirling a helix of her blonde, springy hair around her index finger, chewed her bottom lip again and stared at the floor. Neil and Andrew, trying as hard as possible to emit utter obliviousness, looked across the pub at nothing whatsoever and did their best to be psychically invisible. It was bad enough to have a domestic occurring around the table, but the *very* last thing they wanted was for either party to involve them in some kind of 'appeal to the jury' fashion. Michelle, fidgeting slightly in her seat, looked back and forth between Chris and Katrina, and wondered if she should jump in as a referee – for she had many pertinent observations to make – or if she ought to hold out in the hope of being asked.

In the taut silence 'Alphabet Street' by Prince suddenly started playing from the jukebox. Chris considered whether this was a sign – or could be taken as a sign, at least. His mind did a quick recce of the lyric. Nope: it was utterly meaningless. Damn – the timing was spot-on perfect too. He couldn't help glaring around the pub briefly, trying to guess which idiot had – at *exactly* the right moment – chosen a song from which it was impossible to pull any coincidental insight, or sad irony, or anything whatsoever except the irrelevant, distracting and frankly quite unappealing image of someone jerking their body like a horny pony.

Nevertheless, Chris made the decision (without any help from tiny purple pop singers – thanks for nothing) to be a type of conciliatory. He could go on the offensive, of course – no one would blame him for doing so. But he was a bigger person than that: big enough to be a type of conciliatory. Instead of wading in, he'd soften his voice, and adopt a slightly pained expression, and explain things more fully, and generally go for the type of conciliatory that says, 'I didn't intend to upset you. *This* is what I mean. I hope you understand now. Though, obviously, if you don't like it, you can still fuck right off.'

Chris, like a man steeped in spirituality, struck his pool cue against the pub floor by the black rubber knob on its end and then caught it as it bounced up again.

'The job is doing my head in,' he explained. 'It's … Oh, I don't know. Maybe it's because I didn't take a gap year.'

'I didn't take a gap year either,' Katrina muttered to herself, loudly.

Chris very nearly replied that, as she had done an Art degree at poly, she'd had pretty much one thirty-six-month-long gap year. But he remembered he was being a type of conciliatory and instead offered her the gift of continuing with what he was saying as if she didn't exist.

'I've never taken the time out to decide what I really want, long-term. And I think I ought to do that now, before it's too late. Everything's still open at the moment. I can change direction a bit, or try something completely new, or just sit around in my underpants watching *Brookside* for twelve months – it's all OK.

A year's navel-gazing is no problem at this point, but – Christ – in five years I'll be *thirty*. I need to do it before I'm too old to do anything whatsoever.'

It had the feel of a declaration of intent delivered to the assembled peoples of the Earth, and everyone remained silent for a time after Chris had finished. Andrew tapped the side of his glass with his fingernail, but otherwise no one moved. Cigarette smoke gave a milky hue to the air. In the background Prince assured them all that, if they could hang, they could trip on it.

'I think, Christopher,' Neil said at last, 'that *all* of us will probably be too old to do anything whatsoever simply from waiting around for you to take your shot.'

He smiled through his pantomime of weariness, Andrew gave a snorty laugh, and Chris, grinning, replied, 'Bollocks.'

There we go, Michelle thought to herself.

Chris scrubbed the tip of his cue with chalk then puffed off the excess in a small blue plosive. He bent over casually, and doubled his red into the centre pocket. (Whack! Right in – without touching the sides. He was flooded by an energising euphoria along with a profound sense of achievement: he idly wondered if women felt something approaching this after giving birth to a child.)

'And I'll tell you another thing,' Chris said, unnecessarily chalking his cue again. 'Not only am I telling Short Stick where they can shove their job tomorrow, and not only am I going to give Fluke Boy Neil here a pool lesson he won't forget in a hurry, but I am also going to get totally, completely, and *utterly* wankered.' He reached into the pocket of his jacket and pulled out his wallet, which he tossed onto the table in front of Andrew. 'Get a round in, would you? I'll have a Grolsch to kick off with.' He glanced at Neil.

'I'll give a home to a whiskey.'

Then at Michelle.

'I'm still fine with this, thanks,' she said, nodding towards her drink.

Then at Katrina.

She didn't meet his eyes. Instead, she gave the impression of being so interested in some detail of the decor behind the bar that she was entirely unaware that he was there.

Fine, thought Chris, his nostrils allowing themselves a slight flare. Def me out, then. I can get absolutely pissed without *your* assistance. And he resolved to get even drunker that he'd originally intended, just to teach her a lesson. He shifted his gaze over to Andrew. 'And whatever you want yourself,' he said.

Chris turned round to face the pool table once more. He took a moment to glance at his watch – it was still only ten to eight. With that kind of run-up, he felt sure, he had more than enough time to make one *hell* of a night out of it.

4

Chris's head felt like someone had used it to get very, very drunk.

Though he was aware that he was now more awake than asleep (and that this downturn was likely to continue), he lay unmoving and unseeing with his cheek flaccid against the pillow and did nothing but tentatively attempt to take stock of himself. It seemed as though a skilful attacker were pressing his thumbs – hard – against his temples, from the inside, and he was genuinely intrigued to know how (a small preliminary twitch of the lids had revealed) he had somehow managed to develop toothache in his eyes. His whole body was constructed from sloppy, dull pain occasionally brought into sharper focus at key points, but, even so, it was his head that was making all the running. The icy-hot jolts that randomly streaked across his skull were so flawlessly agonising that there was almost a beauty to them; like the minimalist precision of some lethal virus or the perfect, killing-machine horror of Giger's Alien, Chris's head appeared to have raised crapulence to mathematical art: *this*, he thought, was how BMW would make a hangover.

He tried to recall his journey into this abyss, but it was blurry and fractured. He recollected laughing a lot. Before the curtains came down and obscured his memories entirely, he had images of being almost helpless with completely genuine laughter – that's to say, his good spirits were the honest result of a combination of something not very funny plus a massive intake of alcohol. But there was the metallic aftertaste of other laughter too, from a little earlier, and this he seemed to have been having to work at. He tried to concentrate. Ah, yes. He'd been making a point of how very unconcerned he was, and what an enviable amount of fun he was having, for the benefit of Katrina (who was there, determinedly dour, sitting at a table and trying to snare him in some sort of accusing strop). He couldn't fish out any remembrance of having an actual stand-up shout-down argument with her, but it seemed that all the ingredients had been there, ready and waiting. If the row hadn't happened in the missing part of the previous evening, then it hadn't been avoided; it was merely circling impatiently above them, in a holding pattern.

He had another stab at opening his eyes. Stab, it seemed, was the perfect word for it. The weight of the light on his pupils made him wince, and he clenched his lids shut again.

The world hit a wall. A very loud second ticked by in his head. And he snapped his eyes open once more.

His vision was unfocused and listing, and everything remained too bright to bear. Perhaps it was being only half awake, or perhaps it was the nauseous headache, or perhaps he was still a bit drunk – most likely, he guessed, it was all three. However, though he couldn't see very well, he could see well enough to be absolutely sure that he wasn't in his own bed. He wouldn't have stood a chance of reading the time on his bedside clock-radio, but he would have been able to pick out its glow, at least, had he been in his own bed, in his own bedroom. But this room wasn't his. It was bigger, and had much more furniture in it, and it was the wrong colour. Another thing that was the wrong colour, and which was also preventing him from seeing where – in his own bedroom – his clock-radio would have sat, was the back of the head resting on the other pillow.

It was this final thing that tore his eyes back open. It took a second to register but, when it did, it was like waking up falling through the air. His mind surged full to bursting point with that bit in the *Godfather* where Jack Woltz begins his day by finding the severed head of a horse tucked up in his bed. Chris wondered if it was *just* a head lying there next to him. A fear-filled, split-second glance confirmed that there was a body attached, however. This was an immense relief, yet, somehow, he couldn't completely characterise it as a sign that things were looking up. Encouragingly undecapitated, yes, but it remained a head covered in flowing, dark hair of exactly the type that Katrina didn't have. Moreover, this hair was made up of soft waves – it took on the curves of the pillow and the duvet, rather than being constructed of long determined springs that allowed little interference from the world, like Katrina's. And those two things were on top of it being *here* – which was God knows where. No, this was definitely a stranger's head in a strange bed, and Chris hadn't got the first idea what the hell he should do with it.

Suddenly, from nowhere, a plan to get the situation back on track uncoiled in his mind. Relieved, he closed his eyes and – after a few seconds and a steadying breath – opened them again.

The head was still there. Shit. So much for trying to take the initiative then.

He rolled over onto his back and stared at the ceiling (the ceiling had the benefit of being blank, and thus offered the slight respite of presenting him with nothing to be out of focus or swimming around erratically). His mind raced. Unfortunately, as his mind still had quite a bit of alcohol sloshing around in it, its racing was not only largely directionless but was also quite likely to cause an accident. He wondered why you can be delighted by almost all levels of drunkenness during the evening – from slightly merry to stumbling along in the middle of the road belting out Pogues songs – yet immediately, always and at all gradations, it is vile to wake up drunk. He further wondered how he could *possibly* be wondering this, when far more pressing issues were lying on the pillow next to him. It was probably, he concluded, the drink thinking.

Retargeting his efforts, he wrung out his brain for how he had come to be in the strange bed of a strange woman.

Christ!

Was it a woman?

Absolutely conscious that he was completely fine with any hue from sexuality's large rich palette, and committed to the position that one kind wasn't any better than another, he peeked over at the body next to him in absolute terror. Because it was no big thing – not a thing at all, really – he forcibly prevented himself from letting out a delighted gasp when his double-checking confirmed his unknown bedfellow wasn't literally a fellow. He wasn't so crass as to do a thorough examination, but, ill and disobedient as his eyes still were, the general shape alone was enough to pretty clearly announce, 'Female.' (A voice deep in his head did whisper, 'Or post-op,' but he took that voice into a secluded backroom in his brain and hit it in the mouth with a broom handle.)

Chris turned his gaze back to the ceiling. Ascertaining the sex of the person he was lying in bed with was, he thought, something he felt he probably owed himself, but it wasn't really progress. The last ... whatever it was – a dozen or so hours, perhaps – were still a blank. He remained unable to recall what had happened between then and now; the precise series of events leading from a few drinks to a brunette.

Perhaps, if he speculated – using the known facts – on the probable course of the previous night he might jog his memory. It was worth a try. (And he took heart from the notion that it was, methodically, exactly what Sherlock Holmes would do, if the world's foremost consulting detective woke up in bed with some unknown woman after getting pissed.)

OK, so he'd been celebrating. He and Kat had fallen out – over what he couldn't entirely recollect, but he had the strong impression that it was her fault. Certainly, it had particularly annoyed him that she was being a pain because it was meant to be a good time for him. (It's aggravating if someone bums out your day, but it's especially so – and you take it more personally – if they bum out your birthday.) Given this, it seemed fairly reasonable that Katrina's actions had caused him to sleep with another woman.

This wasn't something he was remotely in the habit of doing. There was no sense in him of a realisation, now he came to think about it, that, Yeah – that's just like me. The previous week, for example, Katrina had clumsily recorded over his video of *It'll Be Alright on the Night 5*, and he hadn't immediately marched out and had sex with someone to balance things up. Had you, yesterday morning, asked anyone who knew him whether they could picture him in the present situation, he was sure they'd have replied that they couldn't. But, working back from what was undeniably the case, it seemed somewhere between credible and obvious that, under the pressure of alcohol and Katrina's selfish sulk, he'd had little choice but to cop off with someone else.

Mind you, he thought on reflection, he probably shouldn't regard himself with quite so little respect, if he were to be fair. Though doing what he had wasn't admirable, it was, let's be honest, pretty admirable to be *able* to do it. He'd never considered himself irresistible to women, and, in this assessment, women seemed to be right behind him. Not that he was some kind of dribbling grotesque. He'd always done reasonably well (*surprisingly* well, he felt) in the girlfriend department, but it was more a steady and gentle succession of them, rather than his constantly having to keep on the balls of his feet in case a woman glanced his profile from her bedroom window and immediately hurled herself out of it at him, unbuttoning her blouse on the way down. If, as seemed to be the case, he'd managed to pick up and bed a woman he'd never met before, right there, from a standing start, practically the minute Katrina had (effectively) dared him to, then that was not a little damn impressive. It was the kind of thing a chap could be rather proud of being ashamed about.

This small bubble of satisfaction burst almost immediately, however, as three more thoughts crashed into his head – all tumbling over each other so that they seemed to be a single big thought with multiple horrifying faces.

One was Aids; the chilling, world-warping plague that stalked them all now. Aids was that iceberg of the adverts – slipping towards you, half-hidden under the dark water. The chances of contracting it from a one-night stand, he knew, were appallingly high. It was everywhere and everyone had it. In a few years sex would probably stop entirely – sex as we knew it, at least. There'd be no romantic liaisons in the back of a Vauxhall Cavalier after the disco; those days were over. By, say, the mid-1990s, people would meet, exchange medical histories, get married and then, after a few years, perhaps transfer semen via their lawyers. The cold, numbing fear that Chris felt about finding himself in this situation, at this dangerous time, was a sickening buzz in his head; he felt almost as though he'd heard his death sentence announced, and was now just holding on to the hope of being given leave to appeal on a technicality.

The second troubling thought was far, far less serious, but that's not to say that it wasn't deeply serious, all the same.

Was she ugly?

She'd been prepared to jump into bed with someone she'd met possibly only minutes before, and (less politically suspect of him to be thinking this, so he stressed it for the sake of his moral centre) that someone was *him* – presentable enough, yes, but he was hardly an opportunity that no woman would forgive herself for passing up. Chris did the calculation in his head, and the result was a high statistical probability that she was ugly. Perhaps very ugly. Unlike whether he was, starting now, going to die slowly and unpleasantly from an appalling disease, the ugly question was easily answered. (Though even asking it produced a wave of unspeakably painful bitterness at the idea that he might not only have got Aids, but that he'd got it from someone really ugly.) However, the consequences of answering it were potentially devastating. Right now there was nothing to stand, conclusively, against the theory that Katrina's childish actions had brought upon herself a situation where he had given in to provocation and lager, flicked off the safety and – within moments – had attracted a gorgeous woman. Or, maybe, a line of gorgeous women, from which he'd picked one. If he didn't open his eyes and lean over to take a peek at the strange woman's face, he could keep that always. Whereas, if he did take a look, what were the options? She might be lovely. This would be pleasing, but beauty is largely symmetry and a lack of conspicuous flaws; as such, its image is smooth and easily slips from the mind over time. Ugly, on the other hand, is jagged and stays with you forever. Try to hear the sound of gentle waves on a beach in your head. Tough. You can get a general hiss, and imagine the *idea* of them, but the actual noise is difficult to recreate in detail. Now, try to do the same with the sound of gears clashing because you've changed without having the clutch fully in. You can hear it *perfectly*. Chris knew that, long-term, the reward of soft skin and appealing features was nothing compared to the cost of a face like a Monday morning in Coventry. It was better he didn't look, he concluded, and was pleased with the personal depth that his making this decision implied.

The third and final thought of the trilogy was, Shit!

To fully understand this you need to have remembered that time is relative. While these many pages have ticked by as we've sat together in Chris's head, in the real world well, well under a minute has passed since he first flopped out of sleep into a jumbled and viscous wakefulness. He hasn't been idling in bed letting his mind drift; he's just woken up and scrambled to get his bearings.

With a sudden Shit! Chris realised that he had to get the hell out of there – *now.*

He jackknifed upright. Doing this generated a selection of vivid sensations, and he would have taken the opportunity to throw up, except his brain wanted his mouth to vocalise the pain tearing apart its every neurone, and he couldn't get drawn into doing that either *because he had to get the hell out of there*. If this woman woke up while he was still in the room ... Well, it didn't bear thinking about. He'd be trapped with her in a post-cop-off car wreck. There'd be interaction, and talking, and God knows what. There could even be dealing with stuff. Just *imagine* if he was suddenly confronted with her, being there, and sentient. It would be buttock-shufflingly awkward even in the best-case scenario (that is, the one in which she was of an unbreakably cheerful disposition, and spoke no English). More realistically, however ... 'Shit!' She could be angry. Or clingy. Or ugly. Or any number of terrible, terrible things that would be unleashed by the single catalyst of her being awake.

He partly clambered, partly rolled to the edge of the bed. It was the hardest thing anyone had ever done. He ached, his limbs were stiff, pain was shagging his head, his eyes were still on a learning curve, he felt sick, he was frantic to go as fast as possible yet scared prickly that any sudden movement might wake up Strange Woman. How could anyone cope with all those things simultaneously? All Edmund Hillary had needed to do to climb Everest was to keep heading up, and (though he *was* from New Zealand) he probably wasn't pissed at the time either. If someone had told the celebrated adventurer that he'd have to deal with the array of (sometimes conflicting) challenges that *he* faced, Chris thought, then the man would almost certainly have started crying like a little girl. It hardly seemed a fitting reward that, when Chris – the Greatest Hero of All Time – somehow pushed on through all these incredible adversities until he was able to swing his feet to the floor and – as quickly as his fear allowed, as slowly as his panic would permit – stood up, his groggy eyes noticed a curious thing.

He was wearing someone else's clothes.

Black socks, jeans (they were unremarkable but, he was sure, they were not his) and, dangling to his thighs as though it were some kind of corporate kaftan, a loose-fitting, dark-coloured shirt. Strange Woman had obviously had him dress up in this manner before sleeping with him. This was a full set of daywear weirder than he was happy with. What was even worse was that he instantly sensed that not even the freakiest of fetish queens would have sought out an outfit that was so obscenely uninteresting. Ergo, his initial thought was literally true in an even more literal way – these were not simply not his clothes; they were *someone else's* clothes. He was, he would've bet now, wearing the clothes that belonged to Strange Woman's partner. She'd dressed him in her boyfriend or husband's stuff. Lord, she must be an unbelievably perverted individual. Yet, on the downside, she was also apparently a person who'd slept with him despite being in a relationship with someone else. That didn't speak well of her general character. It additionally meant, Chris shouted to himself, that her boyfriend or husband might come back at any moment, find him there, and kick the shit out of him. Chris helped himself to another chestful of panic.

He pirouetted rapidly and unsteadily to see if he could spot where his own clothes had been cast down. No part of his body thanked him for this manoeuvre; worse, not only didn't it reveal what he was searching for, it also caused him to topple sideways across the room. Trying to regain his balance, he performed that peculiar arms swinging, legs crossing dance that music hall entertainers liked to use to work their way off the stage; he'd have needed only a cane, a straw boater and a peppy rendition of 'Knocked 'em in the Old Kent Road' from the orchestra to have secured a week of matinees at the Alhambra on the strength of it. Except, rather than ending in appreciative applause, it ended with his crashing into the bedroom door with the top of his skull. The noise this made inside his head could not be measured using human science; it was something like the level of sound you'd hear if you chewed on a hydrogen bomb. Unfortunately, even outside his head, it generated what was, objectively speaking, an awful bloody racket. He bounced back from the woodwork and pluckily wrestled with man's ancient enemy, gravity, in a bid to steady himself.

A few feet away, Strange Woman stirred from her sleep and asked, 'Mmmmeeerrrum-m-m-m?'

Chris would swear on anything you cared to name that, at this point, he actually felt his testicles freeze, constrict and then flee upwards into his abdomen.

He made himself into a statue. On the tiptoes of someone

else's socks, he consciously stopped moving, breathing, blinking, growing hair, generating heat or having any kind of internal dialogue. In essence, he turned himself into the classic movie submarine, which the captain – to avoid the depth charges of a hunting destroyer – has ordered to lie on the bottom while, in an unbearably tense silence, the entire crew does nothing but listen, and keep still, and wait. Chris stood there, lacking only the eerie clang of sonar pulses pinging off his hull.

Strange Woman's naked shoulder rose. She started to lever herself up from the mattress onto her elbow and lower arm. Chris's testicles moved on from his abdomen and up to his throat; in two more seconds, he guessed, they would leave his body through the top of his head and be away down the road frantically hailing a cab. Strange Woman pivoted higher; but then paused for a second at some invisible balance point and, apparently still too much asleep to pursue the answer to her "Mmmmeeerrrum-m-m-m?" question, sank slowly back down into her pillow. As she fell, Chris bent his knees in time with her – willing her into place somehow by lowering himself in unison.

He knew he shouldn't risk moving (and thus perhaps make a noise) until he'd allowed her to return to sleep fully. And he knew he shouldn't wait there, as every instant that passed increased the chances of her naturally reawakening. Chris couldn't begin to resolve the tension between those two needs. The equation rang uselessly in his ears; a jangling mass of discordant sound – like cheap metal wind chimes in a storm. Thinking out of the box, he wondered if it would help if he wet himself.

As it turned out, his legs didn't require his brain to get involved anyway. The decision was made by his nerves, which wouldn't allow him to remain still any longer; they tugged at his muscles, angry at being ignored for so long when they were yelling so hard. Chris began the move again. He crept back a few steps and slowly opened the bedroom door he'd so recently made good and closed with the top of his head. It swung towards him with a deafeningly tiny click followed by the horrifyingly loud small whisper of unassuming hinges. By now, his *sang* possessed nowhere near enough *froid* for him to pull it wide and walk through the resulting hole like a man who was arrogantly blasé about his own feet. Instead, he drew it back just far enough to create a narrow gap, which he then squeezed himself through awkwardly, mentally cursing the difficulty of the operation. Once out of the bedroom, he strode as quickly and silently as he could across the landing. (This seemed to require that he formed an expression in which his eyes squinted, his jaw was clamped together hard, and his lips were drawn back so that his teeth were bared. Chris couldn't imagine how this helped him move any more quietly but decided that, at times like this, you didn't quibble: you just obeyed orders, got on with it, and pulled the damn face.) He descended the stairs as though he were filled with helium – placing as much of his weight as he could on the banister, so that his feet bounced, bubble-like, from step to step.

In the hallway, he paused. The front door – his prize – was right ahead of him now. Though he was next to the escape exit, however, he wasn't quite in the clear yet. For one thing, Strange Woman's absent partner might suddenly appear and open the door from the other side. He'd see Chris's groin in *his* trousers, and, putting two and two together, kick that groin. The reason Chris didn't get out of there immediately was that, though he did thankfully at least have clothes on, he didn't have any shoes. Wandering the streets in nothing but socks didn't seem very appealing; especially as he had no idea where he was and therefore no idea how far he'd have to walk. By the front door, under the coat rack, was a less-than-fully-appalling, untidy semi-jumble of footwear. Some of it was Strange Woman's, some of it her partner's. Chris laid a foot beside one of the man's shoes, gauging its length. Probably pretty close, he thought (not surprising as they were obviously similar enough for him to wear the guy's shirt and jeans). Ever since Chris had realised that it would be too time-consuming and dangerous to find where his own clothes had been discarded, he'd resolved to leg it in the ones he had on and post them back later (absolutely leaving his address off the parcel, of course). That'd allow him to get out of there, but he wouldn't actually be stealing anyone's stuff; just borrowing it out of necessity. But it now occurred to him that this could land Strange Woman in hot water. Not being able to find items of clothing is frustrating, but it isn't that unusual. In fact, as he understood it, if you live with a woman then not being able to find the particular T-shirt or trousers or anything else you're after is more or less the norm. So, there being some missing jeans, a shirt – even a pair of shoes – is more annoying than suspicious. On the other hand, having the postman ... (Chris caught himself and rewound) having the postal worker turn up at your door holding your clothes wrapped in brown paper and hairy string is definitely going to provoke questions. Strange Woman had, Chris must assume, had sex with him. You don't needlessly drop a woman who's had sex with you in trouble with her partner. If a weird, deviant, sexual freak who's into shagging men who are wearing her partner's pants has been good enough to have sex with you, then you're a despicable ingrate if you act in a way that's careless of her welfare; behave shabbily and it'd serve you right if the next weird, deviant, sexual freak who's into shagging men who are wearing her partner's pants has sex with someone else. So, paradoxically, perhaps the decent thing to do was not to return the clothes. This wouldn't be for Chris's benefit; it would be, well ... a 'white theft'.

Having unpicked this moral knot successfully, Chris concluded, as a corollary, that it'd be best to avoid the man's shoes and instead take the pair of trainers lying among the pile in the hallway. The shoes might be expensive (he'd heard of people paying thirty pounds for a pair of shoes), but trainers weren't going to have cost more than a five or six quid. He slipped his feet into them. They appeared to fit well enough, though he couldn't help thinking that Nike were obviously knocking these odd-looking things out on the cheap; they'd even scrimped on the rubber for the heels, which were hollow and mostly air.

He didn't tie the laces; that could be done when he was safely outside. All that was left now was to quietly open the front door, quietly step through it, quietly close it again, and scamper away anonymously into the morning. Being careful to avoid any unnecessary metallic clicks, he twisted the small, smooth, circular handle of the Yale lock (leaning forward, head close to the knob – like a safe cracker listening for the tumblers). He eased it round gently and, when it had fully turned, held the tension of the spring with his wrist so that the bolt was completely free and he would be able to swing the door open without it touching the plate at all. His ears set to pick up on even the smallest sound, he pulled back.

A squealing siren shattered his entire body.

It was penetrating, hysterical and seemingly coming from *every-*

where. Chris flung himself through the open doorway in an instant, but this wasn't any ninja-like, lightning response; it was really just a 'big flinch'. Having, in effect, shat himself out beyond the front door, he found he was in a small porch. It had two doors, each one a wooden frame holding a large clear glass panel. Chris spent a time bouncing around inside this like a bluebottle in a jam jar. He could see the world out there, right in front of him; however, he was currently nothing but panic stitched together with fraying threads of terror and had therefore reverted to a primordial stage where you might as well have asked him to pilot the space shuttle as conceive of what glass was or how handles worked.

Houdini used to escape from the Water Torture Chamber; a glass cabinet in which he was suspended upside down, struggling to break free before his lungful of air gave out. Change a very few particulars, and you have Chris. It's easy to imagine modern audiences thrilling to this man: trapped and struggling for his life in a porch; wildly flailing around in the hope of getting out before he died from fright – or perhaps just from a crushing sense of the unfairness of it all. Luckily, after an eternity of only a few seconds, Chris's clever elbow accidentally operated the door handle and he toppled out backwards onto the paved driveway – landing at the point where his natural athleticism had instinctively placed his arse. The jolt of the impact clacked his teeth together and for a moment or two he simply stayed there, stunned and bemused. He sat like a cloth doll, flaccid from lack of stuffing; his limbs were limp and his mind was stymied by shock and confusion.

Yet, while his brain was flat-lining as far as its output level was concerned, the input meter was off the chart. Motionless, his head moved at a million miles an hour, taking in everything. The siren's song, he became aware, was now the sirens' song; it was a demonic atonal duet. He could still hear the monotone nasal squeal spilling out from the hallway of the house, but this had slipped under the oscillating screech that was coming from the flashing alarm box attached high on the wall of the outside of the building. The two combined into a single clashing whole: perfectly dissimilar – not complementing each other at every possible level, yet forming something much larger than the sum of their parts (like a bomb that combined sharp shrapnel fragments with the feeling you get at the checkout when you realise you've left all your cash in your other jacket). While his ears assimilated the alarms, his eyes absorbed the house. It was semi-detached and in far better condition than the building that contained his own ground-floor flat. To the left of the wet paving where he was currently sitting there was a moderately-cared-for (if currently more or less dead) front garden laid out before the main, bay window. There was a settled look about it – as there was with all the houses in the street. This was a place where people stayed. Silver metal digits screwed to a small wooden plaque by the door said it was Number 114. That would mean something; it would be part of a domesticity that persisted. If wrongly addressed mail came to Number 117, the person at the door would glance at the name and say, 'No – you need Number 114.' Chris wasn't even sure who lived above him; the people from the flat upstairs were unknown and incorporeal – nothing except a creak that moved across his ceiling. Here was a suburban semi with a garage, a red-tiled roof and an unassuming but definite place in the world. Chris saw the guttering; he saw, in the area immediately in front of the door, a slightly uneven paving stone that someone probably tutted over and vowed to sort out at some point . . . he saw the curtain start to draw back from the Strange Woman's bedroom window. In less than a second their exposed, peering faces would collide.

5

Neil had his head under the sink. It's a whole other world down there, under the sink. A place of oddness, mystery and curious thoughts. You're in semi-darkness, semi-concealed, looking up at pipes and connectors and undersides that you hardly ever see – and certainly don't see from this abnormal angle. Removing all the pots and pans from the cupboard under the sink and venturing inside is like entering the wardrobe and finding yourself in Narnia. Except, of course, that your legs remain sticking out. It does limit the potential for magical adventures when you always have to keep your legs sticking out.

Naturally, there's fear under the sink. For a start, who knows what might be there in the fusty gloom, lurking about on its many, scuttling legs. What's more – let's not kid ourselves – this is *their* place: it might theoretically be in your kitchen, but, in reality, you're a long way from home under your sink. Never is your awareness of the undefended gap between your collar and the back of your neck more acute than in those edgy, under-sink times.

In addition to the above worry, there's the U-bend. The facts, Neil judged, demonstrated that he was sufficiently courageous to survive in Lincolnshire on a day-to-day basis – meeting it on its own terms. But he was not foolhardy. He was not the kind of person who, due to a chemical imbalance in his brain or because he childishly had something to prove, would put himself under the sink for no good reason. And when it comes to good – or, unavoidable, at least – reasons for going sub-sink, the U-bend is by far the most frequent culprit. Lying there on your back with its pitiless curve only inches above you makes the hairs stand up on your every hairy place. The U-bend is a focal point of dread. You're probably going to have to remove it – that's what brought you to this unholy place, after all. But what unimaginable horror might be in there – what soup of Hell might *spill out of it*; what foul pus might vomit *down over you* – is an anxiety that twists at an ancient nerve. It is fear as old as plumbing.

Yet, despite these many troubles afflicting the mind (perhaps partly because of them), there are other, more positive thoughts. A general feeling of manliness, for one. Women reveal they acknowledge that fixing something in the arcane, brute, no-second-chances land beneath the plughole is an achievement that tests the very limits of masculinity by being so incredibly, whoopingly, 'Men? Pff – cower before me, you useless dogs' -ly pleased with themselves if they ever do it (having been driven to that extreme either by their partner's calculated absence or death or, perhaps, by the erratic, empowering anger of PMT). Men lie there below the U-bend afraid, yes, but also conscious now of the force lurking in their pectorals and – heady in the cramped, pressure-cooker dark – able to smell their own testosterone. This could be the reason that, in 'adult videos', the actor who will be the male lead (for the following eight minutes or so) classically arrives in the role of a plumber. Whatever the reason, it's certainly true that no erotic film company of any standing would be without a toolbox full of conduit formers and T-fittings in its prop department, nor is it possible for any normal man to get under a sink and not automatically start thinking about porn.

'What are you doing?'

Neil's neck strained to tilt his head up – it rose until his chin hit his chest and prevented it from going any further.

He saw Michelle looking in at him, framed in the V of his legs.

'There's a blockage,' he replied. 'The water isn't draining properly. I thought I'd take a look.'

'The water's been like that for ages.'

'I know.'

'So why are you taking a look now?'

'It's time. I've been meaning to for weeks, but now it's time.'

'Why?'

Neil wagged a finger. 'Never try to understand how I decide whether or not it's time for me to fix a particular problem around the house. I wouldn't want anyone to put themselves in danger like that; the calculations are so complex that they could damage a person's synapses.'

Michelle squinted. 'Synapses?'

'Synapses.' He tapped his temple. 'The gaps that connect everything in the brain. They're what *makes* it a brain, really.'

She leaned in, over his stomach, and grinned at him. 'Gaps? So your brain's made of holes?'

Neil laughed. 'Yes. My brain's made of holes.' He reached down and ran the back of his index finger gently across her cheek. 'That's why I'm always saying that I've got a memory like a sieve.'

Michelle twisted her neck a little, trying to investigate the alien world of Under Sink, but it was too cramped for her to see much. She turned back to Neil and wrinkled her nose.

'It smells like feet,' she said.

6

Chris spun his head around without bothering to consider whether or not his body would be able to keep up with it. It was a frantic, vicious twist – not so much a turn of his neck but more like hurling his face over his own shoulder. His only thought was that he *must not* share a glance with Strange Woman. She mustn't see his eyes; he mustn't see hers. If that happened, everything would instantly be qualitatively different. At the moment, he was merely scrambling from a one-night stand's house, amid the howling of her burglar alarm, wearing clothes he had stolen from her partner. However, hidden within this state of affairs – latent – was the possibility of a really awkward social situation. Only the mercy of their not looking each other in the eyes was keeping this from becoming fatally embarrassing.

A sliver of an instant before Strange Woman's hand fully drew back the curtain, the remainder of Chris followed his head. Pivoting around on the heel of his palm, he hurled himself to his feet, and then away down the drive of Number 114. (His eyes hadn't quite managed to get away from the bedroom window before the curtain had been pulled aside enough to reveal an ear, but that was OK, Chris thought. He could survive an ear.)

His hand, where it had swivelled against the ground, stung hot and sharp; it sent rhythmic burning throbs up along his arm in time with his pulse. Fortunately, however, Chris was provided with some distraction from this pain by every other pain. He hurt all over. More than all over: the pain began in the earth beneath his feet and didn't stop until some distance above his head. That's how it felt, at least. His temples and his eyes throbbed. As he ran down the street, each footfall was like being hit on the knee with a hammer. After no more than twenty yards his breath began to rasp in and out of his chest too – the very air appeared to be tearing at his lungs, as though each snatched mouthful were laced with powered glass.

He sensed rather than saw the people peering at him from multiple windows. The siren had probably opened every eyelid in the street. And here he was, running away: a gasping, hobbling picture of guilt. This hurt most of all. He wanted to stop and shout to the gawping jury judging him in their pyjamas, 'I'm no criminal! I'm an innocent man! I just slept with a sexual deviant because my girlfriend was being stroppy! So, really, this whole burglar image you're seeing here is my girlfriend's fault! OK?!' But he didn't. He just bowed his head and kept running – his face flushed by humiliation and approaching coronary collapse, and with the jarring squeal of the alarm filling his ears.

Come to think of it . . . why had Strange Women set the burglar alarm anyway? Who comes back to their house – drunk, almost certainly – and takes a complete stranger upstairs for freakish, role-playing sex, but sets the burglar alarm on the way? That spoke of a curious combination of erotic recklessness on the one hand and, on the other, a fastidious approach to home security. Man, Strange Woman really *was* strange.

Chris staggered past the sign at the end of the road. TITHE BARN AVENUE. (He couldn't help noticing that the lettering was unaltered. For God's sake, it would hardly have taken much effort to make it TIT BARN AVENUE, would it? Either this was an unusually nice area, or the local children lacked any drive whatsoever.) As he rounded the corner, he let his hand reach out and slide over the flat metal plate of the road sign to help his balance; it was cold and wet. His fingers gathered up the water droplets on its surface as they ran along its length and, when they fell off the end, they sent a splash into the air. Had it rained in the night?

As soon as he'd turned out of the street, and so escaped from the line of sight of anyone in its houses, Chris slowed. He felt he needed to keep moving (a neighbour roused by Strange Woman's house alarm might have telephoned the police when they saw him running away; appearances are deceptive, so it would be a natural thing to do if one didn't know that Chris was actually just an innocent victim of Katrina-based circumstances). However, though his reasoning told him to carry on, every other part of him suggested crumpling into a gasping heap of exhausted, rubbery limbs, and then – if he had the strength – throwing up. He compromised. Maybe the middle ground would work to his advantage anyway: it was unlikely that any responding officers would be on the lookout for a man 'shuffling from the scene'.

As he went along, he clasped his hands to his hips and swayed backwards and forwards a little at the waist – shambling akimbo – while his dangle-jawed mouth pulled in air (he had a definite suspicion the air was pulling the other way). The discomfort tightened his sore eyes into tight slits. It was agony, this ... this ... this *moving*. He promised himself that he would never, ever drink again. He further promised himself that he meant it this time.

Hmm ... The driveway of Number 114 had been wet too, he recalled now that he had some breathing space (if not yet enough breath to fill it). He looked at the pavement slipping, very slowly, under his feet and saw that this was also wet. Again, he wondered if it had rained during the night.

Then he asked himself why his head was giving any room to such a trivial question. There was the Aids issue. There was the issue that Strange Woman's partner might still appear and give him an extensive kicking (Chris had only just left the street, after all, and was now moving so slowly that he thought he might, if he happened to be moving against the direction of continental drift, effectively be going backwards). There was the issue that a squad car might screech up and he'd get arrested for breaking into a house. Well, um ... breaking out of a house, maybe. Actually, he hadn't 'broken' in *or* out. Still, everything he was wearing was stolen. He'd be arrested for 'Leaving a House Rapidly in Someone Else's Clothes'. And that's not the kind of offence that automatically earns you respect from the lifers in B Wing, is it? Not remotely. If you're inside for Leaving a House Rapidly in Someone Else's Clothes then every day is going to be a fight for survival. And let's not forget Katrina. If you looked at it one way, he had been really quite unfaithful to her. He could see how, if she found out, she'd take it badly. There were, then, more than enough serious concerns to occupy his mind, so why should any part of his head care less whether or not it had rained?

He knew why almost instantly. The solution was of the kind that is already there and is actually just trying to attract your attention; so, the answer appears, fully formed, out of the very act of asking the question.

It was bloody freezing. And that was odd; odd and wrong. This weather, this cold wet weather, didn't fit. Hot sickly sweat was sticky at the back of his neck and bubbled across his forehead like fat from frying bacon, but that was down to simple panic combined with a burst of exertion he was in no condition to meet. The day itself was damp, grim and cold enough that it seemed like an attitude rather than a temperature – the air wasn't so much chilly as hostile. With a start, Chris wondered if he was in Scotland.

It was feasible. He could remember only the early evening of the previous day – and not even far enough into that to know when and how he'd met Strange Woman. It was conceivable that – riding on the clarity of purpose that often accompanies several times too many lagers – jumping on a train to Dumfries might have seemed an idea so perfect and brilliant in all its aspects that it would have come upon him like a revelation to a biblical prophet. 'This isn't that ninth Grolsch,' he could hear his earlier self thinking: 'This is the will of God.' It was speculation, but how else was it possible to explain weather this miserable in the middle of summer unless you were in Scotland? Chris searched for evidence.

It came back to him that the garden of Strange Woman's house was mostly lifeless. He looked around now and saw that the gardens of the houses he was passing were the same. Moreover, the trees that irregularly lined the road were without leaves too; they were nothing but bare black branches that looked like running cracks against the sky – as though their trunks had risen up and then, in the cold air, shattered.

Christ. How far north was he? Wasn't it June? Surely, there simply wasn't time for him to have travelled to Inverness?

What hour was it? The colour of the sky's dull blanket of clouds lolled around a mean of school-sock grey, but the level of light generally suggested that the day could do better, if given a little time and understanding. What would that make it, then? Six? Perhaps, six thirty in the morning? (A bit later for every mile beyond Carlisle, but that would be the general area.) There was traffic on the road, and he could see people walking too, though none was close to him yet. Did the world look appropriately busy (no more, no less) for just after six a.m. on a Tuesday? Chris came down very much on the side of having no idea.

Suddenly, two women stepped onto the pavement about fifteen yards in front of him. He saw that there was a pub next to where they'd appeared; they'd come from the car park – possibly having taken a short cut across it – and they were now walking towards him, chatting away enthusiastically. Chris put his 'Not Coming to Any Useful Conclusions about Anything' on hold for a while to try to hear their accents in the hope of that providing a clue to his location. At first he couldn't quite tune in to their voices, but then, as they drew nearer, his ears steadied their footing enough for him to realise that the pair weren't speaking English at all; they were talking rapidly in something Slavonic. Lots of stuff was happening towards the backs of their mouths and, not infrequently, their nostrils became involved. There was only the briefest stumble in Chris's heart at the thought that he'd got so drunk last night that he'd woken up in Gdansk. The street sign, the cars driving on the correct side of road, the litter – he was somewhere in Britain all right.

However, the women's very uselessness as regional indicators provoked Chris into the decision to settle the matter practically, right now, rather than indulge in any more theorising. When they got to about six feet in front of him, he stepped across, putting himself in their path. They pulled up, stopped talking and briefly glanced at one another.

'Excuse me,' said Chris. 'Am I in Scotland?'

The woman on the left made to speak, but then she paused for a moment and – her mouth already open and poised to begin – looked again at her companion, as though seeking confirmation that they were both of the same mind. Her companion gave a slight upward flick of her chin and, relaxed and cheerful now she knew they were in agreement, she turned back to Chris and, helpfully pointing for clarity, said, 'You. You fuck off, you.'

With that, they moved to one side and hurried past him.

'Fuck off,' the woman repeated as she went by – this time her companion taking over the responsibility of saying 'You' and pointing at him.

Now it had been flagged up by his being told to fuck off twice, Chris could see how approaching a pair of complete strangers and asking them if you were in Scotland might come across as a little 'Hello, ladies. I'm a nutter.' It's something that has that kind of quality to it even if your laces aren't undone, you're not wearing clothes you've slept in (had sex in and *then* slept in, to be fully accurate), and you aren't sweating and panting. Watching as the two women worked briskly to put some distance between Chris and themselves, he wondered if he might clear up the misunderstanding by running after them – shouting, perhaps.

He was steered away from that particular chasm by a minicab. Because he'd turned round to look at the retreating women, he saw it pull up at the junction on the opposite side of the road.

Lurching forward, he called out 'Hey!' and waved his arms above his head.

The women glanced back at him. The usual one told him to fuck off. He stabbed a finger at the cab – to indicate that he was yelling to it, not at them. The woman interpreted this to mean that he wanted them to get into the cab with him. She told him to fuck off again. In those parts of the world where it's legal to carry handguns, Chris would probably already have had two or three bullets in his chest by this stage.

The cab pulled out and turned, coming to a halt next to where Chris was standing. Chris found himself thinking that the driver was breaking the law by doing this: only proper taxis are allowed to pick up fares that flag them down on the street; minicabs must have everything pre-booked via their base. It was merely a random thought – Chris wasn't about to make an issue of it, obviously. A driver contemptuous of taxi regulations and Chris himself – a man who frightened Baltic women while wearing stolen trousers – they were clearly part of the same shadowy criminal underclass.

The driver leaned across inside the vehicle and wound down the passenger-side window.

'Yeah? Where to, mate?' he said.

Chris bent over a little so he was at roughly the same level. The driver was Asian, which was comforting; it had been rather a disorientating morning thus far, so he welcomed any contact with reassuring familiarity (and you know you're in Britain if your cab driver is Pakistani). However, it didn't really tell him anything about *where* he was in Britain, and the man's accent was too much of the subcontinent to provide any clue. But, instead of asking

'Am I in Scotland?' again – and thus presenting himself as a madman – Chris decided to play it smart this time.

'Can you take me to Devant Road?' he asked.

'Sure. Jump in.'

Slyly, Chris began to pull on the rear door but then abruptly returned to the still-open window as though snatched back by a sudden concern.

'Oh, that's Devant Road ...' He paused for effect, and then added the name of the area with his face screwed up to indicate his anxiousness at – now all the facts were known – the possibly troubling vastness of the task.

The driver's forehead deformed into ripples of consideration and he peered back at Chris, puzzled.

'Is there any other Devant Road besides that one?' he asked.

This was clear and unambiguous. Which was an almost perfect result: its one defect being that Chris hadn't been prepared for his plan succeeding on quite such a spectacular scale. He realised that he couldn't now reply 'No' or 'It's the only Devant Road *I* know of' without appearing worryingly nutter-like for implying otherwise in the first place. He was hoist by his own petard. He shouted at his brain to give him something to say – and quickly. Infuriatingly, his brain did nothing except distractedly reply that, one day, it ought to get round to looking up what on earth a petard actually is. The knock-on effect of this was that his mouth decided to get all proactive.

Chris heard the words 'I think there's one in Scotland' fall out over his teeth.

The driver peered at him noticeably harder.

There was a precarious beat, but then Chris snatched the initiative and ducked into the back of the cab before the driver could decide that perhaps his foot ought to press down heavily on the accelerator while this scruffy, sweaty, mentally suspect, wheezing bloke was still standing on the pavement.

Once inside the car Chris joyfully sprang open on the back seat. It was more than a simple flop; it was an exaggerated relaxation celebrating his relief. Instinctively, he added a powerful sigh to the moment too – it deserved it.

'Thirty-Seven Devant Road, then,' he told the driver.

As the car started to move Chris let his head fall back. He closed his eyes and allowed himself to enjoy the soothing effect of getting this far without being caught. There were still some sticky issues to be negotiated – he knew that – but at least he wasn't directly in the firing line for the time being.

He wasn't sure how long the journey took; lulled by the motion of the car and a sense that he was, if not out of the woods, then at least no longer in any immediate danger of a big tree falling on him, he drifted off to sleep.

The driver announcing 'Here we are, mate' caused Chris to wake up with a slight 'Nyh!'

In that way that sometimes happens when you've unintentionally nodded off for a short time, he lurched into wakefulness like someone missing a step on the stairs. The driver (who had obviously seen that Chris was sleeping and who had therefore raised his voice to rouse him) had twisted in his seat to look back. Though Chris saw and heard him well enough, he was briefly confused; his eyes and ears were awake now, but his brain hadn't fully joined them. The information passed through into his head, where it merely fell into a hole.

'Right, right. OK,' Chris replied crisply, straightening up. But it was basically a bluff; it was a few moments before he remembered where he was and how he'd got there. Those two or three seconds were surprisingly frightening. Although there was nothing innately terrible about the situation itself (he was sitting in the back of a cab being spoken to by the driver, that's all) it was awful, actually chilling, to be flung into it from nowhere. Even such an ordinary place was briefly fearful when he had no idea how he'd come to be there.

He rubbed his eyes with the heels of his palms (which just made his vision more blurry – does doing that *ever* help?) and, far happier because he'd recalled where he was now (even if he couldn't see it properly), he opened the door of the cab.

'Wait a sec. I'll just pop in and get some cash,' he said to the driver as he stepped out onto the pavement. It had already occurred to him that he wouldn't find the usual ragged handful of cash stuffed into his trouser pockets, because they weren't actually his trouser pockets. They were the pockets of a stranger's sex trousers. So he'd need to get some money from his flat to pay the cab fare. What hadn't already occurred to him, however, was that the pockets of a stranger's sex trousers wouldn't contain the key to his flat either. He realised this, celebrating the moment with a sighed 'Shit' as he loped up the short path to the front door.

He'd have to hope the people who lived upstairs were in, and – though he'd never seen *them* – that they knew who *he* was, or were prepared to believe him when he told them, at least. If they could open the front door for him so he could get into the hallway, then he'd simply have to kick in the inner door to his flat. It wouldn't take much of a kicking. He'd been asking for a better door to be fitted since the day he'd moved in, but the landlord had clearly made the decision that he could deal with the request most economically by a combination of lying and doing nothing. Chris was pleased now that his landlord had felt comfortable about ignoring his demands for two years, and congratulated himself on cleverly being so consistently ineffectual.

He planted his thumb on the top bell and kept it there long enough for the occupants, if they had any social skills at all, to realise that it was a mild distress call – the sound, as it were, of a thumb that needed a hand. He did this twice, and was about to begin a third attempt when the door swung open to reveal what could only be a student.

'Hi,' said Chris. 'Hi. Sorry to wake you, but I'm afraid I've lost my key.'

'Your key?' the creature replied, his voice suggesting that this was a somewhat puzzling concept.

'Yes. My key.' Chris flicked his eyes over to the door of his flat, at the end of the hallway. 'My Key. To my door.'

'Your door?'

'Yes, my d— Look, are there any nouns you *don't* have trouble with? Tell me and I'll work around you,' Chris replied, regretting it instantly. He was tired, ached all over, and had a headful of problems; it was understandable that he'd be irritable. Still, it was poor manners to snap at a person who was helping you out, never mind the questionable acceptability of mocking someone who, it seemed likely, was congenitally stupid. 'Sorry. I've had a bad morning,' Chris said apologetically, but at the same time he pushed past the student and into the house.

He stopped outside his flat, peered thoughtfully at the small round Yale lock, and gave the door a couple of experimental bangs with his hand to try to get a sense of the solidity of it.

'What are you doing?' asked the student, who had followed Chris and was now shuffling about awkwardly at his shoulder looking like he was reluctant to be there but equally reluctant to leave.

'Testing,' said Chris.

'Testing?'

Chris sighed. 'Yes,' he replied, leaning back against the wall behind him and raising his foot to waist height. 'Tes ...' and, on the sharply exhaled, '*ting!*' that followed, he turned away from the student and drove the flat bottom of his training shoe towards the door.

The next bit was absolutely perfect.

Mel had been sniffing a carton of milk to see if it was off when she'd heard someone knock. She guessed that it was one of the guys from upstairs – probably on the scrounge. That was fine, though – they'd only want to borrow a CD or perhaps some lecture notes, and it meant there'd be an extra nose available (there's a vast grey area when it comes to sniffing milk – it's rare you're confident enough to make a decision without wanting a second opinion). So, she ambled over happily. She turned the catch and let her body weight fall backwards to casually, lazily open the door. Her motion here, and Chris's outside, accidentally blended with unearthly precision. Chris had in mind that he wanted to force the door open, not uselessly kick a hole in it with his foot (which would do no good, and be something else to repair too). So he was careful to aim for a flat-footed impact, and also a kind of 'Hai-*yaa*!' approach: applying the full force only when his shoe had reached the door – not so much a kick, more a hefty push with a bit of a run-up.

The coincidental but flawless interlocking of their movements ensured that Mel opened her door and immediately saw an unknown man shouting '*Ting!*' as his foot came forward to lift her slightly into the air and hurl her back across the room into a bin bag full of laundry. Her launch caused her arms, left behind as her body was propelled backwards, to whip up, and thus – from Chris's point of view – an unknown woman had startlingly appeared on the end of his foot and hosed him from groin to forehead with on-the-turn milk. The glorious whole would, under other circumstances, have been considered an important and technically innovative piece of performance art.

'Fuck!' was the consensus.

Mel sat on the floor with her legs splayed out in front of her and her mind empty from shock. She wasn't hurt; simply so completely surprised that her brain needed to reboot. Compared to Chris, however, she was a model of mental keenness. Mel was reacting to something deeply unexpected, that's all; Chris had been confronted with the jarringly surprising, beyond which was waiting the completely incomprehensible. Even as he watched his sole take this woman-who-shouldn't-be-there off her feet and propel her away into some washing, his stunned brain was also picking up that his flat was entirely wrong. Everything in his field of vision – from the flying woman outwards – was a thing that didn't make any sense. The wallpaper, the decorations, the furniture and the personal objects were not the ones he'd left as he'd closed the door behind him the previous night. Everything was different.

The student who'd let Chris into the house pushed him sharply aside and ran in to Mel. 'Are you OK?' he asked, kneeling down beside her, but he turned back to Chris before she'd had any chance to reply and spat, 'What the fuck do you think you're doing?'

Chris barely heard him. Dizzy, he took a half-step through the doorway and looked around. Yes: *everything* was different. The only tiny thing that remained of his flat was the sense that – despite nothing in it whatsoever being familiar – this *was* his flat.

'You fucking nutter,' the student said angrily, helping Mel to her feet.

'Huh?' replied Chris distractedly, as though he'd fallen out of a daydream into the second half of someone's question. He continued to gaze around with a concussed expression on his face.

'I live here,' he said softly, without any particular implication identifiable in the tone of his voice; he spoke as if it was just trivia he'd mentioned for no particular reason.

'Who is he?' Mel asked the student.

Her friend strode over and squared up to Chris in a manner that would have sat well on someone who was three stone heavier and whose hair was far less silly.

'Christ knows. He rang the bell and then barged straight in here. He reeks of drink too. Call the police.'

'What?' said Chris. 'No. Look ... I live here.'

'Call the police,' the student repeated, even more insistently.

Half of Chris wanted to snarl back, 'Yes – call the police. *Then* we'll see who's in the right.' But the other half of him strongly urged against doing this. Impossible as it seemed, maybe he *was* in the wrong place: a completely unrelated 37 Devant Road, in a totally different part of the city, that simply happened – by bizarre chance – to look very similar to his flat. That was hardly plausible, but not as implausible as, for who could imagine what conceivable reason, a Hitchcockian conspiracy where his home had been changed radically and peopled with new occupants overnight. So, his head swirling, he backed out of the room instead, mumbling, 'Sorry. I ... Sorry. I'm going, OK? I'm ...'

The student followed him, maintaining a threatening closeness all the way to the front door. At the step, Chris paused. He glanced towards the road, and then turned to the student again.

'Um ... I don't suppose you could lend me some money for the taxi?' he asked tentatively.

The door slammed in his face.

Chris walked to the cab very slowly and climbed into the back seat once more. He sat there silently for a time, shifting his gaze between his knees and the front of this house that looked very like but, on closer inspection, not quite identical to *his* house.

Eventually, the taxi driver said, 'So?'

'Sorry? Oh ... yes. Erm ... how much do I owe you?'

'There's twenty-seven pounds fifty on the clock.'

Twenty-seven pounds fifty? Jesus! Had he been driven halfway across Britain while he was asleep?

'*How* much?' Chris asked, astonished.

'Twenty-seven fifty.'

Chris had a sudden thought and patted the pockets of his stolen sex trousers. He heard a metallic chink in the one on the right and, reaching inside, pulled out some coins and a bunch of notes. The cash seemed to be British, but many of the designs and sizes were unusual. Maybe it was Scottish money; perhaps he was north of the border after all. Even more unnerving was that, during his search of himself, he also discovered a tiny device in his left pocket.

55

It looked like one of those futuristic communicators from *Star Trek* – the top flipped up to reveal a screen and numbered keys. Hellfire. Who could own something like that? What was Strange Woman's partner? A spy? A space alien? As if things weren't bad enough without the idea that he'd shagged the wife of someone who had a licence to kill, or who was a Klingon. He cautiously pressed a button at random, but the screen responded with 'Keypad Locked'. Better not experiment any further: maybe hitting 7 would blow up the third floor of the Bulgarian embassy or something. Holding it by his fingertips, he carefully returned the device to his pocket.

'So?' the driver repeated.

Chris herded his attention back to the cab. For the first time he noticed (on the dashboard in the front) the driver's ID plate and he looked through the details on it. So, he *was* in the right city. Unfortunately, confirming this removed even the few desperate shreds of any of the half-unterrible explanations he'd been juggling around; it was a clue that left him more clueless about what could be going on.

At a loss for what else to do, he told the driver to take him to the house where Andrew lived. There he found a very nice Bangladeshi family, with whom he had an extremely brief, entirely useless conversation.

No one was home at his next stop – Neil's place. It being empty on a weekday morning wasn't that surprising. It having bay windows and a garage that hadn't been there on Saturday . . . was. The house that contained Katrina's flat had been remodelled too. Rather extensively. So extensively, in fact, that it was now the car park of a garden centre.

Shuffling back into the cab yet again, he realised, with an acceptance that was as unwelcome as it was complete, which house he needed to visit next. It was the logical destination. He *had* to call there, he knew that; but it was also the place he very much least wanted to go.

7

If Ted knew anything, Ted knew people.

'If I know anything, I know people,' said Ted, smiling broadly – the accuracy of one of his opinions again satisfyingly confirmed by the act of expressing it. He picked up the pint in front of him and took a big no-nonsense drink; his rearing lip was visible through the glass as the beer poured under it. To Luke, sitting beside him at the pub table, his mouth looked like the top of one of those kitsch Victorian water jugs shaped like a fish.

Ted wiped his foamy upper lip; the back of his large round hand with its loose mat of fine red hairs could have been made for the job. 'Ahh . . .' he said, and grinned. 'That hit the spot.' He tugged his belt down slightly to allow more of his stomach to lurch over the top of his trousers, where it rippled briefly – giddy with its new freedom.

Luke took a lengthy gulp from his own beer and smiled back. He was unsure whether or not to belch. After a quick calculation, he decided against it. It *could* help cement a bond (Ted, he judged, was a man who belched in pubs, and who did so partly to *declare* that he was a man who belched in pubs), but it could easily backfire too. Ted hadn't belched yet, so it wouldn't be mirroring. No, to be the first to belch was to imply a confidence in oneself and a sense of security with one's place in the general interaction that looked very much like a tacit announcement of dominance. Ted might take a belch at this point as a challenge to his position. Luke cleaned his beery mouth with the back of his own hand, but held the belch in reserve for now.

Three men with nothing remarkable about them walked past, unenthusiastically discussing the previous night's football. Luke peered at them suspiciously and used the end of his shoe to push the hard black briefcase at his feet further under the table. He did this casually, but was certain that Ted would notice it on some level. The intended implication was a sense that vigilance was vital because the contents of the case – its valuable items and guarded secrets – were under constant threat of theft; it invested them with glamour and desirability. In fact, the case contained samples of central heating parts, and catalogues of the same, so inherently uninteresting that Luke cautiously stored it out of sight in the cupboard under the stairs whenever he went home. He had, you see, developed a personal survival strategy based on his being a salesman: a wily, quick-witted operator who could 'sell anything' – snow to Eskimos, or bikini bathing suits, also to Eskimos. He'd focused on the study of bleeding-edge sales techniques drawn from books and seminars. Transactional analysis. Anchoring. NLP. This, sinking himself in a bigger picture of non-specific selling, kept him fit and functional. Whereas, if he ever let his mind settle on the idea that he'd spent the last five years of his life traipsing around the country peddling central heating components to people whose businesses relied on their buying central heating components, then he suspected the same moment would see the return of his drinking problem.

'Some people are full of shite,' growled Ted, his voice like a saw tearing at wet wood. 'I can smell 'em.' He thought for a moment, then added, 'They smell of shite,' and laughed loudly. 'You know what I mean?'

Luke echoed Ted's laugh.

'Aye, of course you do,' Ted continued. 'That's it, y'see. I can tell. You're like me – one for straight talking and straight thinking. Feet on the ground; eye on the ball. No shite.'

'Well, I'd like to think I am, Ted. No argument there,' Luke replied, nodding (lots of nodding, always lots of nodding – induces a compliant state in the client). He was especially pleased with his answer here. The 'no argument' bit was nice – suggesting he *did* argue; that he was a man whose agreement had to be won and was therefore valuable, but that Ted had captured it without reservation. It was the 'I'd like to think I am' he was most proud of, however. Essentially, Ted had said he was a thing, and Luke had replied that it was his *aspiration* to be that thing. Not a simple (and possibly competitive-sounding) 'I'm like you' but a hopeful 'I'd love to believe that I'm like you'. Flattery would lift Ted's mood, and also encourage him to open his pockets wider to maintain the image that he was an important, successful person – someone who wrote big (to lesser people) cheques instantly and without a flicker of concern. Luke admired himself almost to the point of trembling with awe for keeping it subtle and apparently accidental even though he wasn't sure whether this level of soap should be called flattery or fellatio.

'I can't be doing with none of this bollocks where everyone's supposed to pretend they're something they're not, or that things aren't like we know full well they are,' Ted declared. 'All this ...' His lips warped with disdain and he shook his head, but he couldn't seem to find any actual words that were up to the task of continuing. Whatever 'all this' was, there was obviously too bewilderingly much of it for Ted to pick out a specific example off the top of his head.

Then, suddenly, he brightened and reached into the inside pocket of his jacket. Luke wondered what he was going to pull out and braced his face to look surprised and slightly envious if Ted's hand emerged with anything from a ChapStick to an SS dagger formerly owned by Himmler's personal hairdresser.

What Ted was reaching for, it turned out, was his wallet. He placed it on the table and opened it, almost reverently – as though it were a religious book: the basis of his personal faith. A finger turned over a couple of transparent plastic inner sleeves until it reached a photograph, which the same finger pointed at meaningfully.

'My wife,' said Ted, leaning back in his seat, job done.

Luke, playing the percentage shot, nodded.

'She's a cracker, isn't she?' Ted went on. 'Better than most that's half her age. Any man old enough for his balls to have dropped but young enough for them not to have dropped off is going to take one glance and think, Christ – I'd like to give her a seeing to, all right.' He moved forward in his chair again and leaned in close to Luke. 'That's what you're thinking right now, isn't it?'

Luke searched his memory for any sales seminar he'd attended where the speaker had mentioned which was the better answer to give to a potential client: 'I'd like to shag your wife,' or, 'I wouldn't like to shag your wife.' Even just nodding didn't seem a safe option here.

Fortunately, Luke struggled for a reply unobserved because Ted turned away to take another oesophagusful of beer as soon as he'd asked the question and, immediately he turned back, happily growled, 'Yeah – of course you are.' He tapped the photograph with his finger. 'She's what every bloke wishes he had: a wife what other men want to bang. I'm proud of her. How many men can say that, eh? That they're *proud* of their wife. Reasonably satisfied, maybe. Perfectly content with her, even, if you want. But *proud*? Like you'd be proud of a Roller, or owning the most successful central heating business in the north of the region. Something as, when other blokes see it, it takes a little nip at their insides because they'd love it to be theirs but they know it's yours.'

Luke signalled his agreement with a slight, conspiratorial smile – as though they were secretly sharing a Masonic handshake – while his mind raced to think of how the bloody hell he was going to steer all this round to how very reasonably priced his auto condensate pumps were.

'There's loads as would pretend they don't care about that kind of stuff,' said Ted. 'That it's not important to them that no other bloke on God's Earth'd shag their wife for money, in the dark. "How would you like to shag our Lizzie, Ted?" "Under a general anaesthetic, mate." Well, I'm honest about the way things are. You don't get any shite with me. You see what I mean?'

'I certainly do, Ted.'

'That's what I thought.' He took another drink, emptying the glass, and then belched loudly. 'Right. Then get another bloody beer in, and let's have a look at what you've got for me,' he said, beaming.

Ted knew people. If Ted knew anything.

8

Chris stepped out of the cab onto the damp pavement of Tithe Barn Avenue with very heavy legs. The street seemed to have decided to punish his earlier escape attempt by being deliberately eerie, sinister and claustrophobic for his return; everything had quite obviously spent the time since he was last there eagerly practising how to loom. Nothing went so far as to be identifiably satanic, but that was the cruel skill of it. It all looked unremarkably suburban, only a little too knowingly so; the kind of place a happy young couple move to, all smiles, and then – after the first commercial break – discover that the neighbourhood watch is run by Dennis Hopper.

Chris twisted round and leaned his head back into the taxi.

'Wait here,' he said.

The driver replied with a tight nod. He was now fairly used to taking this ragged passenger to some house at which he'd stay only briefly before he got back in again and asked to be driven to another one, where the process would repeat. In itself, it had almost arrived at dull. What kept it from actually getting there was a combination of the rather sizeable charge that was by now on the meter and his unnaturally silent fare showing increasing signs of weirdness behind the eyes. When the driver lined up the facts in his head it was pretty certain to him that they spelled out the word 'drugs'. Chris was making deliveries, and – just to be sociable – taking a bit of what he was selling along the way. This was bad. Drug abuse tore apart individual lives and also corroded the broader fabric of society. On the other hand, though, if he was dealing drugs then Chris would have no trouble paying the otherwise worryingly large number of pounds the journeys had racked up. The driver decided that the two things more or less cancelled each other out. So, as he watched Chris in his wing mirror, he was wary but not anxious.

Chris made his way towards Number 114 as slowly as he was able to while still persuading himself that he was being sensibly cautious rather than just downright cowardly. It was best to proceed with care anyway, he thought, as he felt curiously like he was walking on a bouncy castle. Today, nothing – the ground included, probably – could be relied upon not to deform bizarrely as he reached out to touch it. The way reality was slopping about all over the place this morning made his reason dizzy and, in turn, his legs unsteady.

A man strode out of the house next door to Number 114 – Number 112. He was hurrying but seemed relaxed enough about it; as though he was keenly aware he was late for somewhere he wasn't the least bit interested in being. He swam himself into his coat as he headed to his car and, when he reached it, briskly opened the door while glancing over his shoulder. He spotted the slow-moving figure peering at him from the edge of next door's driveway and, indifferently flicked his chin up in acknowledgement.

'Chris.'

'Yes. I am,' Chris replied blankly, after a small pause. But, by then, the man from Number 112 was already oblivious in his Avensis – starting the engine and mumbling something about his wife as he adjusted the wrongly positioned rear-view mirror.

The last few steps up to the front of the house from which Chris had only recently fled were very tough for him. To the eye it looked like nothing, but to the brain it was a steep incline in deep snow while dragging a sled; if he tripped over that not-entirely-level paving stone just ahead then he might lie there unable to get up until he was accidentally discovered much later, in the fossil record. Nevertheless, he edged forward with great resolve until he eventually reached the doorbell by the side of the porch. Arriving there was not remotely like getting over the crest of a hill, however. It was more like, after an exhausting struggle, finally managing to smash your way into a room that contained a lion. The doorbell was the pin of a hand grenade. It was a powerful but capricious god whose help he needed but whose mood he couldn't guess. His finger was genuinely trembling as he raised his hand – having to consciously will it every inch of the way – and, wrestling with his fear, pushed the button.

It didn't work.

Or did it? Some houses have bells you can hear from outside when you ring them, while others are perfectly loud enough to the occupants but completely inaudible when you're standing the other side of the front door. If you press a doorbell and hear nothing, it could be that it's broken or it could be that you just can't hear it from where you are. The natural thing to do would be to immediately sidestep the problem by knocking loudly instead. Except, that isn't the natural thing to do. It's the *obvious* thing to do, but the *natural* thing to do is to want to settle this doorbell question right now, so it doesn't play on your mind – possibly for years to come. Thus, any normal person won't abandon the bell straight away; that would be practical, yes – if practical's your bag – but it lacks psychological resolution. What a normal person will do is ring again, but this time squinting with concentration and while placing the side of their head close to the door to see if they can pick up any telltale bell sounds. This is what Chris did. So that he was there in a slight crouch, aiming his ear through the glass of the porch, when the front door abruptly opened.

He instantly took his finger off the bell and jerked himself upright – making an untidy lunge for dignity. Where he ended up was that self-conscious, incongruous and innately sad pose – *Chest out! Chin up! Shoulders back!* – that men who've served in the army forty years previously sometimes adopt during moments of great drunkenness.

Strange Woman stood in the doorway and gazed at Chris with a sort of skilful weariness. Her eyes briefly looked him up and down, pausing to peer a little harder at one point – and then she let out a gentle sigh.

'Covered in milk again, eh?'

She turned and, seemingly unconcerned, walked off down the short hallway before disappearing out of sight into a room on the left – leaving the front door wide open before Chris.

Chris had told the cab driver to bring him here because he'd decided that he *must* return to Number 114 and speak to Strange Woman. He couldn't begin to formulate a theory that plausibly explained even half of what was going on (his very best effort was that he was the target of absolutely *the* most ambitious episode of *Beadle's About* imaginable). He'd have embraced with cosy relief the idea that he was dreaming, or perhaps that some passing wanker had slipped LSD into his lager as a joke and he was adrift in a bad trip. But, try as he might, he couldn't persuade himself that either of those theories was true. Many, many things were incomprehensible and disorientating, but nothing felt dreamy or druggy; as much as unanswerable questions had set his head spinning, the cold, damp drabness of the world he was wobbling through identified it as real. No genuine hallucination could under-achieve so badly as to create such an accurate depiction of Britain. Therefore, Chris's feeling was that it would be a similar experience had he, in the middle of popping to the newsagent's, say, suddenly found himself walking on the moon. It would, admittedly, be bizarre and unbalancing personally – like Sting before him, he'd be very anxious that his legs didn't break – but *within its own terms*, it would be logical and consistent: this was how one walked, on the moon. Today, it would fit if, for example, he saw everyone was now driving on the right; it would not fit if he saw them all riding around on the backs of giant, rainbow-coloured centipedes. A key point, Chris sensed, was that, though things were wrong and inexplicable and disturbing, they weren't random. And, if it wasn't dada-esqued anarchy – if there were laws – then there was a chance of unpicking it, and the most sensible way to do that was to start at the beginning. So, as desperately as he'd run away from Number 114 earlier, desperation had called him back again. He just *had* to return to Strange Woman in the hope of getting some clues if he wasn't to spend the rest of his days as one of those people who wear baking foil wrapped around their heads to keep out the CIA's thought-control waves.

He stepped into the house and moved with unnatural care along the parquet-floored hall, like someone treading on ice he hoped was thick enough to hold his weight. When his fingertips gently pushed open the first door on the left, he initially remained on the threshold, not actually entering what turned out to be the living room. Tentatively, he leaned his head in while keeping his feet where they were, in the relative safety of the hallway. Strange Woman was tidying up some magazines and newspapers that were lying about the place (to be exact, dumping them into a V-shaped holder by the coffee table, where they still weren't tidy but were at least all untidy in the same place). Chris examined her.

She was very old. Well ... not *very* old. Chris backed up a little from that position. She wasn't old like, say, Mother Teresa or one of the Fates. No, this preliminary evaluation was more of a flinch than an objective assessment. Strange Woman was in, oh ... her mid-forties, perhaps. She was dealing with that decade pretty well too. In fairness, there was even a womanly elegance about her of the kind you see in refined English stage actresses who've moved out of the love-interest age range and over into habitually playing the wronged wives of Cabinet ministers. In the jeans and T-shirt she had on she looked scruffy in a way that you'd normally suspect involved the input of a publicist – 'at home' with a quietly well-regarded novelist in a *South Bank Show* profile. Now both his vision and the light were better than when he'd first encountered it, he could see that her dark hair was veined with grey, but it was also full and strong; likewise, her skin was lined, yet she still wore it perfectly. He accepted that his instinctive response was wrong. She wasn't old, really; she was just old for *him*. Beer goggles must have led to his winding up in bed with her, but not because they'd made her appear attractive when she was actually ugly. What they'd done was see her in the first place. Under normal cir-cumstances she'd have been invisible. His sober eyes wouldn't have seen a Yes, a No or even a Maybe had they scanned across her in a crowded bar. They'd have seen Somebody's Mother and thus, in practical terms, nothing at all. He wondered (because he couldn't even sketchily remember) what it had been like having sex with her and felt no trace of revulsion; only the kind of purely hypothetical curiosity with which every man, at some point, wonders what it's like to have sex with Hannah Gordon.

He cleared his throat for attention and she stopped consolidating the mess in the room and looked over at him.

'Sorry ...' he said, sheepishly. 'Sorry. There's a cab ... I don't have enough ...' He pulled the small jumble of coins and notes from his pocket and displayed them in a cupped hand. 'Could you possibly ...'

Strange Woman sighed again, heavily, and came forward – moving around him as she headed outside.

'I'll pay you back,' he assured her passing shoulder.

65

He walked over to the window and watched her speak to the taxi driver. There were a few words he couldn't hear, a pause, Strange Woman shook her head, and then she walked back up the drive. She didn't come into the room again, however. Instead, he heard her root around in the hallway (possibly by the coat rack), and then she returned to the cab carrying a chequebook. Chris felt a little crappy seeing this, but turning away and peering around the room instead effectively dealt with that feeling. There was nothing much to see, but more than enough to look at. A sofa; the coffee table; a fireplace; a television (impressively larger, and wider, than he'd ever seen before – and with what looked to be a CD player built into it. His hand twitched to the *Star Trek* gadget in his trouser pocket; maybe the TV was standard MI6 issue). He was scanning idly along the mantelpiece, when his eyes collided with a framed photograph that induced a brief power outage in his legs.

The picture showed what must be Strange Woman's daughter, or a very much younger sister. The cheek of her smiling face was pressed against the cheek of Chris's smiling own. He couldn't think where this photo could possibly have been taken, or even recall having met the woman in it at all. Was it a fake? A creepy mock-up? Was Strange Woman a deranged stalker? Were there, in the cellar, hundreds more photographs of him stuck to the walls? Possibly with the eyes cut out?

Or did he know this family? Strange Woman gave the impression that she knew *him*. Christ – even her *neighbour* seemed to know him. Had he drunk himself into a *Lost Weekend*-style blackout on Monday? An alcohol-fuelled two or three days during which he'd made lots of new friends. And left his now re-rented flat (dumping all his stuff in a skip with an unconcerned, beery grin). And persuaded his old friends to remodel, or demolish, their own houses before they also moved out and . . . No. This was stretching a theory *way* past breaking point. He binned the idea. In its place, he had no other idea.

The heavy clunk of the front door closing knocked Chris out of his theorising. He turned to face the doorway of the living room and stood awkwardly, bracing himself for Strange Woman's imminent return.

She came in and, without looking at him, began tidying again.

He got the impression that the two things were related – that she was tidying partly as a way of not looking at him.

'Sorry,' he said.

She was bending over gathering up some magazines but she craned her head and glanced at him around the side of her bottom, her face emerging from an eclipse. Its expression, he thought, suggested she felt his apology was sarcastic, or so brazenly hollow that it might as well have been. He tried not to let this annoy him. He *was* sorry he'd (temporarily) dumped the taxi bill in her lap. So there was no cause to glare at him just because *she* was ... whatever she was. Perhaps she was embarrassed about having dressed up and shagged a man who couldn't remember having met her daughter somewhere or other. Which, now he thought about it, was as good a place as any to start.

Chris indicated the picture on the mantelpiece by sending a slight flick of his chin in its direction. 'I was just looking at that photograph ...' he said.

Strange Woman stopped shuffling magazines, straightened up, and cast her own eyes over it, briefly. She made a small noise – halfway between a laugh and a sniff.

'Yes,' she said reflectively. She pushed her hands into the back pockets of her jeans. It's not really comfortable, having both your hands in your back pockets. Perhaps that's why people tend to do it when they're not really comfortable.

Chris waited for her to continue, but she didn't. So much for the subtle approach.

'I don't recognise the woman in the picture,' he declared flatly.

She did the sniff-laugh thing again. 'I don't recognise the man,' she replied.

Chris frowned and then stepped over to the photo. He peered at it hard for a few seconds.

'Isn't it me?' he asked.

Slight confusion tumbled across her face for a moment, then she sighed and shrugged. 'Is it?'

'I don't know.'

'If *you* don't know, then how could I?' she replied.

'Because it's your photograph.'

'Oh, it's *my* photograph?'

'Yes!'

'Yes?'

'Well, it's in your bloody house, isn't it?!'

'And *my* house. Of course!'

'What? You live here, don't you?!'

'Fff. Yes – if that's what you call it.'

She was nuts.

She was nuts, Chris thought, and he was arguing with her. That was a good way for him to end up nuts too. He sucked some air in between his teeth and held up first one hand (Stop), then a second (I surrender).

'OK, OK,' he said rolling his eyes. 'Let's drop it.'

'Not discuss it at all, eh?' She nodded, too slowly and too big.

'That's right.'

'Because you don't want to talk about it.' Even larger nods, as though she'd just had her neck hinged and was testing it out.

'No. I've talked about it enough now, thanks.'

'Surprise, surprise.'

Strange Woman stared at him, chewing a little on her bottom lip, and then she abruptly twisted away once more. She bent down, snatched up a magazine that had fallen out of the holder and slammed it back. The force with which she hurled it in caused it to skid out again, taking four others along with it. She looked at them all, spilled across the floor. After considering them calmly for a moment, she kicked over the entire holder – not savagely; more, well … *precisely*. Chris found this collected, considered aspect a little unsettling: there was something of the 'No, Mr Bond – I expect you to *die*' about it.

He decided to move on and kill two birds with one stone by enquiring about his clothes. That would give her mind something straightforward to focus on – hopefully with steadying results – and also allow him to get his own stuff back.

'Where are my clothes?' he asked.

'What clothes?'

'The ones I was wearing before these, of course.' (He'd tried not to add the 'of course', as it obviously meant 'you moron', but somehow he found it astonishingly difficult not to say things that he knew full well were going to antagonise her.)

'They're in the washing machine. *Of course*,' she replied.

'You put them in the washing machine?'

68

She laughed. 'And how likely is it that *you* did?'

'Not very,' Chris freely admitted.

'Then we agree on that, at least.' She smiled tightly at him, unhappily happy to have won this point. Chris nodded. He was pleased to concede it graciously, as it seemed to him a point of the 'Collect four and win a bed with straps on it' kind.

'OK, never mind about my clothes,' Chris said brusquely. He saw her stiffen further at his tone. Carefully, he drew in a breath and then slowly released it, making a conscious effort to exhale any signs of confrontation along with the air. 'Look ...' he said. He took a step towards her and, pleadingly, continued, 'The thing is ... The thing is: I have no idea how I got here.'

Strange Woman smiled at him, quite sympathetically, he thought.

'Yes.' She lowered her eyes. 'I know the feeling.'

'Actually, I'm not even sure where here *is* ... And there's all this stuff that has changed, but I can't figure out how, and ...' He shook his head. 'It's so confusing.'

'I understand.' She moved forward and laid her hand on his arm. 'That's how I feel sometimes.'

This demonstration of empathy really pissed him off. It was like the soft-spoken, hard-nosed evasion you'd hear from the leader of some religious cult.

Q: *'Why are you keeping me chained to this wall?'*

A: *'Aren't we all, in a sense, chained to the walls of our expectations?'*

He remembered he was trying to remain calm, and remembering that made him angrier.

'No,' he said, 'you *don't* understand. If you understood, you wouldn't tell me that you understand; you'd understand that I just need to know *where the fuck I am*!'

Strange Woman withdrew her hand and folded her arms across her stomach. 'You're asking the wrong person,' she replied tersely.

'Oh – believe me – if there was anyone else who might have the answers, but *wasn't* barking bloody mad, I'd ask them. The problem is, I'm stuck with *you*.'

She chewed her lip again, and nodded. 'Well ...' Her head twisted away and her eyes flicked over the various mundane objects they found before them; abruptly switching from one to the next as though she were searching for something. 'Well, I'm glad you've finally said it out loud,' she replied, turning back to glare at him defiantly. 'Now we know what your real problem is, the solution is pretty obvious, isn't it?'

Chris stared back at her. He gave it a few seconds, but it became clear she was simply going to look at him while being angry and emotional – as though that said it all. She *still* wasn't going to give him a straight answer.

'Oh – *bollocks* to this!' he shouted, flinging his arms into the air. 'You're a lunatic. Why am I even talking to you when you're a lunatic?'

'Yeah, right – *I'm* the one who's lost it.'

'I never said you'd lost it. I'm guessing, obviously, but my suspicion is that you've never bleeding had it.'

He started to march towards the door. She stepped in front of him – preventing him from leaving – and snarled, 'Just piss off!' (You couldn't even *see* Rational from her house, Chris thought.)

'*You* piss off,' he countered.

'Do you think I won't?' It was a challenge.

'I've no sodding idea *what* you'll do before you actually do it. Which probably makes two of us.'

'Ha. You're calling *me* erratic?'

'Yes.'

'*Me*?'

'Yes.'

'*M*—'

'*Yes!* Look, I can see your difficulty here, but I'm sure it'll all be much easier to grasp once you've been medicated.'

'You are such a—' She was interrupted by a telephone on the small table by the sofa starting to warble shrilly. Pushing Chris out of the way, she strode over to it and reached down. She paused with her hand slightly above the receiver and looked back at him to finish her sentence ('*wanker.*') before picking it up.

'Yes?' she said to the handset, almost not aggressively. 'No,' she added after a moment listening to whoever was on the other end. Her voice was quieter and she turned away a little as she spoke. 'Yeah – I suppose so.'

She walked stiffly back to Chris and, arm out straight and rigid, placed the phone in front of his chest.

At first, Chris didn't realise that she was offering it to him. He thought she was, well, perhaps 'scanning him with it' – as though it were a Geiger counter, say.

Chris looked at her, then down at the phone, and then back up at her. She sighed and gave the receiver an impatient little shake. He finally took it and raised it cautiously to his ear.

'Hello?' he said warily.

'Hi, Chris. How's it going?'

'Andrew?'

'Yes. I wa—'

'Andrew *Wickham*?' Chris did that thing where he was so surprised that he slightly lost his balance for a second and had put out a hand to steady himself. This was the first time anyone had actually done this outside a television light-entertainment programme.

'Um, yes,' Andrew replied. 'Who were you expecting?'

'Who were *you* expecting?' Chris asked, still stunned. 'You called here to speak to *me*?'

'Obviously,' Andrew responded, with what seemed almost like indignation. 'Of course I called to speak to *you*. Who else am I going to phone there? Trudie?'

'Trudie?' Chris echoed, emptily. Strange Woman turned her eyes to him at this. He looked back at her. 'Trudie,' he repeated – some part of his brain having apparently decided that enunciating it slightly differently would help his understanding no end. He frowned and pressed the phone harder against his head. He spoke to Andrew slowly and carefully. 'Trudie ... Dark hair, blue eyes, getting on a bit.'

'Chris. Regular features, five foot ten, arsehole,' muttered (so it now seemed) Trudie.

'Steady on, mate,' Andrew said in a voice that was somewhere between chiding and embarrassed. 'Let's not have another one, eh?'

'Another what?' asked Chris.

Andrew gave a small 'Do we *have* to?' sigh. This kind of thing, he thought, was a bit adolescent. (Feigned ignorance sounds superlatively goading and sarcastic when it is, in fact, genuine ignorance.) 'Another slanging match,' Andrew replied limply.

'Slanging match?' Chris wondered if he was ever again going to hear a whole sentence that he could fully absorb.

'Or whatever you want to call it. Just try – for me – to go for a few minutes without having one with your wife.'

Well, if there *was* going to be a fully absorbable sentence, then that one categorically was not it.

'My www ...' Chris couldn't climb even halfway up the word. 'Wwww ...' He was stuck at the base-camp W, unable to get any kind of foothold; stranded there pathetically, making a noise like the world's most feeble ghost.

Gradually, he became conscious of the fact that Trudie was watching him. His shoulders were slumped, his expression must surely have suggested that it was the product of a series of quite major strokes, and he was making a gentle but steady 'wwww' sound. Trudie, he saw, was looking at him as though none of this was particularly unusual.

'Andrew,' he said, clasping the phone very tightly, 'I need to see you.'

'Sure.' There was resignation there, but also relief, and perhaps even a hint of careful nudging. That was pretty complex, Chris thought. He'd not noticed Andrew be that complex in all the years he'd known him – had he been working up to this 'Sure' the whole time? Sitting in his bedroom in front of the mirror, practising levels? Then again, it was perfectly possible, Chris conceded, that he'd simply never listened to him so closely before. 'Sure,' Andrew repeated. 'Come over.'

'Where are you?'

'I'm at home.'

'Right.' Chris nodded. 'Right ... And where is that, then?'

9

'Hello, Chris – come in,' said a bubbly middle-aged woman Chris was absolutely sure he'd never laid eyes on before she opened the door and said it to him.

He'd not had to put himself through the humiliation of asking 'Trudie' if he could borrow more money for another taxi because when he'd announced – immediately after the phone call had finished – that he was going to Andrew's she'd wordlessly left the room and, on returning a few moments later, had tossed him a set of car keys. Pressing the button on the fob when he was outside Number 114 caused a blue Ford Something parked close by to emit a beep and flash its lights. He got in and drove away. Doing this might have concerned him more were it not easily one of the least utterly baffling things that had happened to him all morning.

After a number of stops to ask random pedestrians for directions, he'd arrived at a detached house of the kind lived in by people who would describe their financial situation as 'comfortable'. It was this house into which he was now being invited.

'How are you today?' the woman asked cheerily.

Chris shrugged. This drew a sympathetic, knowing smile from her. Though what it was she was sympathetically knowing for his benefit was a mystery to him; so she might as well have shrugged back for all the good it did.

A girl of about sixteen came down the stairs in a teenaged hurry, scrambling into a jacket.

'Hi, Chris,' she said as she sped past him.

'Hi ... you,' he replied.

She laughed and started out of the door.

'Where are you going?' asked the woman.

The girl paused for a second, sighed loudly, and answered 'Ooooou-*t*' while rolling her eyes – exasperated beyond all human endurance by such a relentless interrogation. She then left – the woman calling 'Well, phone if you're going to be late' as the door shut on her words at around the 'if' mark. The woman tutted, but remained unfathomably attached to her smile as she turned back to Chris and said, 'Andy's in the living room. Do you fancy a cup of tea? I was just about to put the kettle on.'

'Er . . .' Chris said.

'Or coffee perhaps?' the woman offered, gently.

'I . . .' Chris began but, before he could get any further, he was distracted by the arrival of the worst moment in the whole of his life.

He had been trying to get his bearings. He'd set his sights low – there was no sense attempting to work out where he stood in the entire, bemusing web of this world – but he thought he might at least be able to make some kind of bearable order of his feet and the things within a yard or so of them.

He'd noted that the hallway had quality carpeting. The woman – slightly dumpy but not enough to counteract the creeping wrinkles – had lively green eyes but her hair was cut in that short style that, on a middle-aged woman, indicates that some key part of her had decided to give up and call it a day. She was wearing a simple flowery dress and was probably, he was prepared to allow, just unassailably upbeat rather than mad as a badger. A cardigan hung over the newel post at the bottom of the stairs. The house smelled of lasagne and candle wax. To his left, on the wall by the door, was a three-quarter-length mirror in a pine frame. Reflected in this mirror, Chris saw now he had spotted it, was a Picture of Dorian Gray in Nike trainers.

'Fuck!' Chris felt as though he'd fallen through a hole in an ice-covered lake. 'Fucking *hell*.'

He stumbled closer to the grotesque caricature of himself. His reflection was carrying well over a stone of abandoned fat, as if he'd gone in for liposuction and there'd been a tragic, body-wide blowback from the jar holding the buttocks of several previous patients. He wasn't at all what you'd call obese, but he'd always been skinny so, relatively, the sight of his plumpish features and escaping stomach smacked into him as much as they would had a normal person woken up to find that – overnight – they'd become American. Even worse, his face had melted. The first thought that

74

hit him was, It's my father, followed by, And my father is dead. Then there were his eyes. Jesus Christ . . . his *eyes*. Filmy, vaguely yellow things under which hung dark, heavy bags – torpid, tired and toxic. Surely eyes like that must hurt their owner – they were like bruises or wounds. He winced looking at them, but almost in the *Ouch!-glad-that-wasn't-me* fashion one would had one happened to see someone else march an unwary forehead into an ambushingly low lintel.

He lifted frightened but perversely fascinated hands up to prod his cheeks. His probing fingers sank into the defeated, blancmange-soft skin and then moved down to flick at the wobbly sack of flesh that had been placed under his chin (presumably to collect the general run-off from his landsliding face).

The woman, watching him examine himself in horror, smiled and clucked. With amusement but without any malice, she offered, 'You always pay for a night's overindulgence in the morning, don't you?'

Chris twisted and looked at her, speechless. He turned back to his reflection. A night's overindulgence? No. No way. It simply wasn't possible to consume enough lager in an evening to do this. This – *this* – was worse than you'd expect even if 'a night's overindulgence' meant a sleepless twenty-four hours sucking lique-fied bacon through a tube while completely submerged in for-maldehyde. He swivelled his gaze away from the mirror and onto the woman once more. Inspired by that special clarity of logic that descends in moments of great stress, he was about to throw a shoe at her when a head poked out from the doorway a slight distance further back.

'Hiya, mate – come in,' it said.

The voice was Andrew's. On closer inspection so was the head it was coming from – possibly. The hair was greying and the face had suffered structural subsidence similar to Chris's, but this could indeed be Andrew if one assumed that he'd suddenly fallen prey to some quite appalling disease.

'Andrew?' Chris speculated out loud.

Andrew's forehead wrinkled slightly. His eyes landed on the car keys in Chris's hand, and from there they flicked up to share a glance with the woman's. 'Did you drive here?' he asked – so very, very casually that it came across about the same as a yelp.

Chris peered down at the keys he was holding. 'Yes,' he replied, after struggling with the question for a short time. 'Trudie,' he added, without really knowing why; he merely wanted his answer to be detailed enough to meet everyone's satisfaction.

Andrew stepped out into the hallway. He was wearing black jeans and a baggy top; various sports references curved in rugged text around his pot pelly. He placed a hand on Chris's shoulder and began to guide him into the living room. 'Come and take the weight off,' he said brightly and, turning to the woman, 'Were you making tea, Gill?'

Chris said nothing and allowed himself to be led, still staring down at the car keys in his hand.

For the following few minutes, he sat, small, on the big sofa in Andrew's living room and failed to take anything in. Andrew remained standing and gabbled on about some war or other, and environmental Armageddon, and a pensions crisis – trivial things that just bounced off Chris's eardrums. It wasn't until the woman, Gill, had brought them a mug of tea each and then left again ("I need to get on with my jobs.") that he was able to speak himself.

'Andrew,' he said, staring into his tea. 'I don't know what the fuck's going on.'

Having got the words out, he looked up, steeling himself to deal with whatever reaction (incomprehension or derision or who could guess what) this statement would provoke. However, instead of it seeming to be any kind of bewildering bombshell for his friend, it was greeted with nothing more than an acknowledging nod.

Andrew put his hands in his pockets. 'Yeah,' he said.

This response, Chris felt, fell somewhat short of being at all bleeding helpful. Andrew wasn't grasping what he was being told.

'No, listen,' Chris said, this time with a slight edge. 'I don't know what the *fuck* is going on.'

Andrew sensed that Chris was after something, but wasn't sure exactly what. He paused for a moment – he didn't want to accidentally end up answering a question he wasn't being asked. He took his right hand out of his pocket and used it to pull on his ear thoughtfully. 'What is it you mainly don't understand, mate?' he asked carefully.

'Well,' replied Chris, '*mainly* I don't understand anything that's happening on Earth.'

Andrew smiled. Chris glared at him. Andrew stopped smiling and said, 'You feel a bit mixed up, you mean?'

'No. I'm not mixed up. The *world* is mixed up. I'm fine ...' The image of himself in the mirror came into his head once more. He wasn't fine – actually, he looked like someone who had been discovered preserved in peat – but that needed to be put aside for the moment. He had to deal with one all-consuming calamity at a time. '*I'm* fine, but nothing else is – nothing whatsoever.'

Andrew looked back queryingly. 'Like what?'

'Like *everything*. You. This house. That Gill woman and the young girl. My place. "Trudie" – God help us. Where's Neil? Where's Katrina? What's happened to bleeding *everything*?'

Chris saw that Andrew's expression had now made the jump from 'quite uncertain' to 'very confused indeed'. In the same way that deep creases radiate out from the point of distortion if you poke a single finger into the centre of a soft cushion, lines had shot across Andrew's skin from anywhere that puzzlement had tightened a muscle. It looked, to Chris's eyes, almost as though his face had abruptly shattered.

Apparently unaware of this facial crisis, however, Andrew merely said, 'Katrina?' as if he suspected that it had been a slip of Chris's tongue.

'Yes,' Chris replied (not without a trace of 'Are you stupid?'). 'Her flat isn't even *there*, for Christ's sake.'

'Katrina's flat?'

'Yes. I went to her flat—'

'To *Katrina's* flat?'

'*Yes*. Jesus. I went to her flat, and it's not there.'

Andrew mulled this over for a time. Then, Chris thought, gave insufficient weight to the matter of a whole building vanishing by replying, 'Why did you go to her flat?'

'Why did I go to my girlfriend's flat?'

'Your girlfriend?'

'My girlfr— You *do* remember Katrina, don't you?'

'Well, yes ... Of course I remember her.'

Chris was perfectly aware that there was an elephant in the room. A Trudie-shaped elephant. On the telephone to him Andrew had called Trudie his wife. Now, perhaps he was being literal there, and perhaps it was just some kind of in-joke. Either way, though, it was something that was likely to have a certain impact on his relationship with Katrina; he knew her, and his having picked up a wife – literally *or* figuratively – was just the kind of thing that would rub her up the wrong way. However, to stave off the advent of curling up in a ball and mewling for as long possible, he was sticking to the one-thing-at-a-time approach.

'There you are then. So why wouldn't I go to see Katrina?' Chris replied. 'I love her,' he added, challengingly.

Andrew looked horrified. 'My God ... My *God*. When ... I mean, I didn't know you were even in contact with her. When did you get in touch again? It must be ... God, it must be getting on for twenty years.'

'What must be getting on for twenty years?'

'Since you went out with Katrina.'

This was the most ridiculous and unexpected thing Chris had ever heard, yet also both self-evidently reasonable and entirely anticipated.

Getting on for twenty years. Though consciously refusing to acknowledge the very possibility of such a thing, he'd actually been awaiting its arrival for some time. It wasn't that it made sense, because the things it was required to make sense of themselves made no sense – but it was at least *consistent* with them, when nothing else Chris could think of was. It was the only possible explanation of the impossible facts.

He sprang to his feet, then sat down again heavily. Doing so took no more than a couple of seconds, but he was nevertheless quite pleased with this act of defiance in the face of the world, and, if pushed, reserved the right to do it again.

Andrew was still talking.

'The last time I saw you with Katrina you were ... I don't know ... twenty-four?'

'Twenty-five,' Chris replied mechanically. 'I'm twenty-five.'

'Twenty-five,' Andrew said, and shook his head – as if there were something amusing about the number. 'God. You were tw—'

'I *am* twenty-five,' corrected Chris, shooting Andrew a glance that implied any contradiction from him would mean trouble. 'What ...' He sighed. (There was no way to do this in gentle stages. He couldn't descend – he simply had to plunge – so he might as well just do it rather than frighten himself even further beforehand by looking down.) 'What year is it?' he asked.

Andrew wasn't sure what he meant. 'Um, what year was it when you were seeing Katrina, you mean? Well,' his eyes flicked upwards as he started the calculation, 'it must have be—'

'No. I know that, *obviously*.' Chris dug his nails into the 'obviously'. For him that 'obviously' confirmed, and demonstrated, that he was functional and lucid: there was, *obviously*, no suggestion that his mind was broken. 'I want to know what year it is now.'

'*Now?*' Andrew let out a breath. 'How much did you drink last night, Chris?'

'What year is it?'

'It's 2006, of course.'

Chris nodded. He didn't feel anything. After a couple of seconds, clutching pathetically at the only shred of straw he could see, he asked hopefully, 'January 2006?'

'December 2006.'

Well, that's torn it, he thought.

He rubbed his clammy palms along the legs of his jeans to remove the sticky sweat. These are *my* jeans, he thought, they must be *my* jeans. But then he added a slippery, but vital, qualification: they are Chris Mortimer's jeans. The crude facts and the complex feelings were summed up as, silently, he said to himself, 'I've stolen my own clothes.' His palms were already sweaty again. He turned back to Andrew.

'Andrew? Are you a good friend?'

Andrew blanched. This wasn't an unreasonable reaction, Chris decided after a moment's reflection. 'Are you a good friend?' apropos of nothing is a question you're most likely to hear just before being asked to lend the speaker a truly vast amount of money, or as a lead-up to something like 'Only, I've got four bodies in the boot of my car, and could *really* do with several alibis and a shovel.'

'What do you think?' Andrew replied, trying, it seemed, to simultaneously mock the very question while also being tentative about his answer. The result was a warble of mystifying inflections – like a Russian who'd learnt his English from listening to albums by German rock bands.

Chris shrugged. 'I think you probably are,' he said. 'I mean, it seems that way, but ...'

'But what?' asked Andrew nervously.

'But ...' Chris clicked his tongue. 'But it's been a long time. It's been a long time since ... Look – sit down.'

Andrew considered this, then with a stiff-limbed cautiousness balanced himself on the edge of one of the squat, quietly-too-expensive armchairs that matched the sofa. Chris fixed him with eyes shamelessly feigning fearless resolve.

'This is going to sound crazy—' he began.

Andrew cut in. 'Things that sound crazy usually *are* crazy,' he said, and gave a tight little laugh that was closer to a dry cough.

'Well, this isn't,' Chris snapped back defensively. 'So just shut up and listen. I really need you to listen to what I'm going to tell you, OK?'

Andrew's hands lay awkwardly on top of his legs. He clenched and unclenched them rapidly a few times, and then he gave a single nod.

'OK,' he said. 'I'm listening.'

10

David's wife, Carol, was planning something special for David's fifty-seventh birthday. She was going over the details of her plans with him, partly because he was the one who'd have to pay for it all, but mostly just because she relished going over the details of her plans with people. It was going to be a party that would induce awe and envy in all the guests. Their delight at its breadth, opulence and imagination would scar them psychologically; unmistakably superior to anything they could have devised or afforded, each new joy they encountered would be like falling onto a blade. The tiny details, the grand sweep; the food, the entertainment and the thematic invention; the easy parking. Everything would be an agony of, for them, unattainable perfection. After seeing the floral arrangements, several of those attending, she was sure, would return home and quietly run a hosepipe between their car's window and its exhaust.

'So, tying in with the whole Roman idea, I'm going to have signs on the different rooms – like THE COLOSSEUM and THE PANTHEON and THE ACROPOLIS,' said Carol, whose artistic vision occasionally outstripped her geography.

David nodded. He wasn't really listening; it wasn't necessary, as a simple trained reflex was sufficient to take care of everything. The subconscious program code for it needed only two lines: 'If sounds are coming out of Carol's mouth, do nothing. If the sounds coming out of Carol's mouth briefly stop, nod.' Naturally, it would be disastrous if Carol genuinely asked him what he thought about something, or if he missed her vital warning of, 'Look out – a tiny meteor is heading straight for your neck!' But neither of those things had happened yet and, as the meteor was the more likely of the two, David was prepared to risk it.

Between – and indeed during – nods his mind was concerned

with things other than his wife's strategies for belligerent hospitality. He was discontented. Aside from the occasional bit of deliberately troublesome interference in his empire's affairs (just so everyone knew that he was, ultimately, still the boss) he'd retired at the age of fifty – visibly realising a goal he'd brashly announced he would achieve thirty years before. He was well, *well* beyond that point where people still talk about what someone has 'earned' and far into the reaches of it being accepted to speak of what they are 'worth'. His personal fortune was of that size that is said to have been 'amassed' or 'accumulated'. Here, again, 'earned' wouldn't do. (Possibly because its suggestion of some kind of parity would seem silly; everyone will allow for brains, and education, and sheer effort, but very few would think it reasonable to explain David's wealth as straightforwardly the result of his being over *five hundred thousand times* more intelligent or better trained or harder working than a postman, a bus driver or, it's almost a statistical certainty, you.) He didn't need to toil to pay the bills any longer. In fact, if he simply sold everything and put his money in the bank, then just the interest could support him, his wife and, say, a sizeable part of Humberside. He was vastly rich and he didn't need to lift a single finger, ever again, to stay that way. And yet, he was discontented.

The first twelve months or so of his retirement had been spectacular. It was obvious to everyone that not only could he look out over contemporaries who faced another fifteen years at the grindstone before they could relax and start thinking about selling their houses to pay for sheltered accommodation, but he could look out over them from the deck of his great big yacht. He was a dream. Not an aspiration, a *dream*. A realistic person couldn't aim to be in David Short's position, they could only fantasise about it.

But, as time went on, it became less and less rewarding. The galling thing about having a great big yacht, for example, was that the very nature of it meant that you rather too frequently found yourself moored next to other people who also had great big yachts. Everything's relative: depending on where you happen to be, having four goats can mean that you're seen as – and feel like – either a powerful, wealthy aristocrat or a hapless wretch who smells of goats. The stateroom aboard his 30-metre Ferretti

Navetta was very comfortable and pleasing, but then so is a beanbag and a library book. If your perception is increasingly that everyone can have a floating stateroom, it's almost the same as everyone being limited to a beanbag; to David, seeing people, everywhere he turned, being able to afford whatever earthly luxury they fancied seemed essentially indistinguishable from the worst excesses of communism.

He tried to tell himself that he was fretting needlessly. He was worth hundreds of millions of pounds, while those he was rubbing shoulders with – though seeming to have it peachy – actually had only a few dozen million pounds to their names. But his attempts to rationalise the problem away in this manner quickly fell into a hole. Now he had the time and the yacht to reflect on it, he realised that he didn't have all that much money. Oh, he could afford trinkets and baubles and the former home of Lord Byron, but so what? He was second – probably third – division. He was no Gates or Abramovich. He wasn't even a *Branson* (who, barely scraping into the top 250 of the world's nearly 800 billionaires, was hardly what you could call a role model).

Realising this led to a spiritual epiphany. What, at the end of the day, was his massive wealth *worth*? What did it mean, in human terms? Nothing. Ten billion – now *that* was meaningful. That meant power and respect and, if you fancied, fear. With ten billion, *governments* would shut up and listen to what you had to say. It was presence – charisma – that you could, as it were, take to the bank. The difference was qualitative. Compared to the *personal* substance of having several billion pounds, his superficial millions were nothing. He'd wanted to be a success, to 'get to the top'; in fact, he'd ended up just being someone who could do a lot of shopping.

And here he was approaching fifty-seven – discontented. Bitterness and regret wormed through him. It was too late now, he was sure of that. He was old and out of touch and didn't have the energy he'd had thirty years ago – never mind that he'd be starting so far behind the field.

He gazed out of the window while Carol jabbered on about her party plans with irritating enthusiasm. How shallow does a woman have to be to relish a financial situation such as theirs? And he didn't find her attractive either. What the hell was that about?

What does it profit a man if he gains hundreds of millions of pounds but his wife is ugly? *Christ*, he'd made a mess of things.

In the unimpressive winter of 2006 David Short sat silently, sad to his soul, and wished he could have had his life over again so he could have made much, much more money.

11

There was a deep pause of a number of seconds, into which Andrew hesitantly dropped a frown. It began as only a slight, questioning corrugation of his forehead but – rather like the way paper folds and twists itself as it burns – grew apparently independently into deep, snaking ranges of incomprehension. He eventually decided that he must be missing something and appealed to Chris for clarification.

'What do you mean, exactly?' he asked.

'Precisely what I said,' Chris replied with an unnatural, almost messianic calmness. 'I have travelled through time.'

'A sort of reincarnation thing?' Andrew scrambled a little, trying to get some purchase on the idea. 'You've lived before? You're the Dalai Lama or something?'

'Do you think I'm the Dalai Lama?' Chris replied, now sighing slightly with irritation.

A little embarrassed, Andrew instinctively responded by defending his position. 'How would I know? Isn't that the point with the Dalai Lama? It could be anyone. In fact, it's probably the person you least suspect – like serial killers.'

Chris looked at him expressionlessly. 'Frighteningly cogent.' He wiped a hand over his face before continuing. 'But, for reference, I'm not the Dalai Lama. And I'm not talking about having lived before. I'm not the Dalai Lama, or Julius Caesar, or, um ...' He shrugged.

'Janis Joplin?'

'Particularly not Janis Joplin.' This was even harder than he'd thought it was going to be. Regrouping, he leaned towards Andrew and spoke with great care. 'I mean that I have literally travelled through time.'

'Like Michael J. Fox in *Back to the Future*?'

'No ... not quite: Anyway, he travelled to the past; I've tr—'

'Not in *Back to the Future II*.'

'There's a *Back to the Future II*?'

From the look on his face this was obviously far and away the most disturbing thing that Andrew had heard come out of Chris's mouth so far. 'Yes,' he replied fiercely. 'And a *Back to the Future III*. What the hell is *wrong* with you?'

'What's wrong is that I went out for a few drinks one evening and woke up the next morning, eighteen years later. Having missed, it seems, any number of *Back to the Futures*.' Andrew didn't reply. Chris explained further. 'But there's nothing wrong with *me* – well ... there *is*, but the *biggest* wrongness is that ... is that it's as if the record's skipped. The needle's jumped right across the bloody thing.'

Andrew didn't reply, again.

'I'm the needle,' Chris added helpfully.

Andrew blew out a long, long stream of air. 'Wow,' he said, amazed. 'Really, Chris – how much *did* you drink last night?'

'Quite a lot, I'm sure. But I drank it last night *playing pool with you and Neil*. Katrina and I were having a bit of a row – about my leaving Short Stick – so I took a walk down the Grolsch path. *That* was last night.'

'It wasn't, mate.'

'Yes, it was.'

'No, it wasn't. Last night I was sitting on that sofa with Gill, watching Gordon Ramsay.'

This created a rather odd picture in Chris's mind, until he made the leap that Gordon Ramsay probably wasn't some bloke whom they'd discovered standing in their living room and had then peered at all evening, for sport, but was more likely a television programme – like *Magnum, P.I.*, say.

Chris shook his head. 'That's what you were doing in *your* time,' he said insistently. 'In real time – my time – you were ... well, I wasn't taking much notice – possibly rabbiting on about *RoboCop* or something.'

'And that'd be the first *RoboCop*, I suppose?' Andrew asked indulgently. Chris narrowed his eyes, but Andrew relaxed back into his chair a little and almost allowed himself a smile.

'This is serious,' Chris said, his voice unsure whether it was a demand or a plea. 'This is really fucking *serious*.'

Andrew opened his arms in a generous, priestly manner.

'It is, Chris. I can see that. But here's the thing: what's more likely? That you hit the JD particularly hard last night – after hitting it hard, let's be honest, for many, *many* nights before that.' He raised his eyebrows and inclined his head, as though this expression alone confirmed something they both knew. 'That you hit the JD, and, well, your memory's still drunk, or you've had a temporary blackout, or ...' He shrugged. 'Something like that. Isn't that a slightly more probable explanation than the one where you're Doctor Who?' (Andrew felt a rush of shame about saying; 'Doctor Who' rather than 'the Doctor' but bravely pushed it aside.)

Chris wobbled inside. He was by nature solidly level-headed and sensible. He was not a person more than happy to be taken in by any nonsense about UFOs, ghosts, gods or goblins. What's more, he wasn't used to sarcasm flowing in this direction when he was with Andrew. But, despite everything, *he knew what he knew.* It was plain what the truth was because he felt it to be the truth so definitely. The task, then, was to dig deeper than the obvious; not to be deceived by superficial facts but instead to take what he was personally sure was the case and work outwards looking for supporting evidence.

'No,' Chris said, non-specifically but firmly. 'It's ... I mean, there are clues.'

'Clues?'

'Yes. Little giveaways. They're there – if you know what to look for.'

'Like what?'

'Like what Chris is wearing.'

'What *you're* wearing, you mean?'

Chris waved his hand impatiently. 'Yes, yes – if you like.'

'I can't recall now ... Back in the eighties did we *all* talk about ourselves in the third person?'

'Stop trying to take the piss and just look at me, will you?'

Andrew glanced at what Chris was wearing. Chris noted that his face wasn't swept by sudden astonishment.

'*Look*,' Chris insisted, flicking at bits of himself. 'Jeans ... trainers ... How old am I supposed to be? People of *my age*' – he said 'my age' in a funny voice for devastating rhetorical effect – 'don't wear scraggy jeans and trainers.'

'What do they wear?'

'Um, you know … shoes, and proper trousers. And a sports coat.'

Andrew rolled his eyes. 'Oh, yes. Until they hit about sixty, of course, when they move on to flat caps and waistcoats.' He laughed. 'When we were young, middle-aged people wore sports coats because that's what they wore when *they* were young. You carry the fashions of your time with you to the grave, mate. We're jeans and trainers. Fifty years from now every granddad in the country will be shuffling around in a hoodie.'

'A hoodie?'

'A sweat top,' Andrew explained, gently apologetic for the oversight. It was, it seemed natural for him to feel, perfectly reasonable that Chris didn't know what a hoodie was.

'OK.' Chris did something dismissive with his lower lip. He didn't actually want it to appear that he was conceding the point, but didn't want it to appear as though he was clinging on to it desperately either. (There are so many facts in my bulging Pockets of Truth, he hoped to indicate, that I can let you have that one, just to humour you.) 'OK, maybe that's possible,' he went on, 'but have you *ever* heard of this kind of thing? *Ever*? Yes, people get amnesia. They get hit by a jib or a bear falls on them or something and they come round not knowing who the hell they are – their memory is wiped. But my memory *isn't* wiped, and I *absolutely* know who I am. I can perfectly remember everything about my life right up to the point when I was … sent here.' Andrew started to open his mouth, but Chris carried on before anything unwelcome had a chance to get out of it. 'And I'll grant you that people get banged on the head by rocks or alcohol and have blackouts. But they lose hours, don't they? At most, days. They don't misplace the nineties. Honestly, Andrew, have you ever heard of *anyone* whose memory is flawless, apart from the precise loss of the nearly twenty years before that morning?'

Andrew lifted his shoulders, held them up for moment, then let them fall back down again – as though this wasn't a situation that required the urgency of a speedy shrug.

'No,' he admitted easily, 'I've never heard of that. But then, to be honest, I haven't really been listening out for it. It's not all that surprising that I haven't seen some weird thing that I've never looked for. However, I bet that thirty seconds on Google would throw up a thousand cases.'

'Google?'

'The Web.'

'The Web?'

Andrew felt increasingly wonderful. 'An absolutely vast, international computer network containing more information than it's possible to imagine. Everyone uses the Web now – you access it from your PC at home or work. It's a ubiquitous phenomenon that's profoundly affected culture, economics and politics at a fantastic rate.'

'Jesus – have you seen all this fat?' Chris asked, looking up from his stomach. 'Where did that come from?'

'Um, I hadn't really noticed. It didn't happen overnight.'

'Yes it did,' Chris replied pointedly.

'If you still drank lager instead of spirits, and if you kept down more of what little you eat, you'd probably be twice as big by now. Anyway, the Web—'

'Yeah, yeah.' Chris shook his head irritably. 'Now *everyone* has a Macintosh Plus, and the whole lot of them are connected somehow. Great. I'm sure cameras take 3D, smell-o-vision pictures and we all have hover-boots too. But I'm not actually that interested in the future's sci-fi toys. I'm far more concerned with *this*.' He prodded his stomach. 'And *this*.' He slapped his hands against the sides of his face (wondering if he'd be able to feel it wobble for the next minute or so). 'And … *Christ*. And where I've left my girlfriend, and what I'm supposed to do with a wife – a wife I've never met at that – and every … single … bloody *thing* about this life of mine that's nothing to do with me!'

Andrew smiled, full of hard-to-suppress excitement. 'Yes. Of course, mate.'

'Imagine *you'd* been flung forwards in time almost two decades. You're twenty-five and have it all sorted. Then, the next thing you know, you're plonked down in your own, clapped-out body; the people around you have disappeared; you're surrounded by creepily intimate strangers; and you haven't even got a clue where the lavatory is in your own house.' Chris's eyes were emphatically wide. 'A computer network has altered the previously accepted dynamics of commerce? I couldn't give a *fuck*.'

'Sure.' Andrew stepped over and put a paternal hand on Chris's shoulder. 'Losing your memory must be really confusing, and frightening.'

'I haven't—'

'Whatever. Humour me, eh? If you've got amnesia and everything comes back to you by this evening then that's fine, isn't it? But if you're right and it soon becomes obvious that the Chris who's been here all these years was actually just a placeholder going through the motions until you arrived straight from the eighties, then you can say "I told you so" as often as you like, OK?'

Chris didn't reply.

'Right then,' Andrew continued. 'The most pressing thing is to decide what we do with you now.'

'*Do* with me? What are you thinking? The circus, maybe?'

'I meant how we deal with the situation. The practicalities.'

'I am *not* being thrown to the psychiatrists. So don't even suggest that.' Chris jerked to his feet and paced around the room agitatedly. He moved quickly and aimlessly, eventually coming to a halt close to one side so that a wall was behind his back. 'There is nothing wrong with my mind,' he said, a little manically. 'It's deadly to get into the hands of those people if you're sane. It's their business for you to be mad – you can't win. They'd say my consistency only showed how ingrained and fundamental my delusion was or something.'

'They'd probably just say you were flat-out nuts,' Andrew laughed.

Chris wanted to tell him that he was a complete arsehole, but felt he'd better not risk it. Vaguely, he wondered what exactly the risk was – this was Andrew, after all. Still, he replied with nothing but some wordless shuffling and a hunted expression.

Andrew let his grin stay for a little longer, then carefully put on a serious face. 'I definitely don't recommend calling anyone in,' he said. 'Quite the opposite, in fact. This is probably a temporary thing that won't last the weekend.' Chris thought Andrew could easily have said this sentence with less wistfulness. 'But, whatever happens, it's not good for you to go public about it – not good at all.'

Chris nodded to indicate that he understood. 'Because people will think I've suddenly lost my mind.'

'Exactly ... Except for the "suddenly" part.'

Andrew pushed his hands deep into his pockets and treated himself to a long sigh. He was full-on avuncular now. Chris couldn't resist and, as it happened, didn't even want to.

'Let's go out and get some fresh air,' Andrew said. 'There are some things you really need to know about Chris, Chris.'

12

is everything ok?

yes. just the usual problems. c u later – when coast is clear.
love u. xxxx.

There can be something quite poignant about watching a cigarette being rolled. Often, with roll-ups the fingers involved are tough and taciturn, not fussy gossips; their skin hardened by manual labour, overtly strong, they are slow, heavy machinery. Yet rolling a cigarette requires finesse and dexterity. Watch these vast hands form a so-tiny-in-them tube (disobedient tobacco strands and a single paper, delicate to the edge of transparency, guided and turned and sealed with a kiss) and it's almost like seeing a bear tend to her young cubs.

Neil's hands weren't the immense, sledgehammer variety much favoured by Soviet art (hands seemingly born to hold flags and seize the means of production), but they were a bit on the rough side. Certainly much rougher than they used to be, he mused to himself absently as he sat at the wide pine kitchen table and watched them roll his cigarette. These were not the hands he would have predicted he'd acquire. He ran a thumbnail across the tip of his index finger and smiled wryly at the idea that nowadays he had thicker skin.

The sudden touch of other fingers on his neck made him start.

'Jesus!' he said, turning around sharply.

Ann laughed. 'Lost in a fantasy? I trust it was about me.'

'Jesus,' he repeated, pressing a palm to his chest to reassure his heart. 'I was out of my body and halfway to the damned Light there.'

'You left the door wide open.' She nodded towards it. 'You

ought to be more careful. It's an invitation to passing women.'

'I wasn't expecting you. You said you wouldn't be able to come until after tea.'

'I ditched James at Robert's. They were absorbed in planning one of their complex schemes so my presence was superfluous.'

'You're sure?'

'Yes, don't worry. I bet that when I go back he'll have hardly noticed that I was ever away.'

Neil cautiously accepted this. 'OK.'

He put the cigarette in his mouth and pulled a lighter from the pocket of his jeans. His thumb spun the tiny wheel across the flint, but several attempts at a flame produced only sparks; he gave the lighter a vigorous shake and tried again. However, it seemed that the problem, whatever it was, was so severe that even shaking couldn't fix it. He stood up and ambled across to a drawer.

'Michelle's still here,' he said.

He poked around trying to find another lighter or some matches. The drawer was full to endless-rummaging-point with things that had earned their place in there by psychologically besting him in some way. Screws, bits of something electrical or oddly shaped pieces of plastic that he couldn't identify, for example. They'd cynically cowed him with their unknown provenance – the worry that they 'might be important' frightening him away from throwing them into the bin, ever. There was also an unbelievable number of pens and pencils. These survived in the same way that the disastrous pull of sugary and fatty foods is an evolutionary hangover from lean hunter-gatherer times when a taste for them gave a gene the edge over its celery-loving equivalent. Neil's childhood hadn't been all computer keyboards and mice, and pens and pencils were then still just about scarce and costly enough to have had some value. So, now, whenever he encountered the opportunity to gain a pen or a pencil, he seized it out of instinct. The things took advantage of the fact that his brain simply couldn't respond appropriately to a world where free promotional biros are near-ubiquitous and where just one visit to Ikea might mean a person experiences, in a single circuit, a ten- or fifteen-pencil increase. Like burrs catching on the fabric of his upbringing, all these unneeded writing implements were carried home to be thrown into drawers or stood in mugs. Which, as it happened, meant he never had a pen or a pencil on him when he happened to be out somewhere and needed one – in his house, *hundreds*; in his pockets, zero.

'Jennifer and Ruth couldn't come,' Neil continued. 'Car trouble. Specifically, um . . .' he turned his eyes to the ceiling as he tried to recall exactly, 'that it's "a hateful pile of shit" and she wishes it was a horse so she could at least enjoy watching the bloody thing be shot.' He glanced over his shoulder at Ann. 'So, anyway, Michelle didn't go to town.'

'Where is she now?'

'In the living room watching a DVD, I think.' He returned to searching in the drawer. Five different souvenir key fobs in a corner at the back, none ever used or ever going to be used. He considered at least tidying their uselessness in a single unit. Perhaps by attaching them all to a sixth key fob.

Ann moved across to behind him and reached her hands around his waist; keen fingers slid over the denim then kneaded his crotch greedily. If you were Neil's crotch, you'd have been very aware that this was actually a bit painful; but that was a minor point, overall. Overall, Neil experienced a fizzing rush of pleasure. When you're a man, if a woman spontaneously starts groping you then it's the thought that counts.

'*Ann*,' whispered Neil, 'what did I just say? Michelle's *in the next room*.'

'Watching a DVD,' Ann whispered in reply, pressing her cheek against his shoulder as her fingers began to unzip the fly of his jeans. 'She's occupied.'

'She might have heard you arrive. Suppose she heard the car and comes in to see who it is?'

'She'd have done that already if she was going to.'

The zip was now fully down and Ann's palm slid serpentine through the opening. Useful as this approach had seemed initially, it very soon became obvious that it was comprehensively rubbish. Ann's fingers were so restricted that they could hardly move (Neil's literally palpable excitement was fast making things even more cramped), a curtain of boxer shorts was denying further access and, to top it all, the teeth on Neil's zip were sawing into the skin on the back of her hand. She made a tactical withdrawal and went instead for a double-sided plunge under the jeans from above:

both arms diving in so deep that their wrists were several inches below the belt line.

'You,' said Neil, tipping his head back and closing his eyes, 'are a disgraceful fornicatress.' He emphasised his disapproval by adding a low, breathy moan that suggested he might not be all that far from slipping out of consciousness for a little while. Ann grinned, bit at his back through the material of his T-shirt, and did something with her index finger that caused him to gasp in the manner of someone who'd just opened a door on an unexpected and truly awe-inspiring piece of art.

He arched backwards and swept his hands around to grab Ann's bottom. As his fingertips sank deliciously into the accepting flesh beneath the teasing cotton barrier of her skirt he twisted his head and the edge of his vision caught Michelle entering the room.

With an explosive burst of huge effort he heaved himself around so as to position his crotch, and Ann's-hands-which-were-attached-to-his-crotch, away from her. Ann herself – arms locked down his jeans – swung around with him, as if she were a big backpack he was wearing.

'What the f—' Ann began, but Neil cut across her.

'Hello, darling,' he said, his voice making sure its nonchalance was clear by opting to deliver it at a shout. He tried to tug Ann's hands out of his jeans, but his abrupt and unexpected twist had almost taken her off her feet so her arms were now fastened in like grappling hooks by her unbalanced body weight. Alerted by Neil's greeting to Michelle, Ann was also trying to free herself. Her attempts were no more successful than Neil's. Significantly less successful, in fact, Neil thought. Ann's struggling felt very much like it was doing nothing but tearing him towards an impromptu Brazilian.

'Haha!' he laughed percussively, purely because he was unable to have that much of his public hair wrenched out without *some* kind of noise leaving his mouth.

'Hi, Michelle,' Ann sang cheerfully. 'How are you?' she asked, hoping that this level of chatty brightness would divert even the keenest observer from noticing that she was helplessly trapped in the underpants of anyone at all.

Michelle fixed them both with an unblinking glare and said, really quite pointedly, 'What are you doing?'

95

'I'm trying to find some matches,' Neil replied, starting to dig furiously in the drawer once more.

'And I'm helping,' Ann added, her head lodged between his shoulder blades.

13

'They legalised cannabis in the end, then?'

Andrew looked across at Chris, wondering if the neurological pile-up that had apparently knocked his friend's memory off its feet was also going to set him talking in non sequiturs.

Chris picked up the incomprehension. 'Gear,' he explained, lazily flicking his head back in the direction of the two young men who has just strolled by them leaving behind, no one with any part of a nostril could possibly miss, a syrupy vapour trail of marijuana smoke. That one sniff wouldn't have meant anything in isolation, but the short walk along this indifferent suburban street had already offered up two other scentings: one from another pedestrian and a second, he was almost positive, streaming out of the window of a passing car.

'Oh,' Andrew replied, now realising what had provoked Chris's words. 'No. It's still illegal. But today's youth has turned it into something mundanely criminal – like littering or parking on the pavement.'

Chris made some eyebrows.

Andrew smiled. He felt ... what was it? It was like being ... like being Morpheus in *The Matrix*. Yes, that was it. Sagacious. Mentorly.

'It's one of their things generally,' he continued. 'Stuff we did now and then they have to do relentlessly, almost as if they're trying to show everyone that they don't consider it anything special. That nothing is any big deal to them. They strive to make everything appear more or less a chore. I can't believe there's ever been a generation quite so determinedly joyless.'

That sounded, Chris thought, like the kind of thing you'd hear someone's dad say. Andrew had never been exactly rock and roll, but perhaps age had, well, aged him. Though, then again, maybe

97

it was the facts, not just the years, talking. Chris was very aware that he knew unnervingly little about this world: whether it was broad, cultural assessments or specific details such as whether or not he had a wife, Andrew was far more likely to be right than he was. Chris knew he had to accept that he himself had ... that he had nothing. He gave a small nod and kept his mouth shut.

Andrew led him down the road another hundred yards or so and into a pub. Chris sat at the corner table where he was essentially placed and waited for Andrew to return; which he soon did with, of all things, two glasses of wine.

Andrew took a sip and eased back into his seat. 'So ...'

Chris squirmed. Then he waited, then he squirmed a little more, before finally asking 'So?' and grabbing his own wine.

'It's hard to know where to begin, mate.'

'Take a stab anywhere.'

'Well ... OK. I have my own accountancy firm now. It's not doing too badly, I must admit. I've been married to Gill since 1989 – you must have just, erm, "missed" her. You were the best man at my wedding, by the way. We have a daughter, Charlotte – Charlie. I think you saw her at the house. Chk – teenagers, you know. I ha—'

'That's great,' Chris interrupted, 'and I don't want to appear horribly self-obsessed, but do you think you could tell me about this ...' He waved his hands at himself. 'This ... this me?'

'Right. Yeah – sorry. Let's see ...'

'What do I do?'

'You're a copywriter. Short Stick.'

'*Still?*'

'Well ...'

'The senior copywriter?'

'Well ...'

'Christ.'

All the changes of nearly twenty years were hard enough to assimilate, but nearly twenty years with *no* change could really make your head spin too.

'I was quitting the damn place,' Chris insisted. 'That's almost the last thing I can recall before I came here. Don't you remember my announcing that I was going to tell them to fuck themselves and leave?'

'Possibly. It's tricky to be sure we're thinking of the same evening. You've been announcing that exact thing about every three months since before half the people in this pub were born.' Andrew glanced disapprovingly at a group of girls by the bar, all of whom looked as though they were wearing their mums' make-up.

'Oh, fantastic. I have a massive row with Katrina about jacking my job in, and it turns out I never did it anyway. If I'd known I could have avoided the whole argument and simply said, "Actually, Kat, let's forget about it. I'll just spend the next couple of decades being the world's saddest wanker instead." I mean, women love stability, right?' He took a gulp of wine. 'So, that's my career covered.' He sighed and rubbed his eyes. 'Tell me about Trudie.'

'You married her in '92. And I was *your* best man this time.'

'You were?' Chris caught himself and tried again, managing to filter out the surprise at the second attempt. 'You were? Cheers. How— Jesus! Do *I* have any kids?'

Andrew shook his head. 'No.'

'Oh.' Abruptly realising this was a possibility had battered Chris with cold horror. Discovering it hadn't happened dipped him into a curious sadness. 'Oh.'

'You can't ...' Andrew straightened up, shifting himself away from the table – only slightly, but enough to indicate physically that he didn't want to get too close to this particular area. 'There's some kind of problem.'

'With me?' Back to the horror.

'Trudie. You both tried a few things – doctors. But ...'

Chris mulled this over silently for a moment or two. 'Are she and Chris happy, generally? I mean, I suppose, if they've – if we've – stayed together, then we must be, yes?'

'Ah.'

'Oh, come *on*. Not at home too? I look like I've been sitting in the bath for twenty years – eating chips – my professional life is slumped barely conscious in a corner ... Give me *something* here.'

'That's what I needed to tell you,' Andrew said, leaning forward seriously.

'That I'm a complete failure?'

'No.' He shook his head vigorously.

Chris stared at him.

'Not completely,' Andrew continued.

'Nice. But you have faith in me, right? You think I could still be a complete failure, if I just work on a few areas?'

'Actually, mate, that's more or less the truth.' Andrew held up his hand, displaying a small gap between his thumb and index finger. 'You're *this* close to sinking like a stone.'

Chris took a good look at the distance Andrew's fingers were indicating. Yes, that really was very small. But then, in the circumstances, was it of much importance? He gave a dismissive sniff.

'This future couldn't really be any worse for me, could it?' he asked. 'Or am I due to be eaten by the Warlocks?'

'*Morlocks*. The *Morlocks* eat the Eloi in the future.' God, it was infuriating when people got that wrong. Andrew took a breath, however, and tried to put this aside for the sake of their friendship. 'But let's pretend that doesn't matter. Things *could* be worse for you, Chris. At the moment you're getting away with it, like you always have – in a way, even more so. But it's by the skin of your teeth now.'

'What do you mean?'

'Well, for a start, you drink. For the past couple of years you've been hitting the bottle with the special kind of blind, unassailable enthusiasm you'd normally see in someone who's found religion. Quite honestly, this is the most sober I've seen you for ages.'

'So you immediately take me to a pub and buy me a drink.'

'Well, I thought—'

'Never mind. Go on: I'm an alky.'

'And not a very good one.'

Chris nodded. 'Figures.'

'You're not morbidly entertaining, or tragic, or even frightening. You're all rambling self-pity and falling asleep on the lavatory during lunch breaks. The drinking's bad, but it's just one part of the main problem.'

'Which is?'

'Oh, in essence, a more than embarrassingly ordinary mid-life crisis. There are two kinds of mid-life crisis – Sports Cars or Despair – and you've plumped for the second one; but that decision seems to have been the end of your personal creative input. After that you just took one off the peg. It's been tediously predictable and obvious.'

'Ahhhh.' Chris scratched his cheek. 'I see.'

This fairly measured response told Andrew that Chris *didn't* see. Not at all. He groaned and rapped the table with his knuckles. 'You're not getting it, mate,' he said.

'Yeah, I am. Mid-life crisis. Chris is having a mid-life crisis.'

'Guh. See?'

'See what?'

'You're not *nearly* horrified enough. That's how I know you're not getting it. Nothing today is more risible than a man having a mid-life crisis. It's almost the only thing anyone still needs to be ashamed about – and it's as though the shame that's been removed from everything else got moved over onto it.'

Chris, it seemed, was still struggling to fully appreciate the concept. Andrew, keen to get the message across, decided to call on the sure-fire tactic of using film and television as reference points.

'*Shirley Valentine?*' he said.

'Who?'

'Damn. That's when it started, really – why couldn't your memory have hung around a little longer?' He ran his fingers back through his hair. 'Whatever. The thing is, Chris, you've probably got some kind of Reggie Perrin idea in your head. Individualistic. Reasserting your human spirit. Almost, well, *heroic*. Those are all accepted as characteristics of a mid-life crisis nowadays, but only if you're a *woman*. It's OK – admirable and encouraged even – for a woman to hit middle age, suddenly wonder what the hell's happened to her life, and to stop wearing shoes and go to India for two years to learn how to juggle. A man who goes through the same thing is now the ultimate figure of fun. The one is laudable, the other's laughable.'

'Why?'

'Because it is.'

'Why?'

'Because it *is*. That's the zeitgeist. We don't govern the zeitgeist, do we, Chris? It governs us. I'm not saying it's morally correct, but you have to accept it. And, where we are on the continuum of cultural evolution right now, being a man and having a mid-life crisis places you roughly between someone who has sex with his vacuum cleaner and Hitler's astrologer.'

Chris tried to clarify for himself exactly how he felt about this. He didn't approve of it, but he could understand it. He (that is, Old Chris) had breached this society's new rules in a way that made him an object of ridicule. Except, *he* (that is, the Chris he knew he was as he sat on this chair in this pub) hadn't really breached anything – he'd arrived there only this morning. So, *he* hadn't done anything to feel guilty about, even if the thing ought to have provoked guilt, which he didn't reckon it did. His feelings, he decided, were these: 'Chris Mortimer has been accused of a crime he didn't commit, which isn't a crime anyway, and he's reading about the case in the newspaper, but it's a different Chris Mortimer, not him, though everyone probably assumes they are the same person.' Yes, that was it, clarified.

Chris nodded.

'I'm sure that your memory will sort itself soon,' Andrew continued. 'But whether it does or doesn't you must *not* flush the last of your chances away because of what you may think is true at this particular moment. You've pushed things in your marriage and in your work right to the edge.'

'You think that this could be the straw that breaks the camel's back.'

'I think that "Hello, everyone. This Chris-Body is a mere host; I'm a time-travelling consciousness from the eighties" would be that kind of straw, yes.'

'So, I should pretend to have massive amnesia instead.'

'Actually, no. Frankly, I reckon that doing that because it's less an indicator of catastrophic mental collapse might be a subtlety lost on anyone but us. One might be more colourful than the other, but either way it'd seem like you had – finally – utterly and completely lost it. And, once people saw that . . .' Andrew slumped back into his seat and threw up his arms. 'Well, that's it. It's all over.'

'Short Stick will throw me out.' Chris nodded again.

'Trudie too.'

Chris accepted this second point with another, more offhand, nod. This visibly disturbed Andrew and he drew in close again.

'Listen,' he said anxiously, 'you might think that losing your job at your age and in your state would be disastrous – and it would be. But losing Trudie would be ten times worse.'

'I don't even know the woman.'

'Then just trust me when I say that she's the best thing that ever happened to you. I'd be no kind of friend whatsoever if I let you screw that up. You'd be lost without her. Imploding as he might be, even the you from yesterday would accept that.'

'Then maybe he shouldn't have let things get to this state,' Chris replied a little petulantly.

Andrew rolled his eyes. 'Judgemental suddenly, aren't you? You were never so hard on yourself in the first person.'

That was a rebuke, wasn't it? A straight-out, full-on rebuke. *Andrew* was rebuking him.

Chris was unhappily surprised to discover that the perfectly obvious 'Well, bollocks to you' reply got contorted and lost somehow on the way to his mouth. It fell by right past it, in fact, and finally appeared in his bottom: now changed into an awkward shifting in his seat.

'Um,' he said instead, 'that's beside the point, anyway. Asking me to bluff my way through at work is a bit of a bloody stretch, but I can't possibly avoid my wife of fourteen years realising that I know nothing whatsoever about her.'

Andrew roared with laughter.

Chris scowled at him. 'Seriously. It's not feasible.'

'If anyone can do it,' Andrew said, grinning, 'you are that man.'

Chris didn't feel that this reply made scowling any less the way to go.

Andrew shook his head and continued. 'OK, OK – seriously. I'm not saying that it'll be easy, but there are points in our favour. First, you almost certainly won't have to do it for long – you could wake up tomorrow morning and, for better or worse, be exactly the Chris you were yesterday morning. I've seen enough movies to know that amnesia is almost always temporary. Second plus: you're a miserable git who spends a good deal of his time drunk. Forgetting some things wouldn't appear out of place and, even better, from what I've seen, Trudie would find it odd if you *didn't* respond to a large number of perfectly reasonable questions with nothing more than a grunt, a sarcastic What-do-*you*-think? look or simply a childish, sullen silence. Third, you can always play for time – say you need a pee or something – and then give me a call. I'll spend the next couple of hours or so briefing you about the basics, but if you get stumped you'll still be able to "Phone a Friend".' Andrew smiled slightly and mimed quotation marks with his fingers as he said "Phone a Friend". Chris had no idea whatsoever why he did this.

Andrew could see that Chris was still less than convinced.

'Look: bottom line,' he went on. 'You have nothing to lose by trying, and everything to lose by not.'

Chris let his eyes fall to the table and considered his options for a while. There weren't many. After a few defeated moments he looked up at Andrew once more. 'OK,' he said.

'Great.'

'Yeah, great.' He rubbed his temples. 'I need a drink.'

'*Plus ça change.*'

14

It had been like cramming. Like he was due to take an exam –
Being Chris. Duration: God knows – and he'd left it until the very
last minute before doing any revision.

However, though no small task in terms of the information that
needed to be absorbed, in another way it was easier than he'd
expected. He found he felt neither reluctant, nor even particularly
anxious, about the ... well, what would he call it? The 'philosophical' – or perhaps the 'spiritual' – side of things. That he was
quite so comfortable about this made him rather uncomfortable.
He was worried it might mean that perhaps there was less to him
than he'd previously assumed.

He'd always been insistent that he wasn't just another cog in
the wheel; asserting his individuality was both a desire and a
compulsion. But he now found himself having the uneasy suspicion
that his determination not to be like everyone else was more of
him than he would have liked. Now *there* was an ugly idea: peel
away what he took pains to demonstrate he wasn't and there
didn't seem to be a great deal of what he was. If true, that was
awful. Looking back (however far 'back' was), he was alarmed by
the possibility that he had, to a distressing degree, been playing
even the real Chris. Had he done and said those things that had
become accepted for a role that had evolved via habit and random
circumstance but, beyond that outline of a personality, there was
nothing very much? Could it be that, to a scary extent, he existed
sufficiently to interact with others, take care of his physical needs,
buy shelving, etc., but that was all there was to him? It was
certainly the case that he'd never known exactly what he wanted
to do with his life; he'd had no consuming passions or goals, and,
though he'd held opinions, he'd never held them in 'Shouted, still,
while led to the gallows for their sake' fashion. Confronted by the

secret police his resistance would have probably topped out at the 'muttering under his breath, from a distance' area. He'd been more than sufficiently introspective, but he couldn't deny that even the really basic questions he'd asked himself, such as, 'Genuinely – *genuinely* – am I a good person?' had never received conclusive answers.

Unsettlingly, it turned out that the prospect of faking it as Old Chris didn't, in itself, cause any alarm. Did the notion of pretending to be someone else not jar him emotionally or scare him with its size because, when it came down to it, publicly playing the Chris he wasn't was probably not going to be any more taxing than playing the Chris he'd always been? Maybe easier. At least he had a little solid direction now: in the sense that Andrew was his director.

On balance, Chris decided that this was bollocks. He *did* know who he was, and that person was solid, deep and almost dizzyingly interesting. It was just that it's unnerving to find yourself, even slightly, wondering if there was ever much inside your skin; and the very *worst* time to have your sense of self wobble is when you've been flung through time into the sagging body of a forty-something deadbeat. He really shouldn't begin having doubts about his own essential existence now – not with this middle-aged stomach to cope with.

A more straightforwardly problematic area turned out to be the sprawling trivia of being contemporary. As part of the 'Phone a Friend' ruse, he had learned that the way this would be done was by using a mobile telephone. These days, it seemed, a portable phone wasn't some ludicrously expensive thing the size of a piano leg for which the battery, if you wanted to walk and talk, required you to hire a couple of bearers and a mule. They were like (exactly like) the *Star Trek* device on his belt. And absolutely everyone used them, absolutely all the time. Yet, given that in general terms they were beyond mundane, it took Andrew *ages* to figure out exactly how Chris's model worked so he could teach him to use it. Almost every fruitless key press was followed by angry frustration then a lengthy period of showing how his, Andrew's, own phone was far better and more intuitive. And it took fifteen messages, twenty minutes and a double Scotch for Chris to move through the three stages of predictive text: 'stuttering bafflement', 'the urge to kill', and, finally, 'acceptance'.

Some things played into their hands, though. Chris had expressed concern that Andrew had given him, he felt, only a very brief outline of current affairs.

'Never mind,' Andrew had replied, dismissively. 'No one's bothered about politics nowadays.'

This was a massive relief. The constant drain of having to be bothered about politics had sagged everyone's shoulders in the eighties – the fashion of the time meant you could find yourself a social pariah if you were unable to name the shadow transport secretary or accidentally revealed you'd missed an amendment to a white paper. That 'just not being all that interested' was now regarded as acceptable felt like being showered with rose petals.

'For reference,' said Andrew, 'you're against Bush, the war, global warming and people starving to death.'

'Bush? *Still?*'

'His son.'

'Oh ... Christ. *Christ.* Oh well, I can easily be against all those things. But—'

'No – don't bother. You won't be asked to expand on anything. You're "against them", that's easy enough.'

'OK.'

'I suppose you might want to be worried by terrorist attacks too. Or – better – say you're *not* worried by terrorist attacks.'

'Right. The IRA.'

'No, no – the IRA don't bomb us any more.'

'They don't? Who does then?'

'Broadly speaking, everyone else.'

Chris took this detail on board without feeling any need to pry into it. It was the sort of thing you'd accept as a matter of course. You might be in a different century, but you were still in Britain, after all; *someone* was going to be bombing you.

'And I suppose,' he offered absently, 'that I don't need to know anything about music, as I'm over forty.'

'Now you mention it, there's some really good music around these days, in fact. You might want to turn on the radio. Just for fun, that is. Being over forty it's fine for you to get the names of all the bands confused, but, being over forty, no one will ever ask for your thoughts anyway so it won't be an issue. As for the last twenty years, they won't come up because it's been ninety-eight per cent dreadful.'

Chris looked doubtful. 'It couldn't have got *that* much worse. It was the Pet Shop Boys when I left.'

'The Pet Shop Boys are now regarded as classic.' Andrew held Chris's eyes. 'I'm not joking.'

This was the part that was daunting: the vast ocean of what was unremarkable for everyone else yet that he couldn't possibly have a chance of guessing at, having not lived through the drip-drip journey there but having instead been hit without warning by a tsunami of Now.

A group talking about *Big Brother* wouldn't be referring to Orwell; they might well never have *heard* of Orwell. People, regularly, bought bottled water (bottled *water*). A glass of lager cost more than he'd have spent on an entire round, yet you could fly to Spain for twenty-five quid. Jonathan Ross *OBE*. Chris's awareness of the phenomenon of Billy Piper was handicapped by the fact that, surprisingly for anyone around in 2006, Billie Piper had held back until she was a few birthdays beyond seven years old. And, when he'd absently remarked he'd woken up to Simon Mayo on the *Breakfast Show* the previous morning – little suspecting what the following twenty-four hours or so would bring – Andrew had mentioned that these days Simon Mayo did a culture and politics show on Radio 5 (Radio 5?).

'Simon Mayo?'

'Yes.'

'I see.' Chris groaned and massaged his eyes with the heels of his palms. 'And I suppose *Newsnight* is presented by Gary Davies, right?'

It was utterly bewildering. Even if he hadn't already taken up the position that the really important jolt of Future Shock lay in his private world not in the public one, he'd have wanted to close the shutters on it all anyway. It was simply too ... too ... too *much*.

'Hello.'

Trudie said this meaningfully.

'Hello,' Chris replied, equally meaningfully. He guessed that if he provided the 'fully', she'd fill in the 'meaning' for him. Let her make assumptions. (The best way to keep her feeling that nothing was out of the ordinary was to allow her to think, 'Tch – *typical*.')

He slumped onto the sofa, aware of his many, many joints. It occurred to him that he'd perhaps been partially mistaken about the reason he'd felt so battered earlier; that maybe waking up the morning after a savage night's drinking at twenty-five and waking up *any* morning at forty-three were almost identical experiences. He'd have to ask Andrew about this later and, if it were true, shoot himself. Right now, however, he needed to focus on making sure his wife blithely accepted that he was actually her husband.

Chris picked up the remote and turned on the TV. He thought that this would be a good way of avoiding any perilous conversation while additionally trawling for titbits of popular culture. However, he soon found that it was also effective for keeping Trudie occupied, which meant that he could stare at her.

So, this was his wife.

Not simply his wife, he'd been told, but also 'the best thing that had ever happened to him'.

Well.

Well ... the first thing that struck him was that she didn't look as old as she had done that morning. Was this because he was looking at her more sympathetically now, or was it something else? He was looking at her with Old Chris's eyes. He recalled having read somewhere that the picture we have of reality is patchy and horribly distorted at best. If you sent the image on your retina to Snappy Snaps it'd come back with one of those 'This is rubbish – be more careful, you idiot' stickers on it. The sharp and useful world we believe we see is actually a construct, overwhelmingly the result of experience and inference. Was he growing into Old Chris's eyes? Were they slowly taking the driving seat?

What you see depends on where you're standing. Even these few hours later, was he standing close to forty-three?

No. Impossible. It was just that now he hadn't got a throbbing headache, and he knew she wasn't merely some random mad woman he'd woken up with. Also, he'd had a few drinks in the pub with Andrew, which, he reminded himself, is something that's well known to make all women look significantly better.

He examined her for some time. Not critically, just curiously – but *actively* looking nonetheless. He was aware of his eyes upon her, consciously guiding them like a blind person would explore with his fingers – running them over her hair, tracing out the shape of her lips, curling around her hands as they lay cupped together in her lap. He was surprised to find it was rather therapeutic: not dissimilar, he decided, to doing a crossword or building an Airfix model of a Lancaster.

'*What?*' she asked abruptly, still facing the TV.

'Sorry? What "what"?' Chris replied innocently.

'Why are you staring at me?' She turned, seemingly with the intention of pinning him by the eyes, but she retreated and dropped her own almost immediately. 'What is it?'

'Nothing. I was just looking at you, that's all.'

'Why? What am I supposed to have done now?'

'You're my wife.'

This landed with a very definite splash on Trudie's face. An expression rippled across it immediately; but, though he couldn't miss it, Chris couldn't read what it meant either. Had it made her angry? Scared? Astonished? Rheumatic, sexually aroused and peckish? He was aware, and a bit disappointed, that he didn't have a file of her expressions for reference. Still, he was pretty sure that it couldn't be outrage. It was quite unlikely that in the world of 2006 it was culturally offensive and/or illegal to look at your wife. Wasn't it?

Not knowing what to do and wanting to avoid an argument, he looked away and took refuge in just peering at his own legs. Doing this reminded him of the less than appealing Chris he was wearing, and so another possibility popped into his mind. Perhaps Trudie, like any woman, didn't relish apparently being leered at by some flabby, decrepit old bloke. He acted quickly to let her know that she wasn't being eyed up, that he was no aged lech.

'I don't fancy you,' he said reassuringly.

Her eyes shot back to him, and it quite rapidly occurred to Chris that she might have taken this the wrong way.

'That is,' he continued, 'I wasn't looking at you sexually.' Then. 'I mean, obviously, I must fancy you, um, *generally*. You're my wife, and everything.'

Man, marriage was tricky.

He wondered what Katrina was doing right now. He missed her. Was she sitting wherever she was at this moment missing him?

'When are you going out?' Trudie asked, her voice perfectly level, like a frozen sea.

'Going out?' Was he supposed to be somewhere? Had he got an appointment? 'Where?'

'I didn't know it mattered. Going out – getting pissed – and falling down. I wasn't aware that the physical location was all that important; I thought it was all about the emotional journey.'

'Oh – I see. Actually, I thought I'd stay in tonight.'

'Stay in?' This seemed to throw her a little.

'Um, if that's OK.'

'Of course it's OK,' she replied curtly. 'Why wouldn't it be? It could confuse the neighbours a bit – if they get up on a Sunday morning and you're not spreadeagled unconscious on the front lawn they might not know what day it is – but you shouldn't feel you're under any obligation.'

'Right. I'll stay in then,' Chris said. He couldn't help an edge starting to creep into his voice. This wasn't exactly fair. *He'd* never passed out drunk on anyone's lawn. Well ... he had, now he came to think about it. But just the once and, most importantly, *she* didn't know about that anyway.

'Fine.' Trudie shrugged.

'You go out, if you want.'

'Where would I go?'

She said this almost as though it were a challenge to him. He wanted to reply that she could do something with Jane, or Clare, or maybe Lucy. But he didn't know if there *was* a Jane, Clare or Lucy; Andrew hadn't briefed him, he realised with a mild panic, about her social life. Chris knew she worked as a health service administrator (so it was possible that she had no friends), and he knew which hospital she was based at, but, other than that, Andrew had used the limited time they had available to let him know how she felt about things – so he could avoid annoying her as much as possible – and had mentioned almost nothing about what she did with herself.

For safety, he reached into his bag of fallbacks, and pulled out 'rolling eyes followed by silence'.

After a chilly pause, this led to her huffing, 'Exactly.'

The feeling seemed to be that she'd won that round, and she turned to face the television again.

The phrase 'battle of the sexes' limped into his head. Was this how it was when you'd been together for a certain amount of time? He and Katrina had argued; it was blitzkrieg warfare, though – explosive but soon over. When lines had been fortified and trenches dug deep over many years did it turn into the Western Front? Attritional; low-level yet relentless; fighting constantly, wearily, over a few feet of muddy ground. It was an incredibly depressing thought, and he resolved that – if he somehow managed to get back to his own time – he'd never let it happen to him. He could avoid it, surely, because he'd be able to see it coming now. Moreover, adding this unique foreknowledge to his already impressive list of qualities would mean he would be a quite breathtakingly desirable partner. Absolutely brimming with insight, empathy and sensitivity. And, if that still wasn't enough to ensure he'd never end up in a less than perfect relationship, well then he could just buy a Labrador and a big pile of pornography. To hell with it: let all the women watch him walking his dog to the newsagent to get the latest edition of *Razzle* and rue what they were missing.

Hmmm ... missing. He was missing eighteen years. Except, he wasn't. He missed being in control. He missed knowing what was going on in his life. He missed Katrina. But he *wasn't* missing what ought to have been the main thing: all that precious time.

He almost jumped to his feet.

'I'm going to the toilet,' he said, with far more enthusiasm than the words usually have lavished upon them.

Trudie looked at him, nonplussed. 'Fabulous,' she said. Then reached across and patted his leg. 'God be with you.'

He sped up the stairs, paused at the top – one hand gripping the newel post – to find some oxygen and allow his heart to edge away from a drum roll of wildly flapping ventricles, and then pushed on into the bathroom where he immediately took out his mobile phone.

'Andrew? Andrew, listen – I've got proof.'

'Proof of what?' Andrew asked nervously.

'Proof. *Proof*. Proof of, of, of ...'

Andrew thought it wiser to leave Gill in the living room with

Wilbur Smith and swiftly moved to the kitchen where he could continue this conversation in private.

'You're just very slightly raving incoherently, mate,' he said, closing the door behind him.

'Of of . . .' Chris struggled to frame it. He was excited and, after those stairs, rather light-headed too. 'Proof of *me*,' he finally gasped.

'Of you?'

'Yes. Proof that this *isn't* simply memory loss. Proof that I'm not middle-aged Chris with a fuck load of amnesia, but that I really *am* the Chris who was playing pool and drinking lager in the 1980s only last night.'

15

She had about her the air of a being who was only in our world due to some manner of elfin misfortune. There was a distracted, elsewhere quality to her – as though she'd come to this time and place as the result of a malicious spell or by falling through a hole between realities and, though her body might walk among us, her thoughts still danced in the fields of her green-sunned homeland. She was a thing one had to reach for; to pull, if only for a moment, out of her dreams and her strange knowledge and her bravely borne magnificent sadness.

'Excuse me,' the man in the hat said again, louder this time. 'Can I help you?'

'Oh.' She blinked and, eyes back in focus now, looked at him. 'Oh – sorry,' she said, smiling in a way that conveyed she didn't wish to burden him with her secret pain nor give away that she was a preternatural mystery and an ineffable enigma. 'Sorry. Could I have a pot of the coleslaw?'

The assistant ladled it into a transparent plastic tub, thumbed a price sticker across the top and placed it on the glass counter. Katrina carefully picked it up and put into her shopping trolley – slowly, soulfully; leaving, it seemed, so, so much unsaid.

After loading the coleslaw, a *Best of Clannad* CD and two avocados into the boot of her SUV, she floated round to the driver's seat. She checked herself in the mirror and, satisfied, started the engine.

The woman who came in to clean once a week was taking crockery out of the dishwasher when Katrina got home.

'Hello, Glynis,' she said, graceful and warm – as though she thought of them as equals; as though the very idea that they weren't would have been incomprehensible to her. She then flopped down heavily into a chair and produced a sigh that lasted for a full five seconds.

'I'm just finishing up here. I'll be out of your hair in a tick,' Glynis replied. She moved like a tiny mammal or a purposeful insect; in a series of darts separated by sudden, almost frozen pauses during which only her head and eyes continued to flash around the environment, checking. Glynis was actually a couple of years younger than Katrina but she looked, and they both behaved, as if she were ten years older. Katrina suspected Glynis felt herself to be almost a mother-hen figure – keen to attend to the mundane domestic necessities so that she, Katrina, could concentrate on enriching the lives of those around her and the world in general. A bit like Flaubert's housekeeper, or the woman who did the ironing for Keats. Glynis herself thought of Katrina as 'Tuesdays'.

'I won't be in next week, remember,' Glynis said over her shoulder while running a cloth around the sink. 'Bill and me are doing Kos.'

'Yes, I remember.' Katrina smiled her courageous smile once more. 'You have a wonderful time. It's so good of you to come in before you go, and on a weekend too.'

When Glynis had left, Katrina made herself a cup of peppermint tea, checked that the pot of pin money in the cupboard didn't look any less full than it had been before Glynis arrived, and then settled down in her studio with a stick of charcoal and one of her pads of sugar paper. She always said that this room was all she needed. Her husband, whenever people were round, would enjoy displaying the size of their home – placing it next to the image of the terraced house in which he'd grown up. It was half as big again as the next largest place in the village, and *that* belonged to Thompson, who was a surgeon – and a specialist at that (ears). It was no mean feat to rise from a terraced house in the arse end of Leeds to fifty per cent higher than a surgeon (a *specialist*: ears), wasn't it? Katrina, however, would roll her eyes and declare that she didn't care about that at all. So long as she had her studio she'd have been just as happy to live in a council flat. It was simply that you couldn't find council flats that had decent studio room.

Katrina's art wasn't created for profit. In fact, she thought using something so personal to generate income would be, well, icky. It would vulgarise it. She did have a nice professionally-designed-and-maintained website, but that was really just so her pieces weren't locked away – like those priceless, exquisite items often lost to the public by being buried in the vaults of some prestigious gallery or other. It would have been selfish to hide her work from those who might gain joy or solace from it. Yes, the pieces were for sale on the site, and a few had indeed been bought, but the price tags she placed on them reflected, she felt, their deeply private, emotional value and so kept them out of the hands of the merely idly curious. The income from a sale wasn't important; she was perfectly satisfied with just, through her art, having changed someone's life forever.

Her husband always praised what she made, which she thought very sweet of him as he clearly didn't really understand it. He was a simple man. Good with worldly matters rather than aesthetic subtleties or anything that required spiritual intuition. But, bless him, he helped her devotedly. Not actual help, of course – not input in the creative process – he simply provided the money required to support her needs; it was endearing, though, nevertheless.

Lately, however, all this had began to weigh heavily upon her. She was troubled. This wasn't the reason for the fey melancholy of her manner; that was, and had been for many years, a sign of her intrinsically fascinating soul – it didn't relate to any specific issue. She couldn't help noting that her natural way was all the more fitting and poignant nowadays, though. The seed of her tragic problem was that she felt ... Actually, it was difficult to find the right words for something so elusive and delicate. What came closest to conveying the essence of it? Languid? Adrift? Bored shitless? Whatever it was, it was making her miserable. And not miserable in a dark, interesting, satisfying-to-put-on-canvas way either. No, this misery was of the sit-in-front-of-the-TV-and-eat-two-packets-of-Bakewell-tarts kind. And she knew that depression was not to be taken lightly when it crossed the line into something that could end up making you fat. So, she was well aware of the danger she was facing, yet couldn't work out how to alter the situation. As stated, though listlessness was the seed of this crisis, it was her circumstances that had made it grow to such a looming size. If you had no money and lived in a damp bedsit with flock wallpaper that was, on closer inspection, just normal wallpaper with furry mould growing on it, then being fed up was OK. You should be fed up. Most importantly, it's very easy to fix – you simply need a good wedge of disposable income and a far nicer place. It's much worse, Katrina was sophisticated enough to realise, if you're all lethargic and pissed off when you have a massive house, a great big Lexus and anything you tell your husband to get for you. Being unhappy in those circumstances reveals how sensitive you must be; which is a bitter irony, as being unhappy without any apparent solution available (as you have everything you could possibly want) is going to hit someone who's highly sensitive *especially* hard.

It was, then, the lack of identifiable faults in her life that really twisted the knife. She knew she was dissatisfied but suffered horribly from not having a clue what she was dissatisfied about. It was very cruel.

The sound of the front door opening toppled her out of her glum reverie and she realised that, without ever seeing them approach, she'd finished off a whole layer of Jammie Dodgers. She scrambled the telltale wrapper and the uneaten biscuits into a drawer just in time – a hot instant before her husband thudded into the room.

'What you up to, princess?' he asked, beaming, fresh from the pub.

'Oh, nothing. Just working on some ideas.'

He grinned and swung his hands onto her hips. She calculated that the Jammie Dodgers wouldn't have arrived there yet (though she should go to the gym later to head them off).

'I've got some ideas too,' he said, sliding his arms round and giving her bottom such a forceful squeeze that she thought he might well have been trying to push finger holes into her buttocks with a view to taking them off and using them as bowling balls.

Actually, she liked that he craved her so intensely that it spilled out of his control; that he became clumsy from desire. Though, given the choice, she'd have preferred it if this could have been made equally apparent without her backside feeling as though she'd just sat down in a bear trap. She'd have got the same gratification much cheaper if, say, the sight of her had eclipsed all else for him and he'd therefore banged his leg on the corner of a table while striding over. Still, better to have that effect and pick up the odd bit of indention than not have it at all.

'You've *always* got ideas,' she replied vampishly.

'Who can blame me, eh? With such a red hot little babe of a wife.' A gravelly laugh rolled around inside his big chest and wobbled his even bigger belly. He'd be fifty this year and never really walked further than was needed to reach a plate of bacon, yet the sheer *amount* of him ensured that he had, still, a powerful physical presence. He was an old-fashioned man's man. If his huge, fat-wrapped heart eventually gave out and he keeled over, when they lifted his body they'd surely find two or three passing metro-sexuals crushed to death under it.

Katrina slapped his arm. 'Hot babe? Stop it. I'm forty-one. You can't be described as a hot babe when you're forty-one.'

'Forty-one you may be, but you'd pass for twenty-five, you would.'

'Get away with you.' Katrina slapped his arm again. 'Twenty-five. Tch.' She shook her head incredulously. *Twenty-five*. My, but he laid it on thick. Thirty perhaps.

Anyway, the important thing wasn't whether she looked as good as she had a decade or a decade and a half ago. The important thing was that he was still so pleased to be with her that it compelled him to extremes of flattery. He praised her appearance because that was the way he expressed his thorough admiration; it was the visible sign of how he valued her in all ways. If she put on some extra pounds, and the years finally managed to ambush the bodyguard of genes that had protected her skin from serious assault – even if they'd had children and she'd been left with stretch marks and a stomach like a badly wrapped parcel half full of old socks – he'd have been exactly the same.

He leaned in, close to her ear. 'Why don't you put on that thing I bought you the other week?' he whispered.

'OK.' She smiled and twisted away, heading for the door. 'Give me five minutes, then come up.'

'Magic.' He looked at his watch, making a show of starting to time her. 'Three minutes, you say?'

'*Five*.' She laughed. '*Five* minutes, Ted.'

16

'Where are you?' Andrew asked, before Chris could say any more.

'I'm sitting on the toilet.'

'Oh.'

'But that's not important,' Chris said impatiently. 'I'm not actually, you know, *going* or anything.'

'That's very much the answer to a question I was *never* going to ask,' Andrew replied.

'I meant that I'm sitting here just so I'm away from Trudie – so that she can't overhear.'

'That's why I was asking where you were too. You know we have to avoid anything that might edge her towards the idea that you've lost your mind. Her listening to you announce that you have proof that you're someone else is exactly the kind of thing we should steer clear of. Though, for reference, her overhearing you sitting on the lavatory with your mobile phone telling someone that you're not actually *going* right now isn't all that much better.'

Chris wasn't about to get sidetracked. 'But I *do* have proof that I'm not this Old Chris,' he responded triumphantly.

'Yes?' Andrew reached over and flicked the kettle on. 'Now, while I'm sure this proof is going to be airtight, before we call a press conference could you perhaps run it by me?'

'OK. Hold on. Wait a minute . . .'

Chris lifted up the toilet lid, which was becoming quite uncomfortable, and sat on the seat instead. He also considered taking down his trousers. It was fine when it'd been the lid, but it seemed wrong to sit on the actual seat with your trousers on; his bottom was suspended in the oval hole, yet still covered. There was, somehow, a curious feeling of depravity about it. However, he guessed that if he went for the more standard approach then

Andrew would probably hear the sound of his fly unzipping and so on, and that'd be too risky. (If you want to be taken seriously, you don't send out the message, 'Right, before I make one of the most important statements of my life, let me just take my trousers off.')

'So,' Chris continued, 'something occurred to me. It was this: here I am having lost the best part of two decades, and I don't feel terrible.'

'You don't?'

'No. I mean, yes – I feel terrible. But not about suddenly being eighteen years older. About pretty much everything else, but not that. At a gut level, knowing that all those years have passed doesn't appear to be traumatising me. Why do you think that could be?'

'Go on – tell me.'

'Because, at a gut level, I know that those years *haven't* passed.' Chris smiled (who wouldn't have?) and swept his fingers down to give the toilet roll a celebratory spin on its holder.

'You see, now you've lost me,' Andrew replied.

'I, *me*, in here' – Chris, almost as if knocking on a door, struck his knuckles against the centre of his chest several times – 'I am intact.'

'But—'

'Just hear me out.' He took a breath. 'You know how Descartes proved he existed, right?'

'Descartes? Um, he thought, therefore he was, didn't he?'

'Exactly.'

'*What*, exactly?'

'The proof that you are – that *you* are – and that you're you, is that you're aware of it. That's the most basic thing. And I think – I *know*, it's my absolutely certain, absolutely fundamental feeling – that in here' – he rapped his chest again – 'I'm Chris, who is twenty-five. I don't have a sense of having lost eighteen years, because I don't feel like someone who's forty-three but who, as it happens, can't remember most of the past two decades. That's simply *not the person I am*. I'm pissed off about having a middle-aged body, and I'm pissed off about having a middle-aged life, but that's mostly because I still *feel* – in my very core – twenty-five. Do you see?'

'Yes. It's a perfect description.'

'Hallelujah.'

'It's a perfect description of a mid-life crisis.'

'It's *not*. Listen—'

'It *is*, mate. *I* still feel twenty-five inside too.'

'You don't. You *can't*.'

'I *do*. That's the tragedy of it.'

Andrew made a conscious effort to sound sympathetic. In this matter it would have been all too easy to speak as if to a small, not very bright, child. But, in this matter, he'd have felt guilty. There was justifiable satisfaction in turning tables; there was none in shooting wounded fish in a barrel.

'When you're young,' he continued, 'you think that old people must feel different. But what really triggers a mid-life crisis is a bloke getting to middle age and realising that he has a middle-aged body and a middle-aged life while, inside, he feels precisely the same as he did when he was in his twenties.'

This was so obviously ridiculous that Chris let out a laugh. 'Bollocks,' he said. 'That's not true. It can't be.'

'I wish it wasn't, but it is. Living isn't like eating.'

'And that means?'

'It means that, if you're hungry, you eat and with each bite you take you feel a little more full – until eventually you're not hungry any more. But you don't get satisfied by time. Each day that passes just . . . goes. You don't hit, say, forty and think, "Phew. I'm stuffed now. I could die as soon as I've seen out this episode of *Holby City* and it'd be fine because I've got all those years accumulated in me." Nothing changes, inside. And that's with people who can *remember* all the things they've done and all the time that's past. You're simply having a mid-life crisis, but are convinced that's not what it is. Which, as it happens, is *another* classic feature of a mid-life crisis.'

Chris considered this in silence. He knew it wasn't true. More than that, in fact: in some way he couldn't quite isolate right now, he sensed that it was politically offensive. However, he was also aware that he needed more evidence if he was going to convince Andrew, let alone anyone else. It is very important, when trying to prove that you aren't mad, that you don't behave like someone who refuses to accept 'the truth' without being able to provide anything to support your position. The smart option was to keep quiet; to go along with what superficially appeared reasonable until you were in a position to prove your case. It's not at all unlikely that no one would have listened to Einstein's theory that time is relative, for example, if he'd previously wandered around raving about leprechauns and aromatherapy; it'd have just been, 'Chk. Wacky Albert's at it again.' So a vital deceit, Chris decided, was to seem to accept what he knew was false.

'OK,' he said meekly. 'I see.'

'Good,' Andrew replied, obviously relieved. 'Because we—'

Chris didn't hear what he said next because the bathroom door suddenly swung open. Maybe Chris had been too focused on his conversation or maybe Trudie had deliberately crept up the stairs. Whatever the reason, her entry caught him completely by surprise. In a reflex provoked by guilty panic at being 'found out', he stabbed a finger at the END CALL button on his mobile and sprang to his feet. Or, more accurately, he tried to. What actually happened was that he lurched forward, discovered significantly later than was any use that his legs had gone to sleep because he'd been sitting on the lavatory too long, and fell flat on his face on the bathroom floor.

Trudie peered down at him.

'What on earth are you up to?' she asked, as he thrashed around doing, apparently, history's least dignified Douglas Bader impression.

'Nothing,' he replied with a testy brusqueness. But as this response was delivered from about the height of her waist while trying to heave himself up by the edge of the sink onto legs lost to some kind of rubber-kneed, Roaring Twenties-style dance, it lacked any real authority.

She looked pointedly at the phone in his hand. 'Who were you talking to?'

'No one.'

That was met by a long, long stare. Long enough for him to eventually scramble his way onto the side of the bath, where he sat, banging his fists on the tops of his numb, bloodless thighs. She seemed to be about to say something – most probably a statement of the type generally delivered in a low hiss while suffocating your husband under a shower curtain – but instead, almost as if she'd decided that even bothering would be a waste of anger, she simply shook her head and sighed.

And then she pulled down her jeans and sat on the toilet.

Chris was horror-struck.

'No!' he shouted, flinging the flat of his hand out towards her – but it was already too late. The sound of pee hitting water rang out at, it seemed to him, a room-shaking level of porcelain-amplified decibels. It was like Satan standing right in his head, raining evil rice down onto every cymbal in hell. *'Don't!'*

'Don't what?'

Chris didn't think he could be described as a person who was afraid of intimacy, but a middle-aged woman he barely knew abruptly going to the lavatory within two feet of him was, he sincerely felt, 'rushing things'.

'Don't *pee!*' he pleaded.

Trudie screwed up her face. Then thinking that maybe *he* was desperate to use the toilet himself (a bizarre idea as he'd been up there for ages, but what other reason could there be?), she replied, 'I'll be finished in a sec.'

'Ewwwww.' An update *on the progress of it* was the last thing he wanted to hear. The embarrassment was already on him like a boiling acid cloud at the pressure of about a billion atmospheres (why did this have to happen when his legs were useless? Maybe he could just drop to the floor and try to pull himself out of there using his fingernails and teeth.) But, even as he thought that its one tiny mercy was that it couldn't possibly get any worse, she rose into a half squat and tore off a strip of paper to pat herself dry.

The entire world rushed into his ears; he was sure that his face actually bulged outwards under the force of it.

'There,' Trudie said. 'Done.'

When, some time later, he'd stopped shaking, Chris began to apply himself to the two things that would occupy the whole rest of his weekend.

The first was television. Even if he wasn't actually watching it, he had it on constantly in the background. He'd have preferred to have had a wall-sized bank of screens all running together – like

David Bowie in *The Man Who Fell to Earth*. TV was, he instinctively felt, the best and quickest way to learn about an alien planet.

What struck him most about the television of his new present was its endemic cruelty. This was calculated but unselfconscious, almost jovial. Its curious nature was a thing so banal yet so invidious that he had trouble grasping the underlying mindset – it was like Pol Pot deciding to murderously impose Year Zero using a vast army of Club 18–30 reps. There were any number of shows where contestants (in some form or other) tried to win whatever prize was on offer. The formats were strange to him – many were real-life situations rather than quizzes – but that was a minor point. Far more striking in emotional terms was that the focus wasn't the joy of the winner; it was the trauma and humiliation of the losers. Often there would be special highlight shows, which discarded the surrounding chaff and concentrated entirely on repeating the moments when brutal dismissal was administered. People sat isolated on chairs, the camera gleefully tight on their faces, while a committee publicly rejected them. These were the shows' *highlights*. Chris wondered what the hell kind of society it was if this was how it liked to be entertained. Television, surely, gives the public what it wants? Even though there were, it seemed, ten thousand channels now, programmes would still be made to satisfy a demand – it wasn't worth risking a budget on the vague hope of *engineering* one, surely? So, in this wonderful future, it appeared that the mob chanting 'Jump! Jump!' up at a suicidal bloke on a ledge was no longer just the shocking hook of a sensationalist newspaper story; it was now the key demographic. This appalled him. Not least because he'd always thought of himself as attractively cynical and blasé – part Oscar Wilde, part Harrison Ford. He really didn't want to be redesignated as some sort of laughable *Outraged of Tunbridge Wells* figure instead of continuing to be widely regarded as the *Sardonic Prince of Cool;* and certainly not be backed into that corner purely because fashionable aspects of the modern world were so patently, egregiously crap that you couldn't *not* be offended by them unless you were either a sociopath or a total fucking idiot.

As they drifted about within him, the many subtly varied parts of this simmering annoyance became almost independent of their original cause. They transformed – gradually, naturally – into ribbons of non-specific background anger, and he wound them, for tidiness, around the ball of the same that was forming some-vague-where between his temples and his colon.

The second area that occupied Chris's time was the Web. He was a bit irked to discover he wanted to learn about this (after, by chance, having used it as an example of the very kind of thing about which he could not possibly care less), but he was irresistibly enticed there by a phrase Andrew had dropped out when they were in the pub: 'Everything's on the Web.' Chris didn't desperately want to know *everything*; but he did, desperately, want to know one thing.

Unfortunately, the thing he wanted to know was not something he wanted Andrew to suspect he was trying to know. It would, he had no doubt at all, have gone down very badly there. So Chris had to grit his teeth exceptionally hard before making the first of several calls to his friend asking for help with the matter. It was demeaning to skulk back pleading to learn about something you'd so lavishly dismissed mere hours before, and it also required a little care so as not to reveal why you wanted to learn about it now.

A little luck fell his way, however. Andrew was so keen to be the sage that he scarcely seemed to consider why his wide-eyed student wanted to know about whatever the lecture's subject was, and he was especially enthusiastic about the Web. Film buffs, TV geeks, conspiracy theorists, secretive, pedantic, disgruntled, passive-aggressive, tightly wound introverts ... these were his people. Equally useful for Chris's purposes – because it meant he had to make just a few, relatively short calls requesting help and information – was the fact that using the Web was easy. Andrew, as though preparing Chris so that he wouldn't be too hard on himself, had repeatedly said that some people, back when it was really starting to take off, had found getting to grips with the Web baffling and arduous. Chris couldn't imagine who these people might have been, but he guessed that they must have had difficulty grasping how buttonholes worked too. It was easily the most straightforward, most intuitive piece of technology he had ever come across. Given the outline of a few general principles plus details of half a dozen specific points, you'd have to be missing whole lobes of your brain to avoid being passably comfortable and competent with it in well under thirty minutes.

If you didn't count digital television (and who on earth would?), Chris had encountered only two modern advances so far. He couldn't help wondering if he'd coincidentally met the extremes right off the bat – as he felt at home on the Web already, but suspected that death would take him long before he ever learned to operate all the possible functions on his mobile phone.

He accessed the Web from the computer in the living room. While objectively this was another marvel of the future, probably, it didn't seem that extraordinary to Chris. Its power couldn't be seen or felt. The screen was flat and colourful, more like a television than a computer monitor, but that was just flashy presentation. Take away the pretty pictures and a few changes to how and where you clicked the (now two-buttoned) mouse, and it wasn't that much different from the Mac Plus he used at work. Unlike more or less every computer he'd been led to expect would exist in the future, it didn't talk, didn't control all aspects of day-to-day life, and wasn't noticeably trying to kill him. It was a bit rubbish then, really. Had it not provided access to the Web it would hardly have been worth the bother of switching it on.

At first, he was hugely uncomfortable about being on the Web when Trudie was in the room. The computer was in the opposite corner to the television. Anyone sitting on the sofa, which was against the other wall about halfway between the two, could (if they cared to look) fairly easily see what the person on it was up to. During his initial period of browsing, the possibility of his wife's peering eyes harassed and constricted his every key press; after being on the Web for twenty minutes he'd forgotten he had a wife.

It wasn't just that almost anything you asked this all-knowing oracle produced at least a few answers expressed through the medium of frantic anal sex. Certainly, that was a reward structure that educational theorists must be wishing they'd thought of themselves *years* ago, but it was the sheer fascination of its luring infinity that was the main thing. He supposed that, if you wanted, you could simply type a word – any word at all – into one of these 'search engines' (Chris found the term quaintly Victorian) and follow sparks of random curiosity through the branching paths of the 'links' until you were overtaken by frail age or dribbling madness. But, hunting for a specific thing, as he was, had a consuming appeal too. It was mental detective work. The Web was like a criminal mastermind who didn't want to reveal his secrets but was prepared to do so if you proved yourself to him. If you were creative and tenacious enough in pursuing clues and leads, the Web's twisted sense of fair play would eventually provoke it to nod, 'Ah – you are a worthy adversary, Mr Holmes,' and surrender the answer. It was subtle game of chess played out on a board consisting of everything, ever.

In the early hours of the morning, when he finally found what he wanted, he was almost deflated. Partly because the sport was finished, and partly because the information was lazily explicit. He suspected that, if he'd had more experience, he could have found it in mere minutes and would have been contemptuous of how carelessly it was exposed. In fact, it hadn't even been hidden: it had been deliberately broadcast.

Almost as soon as he was awake enough to be aware of it (and, given how poorly he and mornings got along, possibly for the first time in his life), Chris opened his eyes wide and without hesitation.

This was an active decision. He felt, the moment he became sufficiently conscious for the memories to spew back into his mind, that many people in his position (if any such people had ever existed) would have kept their lids clamped protectively shut; slowly raising them – hopefully, fearfully – only after a period of preparation and while praying that they'd discover it had all been a dream and they were actually still in their own bed, in their own house, in their own time. But this, he felt, would be the action of a person who was unsure of what reality was and, by extension, of who they were. He was determined not to be that person. 'I know what I'm going to find,' he was telling the situation, 'and you can stick it up your arse if you were rubbing your hands together waiting to see me flinch at it.'

Nevertheless, there wasn't a scrap of pleasure in finding that he was, indeed, lying in Number 114, in 2006; in the bedroom, under the duvet but still in his clothes, exactly where he'd flopped down, foggy and careless with exhaustion, the previous night. His sense of his own dignity was maintained, however. He was unbroken. He remained. He . . . actually, he really stank.

The clothes he'd woken up in hadn't been fresh even when he'd woken up in them the *previous* morning. And since then he'd added physical exertion, nervous perspiration and . . . what *was* that? Ah, yes: and milk. He smelt like a sweaty, homeless, yoghurt addict.

Trudie wasn't around. He was alone in the bed (looking at the clock, he saw it was almost noon) and he couldn't hear her moving about elsewhere in the house. So, he rooted around in the nearby chest of drawers and pulled out some fresh things to put on before hurrying into the shower. There didn't appear to be a lock on the bathroom door. He wasn't keen on been caught naked – and was even less keen to be confronted by another episode of flagrant, spousal lavatory usage – so he intended to get himself washed, dried and dressed as quickly as possible.

The full, doughy catastrophe of his stomach was emotionally painful to soap, but he didn't dwell on that problem for too long as, naturally, his attention soon turned to his penis.

He looked down at it.

Water from the shower was pouring along its length before arcing off the end in a steady, unconcerned stream.

He took it in his hands, and reached out to it with all his heart.

They were still together, the two of them. That was something. Whatever miseries life had heaped upon this once familiar body and its stranger's soul, *it* had stood by him. His eyes welled up.

Nervously, he gave it a little shake.

A moment later he gave it a more vigorous shake. Which quickly progressed to an extended waggle. Then a demanding massage. Then a frenetic wank.

'*Clear!*'

'*Nothing. I've got flat lines across the board here.*'

'*Clear!*'

'*Still nothing. It's—*'

'*Increase the voltage and give me twenty ccs of adrenaline!*'

'*It's no use . . . I'm calling it. The time is—*'

'*No!*'

Thwup!
Thwup!
'Let go. It's—'
Beep. Beep.
'My God! We've got a pulse!'

An erection. Thank all the stars in all the skies: an erection. He wished he could have bent down and kissed it. Actually, he'd wished he were physically able to do that ever since he'd hit his teens, but this time it was with a desire that was unsoiled; driven by nothing except the gleaming purity of absolute love.

He could relax. Standing there under the showerhead's warm rain, clasping his erection in his hand, he was relieved and reassured – *saved*. It was a scene both defining and cinematic. Napoleon on his horse at Grand Saint-Bernard pass; Chris holding his knob in the shower – just two sides of the same coin, really. Anyway, thankfully, he knew that things were OK now, so he could stop the frenzied rubbing of himself.

'Though,' he mused, 'as I've started . . .'

Not very much later, still in the shower but newly saintly (that is, exuding languid calm while experiencing also a tinge of self-loathing), he turned his face up into the water and, eyes closed, indulged himself with a long, lazy-lipped '*Bwerrrrrrrr.*'

Trudie wasn't in the kitchen or the living room. She wasn't in the dining room either. Chris went back upstairs and checked what turned out to be the spare bedroom and a box room full of junk. Trudie-free. He'd glanced out at the back garden (really nothing but a big, slightly scraggy lawn) already, so he knew she wasn't there.

His first feeling was one of irritation. He'd rushed a wank. Because he'd suspected she could be lurking somewhere in the house, and so might appear at any moment, he'd rushed a wank. Bugger.

Wanks are crafted. They are given attention and care and constructed using the accumulated wisdom of long experience. If one can possibly avoid it, they are not simply . . . well, tossed off. Just as any other craftsman will bring the skills and insights learned over years of practice to his work, a man whose mind has been turned to thoughts of masturbation by the appearance of

Opportunity will begin with the ritual of preparation. There is not just his own physical arrangement and the correct positioning of tissues to consider. A door may need to be bolted, or a heater turned on, or a dog sent into another room (no man is able to feel remotely comfortable while wanking if a dog is watching him; and, if a dog is there, it *will* watch). Pornography might have to be orchestrated. Only a bumbling twelve-year-old with little more than a week under his belt would, say, open a random magazine and just 'set off', trusting to luck. Even the relative (and literal) newcomer will have realised that there are magazines and there are *favourite* magazines; the former are fine for casual browsing but the latter will always be chosen when there's a real need to be sure that they'll be up to the job. There are favourite pages in the favourite magazines too. Some method must be found to ensure those pages are instantly accessible; you must know where you are going to finish and be completely confident you can get there right when time and fine motor skills are in very short supply. In the same way, the precise segment of a video might need to be placed within striking distance (having to tread water, waiting, can spoil the moment) but not too close (the build-up is a vital part of the whole; a successful wank isn't a crude spike, it's a graceful arc), and – it shouldn't need saying – the remote control should be within easy reach in case REWIND or PAUSE is needed. You must plan precisely, yet must also always give yourself options. What's more, just as a dance is a general concept to which everyone brings their own preferences and personality – leading to the vastly different results – a man's wank is as individual as his signature. It's formed through trial and error, but then becomes fixed; a smooth yet highly structured ceremony. Over the course of a lifetime several variations can be adopted. Perhaps there's a house move, and the former bedroom setting falls out of favour at the new location – usurped by the conservatory which, kneeling in post-orgasm bliss, affords a fittingly spectacular view over the Pennines. But each era will have its unquestionably dominant wank; it is *never* just a lazy chaos of slapdash masturbations.

Chris, then, was understandably miffed about having been, it seemed to him, tricked into inelegant haste – especially as, given the situation, it had been such an important wank.

His second feeling was how lonely it was in this big house. This big, silent house that had no Trudie in it.

He shook himself. Misplaced guilt, that's what *that* was. Pff. Good luck to guilt if it thought it was going to stop him heading in the direction he'd decided to go. No chance: not when there was no logical reason for him to feel guilty anyway.

Pff.

17

A white car hummed by, brushing the side of her face with its slipstream as though petulantly kicking up its heels at her as it passed. She wondered who was in it; tried to imagine the life that was right now being taken into the distance on four wheels on a Sunday morning. What kind of person has a white car? No one who is quite right, that's for sure. White sets off hells almost across the board. White leather three-piece suites. White jeans. Who has that level of optimism? Nobody normal. It's beyond Pollyannaish and more than simply naive – that wouldn't be enough. There must be an unfalteringly confident assumption of control; and also, therefore, great self-regard. A white leather three-piece suite hints at a hard edge to its owner. White cars are different, though: more complex. The owner certainly isn't going to be well balanced, but it could go either way. White cars are like nine-year-old boys: their natural state is filthy; only constant labour and sleepless vigilance will prevent them reverting instantly into something that looks as though it's just been pulled out of a canal. So, nothing says 'obsessive-compulsive disorder' like a clean white car. Naturally, then, there aren't many of those. Most white cars are similar to the one that had just driven past her: grubby to the point of almost seeming to have topsoil. As it's not credible to suppose that anyone old enough to reach the pedals doesn't know exactly what they're going to get if they buy a white car, those who *aren't* outpatients at a psychiatric hospital must just not care; and not care at a very profound level. They've simply given up. Most likely, then, the owner will be a man who's long ago abandoned all hope of ever having a family, or a man who's had a family for so long that he's abandoned all hope.

She hadn't caught a glimpse that might have indicated whether or not the driver actually was a man. She was satisfied with the idea that it had been, though. He was probably going to visit his mother, who was not so good on her feet any more and starting to forget things. Trudie wondered what would happen when she herself grew old. And what would happen when she died. Who would she be when she existed only as other's recollections of her? It's always the most stupid, tangential things people use as labels for the dead, isn't it? 'Old Harry ... do you remember that budgie he had?' 'Bessie. You know. *Bessie* – always carried a packet of Mentholyptus.' What would the shorthand for her be? Not 'unforgettable', that was for certain. Not 'vivacious' either, and definitely not 'stylish' – she never even had the right coat. She didn't have anything like a big collection of coats, but it was still amazing how they *all* missed the target. Not warm enough, or disastrously short of pockets, or inappropriate, or just a big, shapeless ... *thing*: however many she had, she never seemed to have the bloody one she needed. That would be on her gravestone, she could see it now: 'Trudie Mortimer: lived, died and was buried, in the wrong coat'.

Trudie was a person who chewed her thoughts instead of her nails.

She was also very concerned with what things meant. So concerned that, even if the meaning of something – a phrase someone had used, say, or an expression they'd made – was straightforward, she'd nonetheless often roll it over in her mind later; looking at it from different angles, testing it for a fit with other interpretations. There always turned out to be a few possible alternatives, if she replayed it often enough. And each variation she managed to conceive of made the job of deciding which particular one was correct harder and less conclusive, which, in turn, made her search for meaning all the more demanding.

She'd driven out to take a walk alone thinking that it might help her clear her head but, as usual, it turned out to be like trying to shovel sand with a fork. And there was lots of sand. For one thing, she was not in a good mood with herself. She had made some questionable decisions. Mind you, they were perhaps decisions that anyone might have made, in her situation. Though isn't that the excuse people often use for doing what they wanted to do anyway? 'I'm a victim of circumstance. I didn't choose; I just reacted.' And anyway, taking it further, you can't blame 'having no choice' for your poor choices: the justification eats itself.

She resolved to leave Chris.

There was no future in him – in a literal sense: he was a person who seemed to have lost any sense of the future. That was the root of the problem, and it was a killer. How can you hope to make a life with someone who's decided that their life is over? If she gave up on him then, really, she was simply following his lead.

Anyway, she'd put up with this for so long now. And it wasn't as if she hadn't tried to fix things. 'Chris,' she'd said, more than once, 'stop being such a wanker.' But he just didn't listen to her. She couldn't remember the exact order in which 'sullen', 'self-destructive' and 'drunk' had arrived, but it hardly seemed to matter any more. The three of them got on like a house on fire; they were so flawlessly intertwined by this point that they might as well be considered a single, integrated misery. What was the point in her slogging on? Not only was it joyless, she couldn't help feeling it was not a little unfair too. *She'd* have liked to have been angrier with her life than she was able to announce, as it happened. *She* ought to have been allowed to be pretty pissed off with aspects of the world's treatment of her, instead of having to spend all her energy being pissed off with Chris. This thought bit into her especially deeply as there was a time, not very long ago, when they had hated things *together*. They didn't hate all things – lots of things, certainly, but not all things. Hating all things is appalling – it debases proper hatred. Also, they hated them not as Chris hated things now – lazily and dejectedly – but with real passion. It had been part of their bond: enjoying the closeness of sharing an eclectic multitude of grievances with the universe. Phone votes, button flies, Exmouth, government subsidies for religious schools, and DVDs that list Inactive Menu as a 'special feature'. Graphology, fruit teas, everybody else's ringtone, Alaskan drilling and the second series of *Angel*. Together, they'd get through all of those and more in a single afternoon. Admittedly, these targets are a different kind of animal because they aren't personal issues, but, equally, Chris and Trudie had always chosen to *take* them personally. They would, for example, become so mutually furious about the overprescription by GPs of broad-spectrum antibiotics that they'd very often end up having sex.

The memory of all those years opened up inside her until she felt filled completely by it. It was warming and vital, and she decided that she should stay; that she shouldn't give up, not just yet.

Building on this analysis, she resolved – resolved finally, unwaveringly – to leave Chris, then not to leave him and to instead give it one more go, three times during the course of walking a little over fifty yards.

When she eventually got back to where she'd parked the car she'd sieved through the state of her life, detail by detail, so thoroughly that the only thing she knew for sure was that she was cold and wished she'd been wearing the right coat.

Trudie returned home, dragging her feet through a sort of soggy melancholy, to find Chris sitting in front of the computer in the living room.

He turned round when he heard her come in. 'Hi.'

'Hi.'

Would he ask where she'd been? She hoped that, if nothing else, he'd ask where she'd been. That would indicate a tiny, residual level of interest in her, at least.

Nothing.

He'd probably not even noticed that she hadn't been in the house.

'I've been for a walk,' (as you bleeding ask) she said.

'Right.' Chris nodded emptily.

She stared at him. He felt her do it. A little anxious, he wondered if he was missing a subtext. But what? She'd been for a walk – that's all there was. Even if his relationship with her had possessed deeper roots than simply watching a few hours TV together and seeing her pee, he couldn't discern how this would have changed things. She was a fully grown woman and he didn't own or control her. It would have been unpleasant for him to appear to suggest that she had to explain her every action to him, to 'keep him informed of her movements' like a criminal. He would, under any circumstances, have been very careful not to let her imagine that wanting to know where she had been had occupied his mind for a moment – let alone to start *questioning* her about it when she returned, as though it was clearly his right to receive an explanation.

However, there was that staring, and he had definitely detected a pointed tone in her voice too. Was 'I've been for a walk' their code phrase for something? Perhaps Trudie coming back on a Sunday afternoon when he'd lain in bed until midday and saying 'I've been for a walk' actually meant 'I've killed again.' The unspoken accusation was 'If you'd just bothered to drag your arse out of bed in time to stop me, an innocent hiker would still be alive now.'

He had no idea what it might be that he was, apparently, missing. But, even if he had, he thought, the wisest policy would almost certainly be to keep his mouth shut rather than risk saying something that might accidentally worsen the situation. Best to say nothing. That was the one course of action that was always safe.

Trudie peered at him silently as he looked back at her, equally mute, for several more moments.

'Fine,' she huffed, dropping down onto the sofa. '*Fine*.'

What *was* the point?

'Would you have sex with Trudie?'

There was just crackle. Chris didn't know how reliable these mobile phones were – maybe they stopped receiving sometimes, like radios do when you drive under a bridge. He tried again.

'Andrew? Can you hear me?'

'Look, Chris—'

'Would you have sex with her? If you were me.' He pinched his chin to aid deliberation. 'What do you think? Only, I'm wondering if I should have sex with her in a minute.'

'Where is she?'

'She's up in the bathroom. I think she's brushing her teeth before she goes to bed. So I was— Shit! She's coming.'

'It's me again. Sorry – were you asleep?'

'No.'

'Really?'

'Yes. Why are you whispering?'

'I don't want her to hear that I'm on the phone. I've left her in the bedroom and just popped into the loo here.'

'So ... did you?'

'Have sex with her?'

'Obviously.'

'Of course I bloody didn't. Jesus. What? In fifteen minutes?'

'What's wrong with fif—' Andrew screwed up his face. 'How long do you plan on doing it to her, then? Will you need me to pop in each week and water the plants until you're finished?'

'For God's sake – what does the length of it matter? I hadn't actually settled on an exact duration.' Chris tutted and shook his head. 'Though – amazingly – I *did* blithely assume it'd manage to just blast right through that quarter-of-an-hour barrier. Jesus.'

'First rule of sarcasm, mate: it's not on when you've called someone at half eleven at night to ask if you should have sex with your wife. "Oh, you and your crazy questions, Andy . . . Now, tell me if I ought to do the missus." Not. On.'

'Give me a break – it's hardly a normal situation. I've been dumped into the middle of this. *You* know Trudie better than I do.'

'I do not.'

'Of course you do. I only met the woman yesterday morning.'

'You—'

'Never mind. How long do you think I can spend 'just popping to the loo' before she starts getting suspicious?'

'Dunno.' Andrew sniffed. 'Maybe *that's* regularly fifteen minutes-plus. How's your prostate?'

'Christ, Andrew.' Chris felt a ripple of queasy discomfort roll all the way through him. 'I'm not going to discuss my *prostate* with you. Bloody hell: boundaries. Now will you just listen, OK? I was weighing up the pros and cons of having sex with Trudie. You know – earlier. I was sitting there trying to decide what to do, while she was eating her tea.'

'What was it?'

'Some sort of pasta thing, I think. Is that remotely relevant?'

'No.'

'Then why interrupt me by asking?'

'Hey, if you think it's important for me to know that she's eating while you're leering across deciding how to do her, then I may as well have all the details. I mean, what if – as you were trying to make up your mind – she happened to be having a hot dog? She's giving you your answer. On a plate.'

'She was having pasta.' That was the second time Andrew had

talked about 'doing' Trudie. Chris noticed only because it didn't sit well. Chris himself – though it wasn't exactly his preferred term – could refer to 'doing' someone, but Andrew simply couldn't. It sounded out of place if he said it. Stumbling out of his mouth it had the awkward, forced bravado of a schoolboy's first attempt to get served at the bar. Chris shook his head. 'So, now we sorted that out,' he continued, 'can I get to the point, please?'

'By all means.'

'OK, then. As you've ordered me to set to work improving things between Trudie and Chris, I—'

'When did I say that?'

'Bloody hell, Andrew. You gave me a whole dour-faced *lecture* on it yesterday.'

'I didn't say you should throw yourself into improving things. I said that, as they're in a brittle enough state already, you should try not to *smash them to pieces* by letting slip that, on top of everything else, you've now gone and lost your mind.'

'Well, yes. But if someone tells you that things are precariously crap then "Try to make them better" is implicit, isn't it? You don't normally think, 'Oh, he'll be suggesting I ensure they remain teetering right on the edge, then,' do you?'

'Except, as you pointed out to me only moments ago, this isn't a normal situation. You have about a personal ad's-worth of information and hardly any sense of shared history whatsoever. Your clueless, trigger-happy attempts at rekindling your marriage might easily put it out altogether. Let's face it, even in ideal circumstances, how possible is it to predict whether or not something you innocently say to your wife is going to have her either burst into tears or go for your throat with a nail file?'

'Which is exactly why I'm calling you. I'm absolutely OK about having sex with her; really – I wouldn't mind.'

'Noble.'

'But is it a good idea? It'll look like rejection if we do it every night and I suddenly stop now, but, if we never do it any more, it might seem strange and crass if I start going at it out of the blue.'

'You don't do it any more,' declared Andrew.

'Really?' Chris felt unexpectedly deflated. 'We don't? Did I tell you that?'

'Of course not,' Andrew replied scornfully.

'Hey, I don't know, do I? Maybe things have … There were adverts on the TV – adverts selling moisturiser for *men* – I saw them. Perhaps in 2006 blokes tell each oth—'

'Not in 2006. Not ever.'

'Then how do you know?'

'Because, well … OK, I don't exactly *know*. That you don't do it, *ever*. It's … it's a general impression … that you, probably, only do it really, really rarely.'

'A general impression?'

'Yes.'

Chris considered this for a few seconds.

'Andrew, don't take this the wrong way,' he eventually replied, 'but that's the impression I've *always* got from you. I got it yesterday morning, even – but I bet you and, and …'

'Gill.'

'… and Gill are *relentless*, right?'

'That's not the sa—'

'Christ – I bet the two of you can't get through *Call My Bluff* without becoming a writhing mass of limbs and urges.'

'We're fine, thanks.'

'So it's possible that Trudie and Chris are still doing it as well.'

'It's *possible, I* suppose.'

'Then, if I want to avoid letting slip a real giveaway that things have changed, I ought to do it. Not every night or anything, maybe. Twice a week, do you think? Once a week? What's the percentage shot?'

'Just go and do her, OK! You've quite obviously set your heart on it, so what's the point of this conversation? I feel like a fluffer. *God.*'

'Steady on,' Chris said. 'If you think this is weird for you, just imagine how it feels for *me*.'

He rubbed his temples. It wasn't that he'd have to close his eyes and think of England, and Wendy James – Trudie, thankfully, wasn't unattractive, considering. Actually, she was … (Chris struggled to give a name to, and thereby solidify and understand, the complex mixture of subtle components Trudie's physical side evoked in him but, unfortunately, his 1980s mind had no knowledge of the semantic tool MILF.) Pfff. He could do it; that was all that mattered. But, still, it was … No – he had to do it. Or test the waters, at least. In the circumstances – and especially considering what he was about to do in those circumstances – the last thing he could afford was Trudie getting suspicious about anything. There was no choice: he had to play the hand he'd been dealt, and sleep with his wife.

Chris, picking his way thorough his thoughts, hadn't spoken for a while.

'You're going to do it, aren't you?' Andrew asked.

'Yeah ... Yeah, I have to give it a stab. Wish me luck.'

He hung up, took a deep breath, and strode back into the bedroom.

'Andrew? It's me.'

'Yes.'

'Did I wake you?'

'No.'

'Good. I—'

'You were only seven minutes. Actually, *under* seven minutes.'

'You were *timing*?'

'Of course I wasn't timing. I just happen to have noticed the times.'

'Man, but you're an accountant. Thank Christ I don't have to shag *you* – I couldn't take that kind of pressure.'

'So ...' Andrew massively didn't want to hear how it had gone. Of all the things in the world that might be poured into his recoiling ears, that would be among the ones he'd relish the absolute least. 'How did it go?' he asked.

'Yeah, well, that's why I'm calling again,' Chris replied uncomfortably.

'Ahhh. It went badly, then.' Andrew swapped the phone from one side of his head to the other. 'At least you know now, though – eh, mate?'

'No, that's not it. It didn't go badly.'

'Oh.'

'It didn't go far enough to go badly, or go well, or go anything at all. You might say that I didn't pass Go.'

'Oh, *riiiiight*. That's why you're back so quickly. You, um ... fell in the paddock.'

'What?'

'You know ...' Chris was miles away on the other end of a phone and couldn't see, but, bizarrely, Andrew nevertheless instinctively dropped his eyes and nodded towards an imaginary groin.

Just as bizarrely, Chris seemed to pick this up.

'Are you suggesting I have erectile dysfunction?' He said these words with a level of righteous indignation you'd not imagine would come so naturally to a person whose certainty had arrived only after nervously testing this very thing in the shower just a few hours earlier.

'Ugh.' Andrew winced. 'No. No, sorry – it was a poor analogy, probably ... I meant premature ejaculation.'

'Well, that's *loads* better. Cheers.'

'It *is* better.'

Grudgingly, Chris recognised that he couldn't argue with this. Premature ejaculation was indeed better than erectile dysfunction, much better. But hardly 'gloriously' so.

'OK, OK,' Chris replied. 'I would choose premature ejaculation over erectile dysfunction; but I'd be a bit miffed to have my options limited to only one or the other, all the same.'

'Then what happened?'

'If you'd stop bad-mouthing my knob for one moment, I'd bleeding tell you.' He sat down on the edge of the bath. 'Listening?'

'Yes.'

'Right. So, I go in—'

'Gngh.'

'To the *bedroom*. Christ, Andrew, get a grip. I go in the bedroom, and she's lying there reading her book. Trying to be casual about it, I lift the duvet up quite high as I get into bed – so I can take a crafty look. She's wearing a nightdress that comes down to her knees and woolly socks. I slide in beside her—'

'What are you wearing?'

'Me? I'm not wearing anything, obviously.'

'Aren't you cold?'

'Cold? Of course not.'

Actually, he was a little cold. He'd noticed this earlier, but what was he supposed to do? Wear pyjamas? God ... did Old Chris wear *pyjamas*? Now, *that* must be a moment that sounds like a coffin lid closing: the Moment When You Start to Wear Pyjamas.

And there has to be one. That's to say, you can't gradually, almost imperceptibly, descend from virility to pyjamas. ('There was just a bit of elasticated waistband at first – I thought nothing of it; by the time I realised what was happening, it was too late.') No, one day you must, consciously, perfectly aware of what you're doing, take the decision to wear them. What brings a man to that point?

Whatever it was, it wasn't being pushed further away by sitting naked with his bare backside on the freezing edge of a bath.

'Can I carry on now?' Chris asked. 'It's suspicious enough my coming to the bathroom again so soon. I want to keep this short.'

'Whatever. Go on.'

'So, I slowly inch over closer to her, yeah – until I'm lying right up against her side.'

'Uh-huh.'

'And then I twist, like I'm getting comfortable, but I let my hand come to rest on the top of her leg in the process. Subtle, you know; it could be a move; or it could still just be an accident at this stage.' Chris clicked his teeth. 'But that's as far as you can push things, isn't it? If she didn't think I was her husband, I probably wouldn't even have been able to get to *that* position without it being obvious that something was going on.'

'In bed next to her, naked, groping her thigh, you mean? Yes, women tend to pick up those kind of non-verbal cues.'

Chris ignored him. 'It was crunch time. One more step and I was committed. And, do you know what?' He paused for a long exhalation then, shaking his head, continued, 'I froze. I looked at her – she's still reading, oblivious – and I just froze.' He stood up; his arse was like ice. 'It suddenly hit me . . . I have *no* idea how old people have sex.'

For an instant, Andrew took this as a random thought. He'd been making love to Gill one time and, apropos of nothing and when he was performing what he'd assumed was a wholly engaging manoeuvre, she'd suddenly said, 'Can you remember if I turned off the grill?' He hadn't been much pleased by this, but he recalled how he had once found himself consumed by furiously trying to remember the name of the replicant that Brion James played in *Blade Runner* – which is not unimportant (Leon) but not exactly appropriate when you're at a funeral service. These odd thoughts simply pop into one's brain sometimes, for no reason whatsoever.

So, he took it that this is what had happened to Chris, and it –
'Hmm ... I wonder how old people have sex.' – had naturally
derailed things.

Sex is not at all robust, after all; it almost relies on a blank mind
for success. For example, take that old idea that the ghosts of your
relatives watch over you after death. It's a roundly stupid notion
but, even fully knowing that, if it wanders into your head in the
middle of masturbating then it's a real struggle to carry on. And,
if one can dodge ejaculation by thinking about changing a tyre,
it's evident that the thought of changing a tyre can usurp an
orgasm. All you can afford to have in your head during sex is sex;
otherwise it breaks.

However, the very next instant, Andrew realised that Chris was
talking about *Trudie*. The old people in question were Trudie and,
presumably, himself.

'Have you been sitting in exhaust fumes all day or something?'
Andrew asked. 'Trudie isn't an "old person". You're both forty-
three; that's not "old".'

'I can understand you thinking that, Andrew – from where
you're standing and everything. It's like when one ninety-year-old
says to another, "Doris has died, you know. She was only seventy-
five." But, objectively—'

'*Objectively*, if you can't distinguish between seventy-five and
forty-three then you need some glasses to correct your being
profoundly short-minded. For God's sake. Why – to give you a
fitting frame of reference – do you think people talk about a "mid-
life crisis"? It's because you're in the middle of life; the clue's in
there, really. That's a hell of a long way from *Hot Nights with
Darby and Joan*.'

'Calm down. This isn't personal.'

'Well, it sort of *is*, isn't it? First, as I'm the same age as you,
you're saying I'm old. Not just older, but old, with the emphasis
on desiccated.'

'Forty-three's old if you're twenty-five. It's old to anyone in their
twenties, I'd say. So, basically, it's old to anyone who's young; it's
only not old to people who are, you know ... old.'

'So ancient, in fact,' Andrew continued, as though Chris hadn't
said anything, 'that it practically makes us a mysterious other
species. How do we have sex? Like beetles, mate. How else? And,

once you hit forty-five, it's different again, apparently: when you're over forty-five the woman will bury her orgasm upstream under a blanket of gravel and the man goes by later and—'

'I've obviously hit a nerve here,' Chris said – with surprising forbearance, he thought, for someone who had a wife ageing in the bedroom, an erection on call-waiting, and buttocks that were numb with cold (he'd heard of fingers and toes, but did anyone actually suffer frostbite and lose an arse?) 'But try to take a step back, OK? There *is* a difference; there *must* be. And I need some help. Christ Almighty – how am I supposed to initiate sex with a woman who's lying in bed *wearing woolly socks*? And, even if I manage it, where then? Forty-three-year-olds don't have sex like me.'

'Why not?'

'Because what I do is *filthy*. I'm twenty-five. There's the physical limitations to consider – the middle-aged bodies. If I have twenty-five-year-olds' sex it'll end in a big pile of stress fractures. And what are our lungs like? There could be a suffocation. For all I know, my killer move might *actually* kill us both. But let's ignore the physical stuff for a moment, because there are *psychological* factors to consider here. We probably have to reverse what I'm used to and try to keep ourselves hidden at key points, right? God knows, I wouldn't want Trudie to see my gut wobbling around in her field of view while I'm attempting to guide her to a state of untrammelled bliss. And she might feel self-conscious unless she stays in her nightie, turns the lights off, and puts on a second pair of socks. My simply doing what people do in their twenties would be … unseemly. And wrong. And I want to reassure her, not overdo it and send her into shock. I know that sex is massively important when you're young, but in middle age——'

'In middle age it's *everything*.'

'No it's not. Of course it's not. In your twenties it might be virtually all you think about, but in your forties it's not going to be that central because you have all that other, you know, *life*.'

'That's why, you idiot. Sex just happens when you're young. More or less often, but you accept and expect it as a given. It's a drive. When you're middle-aged it's a constant *longing*; sex means that you're still attractive – a woman *does* still want you. You haven't become nothing but a coat hanger for mortgage repayments and parents' evenings and direct debit agreements that no one cares about or even *sees* as a person worth wanting any more. At forty-three sex isn't a bit of fun; it's confirmation that you still exist.'

Andrew heard footsteps on the ceiling. Gill had got out of bed. He couldn't hope that he wasn't the cause of her waking up – he had, he realised, been shouting by the end of his rant just now. He prayed she'd been roused by the sheer, thrumming volume, however, rather than picking up actual words. He couldn't think how he'd explain why he was alone in the living room raging into his mobile about middle-aged sex when it was gone midnight and he had (he now noted) polished off three quarters of a bottle of wine.

'Oh, great,' he murmured, then snapped into his phone, 'Look – I've got to go.'

'Yeah – sure,' Chris replied, shuffling from foot to foot.

He'd thought having sex in the middle-aged context would be unfamiliar and technically demanding, but he hadn't guessed it'd be quite *that* philosophically complex as well. Hell. When he'd left the world he knew, just finding the clitoris had been enough; now it looked as though there'd be a forty-minute written exam too. This was a load to get your head around without Andrew – Mr Don't Mind Me – suddenly going off on one like the spokes-person for some militant Shagging Seniors pressure group.

'Sorry. You go to bed, OK?' he added.

'I will,' replied Andrew and hung up.

Chris looked at his phone for a time, and then let out a long sigh. On top of everything, it was work tomorrow too. This was a tough night. Oh well: bite the bullet.

He slapped his bottom – hoping to knock it out of cryogenic suspension – and marched, yet again, into the bedroom.

18

You can't stab water.

Well, you can, but there's no pleasure in it. It parts to let the blade in – as indifferent to its new shape as it was to the old one – then, the second you pull your knife out again, it flops back to how it was before. You're frustrated and angry, maybe a little wet too, while, for it, the whole thing might as well never have happened. Water just doesn't give a shit.

This, he felt, was what it was like with Chris. As his boss, he had all the power over him he could have asked for – a whole armoury full of knives. But it made no difference. Unofficial warnings, official warnings, outright, barely legal threats – they all sank into Chris without trace. You couldn't land a blow by taking away what little authority the man had, because he was utterly unconcerned with any authority in the workplace, his own included; it was no loss to strip him of something he regarded as utterly without value. Even calculated humiliation was pointless. What did Chris care if he got given many of the worst jobs and was allocated the most rubbish desk? You could have mocked him in front of clients, made him work in the men's toilets and, baying with laughter, thrown custard over him every hour. Chris's relaxed, now-effortless contempt for what he and everyone else in the company did made such things pifflingly trivial details to him.

Yet, self-starting, proactive, goal-oriented executive that he was, he still couldn't let go of the dream that, one day, he'd break Chris Mortimer – snap the bastard in two and, smiling, dunk him like a biscuit. And, maybe, today would be that day.

Ultimately, of course, he could have fired him. It was within his ambit and, given Chris's repeated behaviour, *easily* within his rights. (Whereas, formerly, Chris had gone in for Pointless Acts of Trivial Rebellion, these days it was more Open Displays of

Nihilistic Sabotage.) But there were a couple of obstacles that kept him from doing that.

One was purely pragmatic. The stuff Chris actually produced (and this was especially galling for someone who loved the mantra 'All I care about is results') consistently delivered the required effect. Not only that, but the man himself had, in their limited world, become a sort of cult. He was seen as a precious, reliably entertaining car crash of a human being; the industry's version of Hunter S. Thompson or Sean Ryder. People had 'Chris Stories'; just *hearing* these made clients feel interesting. Like tales of debauched business trips to Amsterdam, they had a rock 'n' roll cachet. Those clients who didn't specifically and gleefully ask for Chris still often wanted to know 'What he's done now?' at least. His famous indifference and regular implosions made him a memorable and well-liked company mascot. He was, God damn him, an asset.

Still, useful or not, Short Stick didn't remotely *need* him. It was vast and dominating and, totally Chris-less, would have remained vast and dominating. Sack him – or, even better, sack him but put out the rumour that he'd finally gone fully AWOL and had last been seen shouting out passages from the Bible on the Northern Line – and the company would have carried on making obscene profits exactly the same. No, the second obstacle – the really serious one – was personal: Chris must *see* that he was beaten.

There was no sense in firing him if he didn't care whether or not he kept his job there; that was worse than useless – it was, in fact, a defeat. As Chris's boss, he had to get through to him, to make him aware – make him *acknowledge* – what a stumbling, washed-up little pissant he was; have him blanche and realise how incredibly lucky he'd been to have kept his job all this time and, trembling, resolve to toe the line from now on; show appropriate respect; grovel. Only when *that* happened would there be any satisfaction and sense of achievement in telling him to clear his desk and be out of the building before lunch.

There was the heart of the problem in all its nagging, infuriating intractability. He simply *could not* fire Chris until his attitude improved.

It was a new, bigger building in another part of town. (Luckily, Andrew had remembered to tell Chris this, realising that he wouldn't know otherwise.) He recognised none of the people sitting at the many desks. It was obviously (from his point of view) hi-tech. Fundamentally, however, it was the same old shithouse. The braying, smug voices issued from unknown faces; phones rang with unfamiliar (but equally hateful) tones; the crap carpet was a different shade of crap. But (and the irony of this wasn't lost on him) the altered body moved to the pulse of its original miserable spirit.

Without being conscious that he was actually saying the thought out loud, Chris stood with his arms akimbo, surveyed the work floor from one side to the other in a single slow sweep of his eyes, and announced, 'You pack of wankers.'

Several people heard him, but only one reacted to any degree; and even he simply glanced across, then turned back to his computer screen and said, 'You're in early, Chris.'

It had been a question whether or not Chris would come in to work this morning. There were reasons aplenty on both sides, tempting him in opposite directions.

On the Against side, it was a daunting prospect; similar to the worry and uncertainty of your first day in a new job, but magnified many, many times because there'd be none of the understanding and leeway that's afforded to a new boy – as far as they were concerned he'd been working there for decades. Also, it was a foreign age for him. What if he got there and discovered that it was his turn to operate the teleporter? Even at the most basic level it was going to be tough – he'd be expected to know the names of his colleagues, for example. There was easily enough in the Against column to make calling in sick look kissably attractive.

But, speaking on behalf of For, he'd also been told that his – that's to say, Old Chris's – record meant it was a miracle he'd still got a job at all. Pulling a sickie was hardly going to help; and what was the point anyway? He'd have to face it some time, so today was as good as tomorrow or the middle of next week. What's more, he did find himself intrigued. He wanted to see this place that had, it seemed, held him like flypaper for the best part of his working life. It was an urge not unlike the one that makes people carefully examine with fingers and eyes some piece of gristle on which they've almost choked.

The factor that had decided it was probably a general desire to give himself a shake: to stand up and Do, rather than mither around ineffectually Considering *What* to Do. Almost comically, considering how mutually antagonistic the two things were, this desire came from the combination of a pathetic bit of fretting about his furtive plan, plus his handling of the Trudie situation. He'd initially been full of eager impatience about the former but, imagining the actual details and all the possible ways they could leave him looking like an embarrassing sadact, he'd experienced a wobble. As for the latter, well, that was flat out dismal. He'd spent so long vacillating in the bathroom the previous night that, when he'd finally walked into the bedroom – set on sexing up Trudie with significant yet sensible vigour – she was asleep. He'd considered waking her. That might be a good idea – he'd be OK about being woken up if it meant there'd be sex. But then he was twenty-five; he'd be OK about being thrown from a moving car if it meant there'd be sex. Trudie was forty-three so she might just be disorientated or furious. He'd decided not to risk it. (He also decided not to tell Andrew about that particular failure. The last Andrew knew before he'd hung up, Chris was about to bravely launch himself onto Trudie; let him believe this is what had happened. Chris felt that his insistence that he *was* young vibrant Chris wouldn't benefit from Andrew thinking he couldn't pull off basic sex despite an extensive run-up and three calls for advice.)

This morning, then – keen to counter-attack pitiable wobbling and shuffling ineffectuality before they gained unstoppable momentum and took over completely – he resolved to stride into work, without hesitancy; to do so *because* it was so very tempting to back away and hide under the duvet instead.

He was congratulating himself on his choice when a hand clapped him far too hard on the shoulder. It stayed there – gripping him as if to prevent escape – even when he turned round to see who it belonged to.

'Chris! Glad you could get up.' The hand's owner laughed loudly. 'Let's get to it, then – we're all ready for you.'

He pulled at Chris, less guiding and more dragging at him, but Chris resisted. The assaulting fingers clearly hadn't anticipated meeting any level of stability, and they lost their grip and slipped off.

'Euan.' Chris was stunned for a moment. Then he too laughed.

'*Euan.*' His laughter was genuine and therefore landed a much more effective blow than Euan's had. 'Look at you. Out of short trousers and everything.'

Euan's hair was cropped still shorter than it had been, but now there was far less of it to crop. He looked fit and was well dressed but – whether through sun, unlucky skin or simply the cumulative effort of being a tosser – his face was a web of deep lines; it was as though someone had taken a copy in plasticine and then run an Afro comb all over it. The combined effect was bizarre: a brown walnut of a head, avoiding bald on technicalities, atop a body that gym membership and expensive tailoring had bluffed out of a decade. He reminded Chris of one of those children who have that terrible premature-ageing condition, and so present you with the uncanny image of a tiny Malcolm Muggeridge on a tricycle.

The short-trousers remark didn't make any obvious sense to Euan, but that didn't concern him. This was Chris, so it probably relied less on pithy observation and more on Jack Daniels. He could, because it was Chris, rely on the assumption that it was *meant* to be some kind of petty insult, and that was enough.

'Steady,' Euan replied with a Gestapo smile. 'It's perhaps not the *best* idea to get mouthy with your boss right before your performance review, eh? Wouldn't you agree?'

Euan took Chris's expression on hearing this as alarm at the prospect of the review (rather than what it was: simple surprise to hear there was a review happening at all) and his brain released a happy little gloop of endorphins. He gave his own cleverness an avuncular pinch on the cheek too. Always the wily tactician, he'd weighted things in his favour beforehand by making Chris's appointment first thing on a Monday morning. It was win-win. If, as was fairly likely, the git didn't turn up because he was still lying in a kebab somewhere, that was a very serious matter indeed. Euan would have the blankest of cheques with which to cash an endless series of repercussions – one of which might finally make Chris crumple. Even better was the alternative: Chris *did* turn up. If he'd got Chris to arrive punctually – at this hour of the day, at this point in the week – then the man must be anxious about the review. And if Chris was worried and fearful about what Euan might have to say to him, then, well – job done. It meant Chris knew he was looking down into an abyss, and Euan could therefore enjoy pushing him into it.

Chris allowed himself to be led to what was obviously Euan's office. It had a glass front, which struck Chris as a design flaw. The good thing about being the boss, surely, was getting an office in which you could sit and do nothing, unobserved. What was the point of having the job if you put yourself in a glass-fronted office where you couldn't just spend the afternoon reading a magazine while absently spring-cleaning your nostrils if you fancied it? It was like struggling up a mountain so that, at the top, you could start climbing a ladder. And the glass couldn't be there so that you could look out onto the work floor, because who would want to? It was depressing.

There was a desk inside, and behind it a chair into which Euan slid himself smoothly. Across from the desk, rather than any other chairs, was a sofa large enough to accommodate three people. Chris looked backwards and forwards between it and the door through which they'd entered the office. He sat down, frowning.

Euan, his mouth solemn but his eyes smirking, steepled his hands and gazed at Chris's worried forehead for a number of seconds. Seeing Chris concerned was worth savouring. Finally, however, he felt he must move on, and so he sighed and said, 'Well ...' as gravely as possible.

'Euan?' Chris asked. 'How did you get this sofa through that door?'

'I'm sorry?'

'It's solid, right?' Chris got down on his hands and knees and peered under it. This confirmed two things to him: 1) that the sofa was a single unit and 2) that his knees were forty-three years old and he should avoid getting down on them in future. 'That desk probably came in here in pieces,' he said, getting himself back to his feet by using his legs, his arms and – vitally – a short grunt, 'but this sofa ...'

'I had them take the wall down,' Euan replied with irritation.

'You had them take the *wall* down?'

'Yes. The glass panels are only fastened at the floor. No sense them being fixed up there.' He nodded, rallying somewhat now he was describing his ingenuity.

'Why?'

'Wouldn't provide them with much extra support, would it?'

'No?'

'No – it's a suspended ceiling.'

'*Ahh* – of course.'

'So, I had them remove two of the wall's glass panels, get the sofa in, and then refix them.'

'Right, I see.' Chris peered at the panels and stroked his chin. Then sat down on the sofa once more and turned his eyes back to Euan. 'Well, *that* wasn't really worth the effort, was it?' he said brightly. 'You could have got three chairs and saved everyone half a day's buggering around.'

Euan briefly remained silent and concentrated on not bursting into flames.

'This is a performance review, Chris,' he said after a time. 'How would you rate your performance over the past twelve months?'

'Compared to what?' Chris replied evasively.

'Compared to ... compared to what's acceptable.'

'What *is* acceptable?'

Euan gave a little snort. 'Well, we can say what *isn't* acceptable: your performance.'

'Isn't that a circular argument?'

Chris was conscious of how very, very difficult he was finding it to pass by any opportunity to wind Euan up. It was like trying to stop eating a bag of crisps halfway through. What particularly struck him, though, was that, superficially, it was similar to being with Trudie: he knew it was sensible to avoid making waves, but it was easier said than done. However, with Trudie he was unhappy that he was carrying Old Chris's baggage (which was the cause of the problem); he was annoyed with the stranger who was his middle-aged self for stupidly making this bed that, now, *he* had to lie in. In Euan's case, on the other hand, he felt quite an affinity for Old Chris. Anyone who got on Euan's nerves surely couldn't be *all* bad.

His boss jabbed at the keys of the computer on his desk with proactive, goal-orientated fingers.

'Right. Let's keep this simple, then,' he said. He motioned towards the monitor, though Chris couldn't see what was on it. 'Arriving late, or not at all, or arriving late, then disappearing early: too many times to list.' Euan indicated the screen again.

'Drunken behaviour; erratic behaviour; obstructive behaviour; behaviour involving the inappropriate use of foodstuffs: ditto.'

'There may have been a few misunderstandings,' Chris offered, trying to sound both penitent and cruelly wronged.

'Misunderstandings?' Euan reclined in his chair and let his head fall back so that he was gazing at the ceiling. 'You lifted Dave's – and Dave is the head of the whole south-west section, for God sake – you lifted Dave's mobile and changed his voicemail message so he appeared to be saying that thing about Emma Watson – who wasn't even sixteen at the time. The police interviewed him for *two hours*.'

Chris nodded. He wasn't familiar with who Emma Watson might be, but he guessed that he was able to grasp the gist of the matter even with this gap in his knowledge.

'July,' Euan continued, eyes still fixed above. 'I asked you to think about possible campaigns and email the Henderson Group five proposals. Number one suggested a TV makeover-show parody. Numbers two through four said, "Fuck off."' He sighed. 'Number five said, "See Number two."'

Briefly, Chris considered saying something about 'maintaining focus', but he decided against it.

'And how could we forget,' Euan said, finally dropping his head and fixing Chris with a chilly stare, 'the sound file of one of our strategy meetings being dubbed onto footage of baboons mating, and the compelling result posted on YouTube?' He stood up commandingly. 'I've hardly done justice to your vast catalogue of puerile stunts with that small, random selection, of course. Let's put them all aside, however. That way we can give full attention to the fact that the effort you put into the work we actually pay you for has been – generously – minimal. And I mean minimal even if we make allowances because your productive opportunities have to compete with the demands made on your time by not turning up, or being too drunk to do anything, or Photoshopping images of my head onto the bodies of nude, clinically obese, Eastern European women.'

Euan was on the verge of getting genuinely, openly angry. He'd missed his chance, however, as by now Chris was there already and not in the mood to allow him to take over the position.

Oddly, considering the greater age distance, Old Chris –

unconcerned and inured to it in any case – would probably not have been bothered about being talked to as though he were a six-year-old. Chris did. While *wanting* to appear chastised and repentant, he simply couldn't because the beckoning call of Pissed Off was just too alluring. Also, it seemed to him that the one thing you'd think Euan would have thrown at him – 'Your stuff is no good: it doesn't work and the clients hate it' – was conspicuous by its absence. He therefore concluded that he (that's to say, Old Chris – but he'd not be pedantic about the distinction this once) was a maverick genius. OK, he might not, in both his deeds and in his demeanour, embody any company mission statements, but he *must* be delivering the goods. If not, why hadn't this been mentioned? *If not*, how in hell did he still have a job?

Chris stood up as well. He moved to the edge of Euan's desk in two purposeful strides and planted his hands on top of it, leaning forward. Euan stiffened uneasily.

'Let's cut through the crap, Euan,' Chris snapped. 'I do the fucking job right? I may not do it how you'd like me to, but it gets done, and it gets done fucking *well*. Lose me and you'd have to scrape by with some clueless twat who adheres to all your pissy work practices, but who *can't do the work* – at least, not anywhere near as effectively as I can.' This was two thirds bluff and wild guesses, but Euan's silence and increasingly knotted expression gave Chris more confidence with every sentence that got by unchallenged. 'You hate me, and God only knows how much I hate you, but if you have one glimmer of business sense in your shitty little head, here's what you're going to do: shut the fuck up.'

'You can't—' Euan began, but he'd dropped his eyes.

'Shut up,' Chris reminded him. 'In fact, what I'm going to do, now I think about it, is take leave until the New Year. I am not going to come near this crap hole of a building again until 2007. When I come back, I might have relaxed into a new, sunny disposition, or I might have found a fresh vein of foaming resentment. But, either way, I'll continue to put money into the company's bank account by churning out the kind of bollocks clients are happy to pay for. If you think you can fire me and it won't be shooting yourself in the foot, then fire me right now. Otherwise, you have a happy Christmas, you toad-faced bag of shite.'

With more experience (the benefit of age), Chris would have

realised that absolutely no one is indispensable. People who stay at work well beyond their contracted hours – constantly fire-fighting – and who do extra stuff in their own time, and who are wearily aware that all of their colleagues are all bone idle and useless, often imagine that the whole operation would collapse if they were away for two days. But when, after perhaps a decade of frantic nerve-chewing madness (these people tend to stay wherever they are for long periods), they leave, within a fortnight it's as if they were never there. Should they walk past some weeks later, it's astonishing to them that everything seems the same – that the area isn't cordoned off by police tape or nothing but a smouldering hole in the ground. But, that's the way it goes.

Old Chris, at forty-three, might have understood this. Chris, at twenty-five, didn't. And that blazingly flawed view of reality was his salvation.

Euan had entirely lost the initiative. Chris's self-assurance had sent him rocking on his heels. Surely the man must be in a strong position to be so bold; who could be that brazen if all he had was bluff? Lazy disrespect and random pointless insubordination wouldn't have been a surprise, but mounting a coherent attack based on the work he produced, and intimations of how taking that away from Short Stick could look bad for whoever did it, *that* had come out of nowhere. Maybe Chris even knew something that he didn't. At the very least, Euan didn't want to make a snap decision and sack him in the heat of the moment. He might be left looking like he'd put his personal feelings above what was best for the company. That would do him no good at all: he had gained and kept his position because he'd proved himself free of any significant beliefs or impractical passions. His management style was direct, clear and invulnerable to emotional factors; he was thus not only solid personally, but also had a valuable dehu-manising effect on others. What would happen if there was dis-ruption and people believed it was down to his sacking Chris in a red-mist anger? He'd be tainted forever. In terms of the damage it would cause to his reputation for being reliably soulless, he might as well be seen running to the toilets crying because someone had said they didn't like his shirt.

'Get out,' Euan growled through fastened teeth.

Chris didn't move. Not in any way: he just stood there, staring back at his boss. This appeared pretty confrontational of him. Actually it was because he wasn't sure what 'Get out' meant. (But, after his *Glengarry Glen Ross* turn, he couldn't really bring himself to ask, 'Er – sorry – but "Get out" in what sense?')

Euan rounded his desk, marched over to the door and held it open. 'You damn well better be here on the dot of nine after the break,' he said.

Chris nodded. 'OK. Yeah – that seems fair.'

He ambled out of Euan's office and headed for the exit without looking back.

Motionless – wedged in his own doorway by sheer rage – Euan stood and watched him. He noticed that John, who worked in Contracts, was looking across while he did some photocopying. Chris disappeared through the double doors that led to the lifts.

'Suspended his arse,' Euan called over to John. 'He's not allowed to set *foot* in here again until January.'

19

He had three weeks.

Twenty-one days exactly, that was the limit. It was a self-imposed limit, and a tight one in which to remake an entire life, but he was determined to keep to it. When things are tough you're drawn to the timeless classics, so 'by Christmas' was the clear choice. Not having to spend at least a fortnight sitting at Short Stick devising memorably irritating adverts for discount furniture warehouses was a real boost to his preparation time, but there was still a lot do.

He began right away. On his way back to Tithe Barn Avenue he stopped at a catalogue store and bought a home gym. It was demanding – requiring that he stuck with it through sheer will-power even though his muscles shivered with exhaustion and his chest burned – but eventually he managed to get it into the car, and – he was now a *machine* – out again when he got home. The three flat packs contained weights, bars, wheels, pulleys, wires, a bag of around 250,000 nuts and bolts, and assembly instructions apparently translated from the Korean by Professor Stanley Unwin. He estimated that perhaps twenty or thirty men had died constructing the prototype – several of them probably by being catapulted into the distance like boulders from a siege engine. Yet, at a gasp after five o'clock, he stood back, flecked all over by tiny static-sticky polystyrene balls from the packaging, and admired the finished device – noting, with not a little pride, that he had completed the task and yet still had some skin on two of his knuckles.

He sat down on the padded bench with its roaring-tiger logo and pored over the included booklet of suggested exercises.

The first blow came in the opening line, before the list of available workouts had even started. In big bold letters, right at the top, it said, IF YOU ARE OVER FORTY OR NOT USED TO STRENUOUS ACTIVITY, CONSULT YOUR DOCTOR BEFORE BEGINNING TO USE THIS EQUIPMENT. There was, naturally, no way Chris was going to do any such thing.

For a start, it would be embarrassing. He was a man: he didn't want anyone to think he had the *slightest* interest in whether or not he looked like crap; looking like crap was bad, but people knowing that you *cared* about it would be humiliating beyond endurance. What was more: doctors. In a strange way, Chris's attitude to doctors placed them in a similar position to teachers. When he'd been at school, if he handed in a piece of work to a teacher his desire was for that teacher to respond with 'Yes, that's it. Well done.' That's to say, he'd delivered what the teacher wanted and they could part on good terms; like two WWI pilots – one German, one British – who'd tried really hard to kill each other but, both out of bullets, now turned back to their respective bases with manly waves of mutual respect. And, crucially, this exchange *was* what the teacher wanted: the teacher *didn't* want to be in a situation where he'd be saying to Chris 'Comprehensively awful, Mortimer. You plainly lack even the basic educational requirements of someone your age … *Excellent* – that means I get to do my job.' The dream of all teachers is to have pupils who don't require them to teach. This is so obvious that it's hardly worth mentioning. You'll no more delight a teacher by being backward than you will a street sweeper by standing in front of him extravagantly littering. What's relevant here, however, is that Chris, for who knows what reason, extended the concept to include doctors. So, apart from the very, very specific reason for the visit (for which he'd be deeply apologetic), he was always anxious to assure the doctor that he was in robust good health.

'*Any persistent headaches?*'

'*Nope.*'

'*Shortness of breath?*'

'*Nope. Absolutely fine.*'

'*Loss of appetite?*'

'*Not at all, no. No, no, no. Actually, can I move this chair back? I'm just bursting to do some star jumps.*'

But enthusiastically convincing a doctor that you have no concerns which might end up burdening him with having to treat you was next to impossible if you've turned up saying, 'I've just bought a gym. Will it probably kill me?'

Finally, as if there wasn't enough to put him off already, it is widely accepted that doctors are lookouts for the Angel of Death. They identify who is to be marked out for the next round of reapings. If you, for example, smoke eighty cigarettes a day, you'll probably be fine so long as, when your doctor asks you if you smoke, you say 'No.' You are fine, just as long as your doctor doesn't know about it – but, the second he does, he'll grass you up and you'll instantly have whatever disease you've been avoiding by sensibly keeping your head down. Confronted by a seemingly casual 'How much do you drink?' you *must* reply, 'Oh, just the odd glass – socially. Perhaps two glasses, if I've just got married or been reunited with a missing brother.' If you say anything else, then that's it: box ticked; liver failure; you'll be dead within the month.

Therefore, if he went to the doctor, he knew he'd be diagnosed as 'forty-three' – and quite possibly an acute and fiercely progressive forty-three at that. Then – *then* – using the gym really would be the end of him. Right now he was twenty-five and merely needed to remind his body of the fact. Massive, reeling, chest-clutching heart attacks were what other people had; people who were genuinely old.

CONSULT YOUR DOCTOR?

UP YOUR ARSE.

Thus, with a swift psychological swerving motion, he tsked past the health warning. Then past the warm-up, stretching exercises, which looked very dull. Anyway, the (rather pressing) goal of all this was to turn a ditch of fat into a wall of muscle, not the far lesser considerations of 'flexibility' and 'safety'; washboard abs now, being able to touch his heel with his elbow – later.

All necessary preparations carefully skipped, he arrived at the practicalities. Lying at the base of the gym were five flat metal weights. Any number of these could be attached to the pulley system to vary the strength needed to push up or pull down the bits at the other end. Each weight was marked with a number. Though, sadly, this number referred to kilograms, which was an abstract system for Chris. He'd used it in maths problems at school but it meant nothing in the real world. He had internal models of a twelve-stone man or a ten-pound turkey, but couldn't remotely feel a kilogram in his head. Still, he decided that what mattered was simply to start low and build, and so he attached only three of the five weights before lining himself up and attacking the two pec-sculpting bars before him. Instantly and as one, both of the bars failed to move. Chris got up and went to the back of the gym to check that he hadn't inadvertently left something bolted together or accidentally attached not just the three weights but also, say, Australia. Everything seemed fine. He tried the exercise again. Still nothing.

Well, he'd given it a shot. Maybe he should go and see if there was pizza in the fridge now. Selling or returning the gym wasn't remotely worth the hassle of having to dismantle the bloody thing, but perhaps he might leave it where it was and make it available for hire: people could pay for an hour working out in his spare bedroom, young women in tight leotards especially.

No! He would *not* be defeated. This was too important. He reduced the number of weights so that just two were fastened to the pulley and took up his position once more. He stretched his neck by leaning his head emphatically to one side, then to the other. This was something he'd seen muscular action heroes do in films immediately before lifting girders from the legs of trapped comrades so, though he was unfamiliar with the physiological details, he assumed it must be important. To be doubly sure, he also grimaced as he powerfully sniffed a lungful of air up his nose, and then slowly expelled it through pursed lips. (Muscular action heroes did this immediately before forcing open explosion-distorted doors that had trapped them in flooding submarine engine rooms.) Then, spiritually centred, he placed an arm on each of the bars, paused for a beat, and pushed.

This time he succeeded. With immense effort, crushingly clamped teeth and an elongated '*Chriiiiiiiiiiiiiiiiiiist!*' the bars were forced inwards for a distance of, at one point, a full four inches from their starting position.

Chris strained to move them further, but it was completely impossible – he might as well have tried to push over a cathedral. Using all his strength – right down to the very last dregs of the '*isssst!*' he could just about keep them where they were; but he decided he'd probably taken the full muscle-building benefit from doing that when, after a couple of seconds, translucent purple dots began to fill his vision.

'Gnngggh!' He gave his arms permission to surrender. The bars instantly whipped back, and the attached weights plunged down with a floor-threatening crash. A framed photograph fell off the wall. Chris, panting, looked across to where it lay on the floor; a ragged crack ran diagonally across its glass. He didn't recognise the people in the picture at all, so if its shattering at this precise moment was supposed to be ominous or ironic, he thought, then it'd completely wasted its bloody time.

He took off another weight.

This was a bit deflating, but doing it meant he managed to bring the bars together (and do so a total of ten times), which was a relief of sorts as he was already worrying that he might end up having to utilise the gym by simply raising its receipt over his head, possibly after first removing the physically demanding staple from the top of it. On a roll now, he tried some sit-ups. He hit five feeling he had more in him – maybe as many as two more – but contracting his stomach had made him feel as sick as a dog so he stopped; concluding that the better part of valour was not puking into his own crotch.

He was soaked in sweat by this point, but might yet have attempted a bench press or three had not the bedroom door opened and Trudie walked in. He hadn't heard her come home; he supposed that this was because the noise of it had been drowned by blood throbbing against his eardrums, air rattling through his lungs and the thin but persistent wail coming from the ghost of his stamina.

She glanced at him, then took a long, slow look over the gym. It was excruciating. He honestly felt that he'd have been far more comfortable if she'd discovered him lost in riotous onanism; there would have been at least a salvaging audacity in kneeling there, trousers around his ankles, howling like a coyote in front of scattered copies of *Amateur Photographer*. There was nothing except prickly embarrassment in being caught exercising. A hot wash of shame set his skin burning and in its sticky humiliation he felt, for the first time, forty-three.

'What's all this about?' she asked.

Chris, in defensive meltdown, spat out an irritated sigh. He found Trudie's standpoint unnecessarily and unpleasantly probing: it was almost sadistic with relevance. She hadn't pointedly asked how much the gym had cost, or begun to moan that the spare bedroom had been lost to an immovable and ugly pile of metal. These were practical matters he could have met without any loss of dignity, even if, ultimately, he was shown to be spendthrift and insufficiently mindful of hoovering considerations. What she'd done with her 'What's all this about?' was to imply that it wasn't a piece of exercise apparatus but rather a big, die-cast symptom of some psychological situation he had going on, and she expected the nature of *that* to be laid out for her.

He'd known he couldn't hide the gym from Trudie, of course, but he'd hugged the delusion that she'd simply complain it would mark the carpet or some such thing. Insisting he fit protective pads to the gym's feet would have been fair enough – after all, they were, theoretically, husband and wife and sharing a house together. Demanding he expose his personal motivations, however, was unacceptable – it was practically a form of abuse. His psyche was his own business, yet the assumption seemed to be that access to it must be open; that it was community property. Nevertheless, at the same time he felt awkward, almost *guilty* – as though clinging to this basic human right put him on the wrong side of the law. Another first now soaked through him: he felt married.

'You have eyes, don't you?' he snapped. 'What does it *seem* like I'm doing?'

'It *seems* like you're going for a new look,' Trudie replied. 'Except,' she added, 'I didn't know that angina chic was in this year.'

Chris knew it was silly to dismiss this criticism, he felt as though someone were trying to inflate his head with a foot pump – God knows what he looked like from the outside.

'I was doing a bit of cardiovascular,' he lied. 'I'm actually *improving* my heart.'

'Not by hurling yourself right at a gym you're not. People need to move up to weight training gradually.'

(Fff. Like he had time for 'gradually'.)

'Oh yeah?' Chris sneered. 'By starting where?'

'In your condition? Well, I'd say by starting with a little light origami.'

'Bollocks. I know what I'm doing. In fact,' he replied, making the decision in the same instant that he spoke the words, 'I'm going to begin jogging too.'

'Ah – a three-step programme: weights; running; autopsy. You've obviously thought this through.'

'What's your problem? Why on earth does it bother you if I start, um . . . training.'

'It bothers me because I don't want you killing yourself.'

Chris found this unexpectedly touching.

He shrugged dismissively.

'And it bothers me,' Trudie continued, 'because I wonder why you've decided to start now. Is this just a latecomer to your existing mid-life crisis, or is there a specific reason?'

'I am *not* having a mid-life crisis.'

'You're forty-three years old and you've spontaneously bought a gym.'

That was *totally* unfair. Chris recalled what Andrew had said about men getting pilloried in middle age almost as a matter of course. Could you not do *anything* at forty-three without it being classified as a sign of an MLC? You've always wanted that sports car, and you find that now you can afford it, so – why not? – you buy one. Mid-life crisis. You change your haircut. Mid-life crisis. You smile at the dental hygienist. Mid-life crisis. Either you quietly decay, an amusingly pathetic old codger waiting for your slippers and cardigan to arrive, or you do something a bit different for a change – MLC.

'Lots of people buy gyms,' Chris countered angrily.

'OK, to be honest, your buying it isn't quite as bad as your actually *using* it,' Trudie admitted. 'You remember when you spent one hundred and fifty pounds on those running shoes downstairs?'

'The trainers?'

'Yes, the trainers.'

Chris didn't remember this, obviously. In fact, he filed it away as evidence to support his case that he wasn't Old Chris with amnesia. He might have forgotten moving to this house, getting married and the collapse of the Soviet Union, but how he could *ever* forget spending one hundred and fifty pounds on a *pair of trainers* was beyond all credible explanation.

'Those worried me briefly,' Trudie went on, 'but I soon saw that getting them was just another of your temporary lapses into some zealous fantasy or other; it was plain that you weren't going to bother any paramedics by genuinely attempting to jog anywhere in the things. You pulled back from that brink; looking at the state of you now, you've obviously base-jumped right off the edge of this one.'

Chris didn't reply. He faced away from her and examined the pulleys with his fingers; silently; unconcerned; driving home the point that he was not going to reply.

'Well?' Trudie asked insistently.

'I don't want to talk about it.'

'I do.'

'You're out of luck, then.'

Trudie shook her head sadly. 'You never change, do you?'

Chris allowed himself a dry laugh. You'd need a slide rule to design an irony like that; its faultlessly precise wrongness reminded him of the story that Charlie Chaplin had once entered a Charlie Chaplin lookalike competition and come third.

'Well,' Trudie said with a shrug, 'if you're committed to killing yourself, you might at least put on some other clothes in future. Keep your good trousers for work, and in case we decide on an open coffin.'

'Actually, I'm not going in to Short Stick again until the New Year.'

'They'll sack you.'

'No, they won't. It was something that came out of my performance review today.'

'Oh my God.' Trudie put a hand to her cheek. 'What did you do? If it was the mayonnaise thing again then—'

'I didn't do anything – much. Euan and I simply sat down together and agreed that *I* could have an extended break, and that *he* could go fuck himself. It was a fair exchange.'

Trudie's expression upped its worry content several degrees. She looked around at the walls, and Chris sensed that she was probably calculating how long it would be before some people from the bank arrived to take them away.

'Honestly,' he said, 'it's fine.'

He was conscious, and his anger faltered badly because of it, that he did *want* to reassure her.

He felt he'd have preferred to always do that, in fact, instead of bitterly fighting his corner – there was genuine pleasure and fulfilment in it. The trouble was, you can do it only from a position of respect; you need to feel your reassurances will be taken seriously. If it seems like someone has faith in you, Chris thought, then you'll more than happily take on the role of a person who is being looked (up) to for support; whereas, if they appear to be doing nothing but saying you're crap, your reaction is going to be 'No, *you're* crap.' Why say anything else? They're not going to accept it anyway.

Trudie perfectly proved Chris's thesis by replying, 'You think everything's fine when you're pissed. You were probably too out of it to realise that you were being handed stage one of a sacking,' thereby moving him, in two sentences, from gently conciliatory to completely *furious*.

'I was not bloody drunk! *Christ.*'

As it happened, he had examined his lack of drunkenness previously, and with surprise. Old Chris – Chris had come to understand merely by its being brought up constantly – spent most of his time either drunk or working towards being drunk or suffering from having been drunk shortly before. As he'd been landed with Old Chris's body, it was reasonable to assume that it would pester him for the alcohol it expected, just as it loudly complained about being subjected to the exercise it didn't. Yet he had no inclination to unscrew a cap or peel back a ring-pull. He'd had a few drinks at the pub with Andrew, but nothing excessive, and no more (less, almost certainly) that anyone would have done had they been faced with his particular mind-rattling calamity. That aside – nothing. He had no cravings. The off-licence didn't call to him seductively. You could, with absolute safety, have left him alone in a room with a bottle of Diamond White. That was curious. Extraordinary really. He paraphrased his musings on this bizarre phenomenon for Trudie:

'Fuck off.'

Trudie rolled her eyes – as though this was an angry denial she'd heard so often that it was now tragically funny.

'I wasn't,' Chris repeated vehemently. 'Actually, I haven't been drunk for . . .' He wanted to say 'eighteen years' but caught himself and substituted the more narrowly accurate 'three days'. (This lessened the persuasive impact somewhat.)

'Wow. Three days,' Trudie replied. 'I didn't realise you'd converted to Islam. Carry on like this and you could end up at . . .' She widened her eyes incredulously. 'At . . . Wednesday.'

Chris boiled with indignation and resolved there and then that he would never have another drink – *ever*. Just to make her look stupid. The human spirit is a powerful, powerful thing, and there's very little that it can't achieve, if it's out of spite.

'I'm busy,' he said tersely. He lay down on the gym's bench, attempted to push up some handles, was told very forcefully by his shoulder muscles that he should reconsider, and so feigned that he was simply trying to align himself correctly. 'Don't you have some knitting to do or something?'

This was a cruel stab at her age. He was disappointed with himself for saying it. But she replied 'Knitting?' clearly having no idea what he might mean; and he was then also disappointed that the stab had utterly missed. It was fitting, though. The details might vary, he thought, but that was an essentially sufficient description of his life, right there: caught between conflicting disappointments.

But he would change that. *He* would change it – by taking action, by his *decision* to take action. It had started already. Each sit-up had been a palpable declaration of his determination to take control. And, you know, he'd done five of them. That was quite good, really. He must remember that the totals sounded lots better if you thought of them as declarations.

'Knitting?'

He'd almost forgotten she was there. 'Or something. Go and do . . . whatever it is that you do.'

Andrew had checked his mobile every few minutes all day. Each time he was sure he'd find it displaying either the new message notification or the missed call alert. It was quite plausible that he'd not have heard something arrive. His phone used to have a tone that, like one of Chris's adverts, was so grating and shrill that it always got your attention, but he'd recently changed the setting to one that made no sound – only a discreet vibration. However, every impatient examination had revealed that the contact he wanted and dreaded in equal measure hadn't been attempted.

The kind of people who set chat-show psychics rubbing their hands with glee will say that, if you suddenly find yourself wondering what someone is doing, the phone will ring and there they'll be. This is twaddle. What *is* true, however, is that if a person doesn't phone you, then my *word* do you wonder what they're doing. In fact, 'wonder' isn't the term; you construct lengthy, detailed, and relentlessly appalling scenarios to torment yourself with your own version of what they are doing.

Andrew wasn't going to do the ringing himself. That, he felt, would have looked a bit sad and desperate. And anyway, the urge to know and the fear of knowing collided, producing a stymieing, fidgety inertia.

Nevertheless, though his imagination was positively lousy with him, Andrew was surprised to see Chris when he opened his front door at a little after ten p.m.

Chris was sweating and breathless.

'What ... Are you OK?' Andrew asked.

Chris, steadying himself against the wall, nodded and waved the question away with his hand. 'Ye ... ssss ... I'm fine ...' He coughed. It sounded like someone hammering a jellyfish into gravel. 'I ... jo ... jo ... jogged here.'

'You *jogged* here?' Andrew tried to estimate how many miles that was.

Chris nodded again, then flicked his head sideways to indicate his car, which was parked about seventy yards down the road.

Andrew looked at it, and then back to Chris.

'You *jogged* here?' He slapped his own forehead. 'Are you mad?'

'No.' Chris straightened up defiantly. Briefly. Before wobbling away to the right until he collided heavily with the dustbin. 'Though,' he allowed, shrugging, 'I am slightly light-headed.'

Andrew led him through the house and into the conservatory at the rear. On the way, Chris popped his head round the living-room door and dripped a little sweat onto the floor from the tip of his nose while he said 'Hi' to Gill. She was knitting.

'I'll get you a drink,' Andrew said as Chris flopped down on a wicker sun chair. It had a floral-patterned, stuffed-cotton cover; orange. There was another one and a matching two-person sofa nearby. It was the kind of thing that only your wife would buy.

'Thanks,' Chris replied. Then quickly added, 'Water.'

Andrew peered at him anxiously for a second, but didn't reply. He returned a short time later with a bottle of Strathmore, a glass, and two cans of lager.

Chris took a drink from the bottle, exhaled lengthily and then said, 'I decided to come round instead of phoning. Phones aren't . . . Well – take last night.'

'Yes,' Andrew replied coolly.

'So, I thought— Oh, it's not too late, is it? Were you about to go to bed?'

'No. No.' Andrew shook his head insistently. 'It's fine. Stay as long as you like. Anyway: exceptional circumstances, and all that.'

'Great.' Chris smiled. He took another swig of water, relaxed, and glanced around as though getting his bearings. 'These covers are shit, aren't they?'

'Gill—'

'Yeah, so the thing is, I wanted to ask about Neil.'

Andrew hadn't mentioned Neil at all. He'd expected Chris to bring him up; actually, he'd almost had private fun with it. Deliberately saying nothing to see how long it was before Chris asked. That he hadn't until now was, Andrew thought quite surprising, but he supposed that with everything else that was going on it was understandable. Guiltily pleasing, even. The dizzying, in-his-face, immediately pressing matters of an unknown wife, mislaying nearly two decades and so on had obviously eclipsed his oh-so-perfect hero for a time.

'Neil?' Andrew said, his eyes childlike with innocent incomprehension.

'Yes – Neil. What's he up to now?'

'Ahh.'

'Is he still with Michelle?'

Andrew opened a lager and drank slowly before placing the can down on the glass-topped, wicker-legged table to his left. He adjusted its position carefully, minutely and pointlessly.

'No,' he replied finally. 'No, he's not.' He adjusted the can again. 'Oh, well, I suppose—'

'Michelle's dead.'

20

In common with most women, Trudie had lost her virginity twice.

The first time was when she was seventeen. Mark Sanderson. It was clumsy, unsatisfying, and over while she'd still got one leg in her knickers – if brevity is the soul of wit, then the Mark Sanderson Experience was like being shagged by Noël Coward. More mundanely, as displays of 'knowing how to please a woman sexually' go, it was like, well – like being shagged by Noël Coward.

This wasn't all Mark Sanderson's fault, really. Teenage boys are generally as thin as bamboo canes despite eating fatty, sugary, or fatty-and-sugary food almost constantly because of the *fantastical* amount of energy they use up straining to keep themselves from ejaculating from one moment to the next. Girls famously do better at school than boys, of course. This is mostly because boys' brains have to divide their attention, and unequally, between doing lessons and controlling insistent testicles. It's an especially cruel paradox that the mental tenacity required to hold back a climax for an entire double period interferes with a teenage boy's ability to learn maths, but then he'll be advised to do mental maths problems during sex as a means of holding back his climax.

So, in fairness, with Trudie Whittaker lying on a bed at a party (atop a very worried pile of dry-clean-only coats) – wanton from Strongbow, with her blouse undone and her A-line skirt hoisted up over her hips – it was commendable that he got as far as he did. It's frankly a miracle that he didn't reach the finish line two days earlier, while buying condoms in the chemist's.

But, for Trudie, this fumbling, disappointing, blink of an event was so far from how she'd dreamed her ascent into womanhood would be that 'it didn't count'.

Women retain the ability to conclude, and fully believe, that a particular sexual encounter 'doesn't count' throughout their lives.

Superficially, men might seem to take a similar view, given their penchant for a defensive 'It meant nothing to me', should the need arise. But it's not the same. For men, they all count.

It was nearly six months later that (piffling factual details aside) she actually lost her virginity. This time might not have been flawlessly perfect either, but it was sufficient. The floor wasn't throbbing to the pulse of 'In The Navy'. No one was being sick in the lavatory next door. There was incense and dry white wine. Jim Edwards was a worldly nineteen. And, crucially, her expectations were lower.

Trudie had been thinking about sex a lot lately. Not salacious thoughts. Well, sometimes salacious thoughts. OK, pretty often salacious thoughts – but they weren't the motivation. She didn't sit down with the intention of diving into a lurid fantasy or reliving an even more lurid memory (Trudie's memories tended to out-porn her fantasies; a fact that filled her with shame and approval). She would set off into her imagination to consider the *meaning* of sex – what it was and how it affected the things around it. She was moved by a desire to understand its nature, not to entertain herself with its mechanics. It was just that during this broadly ontological journey she did fairly frequently decide that she ought to pop in and say 'Hi' to less philosophical points as she was in the area.

The issue that occupied her was, How important is sex? This simple query rapidly branched off in many complicated directions, however. It was also a question that tricked the unwary into a glib, lazy answer. It affected a slack-jawed, guileless, childish look to lure self-consciously intelligent people into a haughty 'Oh, it's not that important, really' and, from there, straight on into their stammering, qualifying, contradiction-ridden doom. For example, what was the difference between friendship and love? Sex. No other criterion could withstand analysis. Everything else was a variable. The only thing that always held was that, with a boyfriend or husband, sex was (sometimes literally – Trudie was prone to take a detour into memories here) on the table.

Love, then, was *defined* by sex: without a sexual component, romance wasn't romance but just a platonic connection – a different thing entirely. Already 'It's not that important, really' was starting to mumble and hedge. Marching on, Trudie asked herself what happened if sex, and even the realistic expectation of sex, with your partner stopped? Did that mean you were no longer a couple, but merely two people whose clothes regularly shared a washing machine? Could a marriage still justify the name when its key features were reduced to nothing more than proximity, habit, and Daz?

And the complexity of the sex question didn't peak there. Suppose someone was in a relationship from which the sex had disappeared and they then had sex with someone else – but the reason for doing that, they deeply suspected, was to fill in the intimacy gap; it was precisely the sexless distance *here* that provoked the sexual contact *there*. In that case, surely, it was almost palliative. You take an aspirin for a headache, yet it's not really *for* a headache; it's to alleviate a headache. Comforting as it is, it's not done to serve the headache or out of an affection for aspirin, it's done for your head, which you actually, genuinely wish was in its former unmarred-by-headaches state. Your head is still your main concern and the cause of your (re)actions. Superficially, you take an aspirin for a headache, but fundamentally it's because you love your head. The reasoning was impeccable ... but somehow Trudie simply couldn't warm to it.

She thought Chris was intending to sleep with someone else.

Trudie cast aside the metaphors here. Metaphors had their place, but when it came to Chris she felt inclined to go down the literal path: he wanted to fuck some other woman in a dirty, pounding collision of throbbing genitals. The baseness of it clawed at her. And she imagined it, in detail, as basely as she possibly could. (She was not about to wound herself by halves.) Who he might be intending to fuck – wildly, animally, while the filthy bitch squealed and urged him on with shouted obscenities – she couldn't say. It was hard to picture any of the perky young women at Short Stick scheming to herself, 'Cor. As soon as they wake him up and drag him off the floor in the toilets – he's *mine*.' Nevertheless, you can't watch bitter dissatisfaction, sullen indifference, and the purchase of a home gym and conclude anything else. Even the most generous observer, in those circumstances, would have to put two and two together and see that it equalled the intention to shag a giggling knickerless slapper against the bins behind a kebab shop.

It made Trudie angry – physically shaking angry. She was

astounded and sickened by the level that Chris and this woman descended to in her imagination.

Sex? 'It's not that important, really'? Only enough to lift fondness to love, or to induce – by the very thought of it – spasms of clenching rage.

And what piled on the hurt when she pictured the perverse, scamy, technically illegal acts Chris was performing with this empty-headed tart was that *she* would have happily done them with him, if he'd only have cared about her enough to go there. And done them better too. She had the capacity to be three times as filthy as any uninspired, bowling-alley slut, *and* she could make a bloody mushroom linguine as well. Going off with a tit-monster (she saw the woman as having huge unruly breasts, for some reason) when he had a wife who was good with the domestic finances, was able to talk intelligently about everything from Camus to penal reform and – potentially – was capable of scaling heights of creative obscenity that would have turned Henry Miller's cheeks ashen? That was a smack in the face.

Trudie sniffed the air.

Crap. She'd forgotten she had those sausages under the grill.

She ran into the kitchen and hurled the crackling pan – shrivelled sticks of charcoal now virtually melted into its metal – into the sink. Her hand whipped at the tap; the water hitting the grill produced a vast explosion of steam that filled the room in a third of a second (she half expected it to clear to reveal a magician's assistant – *Voila!* – standing on the draining board). Then she immediately raced upstairs and, balancing precariously on a chair, tried to prise the battery from the piercingly keening smoke alarm.

Trudie had been thinking about sex a lot lately.

'Dead?'

'Yeah.'

'In what way?'

'How many ways are there?'

'You mean ... *dead.*'

'Yes, like that.'

Chris wiped his face. The sweat that still covered it had cooled into a slightly sticky film now and, as his hand rubbed across his eyes, the salt stung them. 'Christ.'

Andrew nodded. He wasn't flippant, but he did adopt nothing above a mild, comfortable level of solemnity. Death might shock Chris, but he, Andrew, was a grown man – forged and hardened in the fires of eighteen years of real life. These things didn't faze him any more.

'When?' Chris asked. 'I was talking to her just a—' He stopped himself.

'Well caught. Unless you're Derek Acorah you'll get locked up if you start saying you talked to Michelle a few days ago.'

'Who's Derek Acorah?'

'One of those so-called mediums. He's been given his own TV show.'

'You could have said Doris Stokes – then I'd have known what you were on about.'

'Doris Stokes is dead. And hasn't said a word since she passed over, curiously.'

'Why didn't you tell me about Michelle earlier?'

'It didn't occur to me to. It was terrible at the time, obviously, but that was ages ago. It wasn't in the forefront of my mind – why would it be? Your mate turns up – mental – rambling about having come here by falling straight through a hole in the eighties and not knowing the most basic facts of his current life. I try to put you on the rails as best I can, as quickly as I can, so you don't make the situation worse. Emergency first aid. No wonder I didn't think to tell you about Michelle. It would have been weird if it *had* come to mind, actually. "Ah, Chris, you're having a psychotic episode ... Now, let me mention someone I haven't even thought about for around fifteen years." Fair enough?'

Chris gave a reluctant nod. 'I suppose,' he said, turning his bottle of water around in his hands. 'So, she's been dead for fifteen years?'

'Longer, now I come to think about it. It must have been '91. Or even 1990. Yes, I think it was 1990.'

'God.' Chris gasped. 'That's not all that long after I left and woke up here.'

'Precisely. I remember we said, "Chris was sucked into that time vortex, and now Michelle's been killed. It's just one thing after another, isn't it?"' Andrew rolled his eyes. 'You didn't leave. You were there; you were most *definitely* there.'

'Killed?'

'What?'

'You said Michelle was "killed". Not she "died", but that she was "killed".'

Chris was having trouble dealing with this.

Finding out that – 'Oh, by the way' – Michelle had died was shock enough on its own, but his head swam with the confusion of possibilities that his *knowing* she'd died threw up. If he got back to his own time (and, in every film he could remember, people always did), what was he to do with this information? Naturally, he'd want to warn her. She'd think he was insane. That didn't matter; he'd be happy for her to think that, if it saved her life. But, if he saved her life, she wouldn't die, so he couldn't know about her death in the 'future' and so return – armed with the information – to prevent it, so she would die. And round and round and round. On the other hand, say you *could* change the future by bringing back knowledge from a *possible version* of it. This would almost certainly lead (again, in every film Chris could remember) to repercussions thousands of times more dreadful than the one you'd prevented. It was like a Law of Time, or something. His saving Michelle – via an incalculably intricate rippling outward of variations flowing from it – could lead to Italy being destroyed by killer moths. Could he *ever* make a decision when such things might rest on his choice?

Well, actually, yes. Bollocks to Italy.

He'd feel a bit guilty, but it wasn't as though he'd asked to be put in the position in the first place. Also, no one else would know that it was his fault. That would save a lot of hassle.

'Oh, I see what you mean,' Andrew replied. 'It's just what people say: so and so was "killed" in a car crash. I wasn't implying she was "killed", by someone.'

'Right. Yes, I see.'

'Though ...'

'Jesus – *what?*'

'No.' Andrew shook his head. 'Maybe it's best forgotten. It's the one thing it's good that you don't remember, probably. Let's leave it alone.'

'You can't *really* expect me to leave it alone now you've said that, can you?'

'You could try.'

'True. OK, I've tried – now tell me, you bastard.'

Andrew paused for a mouthful of lager. 'Well, you always had a bit of thing for Michelle, which—'

'No I didn't.'

'Yes, you did. Everyone knew that. Even Neil knew it – which wasn't a problem. At least until she died' – Andrew looked mournfully into infinity – 'and then it couldn't have helped.'

'Are you enjoying this? Because you shouldn't. Having fun by being oh-so-cryptic is a bad move now I've got some oxygen in my blood. Trust me. A man who's just run for the first time since he was sixteen *really* isn't someone you should mess with.'

'Calm down, mate.'

'Tell me what bleeding happened, will you?'

'OK, OK. But remember that I didn't want to. You made me say it and—'

'I am holding a bottle. Do you *see* this bottle?'

'OK, *OK*.' Andrew took up a storytelling position in his chair. 'Michelle was killed in a car accident. Night. Rain. The car left the road. It must have been going a fair clip at the time too; it was totalled. The thing is, Neil was driving. And he'd had a drink.'

'He was pissed? You're kidding? That doesn't sound like Neil. Not driving when he was pissed.'

'No, he wasn't drunk. Neil's perfect, naturally. He was sober ... technically. Below the legal limit. But he *had* downed a lager or two. I reckon he blamed himself. Unfairly, perhaps – though, as I say, he *had* had a drink ... Anyway, the point is that *you* blamed him. I don't want to dissect your psychology, obviously, but it could have been that you overreacted. You know – backlash. Happens when people are shown that their heroes have feet of clay.'

'He wasn't my h—'

'It got pretty ugly. You just kept on picking at it. You never came right out with an explicit accusation; it was low-level, but it was relentless. For a time it looked like you'd *never* let it go ...' Andrew paused and took another sip from his can. 'But fortunately Neil had some kind of breakdown and moved up north.'

'A *breakdown?*'

'Well, not an actual breakdown, I suppose. Though he *did* move up north.'

'When was this?'

'Like I said, '91, I think. Certainly in the early nineties.'

'And that was that? He disappeared, never to be heard of again?'

'Oh no. He and I still exchange perfunctory Christmas cards.'

'Nothing else. You don't meet up ever?'

'Nope. I haven't seen him for God knows how long. Just the Christmas cards – and, really, Gill takes care of all the Christmas cards: sends ours out from a master list she's created, and hangs the ones that come in up along the wall on little washing lines. I bet it won't be long now before she sets aside a whole evening to do this year's mailout, in fact.'

'Do I exchange cards with him?'

'I don't know. Doubt it.'

'Could you give me his address?'

'Why?'

'It might be good to look him up. Pop by for a visit.'

'Pop? It's a bit far for a pop. And, that aside, do you think it's a good idea?'

'Yeah.' Chris did. This was better than he'd hoped, in fact. Well, the Michelle part of it was superlatively awful, but otherwise it was a gift. Anyway, he couldn't quite accept that she was dead. She might be dead *here*, but where he belonged she was still very much alive. She was alive at this moment, eighteen years ago – though three days older than when he last saw her: it was just that he wasn't around because he was in the future 'now' not the past 'now'. Yes, that made sense.

Andrew scratched his ear. 'But you had an unpleasant falling-out and you haven't spoken to him for about seventeen years.'

'Old Chris fell out with him, not me – and I spoke to him on Friday. I told him he was an utter bastard.' Andrew peered at him. Chris shrugged. 'He fluked a yellow.'

'Oh, I see, that's all right then. If I'd known all the facts . . .'

'I could spend a day or two staying up wherever he is. See how it goes.'

Andrew didn't like the idea of Chris going to visit Neil. It spat out a pang of something. Not quite worry or jealousy, but something. Yet it would have its benefits. For one, Chris'd be where he wouldn't cause any serious damage. He could behave as insanely as he fancied and it'd be safely quarantined in the north. Also ... Yes, there were benefits to his going away for a few days.

'Whatever you think,' Andrew replied. 'Maybe it'll do you good to take a break from the pressure of not remembering anything. That lack of stress might even, in itself, help to bring your memory back.'

Before Chris left, Andrew had Gill dig out her Christmas-card list. It comprised page after page in a small, spiral-bound notepad, and Chris sensed that she had special feelings for it. She treated it with an anxious affection, as though it were a parchment containing a family tree she was painstakingly compiling. Though it turned out that what she was doing was almost the reverse of that.

'It doesn't grow nowadays,' she said, smiling broadly as usual but with a hint of melancholy somewhere in there. 'Time was when I was forever having to remember to add new people. But it reaches a peak, doesn't it? You get to a place where you don't gather additions like you used to: you've got a lifeful of friends, relatives and acquaintances, and your lives aren't changing any more; so neither does the list. Yes ... And then ...' She indicated a few entries that had lines drawn through them. Not alterations of address: just lines crossing them out entirely. 'Dead uncles, mostly,' she explained. 'Uncles are the first to go, but that's bound to be only the start. The lines are taking over from the additions now.'

Chris found himself liking Gill, which came as a surprise to him.

'I'm being silly,' she said, changing to fully cheerful again a little too quickly. 'Here we are. Neil. Lincolnshire. I'll write it down for you.'

'Thanks,' Chris replied gratefully. Before he knew it, he'd started to reach out to give her arm a squeeze. Suddenly aware that this didn't seem appropriate – it was only the second time he'd met the woman – his brain leapt in to make a save. Some supportive gesture still felt in order, however, so – as his fingers were sweeping upwards anyway – he imperceptibly revised the movement. It didn't stop at her shoulder but instead continued past it. Up to the point where he placed his hand on top of her head, and ruffled her hair.

In retrospect, the arm squeeze would probably have been the better choice.

Gill, Chris and Andrew stood there for a few moments of static awkwardness, then Gill said, 'Paper!'

'Yes!' said Chris. 'Great.'

That was almost everything, Chris told himself with satisfaction as he drove home. It had been a good day. On top of what he'd already gathered, he'd managed to add three uninterrupted weeks and Neil as a waiting alibi.

All he really needed now was some Immac.

21

When he woke up, Chris's first thought was that he'd contracted tetanus.

Trudie had already left for work. He hadn't noticed her get up, which, when he thought about it later, struck him as something he wouldn't have expected. It suggested a level of ease about being in bed with her that wasn't logical after so short an acquaintance. Perhaps, he concluded, it was down to three factors.

One was that he'd decided it was best not to have sex with her; it was too fraught with scary variables – and, in any case, her prickly manner didn't suggest that she was exactly longing for him to hoist up her nightie and smear her in Nivea. She probably didn't even think about sex any more. Anyway, the important thing was that not fretting about whether – and, if he did, *how* – to have sex with Trudie was a weight off his mind. A second factor was that he was pleasantly snug during the night as (temporarily, just until he became acclimatised) he was wearing pyjamas. The third factor was that he was tired from all the lifting and running.

Last night his muscles had ached. This morning they had petrified. It was unreal – his soft tissue had hardened while he slept. He hadn't even been aware of his tendons before, now every one in his body was speaking to him: they were all saying, 'No.' This was unlike anything he'd previously experienced. He hadn't been on very familiar terms with intense physical activity, but he could recall, say, painting the ceiling of his flat and feeling a bit sore the next day. *Sore*. Not fossilised.

He levered himself up from the bed and, arms and legs rigid, tottered about like the Tin Man. He knew he needed to stretch, but it was a slow, painful process steeped in groans. The only thing that kept him at it – teasing out his ligaments a millimetre at a time – was the belief that, at forty-three, he'd surely have given up. But he *wasn't* forty-three – he was twenty-five, and so he wasn't going to stand for it. It was unacceptable.

After about thirty minutes of bitter combat with his own limbs the situation did improve. Little by little, his muscles regained some of their flexibility until he was finally able to move them freely enough to discover how much moving them hurt.

Flushed with this victory, he immediately went into the next room and did twenty minutes on the gym. His deltoids needed to be shown who was the boss. It wasn't just a determination to get himself into non-appalling shape now. He was Chris Mortimer, and the one thing he would never stop doing was anything he was being pressured to stop doing. Whether it was the bullying nature of blindly accepted social norms, Euan, or bits of his own body attempting to coerce him with threats and punishments didn't make any difference.

Courage may sometimes falter, but bloody-mindedness never blinks.

Chris hadn't been able to find what he needed in the house. He'd checked the bathroom again before leaving, but it was no use. Perhaps it was there, but it wasn't worth the time and annoyance of looking further. There was a cabinet so full with stuff that every time he opened it things fell out into the sink. There was also a small set of drawers simply *rammed* with bottles, tubes, sachets and odd-looking implements. Trudie could probably locate particular items in the apparently random, spilling chaos of medicines and cosmetics, but it was like Amazonian natives being able to lay their hands on food where anyone else would starve to death – it took years of experience and a faintly eerie connection to the landscape. Looking into the bathroom cabinet Chris knew that his plane had gone down, and there weren't even any other passengers to eat. Anyway, long term, it would have seemed unsatisfactory, and a bit creepy, to have borrowed Trudie's even if he could have found it. He was a man. He should have his own depilatory cream.

A quick visit to the chemist down the road tooled him up. It was simple, and would have been free from embarrassment too, had he not – having paid for and been handed the bag containing the shameful lotion – said, 'It's for my wife.'

'Of course,' replied the assistant.

He would never be able to go back there.

Chris may not have previously had any *specific* plans for his life, but he was still almost positive that, had you asked him where he saw himself being at the end of 2006, he wouldn't have replied 'In someone else's bathroom, daubing myself with Veet.'

He felt it had to be done, though. The previous afternoon, having been on the gym for a second session of an hour and half (cross-training: thirty minutes of pumping iron, interspersed with another sixty minutes of trying to catch his breath), he'd gone into the bathroom to inspect himself for abs. It wasn't encouraging. Every major muscle group was a no-show; in fact, the only thing that *was* bulging and taut were the veins on his forehead. But, worse still, a detailed examination had revealed hairs. Hairs in the most fearful places.

They peeked out of his nostrils, and had begun candy-flossing in his ears and – as isolated settlers – dotted his shoulders and back. The situation wasn't severe enough to send him fleeing to live out his days playing an organ in some catacombs (only the odd, errant follicle had activated on his body, and his ears and nose would probably have escaped the notice of any more casual observer). But, still – *Christ.* Something had to be done.

When, aged fifteen, his first proper girlfriend had cruelly dumped him while he still had so much left to give and so much left to feel up, he'd been distraught. Adolescent hormones crashing on the sharp rocks of real life had produced weeks and months of almost unbearable suffering. During all that terrible time, however, he hadn't shed as many tears as he did in the five minutes he'd spent leaning to within six inches of the bathroom mirror with a pair of tweezers up his nose.

The ears had seemed less painful, but he conceded that he might simply have been slightly hysterical by that point. And it wasn't that they were any walk in the park either, it was merely that tearing hair from inside his ears had the saving grace that he was able to think, Well, at least I'm not tearing these hairs from inside my nostrils.

He'd had to stop there, however (you know, before he got a taste for it), because the remaining sets of abominable hairs were cunning enough to have situated themselves on areas of his back where he couldn't pluck – or, as an emergency measure, shave – the things without dislocating his shoulders. A system of mirrors could target them, but they remained out of range to anyone who hadn't been training for a Chinese circus since they were four. Cream was the only solution.

As he stood there naked now, gratefully waiting for the chemical soup to seep into his pores so as to eat away the roots under his skin, he lamented the sweeping power of Hair. It was pervasive; it was pitiless; it was capricious; it was the Spanish Inquisition of middle age.

For decades an abused servant, in this period of life it rose up in revolt and conducted a reign of terror. It occupied innocent, defenceless lands like a malicious army. And Chris knew that an icy *lebensraum* policy wasn't all there was to it. Also (the attack of Hair was many-pronged), he was greying. Not as much as Andrew, but the patches were clearly visible around his temples. Perhaps it could have been labelled 'distinguished', but that didn't help much. He didn't want to be seen as 'distinguished'; he wasn't anywhere near finished being 'unpredictable' and 'thrusting', dammit.

Worst of all was the chilling spectre of baldness. Old Chris's body hadn't stricken him with that particular horror, but he did notice some ominous thinning: more of his scalp was shining in the gaps between follicles than would ever allow him another day of unblemished happiness. He quite literally didn't know how he'd be able to cope with the top of his head being exposed: glassily, publicly, betrayingly nude. It was worse than anything he could imagine. It's said that testosterone is the cause of hair loss in male pattern baldness. Which suggests that you might be able to overcome it with massive doses of oestrogen. He certainly couldn't recall ever seeing a bald transsexual. God. Was the sole way to escape baldness one that meant also growing breasts? He was alarmed that this might be the only solution ... but less alarmed than by realising that, if it *was* the only solution, it wouldn't be an easy decision to make.

Middle age was such an unremitting struggle against overwhelming odds. It was almost more than he could bear to cope with at *his* age. Lord only knew how people in their forties managed to deal with it.

But he would stay strong. He *had* to. He must put the temptation to give in to despair aside because one thing, and that thing alone, demanded all his energy, attention and unshakeable commitment. Three weeks.

22

'Have you done the Christmas shopping?'

Trudie looked up at Chris from the sofa, where – her legs curled half under her bottom – she was sitting in a nest formed from the various sections of the Saturday newspaper.

He stood in the living-room doorway, flushed, sweating and out of breath – but smiling despite that, perhaps even because of it. He definitely exhibited the symptoms of exercise now rather than their exhibiting him. Looking at him, she thought, He seems to be enjoying himself. Whereas, when he'd staggered in – flushed, sweating and out of breath – after his first proper run about a fortnight ago, she'd looked at him and thought, Cardiogenic shock.

This morning he, well ... he glowed. Trudie found herself wondering if he was pregnant.

'The Christmas shopping? Why?' she asked suspiciously.

'No reason.' Chris shrugged. 'Except, if you haven't, I thought it might be good for us to do it today.'

Trudie didn't know how to respond to this.

'Sorry?' she replied cautiously. She didn't want to let her guard down and then discover that she'd missed the sarcasm.

'You know ... go into town and get it all done,' Chris said, adding a second shrug.

'You hate it.'

'What, shopping or Christmas?'

'Both. Shopping and Christmas.'

'How do you know?'

'Because you hate everything.'

Chris was a bit saddened by the idea that left to his own devices Old Chris had descended into a forty-three-year-old man who hated everything. What had gone wrong? At twenty-five he had only hated most things.

'Well, maybe I've turned over a new leaf.'

'You *hate* leaves.'

One of the very first things Chris had resented about his older non-self was that the idiot had stagnated. But perhaps he'd been a bit harsh. Changing, he supposed, could be tough. And it surely couldn't help that Trudie didn't seem to accept that Old Chris could change, even when the person she thought was Old Chris had already changed to the point of actually being someone else entirely.

Tss. She needed a shake to wake her up, he thought. He ought to go for that anti-baldness cure after all: track down a mob doctor and score some oestrogen. Let's see how her rigid assumptions and expectations held up when he undressed for bed and revealed a pair of double-Ds and child-bearing hips.

It was a tiny, passing annoyance, however. He was soaring above the ground on the back of having just run his first full mile. He'd completed it in under fifteen minutes too, *and* he hadn't puked into a hedge when he finished either. He was hardcore. Less than two weeks ago, he'd lowered his head as other runners passed him in the street; now he nodded to them, and they nodded back (ninety-eight per cent of them, he noticed, were in or around their forties). It was a brotherhood. Headphones in. Bottle of water clenched in a stoic fist. Specialist socks. Only those who did it – who had made the decision that it was better to live on your feet than to die with your knees – truly understood. The sad, cholesterol-filled, bovine individuals all around slugged about meaninglessly while *they*, the trotting elite, knew the true spirituality that goes hand-in-hand with conquering pavements in the rain and stretching your hamstrings at traffic lights.

So, he was in a beneficent mood, and also powerfully inclined to give some quality time to Trudie. She was, if she only knew it, a very fortunate woman: a woman who had, standing before her, a man imbued with both idle curiosity and guilt. Thus making him the perfect combination of a lover and a husband.

Chris was fairly keen to find out a little more about the life he hadn't lived. As that life had been one largely spent with Trudie, she was a perfect source of information. But, other than to exchange basic domestic data, they'd scarcely spoken since he'd started getting himself ready. She was at work all day, and he'd been preoccupied when she was at home.

The guilt, of course, was because of what he was about to do. And he felt he owed it to . . . to someone, to understand the woman to whom he was going to do it.

Though, he wasn't doing it to *her*. And he had no reason to feel guilty even if, in a limited, pedantic sense, he was. (His feeling guilty when there was no logical reason, he concluded, was down to the weaving complexity of the situation. It didn't *mean* anything; it was effectively just his conscience playing safe.)

'Look,' Chris said, 'if you've already bought everything or you simply don't want to, then it's fine. All I'm saying is that, if you fancy it, give me twenty minutes to get showered, and' – he indicated his tracksuit bottoms and Lonsdale top – 'to change into something less chevvy, and—'

'What?'

That wasn't the word. What the hell was the word? Chiv. Ch . . . ch . . . chav!

'Chavvy, and we can go and do the Christmas shopping together.'

Trudie carefully picked something that wasn't there off the leg of her jeans. 'Sure,' she said vaguely. 'Whatever.'

'We're going, then?'

'Yes.' She began to gather up the tramp's bed of newspaper pages. 'Yes. I'd . . .' She turned back to face Chris, but he'd already gone. There was only the door, swinging shut. ' . . . like that,' she said.

The day was cold, but bright and clear. It was the kind of weather that pinched you to remind you that you were alive. The blue, polished sky looked like it had made the effort and a crisp chill disguised the air in town so it seemed clean and pure; it provoked you to take in a great lungful then expel it slowly with an invigorated 'Ahhhh.' On such a day the whole city became as tingling fresh as a menthol cigarette.

'Do you think my sister would like this?' Trudie asked.

'I have absolutely no idea,' Chris answered with satisfying honesty. '*I* think it's OK, though. Get it.'

This was almost a pleasure. At Christmas you generally have to schlep all over the place, grubbing about for something you think each person will want. It's hardly a tragedy for the receiver if they don't like it; it didn't cost them any time, effort or money, so it's a simple case of 'For me?' – 'Thanks' – eBay. Yet, the ludicrous thing is that you feel that giving a present that doesn't hit the target reflects badly on *you*. It's a social blunder. Christmas is about giving – that's where the embarrassment lies. So, usually, shopping for presents is a draining misery driven by panic and fear.

But Chris didn't have that problem. He didn't know these people they were buying presents for. The sheer, implacable reality of the state in which he found himself meant he didn't even begin to fret 'Would so-and-so like this or . . .' any more than he would've done had someone told him to get gifts for a list of names pulled randomly from a telephone directory. His limitations here were gloriously liberating.

'Do you think? Really?' Trudie twisted unsure lips.

'Yeah,' Chris said confidently. 'Get two.'

She was soothed and encouraged by his slapdash, baseless certainty and went off to pay while he entertained himself by looking through racks of T-shirts and trying to connect with the dominant cultural themes of the period. It was easy to spot them, but attempting to divine their meaning was a baffling exercise. If he'd lived his way to this moment in history, rather than being dumped here while he slept, then where would he stand on the key issues? Would he be bovvered, or would he be the only gay in the village? Can a person ever truly understand what has evolved without him? Maybe if an archaeologist who'd devoted his life to studying the Sphinx were transported back in time he'd just find lots of Egyptians wandering around saying to each other, 'Hey, what you doing? You great pharaoh-headed lion, you,' and howling with laughter. They didn't have key fobs and mouse mats back then, so they'd built a big statue instead. Four thousand years later and whole university departments are studying what is, in essence, a desk lamp shaped like Mr Bean.

Trudie rejoined him. He took the carrier bag from her and they strolled out of the shop together.

'Do you remember the first thing you said to my sister?' she asked, smiling.

'No.'

Trudie gave him a playful punch on the chest. 'Yes you do.'

'I really don't,' Chris replied.

'You said, "I thought you'd be thinner."' Trudie shook her head. 'I'd mentioned a few times that Stella ate like a horse but never put on an ounce, so, instead of just a normal-sized woman, you'd apparently pictured her as a tiny, wasted wraith.'

'A simple misunderstanding.'

'Yes.'

'And she's hated me ever since.'

'Yes.'

Chris had felt safe enough guessing at the relationship there. Meet a woman; immediately tell her (she infers) that she's fat; she'll hate you. It was hardly a daring assumption.

Trudie laughed. 'Well, not *hate*. You know Stella doesn't *hate* you, exactly ... but it's always going to be there, isn't it? It set the starting point, and that's something that sets quite hard. You can never meet people for the first time more than once, can you?'

'Not generally.'

A crumblingly bored man stood on the corner ahead of them. He was giving out brightly coloured promotional cards to passersby. He thrust one at the closest of the pair of men just in front of Chris, and another into the hand of the unrelated woman who was immediately behind them – she took it, looked at it, and threw it away all within a single stride. He tried to give one to a young bloke walking past in the opposite direction, but was rebuffed with a body twist and a sharp shake of the head. Chris drew level with him; the man glanced at him and didn't bother to offer a card.

'Look at that.' Trudie grabbed Chris's hand and pulled him over to a shop window.

She peered through the glass at something, considering it intently. Chris took half a look, but that was enough to reveal that china or pottery or something ceramic was, at the very least, partially involved and so there was going to be no sense bothering his eyes with it any further. For want of anything else to do, and as his face was pointing there already, he looked at Trudie instead.

He hadn't looked at her properly since his first full examination soon after he'd arrived in this foreign life. From where he stood now, she was almost in profile, but also – reflected in the pane of glass – nearly face-on as well; he saw her from two different points of view at the same time, like one of those split-screen effects film directors were fond of in the sixties. She was a bit of a mess: her hair had been rather neglected, her jeans were wearing thin on one knee, and she'd put on what must, surely, be the wrong coat. She was beautiful.

Not pretty; no, not that. Pretty was too syrupy and trite a word for her – too obvious. Actually beautiful. And she just *was* it: a state, rather than a deliberate look. She *looked* slightly dishevelled, but she had a sort of ... accidental grace.

The implications of this stunned Chris. He cast his eyes over the other people bustling along the street. This was amazing. Amazing, bizarre, and more than a little bit frightening.

He turned back to Trudie and found he was now unable simply to stare at her; it was well beyond the reach of staring by this point. He stood there and gawped.

'It's—' Trudie began, twisting her face towards him. 'What?'

'Uh?'

'What? What is it?' She frowned, and smiled, and pushed her hair back behind one of her ears. '*What?*'

'You're very attractive.'

She laughed. 'Yeah, right.'

'No – you really are.'

Trudie dropped her eyes.

'I mean,' Chris added, 'not you specifically.'

'Ffff ...' She shook her head. 'How very far you've come since the days of "I thought you'd be thinner,"' she said.

'Oh, I don't mean that you're uglier than other women.'

'Stop. Stop now; it's like you're channelling Cary Grant.'

'I'm serious. It's so ...' Chris searched the other shoppers rapidly, his eyes darting. He picked someone out and pointed emphatically. 'See her?'

Trudie followed the line of his finger. 'Yeah,' she replied, demonstrably unimpressed.

'What is she? Seventeen? Eighteen?'

'I suppose.'

'She's *stupid*. A girl. I look at her and I think, I wouldn't want to be with *her*. Christ. She'd be writing my name on an exercise book – doing each letter in a different colour felt tip. But, more than that, she's no great shakes *physically*: she's not really a woman, just on her way to being one. She's too new all round. I bet her skin smells of nothing but soap.'

Chris swung his view from right to left.

'God Almighty!' he said, his voice rising well above the noise of the traffic. 'I don't think there's a single woman here below thirty I want to shag.'

A woman, of about thirty, who had been about to walk past them veered sharply – moving around Chris in a semicircle the radius of which meant she stepped onto the road, where she narrowly missed being struck by a bicycle.

'Thirty, eh?' Trudie replied, speaking much more quietly (and hoping he'd follow her example). 'Freakish. That would mean that when those women were born you'd barely have been in senior school.'

Chris didn't show any sign of having heard her. 'I genuinely find forty-three-year-old women attractive.' He gazed at Trudie, apparently trying to see if this extraordinary discovery had sunk in. 'Isn't that weird? Isn't that just ... *weird*?'

'Off the scale. I've got chills.'

'When I look at you, I don't think you're beautiful, for a forty-three-year-old woman. That you're beautiful, *considering*. I just think, you're beautiful.'

He reached forward and patted her arm.

Trudie stared at him for a long, long time without replying. Then she nodded towards the item in the shop window. 'What do you think of this?'

'It's shite.'

They moved off down the street together. Trudie let her arm fall by her side and threaded her fingers through his.

Chris had five carrier bags and they were cutting off the blood supply: his hands looked like he'd spent two nights huddled in a crevice on K2 waiting for a rescue party. Shopping outside the accepted social codes was the best way, but it was still, after three hours, shopping.

'Let's go home,' Chris said, immediately aware of how homely the word 'home' felt in his mouth.

'But we haven't—'

'Book tokens,' Chris cut in. 'Another day.'

Trudie smiled. 'Not exactly *personal*. What does giving a book token say?'

'It says, "Look, we went and got you this book token, despite it being Christmas Eve and our being utterly fucked off with the whole thing by then." Anyway, it's a present, isn't it? A proper present, because it's some kind of fait accompli at least. It's not as bad as giving them the money so that they can get whatever the hell they want. Now that *would* be unforgivable.'

'Actually,' Trudie said apologetically, 'I haven't got anything for *you* yet. What would you like?'

Chris only slightly realised that he hadn't got anything for her either, because he mostly realised that he hadn't even *thought* about getting anything for her.

He wriggled the question off his shoulders, and then kicked it lazily into the gutter with an 'I'm fine.'

'Come on. I've got to get you something.'

'No, you haven't.' He flicked his nose at the shop they were passing. 'Hey, look at all the crap in there. Have we got a present for Andrew?'

'Bollocks to Andy,' Trudie replied. 'What do *you* want?'

'And his wife too. We need something for Gill.'

'I've already got Gill's present.'

'Have you? Good. What did you get her?'

'A necklace. What does it matter?'

'I just wondered. How much did that cost?'

'And what does *that* matter? God.'

'I just *wondered*, that's all.' Chris shrugged. 'So, how much was it?'

'Why do you want to know?'

'Why don't you want to tell me?' He peered at her. 'Are we having an argument about it now?'

'No. No, it was ... Oh, I don't know ... about a hundred or something.'

'*A hundred quid?*'

'*About* a hundred. I can't remember.'

'That's a lot, isn't it?'

'I saw it, that's all. I was— I'll take it back, if it makes you happy.'

'No – it's OK by me. Whatever you think.' Chris tried to scratch his nose with the back of his hand but it was weighed down with carrier bags. He had to bend almost in half to rub the two together. 'I like Gill.'

'Well, so do I. She's lovely.'

'Yes.'

'We agree on that, then. Now: what do *you* want?'

'Really, don't bother,' Chris replied, so casually that it was almost like someone mumbling in their sleep. 'I'm fine.' He fixed his eyes straight ahead. 'Anyway, I might not be here for Christmas.'

His peripheral vision caught Trudie stop. She stayed exactly where she was as he carried on walking, pretending he hadn't noticed. Eyes fixed. Straight ahead.

23

'Hello.'

'Hello ... God.'

'No, it's not God. I get that a lot, though; you know – when I have the light behind me.'

'Humour. I've read of such a thing, of course, but I never imagined it would turn up here, right on my doorstep.'

'What can I say?'

'My word. You are absolutely the second-last person I expected to see.'

'Who's the last person?'

'I was merely attempting to be colourful.'

'Ah.'

'What are you do ... Has someone died?'

'An interesting question. A very interesting question.'

'Why?' Trudie had asked, six days before. 'Why? Why now, all of a sudden?' She pulled Chris upright – he was in the living room, bending down unpacking the carrier bags. Hiding in unpacking the carrier bags. 'Is this yet another mid-life crisis thing?'

'I am not having a mid-life crisis. I just thought I ought to see him.'

'Out of the blue? Now? You don't even speak for *years*, and then, for no reason whatsoever, right when you're having your mid-life crisis, you abruptly decide to—'

'You know, I reckon that the only thing more annoying than *everything* you do being attributed to your mid-life crisis is everything you do being attributed to your mid-life crisis when you're not, in fact, having a bloody mid-life crisis.'

'Come on. It's a bit bizarre. You can't tell me it isn't. From nowhere, abruptly deciding to make contact again? And not simply by phoning him or posting an ice-breaking note – "Hi, Neil. I've lost my mind. How are you?" – but by driving all the way up there? Unannounced? And planning to stay for *days?*'

'Some things need to be done face-to-face, and to not be rushed. I don't think there's anything strange about that.' Chris casually rubbed the back of his neck and adopted a calm approach. It showed he was merely sifting through facts in which he had no emotional stake, as if they were debating what kind of mortgage to go for. 'Say you had the chance to travel back in time to speak to someone from your past – someone who was a large part of your past. Would you plump for meeting them in person, or dropping them a postcard? And would you allow for things to unfold naturally, however long that took, or would you do it against the clock?'

Chris congratulated himself on how thoroughly he'd backed up his position, especially since it was a total lie. Well, not a *total* lie; there were bits of truth in there. If you're telling a big enough lie it will always contain a few things that, by sheer coincidence, happen to be true.

'Fair enough?' he asked rhetorically, indicating that he thought that was the end of the matter.

'Fuck off,' said Trudie, indicating that she thought that it wasn't. 'For a start, you're simply seeing a former friend; you're not going to "travel back in time", for God's sake.'

'I might,' replied Chris. Adding, as an afterthought, 'In a sense.'

'So, as it's not crucial – as you're not fulfilling an ancient prophesy or deciding the fate of Middle Earth – I repeat: why now?'

'Anyone who does anything whatsoever has to do it at some point. That's how doing things work. Why *not* now?'

'Because it's *Christmas*.'

'And then it'll be New Year. And then I'll be back at work. There's always something there that will persuade you to do nothing, if you let it. If a thing is worth doing, it's worth doing now. And, as it had come up—'

'When did it come up?'

'Um, the other day. Andrew was doing his Christmas cards a few weeks ago, and he happened to say where Neil lived, and I—'

'Andy knew – knows about this?' Trudie looked astounded.

'Erm, yeah. Sure. He was perfectly OK about it,' Chris said.

'I bet,' Trudie muttered.

'Why shouldn't he be OK with my going away for a few days?'

'No reason. Of course not. I just meant that you told him before you told me. *Weeks* before you told me, it seems.'

'Sorry. It didn't seem that big a deal. Obviously, if I'd have known you'd massively overreact I'd have mentioned it sooner.'

Trudie slumped down on the sofa and went quiet.

Chris waited for her to start up again, but she remained silent and still; staring at her hands.

She is *not* going to make me feel guilty about this, Chris thought, guiltily.

He began unpacking the shopping again. When he'd finished, he gathered up the empty plastic carrier bags and went to take them into the kitchen.

'When are you going?' Trudie asked as he was opening the door to leave. She spoke into her lap.

'Friday.'

She nodded.

Chris stood in the doorway, fully prepared to handle whatever was coming next. Nothing came next. She just sat there. He couldn't handle that. So he left, put the carrier bags in the carrier bag they kept solely to store other carrier bags, and then went up to the gym – where he worked with steely determination on his triceps, his pectorals, and his not feeling a bit shitty.

Neil, on one side of the kitchen table, rolled a cigarette. Chris, on the other side, watched him.

Neil's home, Chris guessed, had probably once been a farmhouse. This room was filled with old, natural materials: a red stone-tiled floor, erratically undulating whitewashed plaster walls, wooden almost everything else. The kind of place you see in the magazines that come with Sunday papers and immediately sense speaks of a commitment to a simple life, a rejection of rat-raced materialism, and access to a substantial trust fund.

'What are you up to, nowadays?' Chris asked.

'I'm up to forty-three, nowadays,' Neil replied.

'Right. Was that flippant or evasive?'

'I write books.'

'*Really?*'

'And in answer to what is inevitably your next question: no – you probably won't know any of them.'

'I can absolutely *guarantee* that I won't know any of them,' Chris said. 'In fact, what I don't know about contemporary literature would fill a library. What kind of books?'

'Gardening books. A series of books about gardening, but not really gardening that much. Basically, about just hiding in the shed.'

'What are they call—'

'They're called *Hiding in the Shed*. I'm up to *Hiding in the Shed*, colon, *Weeds for All Seasons*. It's number six. Or seven.'

Chris looked around. 'Well, they must be selling OK.'

Neil laughed. 'The secret of a successful writing career, Christopher, is a love of words, dogged perseverance, and a partner who is a highly paid solicitor. If it were down to the money I make alone, I would have this' – he raised his roll-up between his thumb and index finger – 'and we would be discussing it standing in a field.' He twirled the cigarette into his mouth and lit it.

'Lucky.'

'Indeed. If it wasn't for Ann I'd be ... disastrously me.'

Neil was different.

Physically, the change was obvious. Over the years it seemed that he and a good deal of his hair had drifted apart. And what hadn't left him didn't seem to be hanging on with any great enthusiasm; like a couple in a quietly sad marriage, one almost felt the hair that remained was only staying for the sake of the children. His face was gaunt and heavily lined. Most striking of all, there was a deep scar running in an untidy crescent from just below the outside edge of his left eye all the way down to the corner of his mouth. It was not simply a vein of lighter-coloured skin. It distorted the flesh on that side of his face so it looked as though a thread were being tightened across it, creating a blade-thin valley that deformed the surrounding cheek. This must, Chris thought, date from the crash on the night Michelle had died. However, though Neil's physical changes were immediately evident, Chris felt that the emotional ones were at once more subtle and more profound.

'What about you?' Neil asked. 'Are you lucky?'

'I don't know.'

'You merely have to look at the woman you're with, or not with. The woman he's with is what keeps a man in his mid-forties afloat, or ensures he sinks under his own appalling weight.'

'I'm not in my mid-forties.'

'Ah – one of those. The desperate will cling even to mathematics.' Neil tapped the ash from his cigarette. 'Then, come forty-five, they'll change tack to maintain the denial. Mark my words: I bet at forty-five you'll buy a gym.'

'You're a hard person not to punch.'

'You made that plain a long time ago.'

Chris clicked his teeth. 'No, I didn't.'

'I remember it distinctly, Christopher.'

'I don't, Neil. In fact, that's—'

Chris stopped at the sound of a car pulling up outside.

There were voices, chattering indistinctly, and then a woman and two children bustled in through the door. The girl (aged about eight or nine, Chris guessed) and the boy (older, perhaps ten) hurried straight through the kitchen with nothing more than a glance in their direction and without breaking from the argument they were having. The woman looked at Chris intently while taking off her coat.

'Hi,' she said to Neil.

'Hi,' Neil replied. His roll-up still fastened between them, he pointed his first and middle fingers at Chris, like a pistol. 'This is Chris. Mortimer.'

Ann glanced briefly at Chris, then – still moving – looked back to Neil.

'Chris? The Chris who went freaky ape shit after your accident and blamed you for everything like some mad twat?'

'My partner, Ann,' Neil said to Chris. 'As I mentioned, she's a solicitor – her dream of joining the diplomatic corps didn't pan out.' He turned his eyes to her once more. 'Is everything OK?'

'Yeah, it's fine.'

'Didn't James take a jacket? It's quite cold.'

'He's fine. Shut up.' She scurried across the room. 'Excuse me, Chris – I have children to thrash.'

'No problem. Thrash one for me.'

Ann disappeared through the door that led to the rest of the house.

'She seems ... plucky,' Chris said.

'Yes. She definitely plucks.' Neil flicked his cigarette against the edge of the ashtray again. 'You were about to tell me something. The reason you've come, I hope. Behind this calm and fascinating exterior I'm actually quivering to know.'

Chris shifted in his chair. This wasn't the kind of speech you began before you'd definitely got your bottom comfortable.

'Everyone thinks I'm having a mid-life crisis. But that's not it.'

'OK.'

'I'm actually twenty-five.'

'Fff – well, that much is obvious.'

'I know how this sounds, but it's absolutely, literally, true.'

'Of course. Well, we can argue about the "literally", and the "true", but otherwise—'

'No – listen to me, Neil. It was 1988. Katrina and I were having a row about my leaving Short Stick. In the pub. I was playing pool with you. Andrew and Michelle were there. I got thoroughly wankered. When I woke up the next morning it was 2006 and I'd been married for fourteen years to a wife I'd never even met.'

'I *told* you not to have that sixth lager on an empty stomach.' Neil rubbed his chin thoughtfully. 'Lord – your council tax bill must have been *horrendous*.'

'It comes across as utterly insane, I'm aware of that. *Because* of that, I've had to hide it from almost everyone. But I'm not crazy. The situation is crazy; I'm not. I'm perfectly sane, and – literally – twenty-five.'

Neil slid his thumb slowly back and forth across his bottom lip while considering Chris deeply.

'Hmmm,' he said at last.

'Hmmm?'

'*Hmmm.*'

'What does that mean? "Hmmm"? Do you believe me or not?'

'Oh, I believe you.'

'You do?'

'Yes, certainly.'

'Are you *mad?*' Chris squinted at Neil, openly bewildered. 'I know it's true, because it's happened to me. If it weren't for that fact, there's no *way* I'd buy it. If you said it, I wouldn't believe *you*.'

'Ahhh.'

'Ahhh? So, not "Hmmm" now, but "Ahhh."'

'When I said I believed you, I meant that I don't think you're lying to me. I believe that *you* believe what you're saying.'

'You don't believe that I'm actually twenty-five-year-old Chris, then?'

'Hmmm.'

'Great – we're back there.'

'That's the intriguing question, isn't it? Superficial details such as greying hair and loss of skin elasticity aside, are you twenty-five-year-old Chris? Are you – are *we*, all of us – formed from a character that is innate, or are we the product of the experiences we've had? Nature or nurture? If we're the cumulative result of all the things that happen to us, then you're twenty-five – because if you have absolutely no memory of something happening, it effectively never happened. A short time ago you might, for example, have been debilitatingly claustrophobic and terrified of insects because when you were twenty-six you were trapped for five hours in a cupboard full of beetles. You were a jittery, timid, dysfunctional, forty-three-year-old Chris who had never been the same after that incident. But now the beetle-cupboard episode has been erased, and therefore so have all its effects. You are born anew, free – and at a cost of nothing more than the inconvenience of being a delusional lunatic who thinks he's time-travelled from the 1980s.'

'You're assuming I have amnesia. I don't have amnesia.'

'But,' Neil continued, ignoring Chris's objection, 'even if it's the other way – nature – it's not simple. Say that you're Chris; you were born Chris and you'll die Chris. It's who you *are*; you're not a piece of putty shaped by whatever happens to collide with you. Except who you *are* has changed. You *are* middle-aged Chris now, not Chris in his twenties. How much of who we are inside is influenced by the body outside, and where that body finds itself? For example, an eighty-year-old person isn't more anxious about stairs than a twenty-year-old because he's had bad experiences with them and it's made him less courageous; he's more anxious because, for the twenty-year-old, falling down stairs means an embarrassing sprawl; for an eighty-year-old it means a broken hip, pneumonia and death. Experiences might ricochet off without effect, but your time of life will still make some decisions for you.'

Chris considered this, and then looked sheepish. 'I fancy forty-year-old women,' he admitted.

'Did you always?'

'Chk. No, of course not. Did you?'

'Never mind that,' Neil replied. '*You're* the one we're trying to help here.'

Sometimes, Chris recalled, if you sleep all night on a crease in the pillow then that crease will transfer to your face. When you get up and look in the bathroom mirror you see there's a red fold there on your skin, almost like a scar. It can sometimes take an hour for it to fade. Or, rather, it had *used* to take an hour. It happened to Chris the other day and, with his forty-three-year old face, it had taken until lunchtime. Even though he hadn't gone out anywhere, because he knew it was there, he'd still been very self-conscious and awkward when he'd answered the door to the postwoman and, later, to a deeply confused salesman (he was from British Gas, but was trying to sell Chris *electricity* – his first day on the job, clearly).

Chris wondered how it would affect a person if that scar were for life.

He wanted to think that he was intact and unassailable. Old Chris's body was alarming as a discovery and a nuisance to fix, but it didn't, at any fundamental level, alter how he behaved or felt: his 'self' or 'spirit' or 'soul' or whatever you wanted to call it was entirely separate from whatever physical shell it happened to occupy. And yet ... And yet he found it hard to convince himself that it would have made no difference had he woken up in 2006 not in Old Chris's body, but in Neil's. Or, for that matter, in Andrew's. In Old Chris's body he'd developed an eye for middle-aged women. In Neil's would he have felt a desire to hoe, and in Andrew's started collecting publicity stills from *The Avengers*?

Still more worrying, if his mind was – against his will – going native, would he eventually disappear entirely? How long had he got before Old Chris's body turned him into Old Chris? This was a possibility that had never occurred to him, and it made things more pressing than he'd imagined: it made what he was going to do not just necessary but also imperative.

'Almost everyone?' Neil was rolling himself another cigarette.

'Almost everyone what?'

'You said that you'd had to hide your amnesia—'

'I don't have amnesia.'

'Or whatever. Your curious psychogenic fugue, then.'

'I don't know what that is. But I don't have one of them. I haven't lost my grip on reality. I can *feel* it' – he held up a hand and curled its fingers into a fist – 'and my grip's never been tighter, in fact.'

'As you wish. When in almost every practical sense it may be the same thing anyway – whether you've overcome the confines of space and time or just hit your head on a lintel is possibly little more than a pedantic distinction.' Neil thumbed his lighter. 'Almost everyone?'

'Andrew. Andrew is the only person besides you who knows the truth.'

'How did he react?'

'Sometimes he's seemed a bit pissed off with me – and he's a worrier, as you know. I couldn't have pulled it off for this long without him, though. He's been a lifesaver: giving me information, warning me about dangers, telling me who I'd become so I could play the role well enough. And, for the most part, he seems to find it ... erm, satisfying. I think it makes him feel useful to help.'

'That doesn't bother you?'

'Bother me? Why should it bother me?'

'I'm not saying it should. But ... maybe it's that I've been to more funerals than you – or been to more than you remember.' Neil absently wiped his hand across the table. 'People tell tales at funerals to raise the dead for a final, vicarious burst of life, and one finds that they all resurrect a slightly different corpse. We're one person to our friends, another to our family, or our colleagues, or our partners. Being ... what shall we call it? Rebuilt? Being rebuilt on the basis of a single, unquestioned voice, from a single perspective, seems potentially dangerous, don't you think? The builder might tend to make you just one, tiny facet of your actual self. They could even, perhaps subconsciously, take the opportunity to tell you that you're the person they'd like you to be. If

I'd lost my memory at twenty-five, you might have—'

'Assured you that you were shite at pool and always admitted it. That would have been a joy.' Chris shrugged. 'Possibly. But Andrew has no agenda: there isn't any reason for him to massage the facts one way or the other. He's extremely interested, but completely disinterested.'

'If you say so, Christopher. Really, I'm not suggesting otherwise. I can understand Andrew being enthusiastic. It's a dream come true for him: an episode of *Quantum Leap* happening in his living room, and he's Al. It's a wonder he didn't pass out with ecstasy. No, I'm merely speculating on all the questions the situation throws up because you're such a wonderful experiment.' Neil leaned back in his chair. 'So – why have you come to see me?'

'You're ... you *were* my best friend. It seemed a natural thing to do. Should I have stayed away to continue a feud someone else started with my mouth? Bugger that. Even Marley only had to carry his own chains. I don't care what the other Chris thought – you're my friend.'

'I was. Now, at best, I'm a stranger. I have a different life. I have Ann and James and Michelle, and we—'

'Michelle?'

Neil cocked his head in the direction of the door through which his family had disappeared. 'My youngest.'

'You called your daughter *Michelle*? That's a bit ...'

'Ann named her. After her mother.'

'Oh, right.' Chris nodded, but his expression must have given away that he still thought it was vaguely creepy.

'And, anyway,' Neil said, 'I think Michelle – the ... other Michelle – would have approved.'

Chris decided to let the matter lie. But in a way he was glad Michelle had come up because it cracked a tiny opening into the place he had to go next.

'There is another reason for my coming here,' he said. 'Besides visiting you, that is.'

'What might that be?'

'It's to see Katrina.'

'Katrina? Katrina ...' Neil squinted with the effort of trying to remember. '... whatever her surname was? I didn't know she lived around here.'

'She doesn't; she lives in Wiltshire. But I needed an excuse to be away for a while. Away from Trudie ... Trudie is my wife, by the way.'

'So it didn't work out with you and Louise? I can't say I'm surprised.'

'The other Chris saw a Louise for a while, then?' Chris shook his head. 'The name means nothing to me, I'm afraid. After my time.'

'Never mind. I don't believe you've missed an epic romance there. Still, it's oddly sad to think it's been erased entirely.'

Chris didn't find it sad; he had no more interest in the women Old Chris might have seen in his absence than he had in those of any other vague acquaintance.

Obviously, he'd have quite liked a tour of the unknown former girlfriends by finding a shoebox full of nude Polaroids, but that was purely scientific curiosity.

'Anyway,' Neil said, 'let's leave aside the poor relationships you've had with women in the past and concentrate on the poor one you have with your wife right now, shall we? How long have you been seeing Katrina?'

'Actually, I'm not "seeing" her. I haven't seen her, in any sense, since I arrived.'

'In 2006?'

'Yes.'

'So, not for eighteen years?'

'No. Not for about three weeks. I saw her three weeks ago. Though she hasn't seen *me* for eighteen years.'

'And you want to ... catch up.'

'It's not like that. Not exactly.' Chris sighed. 'OK. Here's what happened. I tracked her down on the Internet – you've heard of the Internet?'

'Vaguely. I think there was something in the papers about it once.'

'Well, I found this site called Friends Reunited. I knew the poly Kat had attended – it's a university these days, unbelievably.'

'Almost everywhere is these days. We lead the world in unbeliev-able universities. So you contacted her through Friends Reunited?'

'No. That would have required complex email stuff and pay-ments. I haven't learned enough about the Internet to be able to deal with that sort of thing yet. And, as it happens, I didn't want to get in touch like that anyway. I believe it's best to jump straight in: start with physical contact.'

'I see.'

'It's not like that. Not exactly.' If he still drank, Chris would have paused for several here. He took a deep breath instead. 'But luckily she'd put the address of her website in the public notes where anyone could see it.'

'That sounds like her all right.'

'She sells her artwork online.'

'The world is surely richer for it.'

'*That* site listed her proper address. And tomorrow I'm driving there to see her.'

'Right – just so I understand this correctly – you're going to meet up with an old flame you tracked down on Friends Reunited, without your wife knowing?'

'Well, technically, I suppose that's—'

'But, just so I understand this correctly, you are *not* having a mid-life crisis?'

'You're a twat, and bollocks.' Chris vowed he wouldn't be defensive. 'You disapprove of me "cheating" on my "wife"?' He made the quotation marks with his fingers. Then quickly added, 'If that even happens – which I'm not planning, actually – so you're a twat, and bollocks.' Obviously, his mouth wasn't going to be bound by his promises.

'I don't have any strong feelings one way or the other. I don't know your wife. That's how it works: one has a position, emotionally, on infidelity only if one knows the victim. It's rather like the difference between a person one knows falling down a lift shaft and hearing on the news that *someone* has fallen down a lift shaft. It's the Law of Shaftings.'

Chris really wanted to make his case well to Neil; for it to receive a nod of, if not exactly approval, at least of understanding. The best way to do this, he decided, was to state it boldly – as if he had no misgivings himself.

'The last thing that happened – the moment this all began – was with Katrina,' he said, in the authoritative, *my reasoning is an unstoppable juggernaut* tone of a sleuth who's gathered everyone in the drawing room at the end of a murder mystery. 'I was with her, arguing: *that* was the fork in the road.'

He paused for effect. Neil rubbed his nose. Chris continued.

'I remember that, when I was small and out shopping or something with my mother, she always used to say that if we lost each other I should return to the last place we were definitely together. That's not just the right thing to do practically, it's also the right thing to do instinctively. You *know* it's right.

'In every story I've ever read of the kind where the character finds a cursed amulet on the beach,' Chris continued, 'he breaks the spell by going back to that very same place to throw it into the sea. I know – I just *know* – that my best chance of getting home is to see Katrina. To return to where all this started.'

'Your internal logic is impeccable. If only more people solved life's problems by asking themselves, "What would Gandalf do in my position?"'

Chris let a hiss of air escape from between his teeth. 'I can't imagine how the other Chris thought he could muddle along without your input.'

'Steady on there, Christopher. Don't cheek your elders.'

'Look, here's the thing: say I'm wrong. Say that all I know and feel is nothing more than hormones and synapses, just an alcohol-and-self-loathing-provoked episode of traumatic amnesia. Still, even then, wouldn't seeing Kat be widely regarded as the way to go? Doing it is probably the thing most likely to trigger the recovery of my memory – isn't that what they'd say?'

'By "they" do you mean an advisory body comprising a select few, highly trained psychoanalysts? Or just lots of people who've seen *Marnie*?'

'That's not an answer.'

'It's a kind of answer.' Neil twisted his cigarette into the ashtray and began to roll a third. (He smiled a little. The established wisdom was that each one took three minutes off his life. He smoked and Chris didn't – yet he'd still ended up eighteen years ahead.)

Neil was highly aware of how difficult he was finding this conversation.

Chris didn't have the unpleasant section of their personal history sitting between them. Which meant that, if Neil fancied being angry, he'd have to be angry alone. Despite knowing this, Neil couldn't shunt the past into a siding as if it had never happened. It was there in his head. No amount of rationalisation could truly silence it. Anyone would find that a hard situation to deal with, and he didn't have the finest record of dealing with hard situations.

So, he was highly aware of how difficult he was finding this conversation: which was not difficult at all.

Strangely, the appearance of the Chris Who Used To Be had smoothly slid him much closer to the Neil *he* used to be. Not all the way there, it was true, but much, much closer. Chris, he knew, didn't want his answer; he wanted his approval. Warmed by the glow of this, Neil had settled comfortably into being comfortable; confidently taken on an easy confidence. It was almost like old times. Michelle had maintained that Chris wanted to *be* him, and that Andrew wanted to *be* Chris. ('That's why there's a constant buzz when the three of you are together,' she'd said once, laughing and throwing her T-shirt at his head as they undressed to get into bed. 'You're a nest of *bes*.')

Chris watched Neil roll his cigarette without interrupting; he could see that he was thinking. He hoped they weren't thinking the same thing. There was no way to know for sure, because he was *definitely* not going to raise it. Because Chris's thought contained, like a grub in an apple, a question no one would ever want to be asked; one that it would be terrible to consider even if you weren't required to answer it.

If Chris's theory proved correct, making contact with Katrina would reset the clock – fix whatever surreal glitch had flung him into the twenty-first century. He'd be back in 1988 and would immediately set about seeing that when he arrived at December 2006 again (the proper way) it wouldn't be as a torpid, broken, bitter, self-pitying, hairy-eared drunk. He would save Michelle's life too, of course. *Of course* – how could he possibly not? But, if he did, Neil wouldn't have his breakdown and move away. And so he wouldn't meet Ann: James and Michelle would never be born. The future could be changed, but for Neil it would only ever be big enough to allow Michelle *or* his children to exist in it. No one would want to sit in a kitchen on a Friday evening, however nice a kitchen it was, and consider those two options.

'Where were you planning to stay tonight?' Neil asked.

'I've booked a hotel.'

'You can sleep here, if you want. We have a spare room. It's full of junk and has a strange smell, but has far less junk and far fewer strange smells than that place you had in the eighties. So it'd be perfectly acceptable – as far as you knew.'

'That'd be good. If it's no trouble.' (It would be useful, Chris thought, to be able to call Trudie later – to call obviously from Neil's place. It would firm up his cover story. She was an innocent bystander in all this and, though he'd never married her, she was still at least enough his wife that he felt a duty to lie to her as effectively as possible.)

'It's no trouble at all. Or, if I suddenly realise that it is, I'll have Ann throw you out.' He stood up. 'I suppose we ought to think about organising some dinner too.'

'You didn't answer my question. Do you agree that seeing Kat is what I need to do?'

'You need to do what you need to do, Christopher. The need is the most important thing. The need is always the most important thing.' He shook his head solemnly. 'For example, right now—'

'You're going to say you need a pee, aren't you?'

'Boh – the very suggestion diminishes you as a human being. No, right now I need to tell Ann and the children that an old friend of mine will be staying with us, and that while he's here they must *not* raise the subject of mental collapse brought on by age-related fears of receding masculinity.'

'Thanks. I'd appreciate it if you would.'

'Feel free to make yourself a mug of tea. And have a think about how you're going to turn up at the home of one of your less significant girlfriends tomorrow, after eighteen years, and explain that you need to have intercourse with her to repair a rift in the space-time continuum.'

'It's not like that.'

'There's milk in the fridge.'

24

Louise Fischer peeled the cellophane seal from the salmon and cucumber sandwich she'd bought at the Tesco Metro on Tomnahurich Street unaware of the vast shadow she cast.

She had the smallest life of anyone she knew. Her house was small, her car was small, her desk at a small insurance company branch office was ... well, it was actually quite big but, that aside, it often seemed to her that she was incidental. A careless afterthought in the scheme of things; improvised. 'Oh, Louise – we forgot you were coming,' the world said, sitting around the table. 'Excuse me?' It hurriedly waved to a passing waiter. 'Could you stick another chair on the end, please?'

She didn't resent this. She'd travelled around a great deal when she was younger – seen and done all sorts of interesting things. She'd got a good education; she could speak Italian fluently; once she'd even queued at the counter in HMV directly behind Patrick McGoohan. Ian, the man she'd lived with since 1998, had left her for a homoeopathist three years ago, but he'd subsequently lost a foot in the Gambia so she really didn't think she could complain. She pottered along these days, automatically circling through her daily rituals quietly and unremarkably, but she wasn't unhappy. If asked, she might have supposed that people she'd once known thought, very occasionally, very fleetingly, very, very idly, 'I wonder what Louise Fischer is up to nowadays,' but no more than that. And she was *certainly* not a huge, formidable figure – a character of mythic proportions – in the mind of anyone she'd never met. If you were prepared to insure both your contents and your building with the company she worked for, then she could save you fifteen per cent, but that was the full extent of her power to impact on the lives of strangers.

Louise Fischer was comfortable being a forty-one-year-old woman of no particular importance to anyone.

'I'm no Louise Fischer – that's the problem.'

Trudie poked at her coffee with a spoon; not so much stirring as cruelly niggling it.

'Louise?' Andrew frowned. 'What's Louise got to do with anything?'

Trudie laughed drily. 'She was the love of Chris's life, wasn't she?'

'What makes you say that? Did *Chris* tell you that?'

'No. But I know it's true. I know there were other women before me, of course. There was, oh ... a Lizzie, I believe, a Katrina, a couple of Claires ... But I think Lizzie and Katrina were only brief things, and every man has at least one Claire – it's a stage they have to go through. Chris and Louise were together for *years*, though. He didn't meet me until after they'd split, and I suspect they would have still been a couple if Chris hadn't gone a bit weird after that accident your friend Neil had. That's true, isn't it?'

'I don't know. Maybe.'

'Gill thinks so.'

Andrew fidgeted in his chair. 'Did she tell you that?'

'Not exactly. But I know it's true.' Trudie put another sachet of sugar into her coffee. She had no intention of drinking it now, but she wasn't going to give it any peace either. 'What was she like? She was wild, wasn't she?'

'Um, I wouldn't call her wild, exactly.' He shrugged. 'Her mother was Italian, I think.'

'*Jesus.*'

'She was just a girlfriend he had. I can't recall Chris mentioning her since you two have been together. I mean, she was attractive—'

'Naturally.'

'Not as attractive as you.'

'Yeah, right. And that's not the point anyway. They had wild, freaky sex.'

'Did Chris tell you that?'

'No. But I know it's true. She was his wild, fascinating, freaky-sex girlfriend and I was the unexciting but safe rebound. He settled down with me – settled *for* me – but she'll always be the love of his life. For a long, long time he went through the motions, but when he set off on his mid-life crisis it's no wonder he started to think that shagging me wasn't worth the bother any more.'

'You had sex with him a few Sundays ago.'

Trudie looked across at him sharply.

Damn, Andrew scolded himself. He'd been absolutely determined that he wasn't going to mention the sex. But not mentioning it had meant holding back more and more force inside his chest every time he spoke to Trudie and she *didn't* mention it. It hadn't so much slipped out as been suddenly propelled from his mouth by a build-up of pressure: his brain had given his larynx a Heimlich.

'What makes you think that?' Trudie asked.

'It's right, isn't it?' Telling her that he knew because he'd been on the phone to Chris when he was in the bathroom psyching himself up immediately before setting off would have invited a lot of questions he'd rather not be asked. Anyway, it was somehow better to imply that he felt it intuitively – that he was sensitive to subtle clues – than to admit he'd unwillingly been manning the Shag Helpline. 'I mean,' he added, picking at a mark on the tabletop with his thumbnail, 'since then ...'

'That's ... I ...' Trudie caught herself squirming. Why was she squirming? She had no reason to feel guilty here. It was, she thought, one of the very few places where she had no reason to feel guilty these days, so she was absolutely not going to waste it. 'It's *not* right, actually,' she said brusquely.

Andrew stared at her. She was lying about it now. That made it even worse. Best not say that, though.

Don't call her a liar outright.

Don't call her a liar, shout 'Ha!' and squirt non-dairy creamer into her face. There had to be another option, surely?

'OK,' he said. 'My mistake.'

'Yes.' Trudie took a moment to let go of the irritation that was threatening to distract her. One can't do angry and fatalistic at the same time; it's one or the other. 'So,' she sighed, back on message, 'this visit to Neil is just the first step. Chris is set on travelling back to his perfect past – to before he was tied down with me. Neil's a stopover on the way to Louise; or, at the very least, the idea of Louise. It's obvious.'

She exhaled and shook her head, as if surprised by the dumb stubbornness of her own idiocy.

'I should leave him. It's no use my staying. It's annoying for him and humiliating for me.'

'No! I mean, no. I'm not saying you should never leave – of course I'm not. That goes without saying. But I don't think you should make a snap decision while you're upset.'

'I'm simply facing the facts, Andy. Why drag it out? He's pretended for all these years, but he can't forget.'

'Oh, you'd be surprised what he can forget.' (Careful. That really wouldn't help.) 'Not that he's gone nuts or anything like that. He's a little confused, that's all. Give him time. We should give him time, and continue to be supportive.'

'Being supportive? Is that what we've been doing?'

'Yes. And no. But yes, and no. It's complex, Trude. Things are complex for all of us now. That's the way it is. We're not twenty-five any more.'

25

It had been unexpectedly easy.

The previous evening hadn't. Though that wasn't because it had been bad, but because it had been woundingly enjoyable. James and Michelle were nice kids; Michelle especially had made him laugh lots. She was that rare thing in an eight-year-old girl: precocious enough to know when to give the precocious thing a rest. Ann he liked too. She was clearly still a little wary of him (as though she'd given herself the job of being Neil's emotional minder), but that made Chris warm to her even more.

It was happy, this family he was set on destroying – that, if he had his way, would never be given a chance to exist at all. He was going to execute them in the morning, and they were sharing jokes together as he loaded the gun. The better the evening had been, the worse it had been. The only break from bittersweet was when he'd phoned Trudie. There'd been no joy in that whatsoever. He couldn't help but think that this might well be the last time he ever spoke to her, and she wasn't very chatty. He rambled about irrelevant trivia, as people tend to when they're lying, or when they're trying to make an awful situation appear soothingly mundane, or when they're doing both. The only response he received that wasn't 'OK', 'I see' or 'Whatever' was when, in a single explosion of loquacity, she replied, 'OK, I see – whatever.'

He didn't want it to end like this, but what choice did he have? He was also aware of the irony that, quite probably, *he* would remember. For everyone else these memories would dissolve into nothing because they'd live other lives in the new world he was going to create; but *he'd* have to carry them around forever. Surely it was just Old Chris's bones exerting their influence again, but he'd miss Trudie. Suddenly, he remembered sitting in a German lesson at school; remembered the unexpected realisation he'd had about his own language when he learned the German for 'I miss you.'

Du fehlst mir.

He grabbed himself tightly and yanked himself away from the memory. He couldn't allow such things in; he had to keep his focus and his resolve.

Still, he couldn't help feeling that the idea of a home without Trudie seemed, of all things, extraordinary. What, he wondered, would be 'the best thing that ever happened to him' in the life he was going to live without her?

The early part of the next day had been emotionally draining too. When you're still trying to reconcile the conflicting moral imperatives placed on your shoulders by temporal anomalies, the last thing you need is the A34.

But, after that, it had been unexpectedly – even alarmingly – easy. He'd booked himself a room at a hotel in the nearest reasonably sized town – nearest to where Katrina lived, that is. He'd gone for a run, read a newspaper from cover to cover (and briefly wondered how he would spend all the money he'd have when he reached forty-three again, this time as the inventor of downloadable ringtones, budget air travel and Google), had something to eat and watched TV. Even when he'd got into his car and driven to Katrina's house, there was no hesitation or apprehension – at least, not of any human kind; he was anxious that his mission might encounter unforeseen barriers, but not that standing at her front door he'd feel like a dickhead. The rather tricky point that she was Katrina Morgan should have troubled him, you'd imagine. She'd been Katrina Ryan. Now she was Morgan, née Ryan – and he'd known about that née since his visit to Friends Reunited. It was a detail, however – an error. When he met her husband he'd bear him no ill will, but neither would it distract him. Chris was almost serene. This had to be done, and its absolute necessity relieved him of any misgivings concerning how he might need to do it.

As in many small villages, there was nowhere to park. Chris considered simply pulling up on the road (thus blocking half of it) and leaving the car there. He wouldn't need to return to it, after all. He was going back to 1988; and, come to that, the moment he did the course of his life would alter and so the car wouldn't be there any more anyway. It's pretty much the first rule of time travel that you needn't worry about getting clamped. However, as Katrina's house turned out to lie at the end of a sizeable driveway, he saw no reason not to drive up and park right in front of it. Another rule of time travel probably advised that, even when you were about to change history, there was no sense risking losing a wing mirror while you were about it.

He pulled up next to an SUV. This instilled in him an extra urgency. The possibility of being fatally absorbed, via Old Chris's body, into his foreign future continued to concern him. Though he wasn't part of this world and its ways, he'd noticed that, recently, each time he saw an SUV he filled up with anger and contempt just like every other right-thinking person in 2006. Sensing that a clock was ticking somewhere, he hurried to the front door and kept his finger on the bell until it was answered.

There she was.

That first sight of her fell against him with the weight of all the weeks that had built up to it. All at once, he blinked, inhaled sharply to recapture his breath, and had to adjust his feet quickly to prevent himself stumbling backwards; it was like being hit full in the face by a sudden gust of wind. The solid, physical reality of her there right in front of him took hold of his body and gave it a shake.

His reaction was especially strong because he'd worried that she was fading. Katrina had been – *was* – his girlfriend; someone to whom, in the past that so recently was, he'd been fairly close. She was not a casual acquaintance, but a person with whom he had a relationship that was sufficiently intimate for them to shout at each other in a pub. Yet she'd been absent since the moment he'd woken up in Number 114 Tithe Barn Avenue. Andrew had diluted her further with his attitude – he'd seemed almost as surprised that Chris should ask about Katrina as he would have had Chris been unable to control his agitation until told what Nicholas Witchell was up to these days. Neil was the same: he didn't regard her as significant either. And, outside Andrew and Neil's indifference, there was no one around him who recollected her *at all*. Moreover, Chris found that he himself didn't dwell on her in the proper fashion any longer. Yes, he was driven and determined to make contact with her again – but it was much more because of what she meant to him theoretically than what she meant to him emotionally.

All this was understandable – bizarre circumstances provoke bizarre reactions – but she paled because of it. In some strange way that simply would not succumb to logic, Chris felt that the natural digestive juices of this life he shouldn't be living were intent on dissolving her, bit by bit; that the psychological and the physical were tied together: as she faded figuratively, she faded literally.

He'd feared that, by the time he finally managed to get to her, she might be nothing but dissipating vapour – a ghost, then gone.

So, her standing there in the doorway – less than two feet from him and not even slightly translucent – was a relief, but also a shock.

'Kat?' he said. He had no idea why he'd put it as a question: there wasn't any doubt whatsoever that it was her.

Though it hadn't been enough to eradicate the years of neglect (and the years of years), he was thankful he'd made the effort to get himself into some bearable kind of shape. By giving up the booze, watching his diet and throwing himself into a demanding exercise regime he'd rapidly got results and, instead of being forty-three but looking forty-eight, he thought it wasn't deluding himself too much to believe that he could now pass for a crappy thirty-nine. The importance of this leapt when he saw that time had apparently been so busy laying fat over his stomach muscles, weighing down the skin on Andrew's face and making off with Neil's hair that it hadn't had any energy left, and had just stood aside and waved Katrina through. Even allowing for her being a couple of years younger than he was, and also mindful of the point that – as he'd recently become afflicted by an attraction to forty-something women – he might not be the most objective judge, she seemed to have aged beautifully. It wasn't that she looked significantly younger than she actually was, exactly; it wasn't that she looked fabulous *for* her age, but that she looked fabulous *at* her age. She was forty-one, perfectly. Her figure didn't appear to have undergone any age-related reallocation of resources and, shining in the porch light, her corkscrewing blonde hair effortlessly camouflaged any grey threads that might have been present. There were a few extra lines at the edges of her eyes and mouth, and the skin around her neck had perhaps allowed itself a little more room to manoeuvre, but she was essentially as he remembered her. She might almost have spent the last eighteen years lying inside a box packed in moisturiser, waiting for him to ring the bell.

He was hugely relieved that his own body, if it came to be naked next to hers, wasn't now as thoroughly shameful by comparison as it could have been had he failed to prepare it. Not that he did have any intention of it being naked next to hers. It wasn't like that.

She squinted. She gasped. She laid a hand on her chest, and she spoke.

'Oh ... My ... *God*.'

A few weeks ago that would have puzzled him a little, but he'd quickly realised that talking like an American (and also, quite probably, with the rising terminal intonation formerly confined to young Australian women) was near enough standard these days. Everyone sounded like that. (Apart from Neil, but he hadn't sounded like anyone else in the eighties either.)

'*Chris?*'

'Hi, Kat. How's it going?'

'Great. Totally great. I'm ... Oh. My. *God*.' She stepped forward, more accurately *lunged* forward, and hugged him. 'This is *so* cool.' (OK, Chris thought, this was now rather more American than usual. But ... well, maybe she'd got Sky.)

He had a stab at hugging her in return, the best he could – being careful to keep a clear six inches of platonic air between their groins (it felt curiously appropriate to do this).

'I was in the area,' Chris said. (Which, of course, was demonstrably true.)

'But how did you— Oh, come in, come in – let's not stand on the doorstep.' She grinned and tugged him into the hallway, then pushed him – her hand on his shoulder – through to the living room.

Chris did a quick viewing-twirl, nodding appreciatively as he revolved.

'Nice place,' he said, because that's what you do. Actually, he thought it horrifyingly awful; ugly in a way that's possible only when money is no object. Maybe Katrina had moved in quite recently and so hadn't had a chance to change the furniture and decor left by the previous occupant; who, Chris guessed, would have been Hugh Hefner.

She glanced around, as though she'd never noticed her living room before.

'Yeah,' she replied, wrinkling her nose. 'It's OK, I suppose. I don't take much notice. A house is just a house, right? I'd be as happy in a tent, quite honestly – you know me. This is fine, but I don't really care. That fireplace cost two thousand pounds. Can you believe that?'

'Well, it's certainly very ... big.'

Chris's eye rested for a second on the photograph that was on the mantelpiece. There was a photograph on the mantelpiece of 114 Tithe Barn Avenue too – he'd seen it, and been nuked by confusion, that first morning in 2006. The Tithe Barn Avenue photo was a hasty, compositionless snapshot of Trudie and him side by side, laughing at something together. The photograph here was a large, professional-looking, solo portrait of Kat.

'Yeah. Two thousand pounds,' Katrina continued. 'But I don't really care.'

Energised by her indifference, she launched herself and almost Fosbury-Flopped onto the sofa. It exhaled sharply, winded, as she landed on its plump, soft, cream-coloured, leather surface.

'But never mind that,' she said, patting the space beside her in invitation. 'What about you? It's *so* amazing to see you after all these years. How long has it been?'

'Getting on for a couple of decades.'

'*God*. It doesn't seem like that.'

He sat down beside her. 'No.'

'Where does the time go?'

'Search me.'

'What are you up to now?'

'I—'

'I've done— *God*, well, you know me. It's been *crazy*.' She rolled her eyes. 'Don't ask. Just ... Don't ... *Ask*.'

Chris didn't ask, but she told him anyway. However, it was difficult to follow her account because she ricocheted around the timeline – often without giving any indication of the transition between one point and the next. Chris would only gradually realise that what she was talking about must have happened, say, five years before what she'd been talking about a few sentences previously. And, by then, she'd probably have jumped to yet another era anyway. Also, she was prone to give unclear and cursory accounts of things in favour of detailing at length how she felt about those things. On several occasions – when she paused briefly to look at him for, he thought, agreement or understanding – he found himself saying 'Of course' or, 'I can imagine' without having any real idea what he was supposed to be, of course, imagining.

The best he could make out, she'd spent some time in Ireland (very spiritual), and Africa (*amazing*), and India (*amazing*, and very spiritual). Due to her commitment to vagueness, Chris wasn't sure of the order, or whether or not she'd lived in a particular place for a number of years or just gone there for a long weekend.

She sold her art; people absolutely *loved* it, though she didn't really care about that – she did it for herself; but, to repeat, people absolutely *loved* it. She couldn't believe what some collectors (she used the word 'collectors') paid for her pieces; she was dumbstruck that anyone would spend that amount (the asking price) and she, personally, was sure they weren't worth it (the asking price), but collectors obviously thought they were, so who was she to argue? Anyway, it wasn't about the money; the proof of this being that she couldn't have lived off what she made from selling her work – she wouldn't want to, it was *not* about the money. Somewhere around here she mentioned that she was married to Ted. She gave a long-suffering smile, shook her head and sighed immediately after saying his name, as though he were a slow, orphaned nephew she'd taken it upon herself to look after. Chris worked out – again by inference and complex mental cross-referencing – that Ted was her second husband. At some previous point, for an unspecified amount of time, there'd been a Gary. Gary had smothered her. Though not, Chris assumed, literally.

It was tricky for Chris to keep up. Listening to her was like watching a movie written by David Lynch, then edited by Yoko Ono – but there was more to it than that. He was expecting a clap of thunder. The sudden, concussing chime of a huge bell. A blinding, white-out flash. The shopkeeper from Mr Benn to appear. *Something*. Some dramatic, signalling event that would explode, envelop and then almost instantly vanish, but leave him now – possibly dazed, probably dizzy and hopefully with forty per cent-tauter skin – standing once more in 1988. Expecting it pulled at his attention. Listening to Katrina, when the Big Reset might burst upon him at any moment, was a bit like trying to read a magazine feature in a dentist's waiting room. Worse, in fact, as he couldn't even reread the same bit four times when he realised it hadn't registered. If he had a few moments distracted absence, she'd forge unstoppably ahead and his concentration would return to find her in another country or with a different husband.

He'd half supposed that the instant he saw Katrina would be the trigger. When nothing happened then, the instant they first touched became his next guess. But the Big Reset had been a no-show then too. As time and Katrina went on, he began to accept that it wasn't going to be that simple.

Something was missing. He was in the right place, he was sure of that, but he had not yet located the vital catalyst. Perhaps it was a word, a phrase or the appearance of a special, shared memory. Maybe a thing remained for him to learn; a moment of insight could be the key. In ghost stories, the haunting continues until the haunted person suddenly realises why the troubled soul can't move on; fables turn on the character's arrival at wisdom, or humility, or some such deep, personal change. It could be that he simply had to sit there, listening to Katrina talk shite, until he achieved a Zen-like eradication of the self – but at least that collapsing surrender of his defiantly resisting spirit wouldn't take long, he thought, if had to suffer much more rambling bollocks about Celtic mysticism. He was ready, and just wished that what-ever unseen entity was judging his new-found pious serenity would get a bleeding move on.

'So, anyhooo,' Katrina said, at (hopefully) last. 'That's me – in short. What about you? *God.*' She laughed. 'The last time I saw you, you were doing that crappy little job at Short Stick. What are you up to now?'

'I work at Short Stick.'

'Oh – right. Sure. What do you—'

'The same thing.'

'Oh.'

'I mean ... it's at new offices now.'

'Cool.'

Why did he feel he needed to mount a defence? He'd done nothing. That is, Old Chris had done nothing. Why was he trying, in any way, to excuse what he found inexcusable himself?

'Ted, is it?' he said, changing direction. 'Your husband?'

'That's right. Ted.' She pulled up her dress slightly to curl one leg under her bottom. 'He's away until tomorrow afternoon. He's away a lot – for work.'

'That must be hard.'

Katrina pushed a strand of hair back behind her ear. 'Hey! I haven't even offered you a drink – how bad is that?' She stood up. 'What do you prefer? Red or white?'

'I don't ... Well, just the one glass of red, then. If you're having one.' It was another world here; there was no sense keeping to rules he'd formulated for everyday life – not to mention that his liver would almost certainly be eighteen years away before the alcohol could find it.

Anyway, no one would object to a person having a steadying glass of wine when they were about to return to a Britain where Sonia was still in the charts.

'Do you ever think about how your life could have been completely different?' Chris said, slicing through the plastic seal on the third bottle with the pointed end of the corkscrew. He had no idea how late it was now; he'd indulged in a little rambling himself and the time had flown by.

'Yeah, I *so* do,' Katrina replied. 'Like, if I'd been the daughter of a king or something.'

'Well, yes, there's that. But I meant how it might be – how it, and maybe *you*, in yourself – might have gone along a completely different path if you'd made different decisions. Perhaps just *one* different decision.'

'Hmmm.' She ran a fingertip slowly around the rim of her wineglass. 'I think I'm pretty lucky, really, because I have very good intuition. Mostly, I know what the right decision is at the time.'

'Ahhh,' Chris said pointedly, smiling and with a profound,

professorial air. Then he dropped the corkscrew and had to fish around under the sofa for it for quite a while – it was made hard to find by the amount of wine he'd drunk, which also insisted he bang his head on the coffee table during the search. Eventually, he retrieved it and fell unsteadily back into his seat. 'Ahhh,' he repeated, '*at the time* . . . But suppose you could see those decisions not just from your position at the time you took them but from many years later. See where they led, have information you didn't *have* when you made the choice. If you could, would you go back and change any of them?'

She looked at him silently while she sipped at her drink. 'Maybe.'

Chris filled his glass, emptied it, filled it again, leaned back on the sofa and stared at the ceiling. Katrina wriggled over closer to him. She reached forward and ran her hand through his hair.

'Why did you come here, really?' she asked.

'Really?'

'Yes.'

'*Really?*'

'Yes.'

'Because I was with you the last time I remember being the proper me.'

'*God* – that's *so* sweet.' She stroked his ear. 'What were you doing?'

'I was calling you a silly cow, I think.'

Katrina smiled sympathetically. 'I must have hurt you *so* badly,' she said earnestly. 'I didn't mean to – honestly.' She laid her head on his shoulder. 'I never thought for a second that you still wouldn't be over me after nearly twenty years. *God.* Was I on your mind all this time? Even when . . .'

'When what?'

Katrina turned towards him, took one of his hands, and clasped it tightly between hers. 'You know . . .'

She slowly raised her eyes to his, paused for a second, and then leaned forward and kissed him. At first it was with a kind of mournful softness, moving gently, but soon her tongue slid between his lips and the intensity grew. She drew herself tightly against his body; her right hand stayed gripping his, though harder now, while her left took hold of the side of his T-shirt and clenched the material in its tight, twisting fist. The kiss lasted a long time; Katrina was breathless when she finally pulled away for a moment and looked at him.

'No – when what?' Chris asked.

'Eh?'

'On my mind even when . . . what?'

'Um. Even when you were with your wife, of course. Even when you got married. It must have been so hard.' She ran her fingers over his cheek. 'Was the thought of me calling to you as you said, "I do"?'

Chris thought it pretty unlikely, but he couldn't honestly say that it wasn't. For all he knew, that other Chris might indeed have been thinking about her as he took his marriage vows. He might have been thinking about her, or that he needed to get a loaf on the way home, or that his underpants had ridden up. There was no way Chris could know for sure.

'Possibly,' he admitted.

Concern creased Katrina's face; the thought of him being in that situation obviously plunged her into a rapture of agony.

'*God*,' she gasped, and immediately pushed him down onto his back.

She lifted her dress over her head and off in one unbroken, peeling movement, threw it aside, and then crawled on top of him. As soon as she was high enough, her mouth dropped to his neck, and began kissing and biting its way up and around.

Chris reached the conclusion that he'd probably have to shag her.

It would be impolite not to. If a woman is writhing above you in only her bra and knickers then not to shag her would be the most appalling manners. He might not be perfect, Chris told himself, but never let it be said that he wasn't gentleman enough to slide his hand into Katrina's underwear and knead her bottom.

Anyway, he thought as her lips reached his once more, what did people call it? *La petite mort*. (People, here, being the French – but who knows more about unintelligible, surreal weirdness than the French?) Perhaps, as everything had so far failed to detonate the Big Reset, *this* was to be the thing that would do it: the little death.

Death.

Rebirth.

It made sense, in a way. He would, he concluded, have to shag his way back to the Major government and fifteen per cent mortgage rates. What choice did he have? Etiquette and the mechanics of temporal shifts had him trapped in a pincer movement. As, come to that, did Katrina's legs.

However, all these things – quite oddly – were not entirely pushing at an open door. It wasn't as bizarre as his wanting not to have sex with her; that would have been ludicrous and, for that matter, rather worrying. He didn't wish he could avoid it but, even as he brought a second hand to bear so as to give Katrina's other buttock a comparable level of attention, he was aware that he wouldn't have minded *not* having to do it.

He was surprised by how Katrina tasted. It wasn't unpleasant, though it certainly wasn't delicious either. The curious thing was that he was conscious of it at all. It was the same with the scent of her hair and skin. He recognised the aromas but, rather than their being familiar, they seemed . . . recalled. It was like returning to your former school as an adult and thinking, 'Ah, yes – this is it,' as your senses encounter the old, previously ordinary landscape; yet now not finding it that natural to sit in a room that smells of exercise books and chalk, nor being able to eat a lunch made up of crisp sandwiches, a Penguin bar and a couple of Dairylea cheese triangles without any introspection.

Also, everything seems much smaller than you remembered.

It had been easier to go Christmas shopping with Trudie, his unexpected wife, than it was kissing Katrina, his unfinished girl-friend. For the first time, the past everyone else regarded as distant felt distant for Chris too.

Chris's reaction to these feelings was creditable. He wriggled up half out of his jeans as Katrina hastily pulled them open; he *made* himself – displaying vigour and determination. This, he knew, was a test of his character. He must have sex with her, and do so with the appearance of commitment, gusto and vim; to do anything else would be to let both Katrina and himself down.

Thus, he threw himself into it. Temporarily pushing Katrina aside so he could work unobstructed, he boldly tugged his jeans down; grabbing them by the waistband and rolling them off. Well, almost off. They were off most of him, but couldn't clear his trainers, which were trapped at the bottom of the now inside-out legs. He bent down and, head between his knees, pulled at the jeans with all his strength. This didn't shift them at all, but did give him a nice display of coloured lights and a hum that took him on a brief tour around the edge of a slumping faint. (Maybe, he thought as he resurfaced, this was the reason older people did less drugs: if they ever wanted a quick buzz then all they had to do was try to take off their bleeding trousers in a hurry.) His efforts hadn't been completely without effect, however. When he abandoned attempting to wrench the jeans free of them and changed tactics to removing the trainers first instead, he found that the denim was now stretched over them so tightly that he wasn't sure whether he could pull the legs back *up* enough to get at the laces either.

Katrina, optimistically expecting Chris would be able to undress himself, had stormed ahead. She'd slid out of her bra and knickers in an instant, and was now sitting on the sofa beside him, waiting. Chris could see her perched there out of the corner of his eye, and sensed that he was losing the moment. But he couldn't carry on while he was like this. Never mind that if they changed location he'd have to waddle along after her as though he'd escaped from a chain gang, it was also fatally unerotic even if they stayed put. Well, it was unless she had a secret fantasy about being ravished by a man whose feet were trapped in a wind sock.

He yanked, strained and grunted his way a little closer towards hysteria. Katrina sat beside him on the sofa, marooned in the awkward hiatus. She obviously didn't know what to do, and it was becoming increasingly odd just sitting there pretending nothing was wrong as the seconds ticked by and Chris's struggles became more and more desperate. Yet what alternative did she have? Pour herself a drink? Read a magazine? Whistle to provide some accompaniment?

'Can I—' she began tentatively.

'No, no – I'm fine,' Chris replied with no small amount of defensiveness. The embarrassment was crashing over him in scalding waves already; sympathy and offers of help were the last things he needed. Christ, next she'd be saying, 'It doesn't matter. It happens to all men at one time or another.'

'Maybe I could—'

'No, really. Just give me one second,' he insisted – one second away from asking if he could have a pair of scissors; perhaps to cut himself out of his own trousers, perhaps to just stab himself through his heart and be done with it.

But then a last, draining, face-purpling pull finally set him free. His left trainer came off in the process and remained wedged in the leg of the jeans, but that didn't matter. He stood – in a T-shirt, no underpants, a sock on one foot and the other still in its shoe – and roared with manly triumph like the victorious hero in a Greek myth. Katrina, swept by relief, gave him a spontaneous round of applause.

Quickly, he stripped his feet – nudity seeming like an achievable goal once again. He faltered a little before the last jump (his T-shirt), however. His stomach was better than it had been when it'd been plonked (almost literally, he felt) in his lap a few weeks ago, but he still didn't regard it as anything he wanted to blithely unveil in front of a woman without a counsellor on hand. But then, he couldn't keep his top on. For one thing, doing that leapt away from 'elegant' without landing anywhere near 'excitingly feral'; it was simply rubbish. For another, it would probably emphasise his bottom. Chris hadn't really examined his bottom. If you're middle-aged but retain at least *some* kind of grip on reality, you aim to make yourself look reasonably good from one angle and then try to use movement and terrain so you remain at it (at Old Chris's age any threesomes wouldn't merely be difficult to come by, they'd be nightmarishly complex to choreograph anyway). So, despite not having surveyed the area enough to give him a clear picture of it, he was sure that his bottom wasn't something he wanted to introduce at this point – just when things were picking up. By far the best idea was not to highlight it with the hem of a T-shirt, and to try to keep it out of view by sort of 'orbiting' Katrina.

As though gritting his teeth and tearing off a plaster as fast as possible, Chris whipped away his top. Fantastically, however, it turned out better than he could have hoped. Completely naked now, he glowed with pleasure when Katrina, quite unmistakably, didn't scream.

Relaxed by the knowledge that she had looked upon him for several seconds and there she still was, lying on the sofa – rather than having locked herself, sobbing, in the bathroom – Chris ran his eyes over her properly for the first time. There was an instant of cold, queasy horror as he arrived at her crotch. Oh ... God help us. The years might have taken the lion's share of Neil's hair away with them, but *Katrina was totally bald.*

It was unappealing sexually, obviously, but the bigger problem was how should he respond to it on an interpersonal level? Pretending there was nothing wrong would only exacerbate the awkwardness. It would make Katrina's vagina the elephant in the room. What could he possibly say, though? Where was the acceptable middle ground between ridiculously refusing to acknowledge the situation at all and recoiling with a loud 'Arggh!'?

In what wasn't the most stylish manoeuvre in the history of his sex life, he bent over and squinted at it.

On closer inspection (Katrina – with the forbearance of every saint who's ever lived – lay there doing nothing more than clearing her throat a couple of times as he peered investigatively), it appeared that the hair had been deliberately removed. Was this the equivalent of a man opting to hide his thinning middle by shaving off what remained on the sides? Had she chosen to do this merely because it was preferable to a comb-over? Or maybe she'd recently had an operation. There was a third option, but Chris couldn't bear to contemplate that – and it wouldn't have been necessary anyway; surely one could buy ointment for that?

Finally, it dawned on him that, incredibly, it might be an active choice. He'd run into this kind of crotch on the Internet. It was hard not to. Especially if the third thing you did when you'd discovered what a search engine was for was to type 'photos of naked women' into it. Which was the second thing Chris had done. He hadn't thought much about the frequency of pubic baldness back then, as these were porn models. The lack of hair was for speed: it meant that one quick wipe with a moist towelette like you got from KFC and they were good to go again. But why would a woman do it otherwise?

Utterly baffling. Still, it was by the by. He couldn't, and wouldn't, back down now. He *had* to shag her – at least one person's life depended on it. He had a mission to fulfil this night, and much relied on his seeing it through. This was bigger than Katrina's vagina.

And so, with no more than a slight 'Oh well' click of his teeth as he finally looked up from her groin, Chris lay down face-to-face with Katrina and, at last, they had sex. Beginning in the living room and reaching its raw, sighing, exhausted end in Katrina's bed, Chris did what he had to do; sometimes – if not consistently – closing his eyes and thinking of another, earlier England.

26

The clock-radio poked Cliff Richard singing 'Mistletoe and Wine' into Chris's sleep as if it got some kind of sick pleasure from doing it. Aching, he winced half-awake and a groan like a creaky door rolled about in the dark alcove inside his head where his throat and nose met secretly to plot phlegm.

He rolled slowly onto his side and, so as not to commit himself to a morning, opened just a single eye to peer at the clock. It didn't help. The sickly numbers on the display weren't visible because, as was always the case when she stayed there, Katrina's coils of swirling blonde hair were in the way. He'd have to lift himself up and look beyond her to know what time it was; but that would mean moving and, before that, making the decision to move. He allowed the lone eye to shut again.

As soon as it closed, Chris immediately slumped back into that boiling mass of criss-crossing randomness that swills about just below consciousness. He was in Egypt and he needed, urgently, to buy batteries, but it was a Wednesday so all the shops were buried underground and he didn't have a shovel, which was making his companion – Meryl Streep – absolutely furious with him (like it was all *his* fault), and she was bawling and ranting and insisting that she'd dig herself, dammit, if only her shoulders weren't made of jam.

This went on for minutes or months until, gradually, like pulling wellington boots out of mud, pieces of his brain heaved themselves free of the sticky dreamscape and up into reality. As their number rose, they began to arrange themselves into a second dream. Chris foggily accepted that he'd woken from one only to recall another; it had taken place amid a weird world in which he'd inherited a life that wasn't and was his. He'd had a wife there – Trudie. A ubiquitous computer network spanned the world; people had personal, wireless telephones on them at all times; CCTV cameras were everywhere; and – in that 'you know it is, even though it doesn't look like it at all' way you get in dreams – there was a Labour government. Alarmed at how vivid it had been (he could still feel its residue on his skin), he opened his eyes and locked them into Katrina's spilling hair to regain his balance. He sighed, rolled over onto his back and stared up at his cracked white ceiling.

Except it wasn't cracked, or white, or his. It was flawless and mauve, and – it was bleeding *mauve* – definitely not his.

'Fuck!'

He sprang up into a sitting position and the room assaulted him from all sides. It felt like pushing his head into a spin dryer. The most unimaginable, unbelievable, inexplicable thing had happened: nothing.

Beside him, Katrina stirred, parted her eyelids and smiled. Tiny, stunningly massive lines were etched into her face; bloodless cuts from two dozen of the finest razor blades.

Chris went cold with the terror of panic. The terror of failure. The terror of helplessness. The terror – off to one side and whispered, but most jolting of all – of relief.

Sometimes you stumble out of a dream and curse whatever must have wrenched you away from it. It might not have been a particularly pleasant dream. It might even have been a nightmare. But you were engrossed in it. However nonsensical it was, it made sense *there* – and when you were in it you knew what you needed to do with empowering clarity. For all its monsters and peril, it was intriguingly unusual and engaging. It was – though you were falling through miles of air towards an icy lake with your pockets full of vampire rats when you left – better than the flatness of waking in your bed on yet another Tuesday morning; lying in the muggy heat under the duvet; the smell of yesterday's onions lumbering in from the kitchen. So, you're not glad to be back, and there's fury at the selfish ringing of the telephone, perhaps; the barging, thoughtless intrusion of a doorbell; the special, bitter rage which only the bin men can provoke. You grumble incoherently, wriggle your face deep into the pillow, and try to return to the place from which you were cruelly snatched. It rarely works. But imagine if it did. Imagine if you found your way back there but, in the same moment as you experienced the scary euphoria of returning to its strange, energising otherness, you knew for certain that you would never be able to wake from it again.

'Hiya,' Katrina said, her voice croaky with sleep.

'It's still 2006, isn't it?' Chris replied. It was more a statement than a question.

She laughed. 'I'd guess so. That is, unless we've been asleep for over a week.'

He swung his feet out to the side with the intention of getting up and finding his clothes, but the moment he tried to rise nausea rushed forward and pushed him back onto the bed. He took some comfort from that. It meant he must have been drunk. Alcohol's greatest gift is to have it to blame for what you've done the night before; quite often people will get plastered specifically so they can lay the responsibility for what they're going to do later on having been plastered at the time.

'Are you OK?' Katrina asked. 'Mistletoe and Wine' finished (one small mercy, at least) and the DJ on the radio was gabbling something about it being Number Twelve in their Christmas hits special as Katrina switched him off.

Chris wiped a hand over his face then arched forward, his elbows resting on his knees. 'No, I'm not OK,' he replied. 'I'm ...'

She moved across and touched his back. 'What? Are you ill?'

'No. Well – yes, I'm ill: I feel like I've swallowed a bagful of eels. But it's ... it's not ... I'm *married*,' he said.

She leaned closer and hung her arms around him.

'It's that bad, eh?'

He didn't respond. It was bad; it was bad because it really wasn't that bad at all. Even though Old Chris had damn near kicked it to bits before passing on the baton, it still wasn't bad.

It was good to lie down to sleep next to Trudie, with her soft, slow breathing and her occasional murmurs and her woolly socks. 'Hello, darling – how was your day?' existed only in American TV shows; he carried on with what he was doing elsewhere in the house and never said a word, but every time he heard the door open when she returned from work, he felt as though a vital piece was slotting back into place. Maybe it was the creeping occupation of him by Old Chris's body, but, if it was, then he didn't care. In fact, he was thankful for it. He was pleased that – right now, sitting on the bed with his spine between Katrina's breasts – he felt horribly guilty. It hadn't been his fault – he'd needed to try to get back to where he belonged; or where he'd thought he belonged. And it wasn't his fault – he'd been plastered. But, nonetheless, he felt guilty; and that felt right.

'I think,' he said anxiously, 'that I might love my wife.'

'*God*,' replied Katrina. 'Of *course* you do. Not in the same way you love me, maybe, but definitely, *definitely*, you know … a bit. It isn't as intense, but—'

'Love *you?*'

'Yes.' She laughed again. Chris couldn't see her face, but he guessed she was rolling her eyes. He could sense it, somehow – perhaps by touch. He concentrated on her prodding nipples with his back, trying to make out if they were chiding him. '*Don't* you?' Her voice was a swooping tease.

'Did I? Ever?'

She hopped from the bed and stood in front of him. There was her crotch again; or, rather, the eerie blank space where her crotch should have been. It was directly level with the bridge of his nose. He shifted from side to side, but it followed him around, like the eyes on the *Laughing Cavalier*.

'You totally bloody did, yes,' she insisted. 'Why else did you come here after all these years? Revenge?'

'Revenge? How could it be revenge?'

'Exactly. It wouldn't make any sense, would it? As if, just because I slept with someone else, then you sleeping with me when I'm married – twenty years later – would even the score or something? That wouldn't—'

'You slept with someone else?'

Katrina folded her arms tightly. One of her breasts slipped below them, and the other popped out above. It looked very untidy. 'There's no need to be sarcastic. I know it hurt you, but it just … happened. I can understand it made our split quite nasty, because you couldn't deal with it, but you can't be *still* be angry about it now.'

He wasn't angry about it. He was angry with himself. On a hunch, he took a swing …

'Why did you and your first husband get divorced?'

'Fuck off.'

… and hit.

Like an image through a lens suddenly twisted into focus, Katrina resolved; resolved and shrank, in the same manner as the short, simple answer to a superficially complex equation. And she wasn't that interesting. She wasn't that interesting, but, good Lord, how badly she wanted to be.

He didn't hate her for it. In a way, he actually felt quite sorry for her. It would never have lasted between them, though. She was a bit of a wacko. She was just Katrina: one of his less significant girlfriends. She was, absolutely, no Trudie.

'I think, Kat,' Chris said, 'that you need drama a little too much.'

'And you, *totally*, don't know what you want at all,' she spat back.

He nodded. 'That was true, I'd say. It *was*. Past tense. I don't get to use the past tense as often as most people – trust me about that. But I recognise it when I see it.'

Katrina snorted and swung her vagina around to face away from him. 'I think you'd better leave.'

'Yeah,' Chris replied quietly. 'I think you're right. You ... You take care of yourself, OK?' he said to her bottom.

He meant it sincerely, and it was – despite everything – a pretty darn good bottom, so closure probably didn't come much better than this.

He turned the key in the ignition. Like the sound of a smoker in the morning, there was a high, wheezy rasp from the starter motor before the engine caught and took over, deeper and louder. Chris sat for a moment and looked out at Katrina's place one last time. This was her house; it would never – whatever he'd have done differently had he been able to go back to 1988 and make alternations – have been his, have been theirs. He didn't believe in fate, but some things were never meant to be. It isn't that they're not in your destiny; they're simply not in *you*. You can't exactly decide the path your life will take – some paths are blocked off or never offered to you in the first place – but the type of person you are means that you won't walk down whatever is in front of you either. It's not passive. We don't get to choose our options. We do get to refuse to take a few of them. Running water carves into stone over time – shapes and changes it; nothing can prevent that.

But the result doesn't depend on the water alone; it also depends upon the kind of stone it meets.

There was no way – not in a million multiverses or a billion parallel realities – he would have ended up in bloody Wiltshire with a bloody SUV and a bloody mauve bedroom.

He slipped the car into gear and began to drive home.

27

Andrew faced away as he pulled on his underpants. Pulling his underpants back on was always an awkward point. Taking them off was easy: he was motivated, in high spirits and free of very much self-consciousness when taking them off because he was focused on the underpantless things to come. Such feelings had evaporated when the time came to return to them, however. Re-panting was a melancholy, sombre experience; always uncomfortable and where full, ghastly embarrassment was never more than a snagged toe away.

'When will he be back, do you think?'

Andrew aimed at sounding conversational and light. He got quite close, but this just made it seem weirder because the mood wasn't conversational and light. The faux reasonableness caused it to stand out all the more. He sounded like a Hare Krishna at a prison riot.

'I don't know.' Trudie was already dressed. But then, she'd never actually been *un*dressed. Her jeans had been down – concertinaed at her ankles – and her T-shirt had been pulled up to under her armpits. She'd been sort of temporarily 'opened', like a pair of curtains; but she'd never really been undressed. 'I told you,' she said in a slightly irritated monotone. 'He refused to tell me exactly how long he'd be away.'

Andrew zipped up his fly quickly. It made an annoyingly loud (and annoyingly comic) noise in the tetchy silence.

'Yes,' he said, 'but I wondered if you had a general feeling.' Andrew had called his friend the previous evening but Chris hadn't wanted to talk and had been evasive even in what he did say, apart from mentioning he was confident he'd be back in 1988 very soon now. 'If it seemed to you,' Andrew continued, 'like he intended to be two days, or three, or whatever.'

'It seemed to me like he didn't know himself.' She rounded up her hair with one hand, folded it in half and threw it loosely through an elasticated tie she'd been carrying on her wrist. 'Maybe he's not sure how long his stamina will last out. He knows he won't return from the grubby orgy he's having at Neil's with Louise sodding Fischer until he's too exhausted to manage another thrust but he's not sure how many days that will take – not now he's been in training for it.'

'I really don't think that's likely, Trude. I don't know why you've got it in your head. I doubt he can even remember Louise Fischer.'

'Pff. Anyway, he can remember thrusting, I bet. If it's not Louise Fischer it'll be someone else. Christ, it can't be that difficult. They're *everywhere* nowadays.'

'Who are?'

'Women.' Trudie gave herself a quick once-over in the bedroom mirror to check that she didn't look like she'd just been hastily shagged. 'And, before you say anything about my having no right to be angry with Chris considering what we're doing, it's not the same thing at all.'

'Gosh, no,' exclaimed Andrew, keen to reassure her that he was distressed she might believe he thought that. 'With us it's never just been about sex. It's far more than that.'

Trudie realised that what she'd meant was it wasn't the same because Chris would be enjoying himself. *He* would be loving every second of it, the selfish bastard – that's what she resented. This thought had enough momentum that it very nearly crashed out of her mouth, but she caught it just in time and dragged it back, for Andrew's sake. She felt responsible for him.

She was responsible for him because she was responsible for the situation. She had allowed this to happen. She hadn't resisted the first time because at that particular point in her life it had seemed like a perfect opportunity; a chance to offer the scathing challenge 'Why the hell *shouldn't* I, eh?' to, pretty much, the universe in general. The second time had gone by, as best as she could recall, almost entirely on the basis of shrugging to herself 'Well, you've already done it once, Trudie . . .' The second time was sort of the original's tag-along. 'Hi,' it had said, standing at the door and peering round her to the party inside as it spoke, 'I'm Angry

Infidelity's plus one.' Yet, by allowing a second time, she'd set a pattern; raised a legitimate expectation; concluded a tacit agreement. What could she do? She'd made her bed; she'd just have to be laid in it.

That said, Trudie fully accepted that there had, early on, been a thrilling side to this. Illicit sex – secret liaisons – all that stuff. There was the delight of revenge too. That had perked her up no end and, she felt, done so in a wholly beneficial way. Revenge seems to have got a reputation for maniacal cackling while smearing yourself in your victim's blood (black in the moonlight), but achieving it had left her wanting to make daisy chains and, perhaps, skip. Chris had been a tosser for ages, and now she was having sex with someone else. This proved there was a measure of justice in the world after all – and that reassurance always has a civilising effect on people. He deserved this, and now he'd got it. This – this which she hoped he'd never even suspect was happening – *this* would show him. There was also the wonderful, intoxicating, addictive, vain and self-centred gratification of making someone happy. She had the power to make Andrew *deliriously* happy – and to do so with almost lazy ease; like the trailing overboard hand of a goddess painting lilies into life on the surface of a lake. So, yes, Trudie accepted that, for two or three weeks, the situation hadn't exactly been a burden she'd borne through gritty stoicism alone. She hadn't planned it or intended it; she didn't eagerly encourage or avidly intensify it; but what she mostly didn't do was stop it. While shaking her head lamenting that it was happening, she never quite managed to shake it enough to say 'No.'

Yet the sparkle it had possessed had begun to tarnish very quickly. One particularly terrible watershed moment had been when Andrew had first said that he loved her. Well, not exactly the first time, but the first time it wasn't said within the Zone of Disqualification that surrounds ejaculation. Anything uttered inside the Zone obviously has no relevance whatsoever outside it; that's nothing more than common sense. For example, however sincerely a man may have made the request while in the Zone, it's a safe bet that he doesn't want you to twist his nipples and call him Julie as a general rule. In the Zone – good; in the queue at Halford's – bad. The first non-Zone time Andrew had said he loved her had been at what he called 'their table' in what he called 'their place' (even though it was clearly Coffee Republic's table in Coffee Republic's place). To Trudie, it had felt like someone had walked up behind her, pulled open the neck at the back of her dress, and poured a bucketful of chilled worms down it. She'd just sat there, staring at him. Maybe he'd wanted her to reply, 'I love you too.' He'd got staring: silent staring. If this disappointed him then he didn't realise how hard 'silent staring' had needed to struggle in Trudie to stay in front of 'striking across the teeth with a spoon'.

Not only didn't she love Andrew in return, but now, instead of basking in the ability to make him foolishly happy, she had apparently been fitted against her will to a dead man's handle that would cause him to be horribly, horribly unhappy if she let go of it. And, after that first time he'd said it, the others followed without inhibition. In person, or on the phone, or in texts; he loved her multiple times each day, the bastard.

This is when it'd had truly become something that made her spirit sag each morning as she woke up and remembered it. Terrible guilt had fully arrived then too. She'd felt guilty before, but now it was in her blood like a chronic illness. She wouldn't simply 'feel guilty' in an abstract kind of way, she'd find herself struck by it – it would rev up her pulse, set her face burning and constrict her lungs; it was shame that aspired to malaria. She felt truly guilty about being unfaithful, though perhaps more as a concept than about being unfaithful to Chris, specifically. However, she was twistingly guilty about Andrew's wife. Whenever she thought about Gill it was like someone was going over her with one of those spiked things they use to aerate lawns.

So why did she allow it to continue when there was no longer any pleasure in it? Partly because she feared how devastated Andrew would be if she called a halt – he might do something crazy – but probably also *because* there was no pleasure in it. She was unhappy, and unhappiness gives you quite a taste for the painful and the self-destructive; if you feel horrible enough, choosing to inflict them on yourself can even provoke a sort of bleak elation. People often overlook that about misery: it's really quite moreish.

'Has it?' repeated Andrew. She saw from his expression that he was anxious for confirmation. That was clear. Now if only she could recall what he was talking about before she'd drifted away for a couple of seconds and a few hundred miles.

'Has what?'

'The sex. It hasn't been about it. Ever. Has it? With us.'

'Oh, right. No. Definitely not.'

Andrew nodded, reassured. Then looked anxious again – even more anxious in fact. 'But the sex *has* been great, though, hasn't it? You've— not every time, I know, but you've—'

'I'm leaving Chris when he gets back.'

'Calm down, Trude.'

'I've never been calmer.'

'We've talked about this. Things are really difficult for me, what with—'

'I'm not leaving him for you, Andy – don't worry. I'm just leaving him.'

'Trude. *Trude* . . .' Andrew opened his arms imploringly, thought for a moment, then added, '*Trude*.'

'You ought to go. Gill will be wondering where you are.'

Andrew looked down and his eyes flicked from side to side, as though there were two bear traps on the floor and he was trying to decide which one to step in.

'Yes, OK. But I'll call you later. Don't do anything you'll regret.'

'Nice one. I'm sure there's a niche in the market for a service like that: "good advice many years too late".'

'Seriously, Trude.'

'Seriously, Andy: leave it. I've made up my mind. *Finally*, I've made up my mind.'

Andrew stared at her and knew it was worse than that. She hadn't simply made up her mind; she'd made up her mind to make up her mind. He could see it in her face: immutable, self-sustaining, that's-fucking-*it*-ness. There was no point trying to persuade her to take a different path, because the direction she'd chosen was almost less of an issue than her decision, lashed to the wheel, to stick to it.

He hoped this wasn't going to get messy. No – no use even hoping that; it was going to get messy. He hoped it wouldn't get messy over him. He'd tried *so* hard to maintain the rickety equilibrium of his friend's marriage. He'd soothed and advised and encouraged and done pretty much everything imaginable short of not having sex with Trudie. He really, really, *really* didn't want this to get messy over him now and destroy his whole life. It would be incredibly unfair. He didn't deserve to have everything collapse beneath his feet. Stalin – after a good meal – had died in his bed, aged seventy-four, with his daughter by his side. Where was the fairness in that? OK, technically, putting quite a lot of time and thought into the project of sleeping with the wife of your best friend, and cheating on your own wife in the process, might be regarded as a bit iffy, especially out of context – but did that make him *worse than Stalin?* He was, frankly, feeling not a little victimised here.

'Where are you?'

'On my way home.'

'Really?' said Andrew, glad he hadn't stayed with Trudie.

'Yeah. I reckon I'll be there in ten or fifteen minutes,' Chris answered cheerfully.

'Really?' Andrew said again, promoting his gladness that he hadn't stayed with Trudie to the bowel-loosening level. 'You're on the road now?'

'Yep.'

'Um ... are you driving while using your mobile?'

'Yep. Man, it's tricky, isn't it?' Chris let go of the steering wheel entirely for a moment to change gear, and idly wondered if showing you were able to use the phone while driving was part of the test these days. 'How did you know I was here?'

'I didn't know where you were. I don't need to know where you are if I ring your mobile, remember?'

'Chk – obviously. I'm not an idiot. I meant how did you know I was *here*, still in 2006? I could easily have been back in 1988 by now.'

'Easily. I suppose I just got lucky.'

'I *am* definitely still in 2006, by the way.'

'Phew. That's a relief – the charges are steep enough even for calling internationally. Lord knows what it'd cost me to call the eighties, especially when I'm not on that plan.'

'I think ... I think I'm going to be here for good.'

'Well, erm – "sorry", mate. Hate to say, "I told you so," but . . . And, actually, that makes—'

'No need for sorrys. I'm moving towards the opinion that it might not be that bad a thing, in fact.'

Du fehlst mir.

What had struck Chris, all those years ago, about how one says 'I miss you' in German was that it was essentially the same as the way one says it in English. It wasn't like some phrases, where the literal translation of what you're saying is totally different – The weather is fab – *Das Wetter ist affen titten geil* (The weather is monkey-tits horny). In English Chris had always talked of missing someone without really listening to what he was saying. Missing someone, his emotional grammar had simply assumed, was something that one *did*, an action one engaged in. 'I'm missing you' was, in that way, the same as 'I'm pulling you' or 'I'm calling you.' But *fehlen* – to miss – had made the real sense clear to him: *fehlen* – to be absent from. 'I miss you' is really 'You are missing *from me*.' It's 'I'm incomplete because a part of me isn't there, the part of me that you are;' 'This hole in me is the hole left by your being away.'

Du fehlst mir.

This is the phrase that had abruptly gate-crashed his thoughts when at Katrina's he'd faced returning to a life – to a Chris – that had no Trudie in it.

'Honestly,' Chris repeated, 'it's not a bad thing at all.'

'Chris, you should probably know—'

'I mean, there's—'

'God! Will you just shut up and listen to me?'

Andrew sounded as though he was perilously close to having a fit. Chris's immediate concern therefore was to wonder what he could say to nudge him over the edge into all-out, warbling meltdown – after all, as Andrew's friend, he did have a duty to push things in the funniest direction. But, what the hell, let this one go, eh? It was Christmas.

'All right,' Chris replied appeasingly, 'you fuckwit. I'm listening. What is it?'

'Right. Well, you should probably know . . .'

'Yes?'

'You should probably know . . .'

'What? *What?*'

Andrew leaned back into the chair in his conservatory and closed his eyes. 'You should probably know that we're stuffed.'

'Who? How? Why?'

'Us. Completely. Bad luck – just rubbish, rubbish luck.'

'I see. Yes, I see. Thanks. Now only the detail of what the fuck you're talking about remains slightly unclear.'

'It's ... it's our generation, mate. We're battered. We're the weary result of just one damn thing after another. All the way from puberty to middle age we've had it.'

'Had what?'

'The *lot*. Do you remember when we were teenagers, and we thought nuclear Armageddon might arrive at any moment? Not that it was a worrying *possibility*, mind you, but that it was near enough a sure thing. Each second the sirens didn't start to wail was a surprise. That was the start of us. Then we had the Falklands War – which wasn't how it's reconstructed in retrospect from newspaper headlines; it was depressing, scary and grim. Still, not to worry, because after that along came Aids. What else might we fancy, eh? BSE, mass unemployment, negative equity, terrorism, international terrorism, state terrorism and home-grown terrorism – we haven't missed a *single* terrorism. The ozone layer. The *ozone layer*. "Good morning. Today's news: they've *broken the sky.*" From there to global warming and general ecological collapse. MRSA. Legionnaires'. E. coli. C. diff. Bird flu. The world's most ill-considered war. Hold on – are we starting to think about our retirement now? Right then. Line up a pensions crisis. Knife crime, gun crime, gang crime – plus identity theft and happy slapping: new crimes invented just for us. Deforestation, overfishing, coastal erosion, falling sperm counts, postcode lotteries, religion – back again and as mad as ever – pesticides on fruit, meat full of steroids, oestrogen in the water, compensation culture, cyber stalking, downsizing, outsourcing and globalisation. And the already-announced coming attractions? Well, take your pick from a crippling fuel shortage, the Ebola virus or a planet-destroying meteorite.

'Never, Chris, *never* has a generation had such a relentless succession of blows to the spirit. We're troubled and anxious because we've been moulded by troubles and anxiety since adolescence.'

'*I* haven't,' Chris replied. 'I'll grant you I got hit by a few of those things you mentioned, but the others mean nothing to me. I've skipped past nearly twenty years of them.'

'Nonsense. You might not remember it, but it's in you and sooner or later it'll make itself felt. And then, you're here with the rest of us: stuffed.'

'Even if you were right about my having amnesia – which you're not – how can you be shaped by what you can't remember? It's not in you as an experience. It can't affect who you are because, from your perspective, it never happened. And, anyway . . .' Chris paused, recalling Neil, and also, as he was doing a bit of recalling, Katrina. 'I believe that people are altered by what happens to them, but *how* it alters them depends on who they were in the first place. The same experience might change people in completely opposite directions: we're all we've known placed in the hands of all we are.'

Andrew didn't reply.

'Are you still there?' Chris asked.

'Imagine what you want, but you're among us now.'

'Woo, "*You're among us now.*" That sounds vaguely satanic. Should I get a cowl?'

'You are where you are. And you're here with us: forty-somethings who've come to expect the worse, and never yet been stood up by it. You need to prepare yourself or it'll be all the harder on you. Ditch any optimism, mate – it's a liability.'

Chris frowned. 'Is there something specific you're trying to tell me about?'

'Specific? No – God, no. It's just a general piece of advice.'

'You're simply calling to tell me that everything is awful? You're simply calling me for no particular reason on Christmas Eve to tell me that everything is awful and I should erase all hope from my soul?'

'Yeah . . . There's never really a good time to say it.'

'Anything else? Or is that it until I'm close enough for you to throw a puppy in front of the car?'

'I'm trying to help you out, mate, that's all. Prepare you so you don't go overreacting to any unfortunate situation you might encounter. As you're bound to encounter one. Bound to, statistically, that is.'

'You know, Andrew: career success, a family, and nearly two decades haven't made you any less weird.'

28

There was a bin bag in the hallway. It was leaning, half full, against
the wall next to the front door and Chris peered at it as he took
off his jacket and threw it over the newel post. It wasn't something
that he found deeply intriguing – it provoked a small, passing
curiosity, that's all. Perhaps it contained rubbish Trudie had been
carrying to the dustbin outside when she'd been distracted by
something. She'd put it down to answer the phone or some such
thing, and had forgotten about it. It was, he knew, amazingly easy
to forget about domestic chores in the middle of doing them.
Simply walking past the television is often sufficient to wipe your
mind; eyes entranced by the screen, you lower yourself slowly onto
the sofa, and it's hours later before you gaze down and – like a
forensic archaeologist – try to work out why the hell there's a
duster in your hand. It's notoriously hard for the human brain to
retain sinks too: Chris couldn't even bother trying to guess at the
number of times he'd shuffled into his kitchen just before going to
bed and, 'Ah, yes – there was all that washing up.' So, a bin bag
in the hallway was unusual, but hardly mysterious or significant.

Trudie had placed the bin bag there with a determined and
ruthless sense of purpose; knowing that it was a sign Chris couldn't
miss. It was a clear warning. Not one meant to help him to brace
himself for what was ahead, however, its role wasn't to soften the
punch, but to enhance the trauma of the experience as a whole by
adding some fearful expectation to the pot. Exactly where to
carelessly dump it had required a good deal of thought, and it'd
been an arduous journey even to get to that point because filling
the bin bag hadn't been easy either. It wasn't a plastic bag loaded
with stuff; it was a plastic bag loaded with messages. As an
illustration, take his blue shirt. Trudie liked his blue shirt. She'd
said more than once that it suited him. So, putting that in the bag

was an unqualified rejection: The best you have is nothing to me. Except Trudie had given her lip a good biting over whether it might be taken as thoughtfulness: There . . . I've put your best shirt in for you. In fact, she'd loaded everything into a suitcase and was about to carry it down the stairs before, with an exasperated roar, she'd realised that this looked a bit like she'd 'packed for him'. She'd had to take it all out again and move it into a bin bag to strike the right note of dismissive contempt. Conveying flippant indifference requires sustained effort and attention to detail. On top of that was the issue of afterwards. Though she might be angry, she wasn't doing this because she wanted Chris to be unhappy; she was doing it because *she* was unhappy and couldn't take it any more. It was *for* her, not against Chris. That said, the very worst possible thing would be for him to leave and be fine. She didn't want him to end up on the streets, or in prison, or dead. But she certainly didn't want him hooking up with a giggling twenty-year-old he'd pulled in his blue shirt either. A good balance would be if he got himself together and salvaged his career at Short Stick, but then spent his evenings alone and miserable and given to bouts of uncontrollable weeping.

Trudie heard Chris open the front door. She wriggled herself into a better-looking position on the sofa and concentrated on her expression to make sure it was expressionless.

Half a dozen seconds passed. The living-room door didn't open. What was Chris doing? Trudie strained her ears. Christ – what if he didn't come in? What was she supposed to do then? She'd seen the moment perfectly in her mind: Chris would spot the bin bag, look inside, realise what it meant and become a little queasy; he'd then step fearfully into the living room, where she – expressionless – would declare, 'I'm leaving you.' Perfect.

But was Chris going to bugger up even this? What if he plodded off through the house without poking his nose into the living room at all? What if he went right to the shower, or to his stupid gym, or to cook himself something? She'd be left sitting there – expressionless, and primed, and like a prat – while he slouched at the table in the dining room eating a crispy bloody pancake. What could she do then? She couldn't go and search him out – that would shift the balance horribly. He needed to come upon her and her cool, imperious presence. If she had to trot after him it'd be rubbish. Damn. Why hadn't she considered this? Basically, all he had to do was keep out of the living room and she'd have to stay there waiting – expressionless – until dehydration overtook her.

'Oh – you're here,' said Chris.

For Christ's sake. He'd waited just long enough for her concentration to slip; just long enough for her to get lost in her thoughts and her expression to drift from expressionless to utterly, utterly gormless. She straightened her back and brazened it out.

'I'm leaving you.'

Chris squinted at her. She saw him out of the corner of her eye, but resisted the temptation to turn and examine his face more closely quite yet.

'Have you been waiting here to tell me that?' Chris asked.

'Yes,' she replied coolly.

'You've been sitting there waiting, so that you could tell me you're leaving? Isn't that a bit ... I mean, you could have simply left, couldn't you? It would have saved time.'

'It ...' Trudie had almost forgotten how infuriating it could be arguing with Chris when he was sober. At least when he was drunk he argued properly – rambling, irrational, emotional. When he didn't have a few whiskies inside him he was a different person, and getting into a disagreement with him could be risky for her: she might easily pop a blood vessel from the sheer, pumping rage of rowing with a man who didn't have any qualms about not losing his temper. Thinking quickly, she veered away before he could trap her with details. 'When I say I'm leaving you, I don't mean I'm leaving this house. *You're* leaving the house. I've put your stuff by the door.'

'Which door?'

'The front door.'

'Really? Where?'

'In the bloody bin bag!'

'Oh – that's what that is.'

'You didn't even have a look what was in it?'

'Why would I? It's a bin bag. Who goes round peering into bin bags?'

This wasn't remotely the homecoming Chris had hoped for. Bin bags were not something he was very interested in – he'd have happily left them out of the discussion entirely – but as Trudie seemed to be curiously fascinated by the things, he resigned himself to the fact of having to deal with them.

'Anyway,' he added, 'there was a knot. It was knotted at the top. I couldn't see inside.'

'You could have undone it. It wasn't even tight – just looped through itself once.'

'Once is more than enough, if it's a bin bag. You don't go "Hey, it'd be fairly easy to lever up the grating over there – reckon I'll have a root around in that drain, then." It's a bin bag.'

'It's a bin bag *in the hallway*.'

'Which is directly between—'

'Jesus – never mind the fucking bin bag! I'm leaving you!'

She glared at him and, furious and fragile in equal measure, tried to look commanding while also trying to hold herself together.

Chris lowered his gaze and shook his head sadly, as though he were desperate to understand the situation but couldn't manage it because it was simply beyond his grasp.

'But you,' he began, 'were the one who brought up—'

'Never mind *the fucking bin bag*!'

Trudie rose angrily to her feet and, barging Chris out of the way, stomped from the room.

In the hallway she stood with her hands on her hips, breathing rapidly, and was confronted almost instantly with the ghastly realisation that she hadn't finished. It was impossibly dispiriting when she did that: made the dramatic gesture of ringing finality, then found she simply *had* to add a few extra points.

She stormed back into the room. (She was well aware that this was awful, style-wise, but the alternative was to be left holding things she still wanted to say – which was so appalling it couldn't be seriously considered as an option.)

'But then, why should I have expected anything else?' she asked scornfully.

The rather stunned look on Chris's face told her that what she'd just said hadn't registered. She was right. When she'd crashed out through the door he'd absolutely not expected her to crash back in and start talking again almost immediately – her words were washed away in the surprise of it.

'Sorry. What?'

'Why should I think for one second that you'd have any curiosity about anything? The only thing you're interested in is yourself. You're completely self-obsessed.'

Chris clicked his teeth. 'There's a measure of truth in that,' he admitted.

This was so far from the kind of reply Trudie had prepared herself for that her mind went blank. Her mouth opened and closed a few times, like a shed door in the wind, but she couldn't think of a single word to send out of it. So, just so she didn't continue to simply stand there looking like a slow-witted fool, she strode across to the coffee table, picked up a magazine, and threw it against the wall.

It struck Chris that this really wasn't the sort of behaviour he'd expect from a forty-three-year-old and, as he wasn't forty-three years old either, he smiled at the idea of it. They were a fitting pair. Trudie saw him smile, and, as a result, found her thoughts were no appreciable distance from a desire to be kneeling over his body with a bloodied poker in her hand.

Her face tight with rage, she growled – actually *growled* this time – 'I'm leaving you.'

Chris sighed deeply. He looked off to the side at nothing in particular for a moment, then turned his eyes back to her and scratched his cheek. 'I'd prefer it if you didn't,' he said.

This, Trudie thought, was hardly a declaration of love that would echo throughout eternity. It could easily be argued that though it contained an element of 'Please stay,' it was mostly made up of 'but I'm not that fussed, mind.'

However, there was curious sincerity to it. Chris seemed slightly embarrassed – it had about it the awkwardness and discomfort that indicates a man must be telling you something that he genuinely feels.

She decided not to speak – to wait for him to continue instead. 'Well, that's lovely, Chris, but being a vague "preference" isn't enough for me, I'm afraid,' she said. (Not speaking was *really* difficult to pull off.)

Chris gazed at her and rubbed his fingers slowly back and forth over his lips for what seemed, to both of them, a long, long time.

After intense consideration he finally, visibly, reached a conclusion. His posture changed so that he now appeared resolved, almost noble.

'Bollocks,' he replied.

He moved over to Trudie; close enough to touch her (though he held himself back from doing that).

'Here's the thing,' he continued with quiet gravity. 'I know you believe I'm the Chris you married, but, actually, I'd never even met you until a few weeks ago. I'm Chris Mortimer, but an earlier Chris Mortimer. I was in 1988 and the next thing I knew I'd been thrown through time and I woke up here, in this body. I'm not sure whether or not that makes me your husband. Probably it's a bit of a legal grey area. But—' It was here that Trudie kneed him in the groin.

Chris folded in half and stumbled back into the computer table as she ran from the room.

In fact, he'd been quick with his flinch and so she hadn't actually managed to catch him – her knee had merely brushed over its target before going on to uselessly hit his leg. But a near miss will still shake you up. *Oh* yes. It's no small thing, psychologically: *almost* being struck in the testicles is like the soldier standing right next to you getting killed. Chris needed a few moments to process events and come to terms with how he'd been little more than a millimetre from a heart-chilling collision and then pull himself together. By the time he'd done this Trudie had pitched herself out of the front door and was half-sprinting, half-falling down the driveway. Chris saw her through the living-room window and started off after her.

When he reached the pavement in front of the house she was already ten yards away down the street – haring along full-bloodedly despite looking like someone who was having a go at running on the basis of nothing more than having seen someone do it on TV once.

'Trudie!' he called.

'Bastard!' she called back.

'Chris,' said the man from Number 112, flicking his chin up at him as he pulled carrier bags of shopping from the boot of his Avensis. Chris raised his hand and flicked his chin up in reply.

Chris's knees were a little sore and his left ankle was 'clicking'. He was someone who ran now ('ran' – not 'jogged'; never 'jogged'). That meant he'd raised his legs to a level of fitness where there was always at least one thing wrong with them: a strain in his calf, an Achilles tendon problem, that peculiar ache at the base of his buttocks, etc., etc. However, though Trudie's muscles might not regularly set almost solid overnight so the first ten minutes of every morning were spent moving about as though one had only as many joints as a cheap action figure, they were no match for his in this situation. His heart and lungs were better too. While Trudie's would pull her up from pain in a few dozen seconds, Chris's could keep him in pain for thirty minutes or more without his needing to stop. Next to her, he was as an Olympian god.

She'd scarcely reached where Tithe Barn Avenue curved into the main road before he was alongside her. He kept pace, looking across but not speaking.

She seethed. It was maddening, this apparent ease with which he was loping along at her shoulder when every breath tore at her throat. Her chest burned with resentment, and burning.

Even before this moment she'd hated his running, as she'd hated his getting himself into shape with his gym. Everything she did, or would like to do, was surrounded by repelling bands of dilemmas or lack of time or guilt; she fretted herself into a corner over and over again trying to reconcile all the factors she felt were pressing on her. Chris, on the other hand, just did what the hell he wanted. It was typical, bloody *typical*, that he'd stopped being a useless, self-pitying drunk. If he fancied being an alcoholic, he was an alcoholic; when he got bored with that and decided to be healthy instead, well, that's what he did. The *bastard*.

And all this was boiling under the immediate anger caused by his mocking her. She'd finally done it: laid her feelings down before him. And what had he done? Made a stupid joke. At the very moment when she was most serious he'd amused himself by treating her like a three-year-old. It was as though she'd staggered from a car accident that had smashed her mouth into the dashboard and, when she'd come to him, shocked and bleeding, he'd grinned and said, 'Hold on – I'll just call the tooth fairy.' She was used to him been self-centred, but she'd never thought he could be deliberately cruel.

Her legs were starting to go now. The crashing squelches of her heart and her lungs' raw rasps were, she'd thought, merely emissaries of death. She couldn't quieten them, but she assumed that they'd do no more than kill her. Her legs were different. You can't die of legs. They weren't threatening her life; they were, increasingly, simply choosing to ignore her. Beyond wobbly, is refusal; it was as if the messages from her brain calling for continued movement were left standing outside the door. 'Speed up!' Nothing. 'Move! *Move!*' Nothing. She knew that her only options were either to come to a standstill or to fall into a heap. She chose the former, just in case (it seemed unlikely, but maybe she had a tiny sliver of dignity left that she wasn't aware of).

Trudie was near the entrance to the pub car park by now. She let herself keel sideways until she'd semi-toppled close enough to the first in a line of concrete bollards to be able to sit on it. Chris followed. He walked across to the next bollard along and sat down; he looked over at her, hands on his knees and leaning forward slightly.

'Well,' he said, 'you took it better than I expected.'

She tried to glare at him, but she hadn't got enough energy to manage it. The air was cold on her hot wet face, and all she could do was gasp, and sit, and sweat.

'Maybe I should have told you before,' Chris continued. He was a little out of breath, but not very much and recovering greatly with each half-second that passed. 'But I think it's one of those things where the timing isn't going to make a great deal of difference anyway. I think that, whenever I'd told you, you'd have tried to kick me in the groin.' He shrugged. 'That only leaves not telling you at all. And I felt . . . I don't know. I felt that keeping it from you that actually I'm twenty-five and not really your husband was a bad thing, in the context of a marriage.'

Trudie wondered if there'd been a dangerous build-up of carbon dioxide in her bloodstream because she couldn't help but think he was being serious. Had she misjudged him? Perhaps he wasn't uncaring and sarcastic; perhaps he was just completely fucking mental. She took a deep breath and (using it all) tested the waters.

'Are you completely fucking mental?'

'No.'

He seemed calm and lucid. She decided to double-check.

'Are you *sure* you're not completely fucking mental?'

'Yes, completely. No thinking I'm a teapot or anything.'

Trudie had herself a little cough. Her lungs were jealous of the attention she was giving Chris and wanted to remind her that they were still there and still hurt. When she'd finished she rubbed her forehead and croaked, 'I don't understand. What are you trying to say?'

'Look,' Chris said gently. 'I know this is a lot to take in on a Sunday morning on a bollard, but sit there and hear me out, OK?' He dipped his head and looked at her for confirmation. 'OK?'

She nodded. 'OK.' It was not a difficult assurance to give; she was still too exhausted to walk away in any case.

'Right – briefly – this is what's happened. It was 1988 and I was in the pub with my friends. I got drunk, so the latter part of the evening is a bit blurry, but when I woke up the next day, the next day was in 2006. I was in bed with you. I had no idea who you were or where I was, let alone *when* I was.'

'You had amnesia?'

'No.'

'So, you *could* remember?' Trudie's forehead wrinkled. 'But you just said you had no—'

'Amnesia is when you have no memory what you've done.'

'Yes. So, you had amnesia.'

'No. I hadn't done anything to forget. I'd travelled through time.'

'You're completely fucking mental.'

Chris sighed in a vaguely superior way. 'Do I *sound* mental?'

'Well, let's see. Say "I travelled through time" again.'

'That's what happened. I was hurled into the future, right into the body of a Chris who was eighteen years away from me.'

He genuinely *did* seem to be serious. Trudie was almost completely positive that he actually believed what he was saying. She suddenly felt horribly vulnerable.

'Chris, I need you to swear to me that you're telling the truth. If this is some kind of outlandish wind-up, then say now – *please*. Because if I allow myself to believe you, only to have you laugh and shout "Gotcha!" in a few minutes, then ...' Her voice became so quiet that Chris could hardly hear her. 'I couldn't take it.' She bit her lip. 'There are no threats left that I can make. So all I can do is ask that you do it out of ...'

'I swear to you I'm telling the truth.'

Trudie sat up straighter, inhaled deeply and nodded.

'Right, then,' she said. 'So, if you're not joking—'

'I'm not.'

'— and you're not completely fucking mental—'

'Ditto.'

'— then you *obviously* have amnesia.'

'Argh!' Chris got to his feet and threw up his hands. 'I do bleeding *not*!'

'Come on, Chris. It's obvious. It's not just that the time travel explanation is ... well – shite. It's also that amnesia makes perfect sense. There you are: depressed, confused and relentlessly battering your brain with alcohol. It's easy to understand that you had some kind of ... whatever – "episode". And it's easy to understand that your mind went back to a point when everything was secure and straightforward: a night you remembered from your past when you were with your friends, and young, and still had your choices ahead of you.'

'Yeah, that'd be so, so *easy* to understand, wouldn't it? That'd have everything boxed up and labelled in a second. My, but that would be easy for everyone.'

'Well, look at it this way: what difference does it make? Really? We can disagree on the facts but – in practical terms – isn't it identical for all involved whether you're an amnesiac forty-three-year-old, or a time-travelling twenty-five-year-old?'

'I am *impossibly* glad you asked that,' Chris replied, beaming with a sort of bitter triumph. 'Here's all I ask: simply take that exact same question and put it to yourself. Is your attitude to me – even though, externally, the two things might appear identical ... Is your attitude to me the same whether I'm a time-travelling twenty-five-year-old or an amnesiac forty-three-year old?'

Trudie didn't have to think about it – it was too plain to require even a second's consideration. A twenty-five-year-old man who finds himself in the body and the life of a forty-three-year-old and reacts against it accordingly (rather than just collapsing into shuffling acceptance) is admirable; commendably dynamic – you might even say he was brave. A forty-three-year-old man who appears to believe he's twenty-five and behaves as a person of that age is, on the other hand, a sad, ridiculous clown.

'Yes,' replied Trudie. 'My attitude is exactly the same either way.'

Chris smiled and, taking her hands in his, helped her to her feet.

'You're a wonderful liar,' he said. 'I mean, I knew you were a health service administrator so . . . but still – such conviction, such boldness.'

Trudie looked at him. She wanted, and didn't want, to ask, 'What do we do now?'

While not asking still had the edge, Chris said, 'Let's go home. I'm getting cold. Are you getting cold?'

'I don't know,' Trudie replied, which was as ridiculous as it was true.

It felt strange, sitting in their living room with this man.

Although he looked exactly as he had done only a short time earlier, the sense that she didn't know him was what dominated. She could have believed that inside that familiar skin he really was twenty-five, if she were still the kind of person who believed things.

What was more, she was aware that *he* didn't know *her*. This was especially troubling, because she couldn't decide whether she thought it was good or bad; a calamity or a gift.

But what was most curious of all was how Chris 'changing' changed *everything*. Changed it in the same way that you see your own town with altered, sympathetically foreign eyes if you're showing a tourist around it. In the same way that abruptly learning at eighteen that you were adopted makes you view your childhood differently. In the same way that things become sharper – brighter, more vivid – if you're sitting in your living room with someone who might just be deranged.

'God, I feel good,' Chris said, inhaling deeply – in the way you do when you've just reached the top of a hill: claiming the air. 'I know it was sensible that we decided to keep this secret, for all kinds of reasons, but—'

'We?'

'Oh. Andrew and me. I told him, on the day I arrived.'

'Andy's known about this *for a month*?'

'Yeah.'

'The . . .' Trudie's lips visibly struggled.

'The what?'

'I don't know . . . . Something worse than fucker. What's worse than *fucker*?'

Chris laughed. 'Calm down. He's harmless enough. Poor old Andrew – he's always been harmless.'

Trudie's jaw clenched.

'And it was for my sake that he helped conceal the situation from you,' Chris continued.

Trudie's jaw clenched even harder. She could have bitten through a bike lock.

'But, now it comes to it, it feels really good to tell you everything. Freeing. It's like stretching out after being bent double for weeks.'

And Chris did indeed proceed to tell Trudie absolutely everything, omitting nothing except that Katrina had been there on the night he'd left the eighties, and he'd thought she was the key to his returning, and he'd visited her the previous evening, and they'd had drunken sex across two different rooms.

It was great to be honest, thought Chris, but there was no sense being a bloody idiot about it.

'So,' Trudie said, 'seeing Neil wasn't the solution you were hoping it would be.'

'Not the one I was hoping for, but a solution all the same. I'm still in 2006, as you can see; but I'm *glad* I'm in 2006. I'm glad I'm here with you.'

'You'd "rather I didn't leave".'

'No, I'd really rather you didn't. Anyway, if you do, you'll be leaving the wrong person.'

'By that logic, if I stay I'm being unfaithful,' Trudie replied, though she couldn't quite look him in the eyes as she said it. She moved on rapidly. 'But why would you care? What's so special about me?'

'Well,' Chris said, 'for one thing I find it endearing that you'd fish for compliments as blatantly as that.'

'Despite the memory loss you haven't forgotten how to be a wanker then.'

'I just . . . I mean, I find you attractive – even though you're old enough to be my—'

'Wife. And that's it, is it? I suppose it must be. You can't remember—'

'Not "I can't remember"; "It never happened to me."'

'Whatever. Let's agree to disagree there.'

'Fine. I know it's true; and what I know and what's true are important to me, the same as they're important to anyone. All I ask is that you don't expect me to feign that I believe otherwise – not to you. OK?'

Trudie nodded.

'Anyway,' Chris continued, 'it isn't simply that I seem to have a thing for older women now. It's ... I don't know – it's hard to reduce it to words.'

He clicked his teeth and, frowning, tried to describe how he felt.

'I'd rather go to sleep with both of us lying there pissed off than be in bed without you.'

He tried again.

'I know what a nightmare you can be, and it doesn't appear to put me off you at all.'

Still not perfect.

He sat down on the coffee table so that their eyes were level and he could lean closer to her. He spoke softly.

'I never wish you weren't here generally, however much I wish you'd shut the fuck up at specific points.'

Trudie laid her hand across her heart. 'Well, it's barely any distance at all from there to a sonnet,' she replied. 'How deeply glorious.'

'It *is* glorious.' Chris got back to his feet, springy with energy once again. 'Maybe you can't see it because you're in your forties and it's crept up on you, but *I* find it amazing. Who doesn't want to be with someone when everything is moony grins and all the sex you can eat? But to be scared of the very thought of not waking up with them even when things are not so good – *that's* amazing. OK, perhaps how I feel is at least partly due to Old Chris – that is, your Chris – erm, *contaminating* me. I'm in his body, so a few bits of him are bleeding over. A very few, though. And if, when so much else is lost completely, his love for you still remains, and remains this powerfully, well – *that's* glorious too. Don't you think?'

Trudie did. The thought of it filled her throat.

She made a dismissive shape with her lips and shrugged non-committally.

'Look,' said Chris. 'This is the situation. I'm OK. You'd think I'd feel gypped out of half my life, but I don't. Quite honestly, I reckon that those people who can look back at their twenties and thirties feel more sadness and loss than I do. From what I've seen, if I'd come here by the usual route I'd be just as bemused and at least three times as bitter.'

'So, you're pleased that there are things you don't know?'

'Wouldn't you be? If it's shit, why do I want it in my head? If it's good, why condemn it to being a memory? So I can't remember marrying you. Well – fuck it: I can marry you again.

'I haven't had eighteen years draining the ability to look forward out of me. I have an unobstructed view of the future. It seems to me that, at forty-three, that's almost like having a super power. Christ – I might just get myself a cape and fight crime.'

Chris's enthusiasm was alluring, so instinctively Trudie resisted. If she could defend herself from its attractiveness long enough to analyse the situation fully, then she could neutralise it. (There was nothing so clear and simple that she couldn't make it confusing and uncertain by determined analysis. Give her a quiet ten minutes to think and she would always be able to reach the point of no longer knowing what the hell she wanted.)

'The question,' Chris went on, 'isn't me – I'm better than splendid about things. The question is, how do *you* feel?'

Well, *that* was an easy one.

'The answer is: I don't know.' Trudie stood up, then sat down again. 'It's so complicated. I don't even know where to start unpicking the implications of all this, it's simply too ... Philip K. Dick.'

'Let me make it easier. I spy on you in the shower.'

'Right.' Trudie nodded. 'That's ...'

'What? *What* is it? Here's what I've learnt about women in my twenty-five years on earth: they are completely subjective. A man who keeps calling, sending flowers and so on despite receiving no encouragement is either the gorgeous romantic they've always dreamed about or a creepy weirdo who won't leave them alone – entirely based on whether they fancy him or not. I – a man you only *thought* was your husband – has been sneakily peeking at you in the shower. How do you feel about that? Not generally, but with me; subjectively. Are you horrified?'

Trudie shook her head. 'Well ... no.'

'Angry?'

'No.'

'What then?'

'You know what. Don't make me say it.'

Chris smiled. He sat on the sofa next to her and took her hands in his.

'Then we can make it,' he said. 'I'm an accidental time traveller, you're some kind of weird, horny exhibitionist. That's something we can really build on.'

Trudie laughed and reached up to touch his face.

'You fucking idiot,' she said. She shook her head and tutted. 'You remind me of someone I married once.'

Sliding his hand up around the back of her neck, Chris leaned forward and (terrified – absolutely *terrified*) kissed her. Trudie kissed him back. He felt fourteen years old.

'It dug into me – my going back to the eighties – when I thought that, as I left, Old Chris would probably return,' he said when they parted for oxygen. 'Even if I couldn't be with you, I hated the thought that you'd get stuck with him again.'

'Where do you think he is now?' Trudie asked half seriously, playing along.

'Perhaps we swapped. Perhaps he's stuck in a crappy ground-floor flat watching *Junior Kick Start* with one of my less-significant girlfriends. Serves him right.'

He put his arm around her and lay back on the sofa, pulling her down beside him.

They stayed there together, silently, Chris slowly combing Trudie's hair with his fingers.

'I haven't got you a Christmas present,' he said apologetically.

'I smashed all your DVDs this morning,' she replied.

They began to kiss again.

CHAPTER ONE

Before too long, Chris accepted that he wasn't *really* a time-travelling twenty-five-year-old and must indeed have suffered from sudden, massive amnesia. You'd think. But that just shows how much what *you* think is worth, eh? In fact, to this day he still maintains his original position happily and absolutely. Which, at the very least, means we have to consider the possibility that he's right. (I'm certainly not going to say it's one way or the other. If you can't bear not knowing which is true, then don't blubb to me about it; I'm the narrator, not your mum.)

To avoid tiresome bother and silly questions, however, Chris's belief is not something they air publicly. Publicly, it amuses Chris to maintain the outrageous pretence that he hasn't travelled through time at all. Most evenings, sitting together on the sofa just before going up to bed, Trudie gives him a tale from 'their' past, to fill him in on the back story and so help him maintain his cover. She enjoys telling him these stories, and he loves listening to her. One of the first she ever told was the story of how they'd met – on the Tube, with her stepping out to take him down a peg or two, just as the doors were closing.

'You're *kidding*?' said Chris, beaming across the whole width of his face. 'Did I ask you to marry me? There and then?'

'What? No – absolutely not.'

'Did you call me a twat?'

'Yes.'

'Close enough.'

Chris filed this away for operational purposes but, as far as he was concerned, the way he'd really meet her was that he'd just woken up one morning, and there she was. As simple and as perfect as that.

Chris and Trudie celebrate on Christmas Eve every year. How

they celebrate is not important, and is – as it happens – shockingly obscene; what matters is that they both savour the idea of celebrating then rather than on Christmas Day. Of celebrating things to come.

They regularly see Andrew and Gill. Trudie knows that every day she doesn't seriously think, I'm going to tell Chris about Andrew; it's the best thing to do and will allow us to re-establish our relationship on a totally honest footing, is a great day. The day she does, she'll have gone hopelessly senile and will need putting in a home. Love is (as Chris has already demonstrated) not being a bloody fool about things.

Andrew is now more attentive to Gill than at any time since they first met. It's not just guilt. It's gratitude. Sometimes the thought of how outrageously lucky he is to have her makes him actually laugh out loud. He'll stand there – in the garden, perhaps – alone, laughing out loud. If her friends are around, it embarrasses the hell out of Charlotte.

Humans make mistakes. Fortunately, to compensate for this failing, they also have the capacity to keep secrets and to lie. It's beautiful, really, if you think about it.

Chris and Trudie sometimes see Neil and Ann too. When they do, Trudie and Ann often sit side by side, listening to Chris and Neil, and wondering whether – if they'd met them when they were as they are when they're together – they'd have ever got involved with them.

Given your track record of assumptions, you might think that Chris left Short Stick – in a set-piece scene of a dramatic, ego-waving fashion – and became a skydiving instructor or went backpacking around China or some such thing. He didn't. Almost everyone hates that they have to work, and almost everyone has to work harder than Chris does. His actual response was far more unusual – very nearly unprecedented, in fact, in a forty-something man in a media-related field: he went in, did his job, and stopped being such a precious, whiny tosser about it.

Spending half your life resenting your job is just letting it define you by the back door. Chris turned up, did his stuff, and then walked away at five o'clock without a second thought but with another day's worth of money heading for his bank account. Aware that he actually earned enough to live perfectly acceptably by doing nothing that painful, really – rather than, say, getting just 50p after sitting in a hut in Nairobi seven days a week making sandals out of old car tyres – he Got a Bleeding Grip. He even made an effort to avoid annoying his colleagues, if he could help it. He feigned admiration for their projects; he smiled sympathetically when they told him their troubles; he secretly placed – when the air conditioning had broken down and the heat was relentless – an open, out-of-date tub of coleslaw behind the filing cabinet in Euan's office. (Sometimes, you *can't* help it.)

Trudie spontaneously and for no remotely identifiable reason took up kendo, the Japanese sword-fighting martial art. That he had a wife who, spontaneously and for no remotely identifiable reason, should take up, in her mid-forties, something as spectacularly pointless as kendo filled Chris with a brimming glow of unspoken pride. Sometimes he went to watch her. He occasionally suspected that for Trudie, in a complex and uncertain world, there was great respite value in any time spent simply trying to hit someone with a big stick. But mostly he was satisfied to know nothing more than that an hour of it always meant she was, when she got home, so horny that he excitedly, breathlessly and eagerly feared for his life.

But the very best thing of all was the nights. Chris would lie there with Trudie's soft warmth curled against him, unable to smell her neck without letting out a relaxing, involuntary 'Mmmm.' He very much suspected that, as the years went on, he'd start getting a bit of a thing for a fifty-year-old woman. Then a sixty-year-old. This was just the start.

And, as far as he was concerned, wherever he was, it would always be just the start. If they called that a mid-life crisis, then they could take away his mid-life crisis when they prised it from his cold, dead hand.